The Sympathy of Christ with Man

SALZWASSER
VERLAG

Octavius Winslow

The Sympathy of Christ with Man

Reprint of the original, first published in 1863.

1st Edition 2022 | ISBN: 978-3-37500-288-6

Verlag (Publisher): Salzwasser Verlag GmbH, Zeilweg 44, 60439 Frankfurt, Deutschland
Vertretungsberechtigt (Authorized to represent): E. Roepke, Zeilweg 44, 60439 Frankfurt, Deutschland
Druck (Print): Books on Demand GmbH, In de Tarpen 42, 22848 Norderstedt, Deutschland

THE

SYMPATHY OF CHRIST WITH MAN:

Its Teaching and its Consolation.

BY

OCTAVIUS WINSLOW, D.D.

"His hands are as gold rings set with the beryl; his belly is as bright ivory overlaid with sapphires."—*Solomon's Song*, v. 14.

NEW YORK:

1863.

PREFACE

One, and the chief, design of this volume is to exhibit and illustrate the *practical* character of our Lord's emotional nature — thus linking Him in closer and more personal actuality with our circumstances. Every endeavour to bring into more proximate communion the *personality* of Christ, and the *individuality* of the Christian, cannot fail, however imperfect the execution, to promote the holiest interests of experimental Christianity. Much that passes for sympathy, and is really so, as commonly understood, is deficient in this one essential element, and needs to be remodelled. There is poetry and there is beauty in real sympathy; but there is more— there is *action*. True sympathy may exist impotent to aid, we concede, and its *silent* expression may not, in some instances, be the less grateful and soothing; but the noblest and most powerful form of sympathy is not merely the responsive tear, the echoed sigh, the answering look—it is the embodiment of the sentiment in *actual* help. It identifies itself with the object of its commiseration so personally and so closely as to realise the apostle's beautiful idea of true sympathy: "*Remember them that are in bonds*, AS BOUND WITH THEM; *and them which suffer adversity, as being yourselves* ALSO IN THE BODY."* This was pre-eminently the character of Christ's compassion when on earth. He was willing Himself to wear the chain He came to loose, to share the sorrow He came to soothe; and the remembrance that He was likewise "in the body" constantly forced itself upon His mind, imparting to His deep sensibility and tender compassion the power and the lustre of an actual and personal participation in the calamities He repaired, the wants He met, and the griefs He assuaged. Thus, from His practical sympathy, who is the Great Teacher of the Church, and the "Consolation of Israel,"

* Heb. xiii. 3.

may we derive lessons of holy instruction, and streams of the richest comfort.

To aid this object, the present volume is, with diffidence, offered to the Christian Church. Composed under the pressure of important ministerial, extended pastoral, and continuous public labour, it necessarily partakes of the imperfections of a work thus written, and often at a season when the jaded powers, both of mind and body, demanded the restorative of sleep.. But if the "lame take the prey," the author may humbly hope that this lowly attempt to present the Saviour more vividly to the personal realisation of the reader, and thus render Him more loved and precious, and His example more closely studied and imitated, will not be without acceptance and blessing to the one Church of God,—the sorrowing, suffering Body of a Divine and sympathising Head. The TRIUNE JEHOVAH bless the work, and to the Sacred Three in One shall be the glory! Amen.

BATH, *June* 1862.

CONTENTS.

THE

SYMPATHY OF CHRIST WITH MAN.

CHAPTER I.

SYMPATHY, AN ELEMENT OF CHRIST'S NATURE.

"In all things it behoved him to be made like unto his brethren, that he might be a merciful and faithful High Priest."—HEB. ii. 17.

IT was a noble sentiment of TERENCE, the utterance of which electrified the Roman senate, "Homo sum, humani nihil à me alienum puto;"—"I am a MAN, and nothing that is *human* is foreign to me." With what higher sublimity and profounder emphasis of meaning might our adorable Lord—the Divine Man—have pronounced these memorable words! His whole life was a living, luminous illustration of the thought. He was the highest type of humanity. Essential

God, He was not the less, but all the more, perfect man. He owned to all the sympathies of manhood. Descending from a pre-existent state of glory, He made His advent to our nature, assuming everything that was essentially human, while relinquishing nothing that was essentially divine. He was intent upon being man, because He was intent upon redeeming man, and "very man of very man" He was. With that one joy set before Him—the joy of saving the lost—and oh, who can sound its depth?—no stoop, no humiliation, no suffering, should deter Him. His first step was to descend to the nature which He was to ransom and exalt. Around the solar rays of His Godhead He cast the darkling vesture of our manhood, shading and softening, not extinguishing or lessening, the glory of His divinity. In that marvellous, that fathomless descent to our nature, there was one exception we must ever, in our study of this subject, keep in view. He assumed all that was human but the accident of *sin.* "*He knew no sin.*" The drapery of "flesh" which hung in such ample and graceful folds around His hidden and superior nature, was morally untainted and untinted by transgression. Its entire texture, woof and web, was as essentially pure and undefiled as the divine and ineffable glory it sought in vain to conceal. Let it be remembered that sin, as we have just remarked, is an accident of, and not a property essential to, our nature. It was not necessary, nay, it was not possible, that in creating man God should create him *sinful*. SIN is a foreign and alien element, not originally entering into the formation of Adam, but exported from some dark and unknown clime into our humanity, since God first created it in His own holy and ineffable image, and then pronounced it very good. So far, indeed, from sin being a necessary and original element of our humanity, we became *less human* when we became *less holy*. In proportion as we recede from the prototype of our creation, we descend in the scale of God's workmanship, and sink the rational in the animal. Sin, despoiling our lower nature, reduces us to a level with the brute creation, from whom God bids us learn: "*Ask the beasts, and they shall teach thee!*" (Job xii. 7.) Are not all our faculties and powers paralysed and prostrated by the Fall? Have we not lost those fine and noble instincts, those traits of beauty, sensibility, and power, which, though human, once looked so divine? Is not our humanity materially changed and essentially deteriorated by sin? Most undoubtedly we are less human because we are more sinful. We think the less profoundly—reason the less accurately—feel the less intensely—act the less vigorously—and achieve the less nobly, because we were shapen in iniquity and conceived in sin. This train of thought will serve to place in a clearer and more impressive light the great and precious truth it is intended to illustrate.

Christ, as we have remarked, was the most perfect type of our humanity. Essentially and entirely free from sin, He was the purest and most exalted specimen of man. The difference between the original formation of His inferior nature and ours is strikingly suggestive. His human body was not, as Adam's, framed of the dust of the ground, but proceeded from ours by the miraculous power of the Holy Ghost; so that, while partaking of all the natural properties of the human, it likewise partook of all the essential sanctity of the divine. He was that "*holy thing*" that knew not and could not *sin*—"*the holy child Jesus.*" The thoughtful reader will at once perceive the object at which these remarks have pointed. We are about to unfold in these pages the perfect HUMAN SYMPATHY of Christ with man. And in order that the fact may have all the force of which it is capable, we have sought to present it in the light of its *perfect sinlessness*, seeing that, as our humanity becomes freed from the brutalising influence of sin, its emotional feelings, its sensibilities, and sympathies become all the more unselfish, intense, and exquisite; so that we are prepared to find in our Lord Jesus Christ a sympathy with our sorrows and infirmities such as it would be impossible to find in any other being. Every Christian grace in the believer has its opposite, every human virtue its foil. If we have faith in God, it is assailed by unbelief. If we love the creature, our affection glides into idolatry. If benevolent, we are exposed to prodigality. But not thus was it with Christ. Every divine grace, and each human excellence, dwelt in Him pure, simple, and unmixed. He could love, without adoration; confide, without suspicion; be cheerful, without levity; be humble, without meanness; be mild, yet not timid; be firm, yet not tyrannical; secret, yet not crafty; generous, without waste; and tender, compassionate, and sympathising, without the slightest approach to weakness or unmanliness. And all this because —"*He knew no sin!*"

Now, the *emotional*—an essential element of our humanity—belonged to Christ, as we have remarked, in its purest and most intense form. Our nature is essentially and highly *sympathetic*. The curious and delicate network of nerve which transmits from the sensorium to the extremity of the body each thrill of pleasure or of pain, is not more electrical in its influence than is this sympathetic principle of our humanity. Its relation to the intellectual part of our nature is intimate and reciprocal. Not less independent are they of each other, than both are dependent upon God. The history of our race supplies many illustrious evidences of the union of the loftiest intellectual powers with the finest sensibility. There is no necessity whatever why the *mind* should not act in perfect union with the *heart*: why we should be less reflective because intensely feeling. In the words of a deep thinker,—"Emotion is always attached to some conception formed by the intellectual faculties. Man is so constituted that the conception of certain objects is accompanied with emotion, or, as we would rather say, that certain conceptions are emotional. The conception of probable pain produces fear, and the conception of ill-usage inflicted produces anger. Emotions are thus mainly dependent on the intellectual conceptions to which they are attached. But still, as consciousness attests, they are something more than the mere mental conceptions upon which, as well as upon the general train of association, they exercise a powerful influence. The Author of our nature, in making the conception of certain objects emotional, has added vastly to man's capacity of enjoyment, and has also provided for Himself a powerful instrument of government. The basis of every emotion is a conception. But all conceptions do not raise emotions. The conceptions which raise emotions are all conceptions of objects supposed to be good or evil, or supposed to be connected, for instance, with pleasure or pain, with right or wrong. We thus see the importance of right principles or motive powers in the mind. In a mind of right principles, that which is good is always conceived of as good, and that which is evil as evil, and the emotions flow responsive to the guiding principle. When the motive power is allowed by the will to become perverted, and the objects are conceived of as good which are evil, and as evil which are good—the result is a divided sensibility, disturbing the whole equilibrium of the soul, and like the wind carrying it away."*

No fact will be more vividly brought before the mind of the reader, as we proceed, than the *personality* of our Lord—a truth but imperfectly realised, and yet of surpassing interest and preciousness. Each emotion of His nature, as it passes before the eye, will bring us into the closest contact with Christ as a distinct and real person. There are teachers who speak of Christ as a traditional and historical being, and yet others as a visionary or ideal being,—a mode of instruction well calculated to transport the learner far into the mysteries of cloudland. It may be true to a certain extent that our Lord is a historical being, for His whole life is history, and history teaching by the purest, loftiest example, which has been defined the truest philosophy. His gospel has supplied the world with truth, His life with history, and His character with a living model of every divine perfection and human excellence. But our nature craves for more than this. We want fellowship, not with a sentiment, nor with a tradition, nor with an ideality, but

* M'Cosh.

with a real, living, *personal* being. We seek communion with, and sympathy from, a Saviour in alliance with our veritable nature, endowed with real, deep, holy sensibility, disciplined by personal sorrow like our own, and thrilling with a quick response to every note of

> "The still, sad music of humanity."

We must know Jesus as once tabernacling in the flesh, and dwelling among men as man,—hallowing earthly spots with His presence—entering the dwellings of men—sitting with them at their tables—noticing and blessing their children—mingling in the scenes of domestic life—smiling upon our loves—sanctioning our marriage-feasts—healing our diseases—pitying our infirmities—weeping at our tombs—consecrating our loneliness and solitude; in a word, unvailing a bosom the perfect reflection of our own in all but its sinfulness. Oh, it is this fact of our Lord's personality that brings Him so near to us, blends Him so closely with our individual history, and which imparts to His presence and sympathy a reality and preciousness so inexpressibly great and endearing. Read in the clear, steady light of this fact, what meaning and what beauty appear in these inspired declarations concerning Him: "*Forasmuch then as the children are partakers of flesh and blood, He also Himself likewise took part of the same.*" "*Verily He took not on Him the nature of angels; but He took on Him the seed of Abraham.*" "*The Word was made flesh, and dwelt among us.*" "*In that He himself hath suffered being tempted, He is able to succour them that are tempted.*" "*We have not an high priest which cannot be touched with the feeling of our infirmities.*" Such, my reader, is Christ, and such His sympathy with you! And in all the circumstances of your Christian life it is an instructive and consolatory thought, that your humanity is represented in heaven by the Head of all creation; that the Lord Jesus—the "*first-born among many brethren*"—is still clad in our nature, and occupies the central throne in glory, exalted "*far above all principality and power, and might and dominion, and every name that is named, not only in this world, but also in that which is to come.*" From that elevation of dignity, glory, and power, encircling spirits hymning His high praise, there flows down to you a continuous stream of sympathy, grace, and succour, meeting your every circumstance, supplying your every want, soothing your every grief, and shedding the soft and cheering lustre of a personal presence on your homeward path to glory. And although we no more *"know Christ after the flesh,"* yet, dealing by faith with His personality, we may realise that we possess a Friend, a Brother, and a Redeemer, in whom are mysteriously yet truly united—the SYMPATHETIC NATURE OF MAN, with the INFINITE MIND OF GOD.

CHAPTER II.

THE SIGH OF CHRIST.

"And looking up to heaven, he sighed, and saith unto him, Ephphatha, that is, Be opened."—MARK vii. 34.

THE sympathy of our Lord evaporated not in mere sentiment—cold and unpractical. It was always expressed and embodied in acts of benevolence and in works of power, which, while they conferred upon their recipient a real and permanent good, confirmed His Messiahship, illustrated His boundless resources, and gratified His own manly and man-loving nature. Unlike the volatile pity which sublimates into thin vapour—hollow, heartless, unsubstantial—Christ's sympathy, wakeful to every sigh of sorrow and spectacle of suffering, flowed in streams of real and abiding blessing; and of Him it may in truth be said—

"He lived in *deeds*, not words—in *thoughts*, not years."

And as we proceed, dear reader, in unfolding the precious truth of this volume—Christ's *practical sympathy* with man—let the fact be constantly before your mind, that you are not reading of a Saviour who *was*, but of a Saviour who *is;* that the Lord Jesus is moved by the same sympathy, is possessed of the same power, and is as quickly and as tenderly responsive to the appeal of the sorrowful and the necessities of the needy, as when the tabernacle of His humanity adorned and consecrated our earth, and when to its asylum thronged earth's sons and daughters of suffering and of woe. Oh, it is a truth as replete with comfort as with wonder, "*Jesus Christ, the same yesterday, to-day, and for ever.*" Beloved, cling to this Unchanging One! No ebb in the tide of your affection, nor trembling in the needle of your faith, has created, or can create, the slightest variation in His love or faithfulness. Your waywardness has not chilled it, your fickleness has not affected it, your sinfulness has not forfeited it, because He is essentially, immutably, and eternally the same. "*Though we believe not, yet He abideth faithful; He cannot deny Himself.*"

The first view of Christ's sympathetic nature which we present, brings Him into close relation with the more pensive and subdued feelings of our humanity—the *sigh* of Jesus. "*He sighed.*" How near will this bring the Saviour to many a heart! To some minds of delicate sensibility and perception there is no emotion more eloquent and touching than *a sigh*—nothing which carries so deep a meaning, or penetrates the heart with so irresistible a force. What feelings does that sigh betray! what volumes does it speak! Turn we to the Saviour. "*Looking up to heaven, He sighed.*" Never did He appear more human, or with our humanity more sympathetic! Let us examine the occasion which gave birth to this emotion, and receive from it spiritual instruction.

There was brought to Him for His healing a man bereft of two bodily senses, the deprivation of which entails so much loss of exquisite enjoyment. As if to illustrate our Lord's illimitable power over the physical and mental infirmities of our nature, and thus to confirm our faith in His deity, there was no species of disease which He did not combat and conquer. But a bodily healing was not the end of His interposed compassion and power. There was a hidden and deep significance in every cure He effected. He had come the Divine Healer of a more woeful malady

—the Physician of a nobler, more diseased and imperilled part of our being. He had come to heal and save the *soul.* And while all physical disease fled at His command, vanished at His touch, He sought thus to illustrate His deeper compassion for, and His higher power over, the *spiritual.* The case before us is replete with gospel teaching.

Take the first infirmity mentioned. This poor man was—*deaf.* The tympanum of the ear was destroyed, and thus a direct and exquisitely constructed inlet to the soul—one of the most beneficent creations of God—was closed. If for a moment we reflect—gathering the evidence from our own experience—how the soul is stirred to its depths by the accented sounds of the human voice—the breathings of love, the words of friendship, the strains of eloquence, the melody of music—we may form some idea of the severity of the loss which the deprivation of this sense must entail. Take a single illustration—one of the purest enjoyments of which this sense is the avenue—the power of *music.* I say the purest, for it has been well defined the only sensual gratification which mankind may indulge to excess without injury to the moral feelings.* The

* Addison.

power of music in tranquillising the mind, calming the spirit, and waking the whole soul to elevated thoughts and feelings, is marvellous. Milton, with a licence of expression ceded to poets, speaks of it as "creating a soul under the ribs of death." Luther's remark is, perhaps, less poetical in its conception but more true in idea:—"Music is the art of the prophets, the only art that can *calm* the agitation of the soul: it is one of the most magnificent and delightful presents God has given us." A modern writer, forgetful of his own marvellous power as a poet, generously awards the palm to music:—

> "Of all the arts beneath the heaven
> That man has found, or God has given,
> None draws the soul so sweet away
> As music's melting, mystic lay;
> Slight emblem of the bliss above
> It soothes the spirit all to love."

Its necromantic power to reproduce, as it were, the past,—to summon back its sacred reminiscences, its holy loves, its precious and undying memories, has been exquisitely and touchingly expressed by a master in the sister art:—

> "Mysterious keeper of the key
> That opes the gates of memory,
> Oft in thy wildest, simplest strain,
> We live o'er years of bliss again!

"The sun-bright hopes of early youth.
Love, in its first deep hour of truth,
And dreams of life's delightful morn,
Are on thy seraph-pinions borne!

"To the enthusiast's heart thy tone
Breathes of the lost and lovely one,
And calls back moments, brief as dear,
When last 'twas wafted on his ear.

"To gloom of sadness thou canst suit
The chords of thy delicious lute;
For every heart thou hast a tone
Can make its pulses all thine own!" *

There is one view of music which to the Christian mind gives it a transcendant place among the arts—I refer to its *truthfulness*—especially as an expression of *religious* feeling. Poetry, sculpture, and painting—faithful as may be their delineations—deal more closely with the ideal. The loftiest and sublimest soarings of their genius are upon the eagle plume of fancy, and they delight to revel and to sport amid brilliant worlds of their own creation. But, withdrawing us from the unreal, the gorgeous fancies and subtle refinements of poetry and painting, music brings us into closer communion with the true, into closer communion with ourselves.

* A. A. Watts.

To both the sister arts of poetry and music the Church of God will ever acknowledge its profound indebtedness. Sanctified by the grace of God, and consecrated to the high and noble purpose of expressing religious sentiment and pious feeling—the holy thoughts of the mind and the spiritual feelings of the heart—the saints in all ages, including Moses and David, Solomon and Job, have poured forth their noblest thoughts and loftiest aspirations through the medium of these divine gifts. The *poetry* and the *music* of the Bible were, in the absence of all other evidence, alone sufficient to stamp it as a Divine Book,—to authenticate, beyond all doubt, its Divine inspiration. From whence but from GOD himself could those historians, poets, and musicians have derived their sacred annals, lighted their holy fires, and learned their entrancing melody? Truly, their minds were instructed and their muse was kindled and their harps were tuned from other than a human source, and by other than a human hand. And yet there are, styling themselves "Masters in Israel," who would reduce this divine and sublime Book to the level of a human, nay, a false and spurious composition, and compel us to receive it, not as it is in truth, the Word of the Most High God, but as an invention of man, "*a cunningly-devised fable.*" With regard to music, let the saints of God be jealous of its true glory, which is, its high and holy consecration. "*Speaking to yourselves in psalms and hymns and spiritual songs, singing and making melody in your heart to the Lord,*" you employ the gift in the noblest service, and consecrate it to the highest end on earth. "PRAISE *is comely.*" And God has said, "*Whoso offereth* PRAISE *glorifieth me.*" A *praiseful* spirit is one of the most deeply sanctified emotions of the soul—*praise* one of the holiest engagements of the Christian. The service of heaven is the service of *song;* the chief employment of the glorified is—*praise.* It behoves us, then, to give the holiest, the highest consecration possible to this noble art. Carnal, worldly music breathing from the lips of a saint of God is as incongruous and inharmonious as a bacchanalian song breathing from the lips of a glorified spirit. Nothing but what is holy in its sentiment, spiritual in its tone, and edifying in its influence should be uttered by a Christian's lips, should vibrate from a Christian's harp. The magnificent composition of Handel's MES-

SIAH supplies no exception to this rule. Admitting the Divine inspiration of the words, the transcendent genius of the composer, the sublime character of the oratorio, and the elevating influence of its skilful and masterly execution, we must yet maintain that the music of the MESSIAH, as performed in modern times by the unholy and the unsanctified, should be as distasteful and painful to the Christian and spiritual mind, as it is, unquestionably, unacceptable and dishonouring to God. What spiritual mind can listen to the solemn words of Christ, expressive of His heart-sorrow, His soul-anguish, His bodily sufferings, sung by voices and breathing from instruments of music in a *cathedral*, wont to wake the echoes and the plaudits of a *theatre*, without indescribable torture of feeling and the most depressing sadness of spirit? Could we thus listen to a recital of the humiliating insults, the lingering tortures, and dying agonies of one the nearest and the dearest to our hearts? Never! Beware, then, of the unholy fascination of music. It may lead you from God, allure you from Christ, draw you into the world. It may become an easy and a fatal snare to your soul. Seek the deep sanctification of the gift, and its holy and supreme consecration to God. As such, *sacred* music, breathing from a spiritual mind, a Christ-loving heart, may be a valuable aid to the soul,—soothing, sanctifying, elevating. God can give you a night-song,—a song in the gloom of your sorrow, loneliness, and woe,—a song of His love unchanging, of His faithfulness unfailing, of His presence sweetening your sorrow, soothing your grief, cheering your solitude, making you submissive, happy, and cheerful in the darkest and most painful path along which your covenant God is leading you. Beloved, the chief employment of heaven is *music.* Oh, what melody floats through those bowers, rings through those mansions, reverberates through that dome, from the spirits of just men made perfect! They sing the song of Moses and the song of the Lamb. They sing of the everlasting love, of the atoning blood, of the sovereign grace that brought them there. Around the Lamb once "slain" they cluster, and upon His head, once filled with bruises, torn and bleeding with the thorn-crown, they bind the diadem of their praise. And, oh, how worthy is He of their sweetest anthem, their loftiest song, their loudest hallelujahs! So resplendent will be the unvailing of His divine glory, His human beauty; so great will appear His love, so glorious His work, so rich His grace, and so precious Himself to the heart, that from every creature which is in heaven will be heard the anthem, "*Blessing and honour and glory and power be unto Him that sitteth upon the throne, and unto the Lamb for ever and ever.*" Then, O disciple and follower of Christ, separate yourself from all secular, carnal, worldly music, and learn on earth, in the house of your pilgrimage, in the strange land in which you dwell, and amid your trials, sorrows, and conflicts, the song of Moses and the song of the Lamb, which will employ your tongue throughout eternity. "*It is a good thing to give thanks unto the Lord, and to sing praises unto thy name, O Most High: to shew forth thy loving-kindness in the morning, and thy faithfulness every night, upon an instrument of ten strings, and upon the psaltery; upon the harp with a solemn sound.*"

But to return from this digression. What a deprivation, then, is the loss of the sense of *hearing!* To such a one all nature is mute, all beings dumb—signs instead of sounds conveying intelligence to the mind and love to the heart. The feeling, too, of isolation and loneliness, the pensive sadness which the loss produces, is often extremely painful and depressing, and should awaken in our heart, on behalf of its subject, the tenderest sympathy and the most delicate attention. Happy, indeed, for such if the trial is so sanctified as to sequester the heart more entirely from others, entwining it more closely with Christ!

Turn we now to the *spiritual* teaching of this part of the narrative.

There is a still more marvellously-constructed and delicate organ—*the ear of the soul.* Through this enter, not the accents of man, but the voice of GOD! And when *He* speaks with commanding, irresistible, and saving power, the human soul is yet more deeply conscious of the fact than it ever was of the breathings of love and the words of kindness and sympathy. But this spiritual organ is sealed to the voice of God. The fall of man produced a moral concussion of the soul, and from that moment its ear has been closed to the most glorious announcement, the sweetest melody, the most powerful voice that ever chimed upon the ear. We will confirm and illustrate this fact by a reference both to the *law* and the *gospel.*

The *law* of God speaks authoritatively, powerfully, solemnly. It commands perfect obedience —demands supreme love—threatens eternal judgment—thunders the divine curse; but although its dread artillery peals above the sinner, although it confronts him with its commands at every step, exclaiming with imperative tone, "*Pay me that thou owest;*" not a sound strikes upon the spiritual ear of the soul! The sinner heeds not the voice of justice, and of wrath, and of condemnation. He is as a deaf man that cannot and that will not hear. So with the *gospel.* The gospel is the voice of JESUS speaking in mercy, grace, and love. It is the voice of pardon, of peace, and of hope. It affirms the most astounding fact that ever startled the universe, that, "*God so loved the world, that He gave His only-begotten Son, that whosoever believeth in Him should not perish, but have everlasting life;*" and still the natural man receives not this saying, heeds not this voice, is deaf to this sound. Jesus speaks from Calvary in tones that encircle the earth, that darken the sun, that melt the rocks, that wake the dead, but all is still and motionless as the cemetery of the sleeping dead, over whose graves floats unheeded the music of the spheres. "*They have ears, but they hear not.*" With many the case is judicial. In them is fulfilled the awful command of God—"*Make the heart of this people fat, and make their ears heavy, and shut their eyes; lest they see with their eyes, and hear with their ears, and understand with their heart, and convert, and be healed.*" (Isa. vi. 10.) That is, leave them to the consequences of their wilful rejection of the Saviour and His gospel; give them over to a reprobate mind and to judicial blindness of heart. My reader, God has but to leave a sinner to his wedded idols, to "*let him alone,*" and the unchecked, unbridled, unrestrained passions of his fallen nature will work out their legitimate, certain, and appalling result—judicial hardness of heart here, and eternal destruction from the presence of God hereafter! What is the case with *you?* Examine and determine,—it is for your life! But glance once more at this condition of the soul. Is it a calamity to be deaf to human sounds—to hear not the soft breathings of affection, the entrancing strains of music, the spirit-stirring sounds of eloquence? Oh, infinitely greater the calamity to have the ear of the mind closed to the voice of God, of Christ, of the Spirit, of the gospel! To hear not the voice of life and love, of providence and grace—the melting accents of Calvary, the lessons of adversity, the solemn warnings of bereavement, the imperative tones of death—this is a calamity and a crime the magnitude and the guilt of which distances all thought and defies all expression. Sinner! the hour is coming when you *must* hear the voice of Jesus speaking to you—not in the all-gentle, all-persuasive pleadings of a *Saviour*, but in the terrible, overwhelming thunders of a *Judge!* Believer in Jesus! blessed are your ears, for they hear. You have heard the Shepherd's voice, and it has won your heart, enkindled your affection, and bowed your whole soul to its gentle and gracious supremacy. Oh! is there, amid the voices of the universe, one like unto Christ's? Is there one so powerful, so winning, so gentle, so sweet? Lord! were all other sounds hushed in the profoundest depths of eternal silence, all other voices for ever quenched in the stillness of everlasting death, to hear Thy gentle tones of pardon, peace, and love quelling my fears, soothing my sorrows, assuring me of an interest in Thy salvation, calling me Thine own, and promising that I shall be with Thee ever,—oh, that were enough for the eternity of my being!

To the loss of the sense of hearing was added, in the case of this object of Christ's compassion, the loss of the faculty of *speech*. Language is a divine gift. The power of communicating by articulate and intelligent sounds our thoughts, and feelings, and wants, is one of God's most wise and beneficent arrangements. It is by this faculty we hold intercourse with intelligent beings. The *tongue* is a mighty instrument for good or for evil. Solomon reminds us that "*life and death are in the power of the tongue.*" There is *life* in it when it speaks a word in season to him that is weary—when it drops into the ear an accent of kindness—when it speaks of Jesus' love and compassion to a sad and mournful heart—when it quotes a promise of God to a dejected, disconsolate mind—when it gives utterance to thoughts that elevate, to counsels that guide, to the breathings of encouragement and sympathy. Oh, what *life* is there in the faculty of speech when, holy, and wise, and gentle, it is employed for the good of our fellows and for the glory of God! There is *death* too in the power of the tongue when it is employed as an instrument of evil by the whisperer, the backbiter, the slanderer, the tale-bearer, the untruthful—death to reputation, death to character, death to usefulness, death to happiness. The poison of asps may be under the tongue, and death to some injured one may be the consequence! This thought finds a yet more awful illustration in his case who, as a professed minister of Christ's gospel, gives utterance to doctrines fatal in their tendency and effect to the well-being of souls. God holds us responsible for the use of this faculty, for He writes, "*By thy words shalt thou be justified, and by thy words shalt thou be condemned.*" Oh, see that your speech is seasoned with grace, administering instruction and edification to the hearer. Let no corrupt thing, no false doctrine, no untruthful statement, no harsh, unkind, unsympathising, heart-wounding word flow from your lips. Speak for God, for Christ, for souls.

But this poor man was dumb, or was afflicted with an impediment in his speech, which rendered the faculty distressing if not useless. There is something touchingly affecting in the sight of a mute! He stands apart, insulated and alone, from his species. All beings, all things, all events, seem to have a language and a speech but him. And yet, perchance, cloistered deep within the recesses of his soul, there are great thoughts reposing, and noble purposes forming, and tender feelings and sacred sympathies welling up, to which his lips, mute and soundless, can give no utterance. The musings of a mother, bending over her dumb and only child, are thus vividly, and with great poetic beauty, described :—

"'Twas long ere I believed
That this one daughter might not speak to me;
Waited and watch'd, God knows how patiently!
How willingly deceived!
Vain love was long the untiring nurse of faith,
And tended hope until it starved to death.

"Oh! if she could but hear
For one short hour, till I her tongue might teach
To call me '*Mother*,' in that broken speech
That thrills the mother's ear!
Alas! those seal'd lips never may be stirr'd
To the deep music of that lovely word.

"I've watch'd her looking up
To the bright wonder of a sunset sky,
With such a depth of meaning in her eye
That I could almost hope
The bursting soul *would* burst its binding cords,
And the long pent-up thoughts flow forth in words.

"Wills He the mind within
Should from earth's Babel-clamour be kept free?
Even that His 'still small voice' and step might be
Heard at its inner shrine,
Through that deep hush of soul with clearer thrill?
Then should I grieve? O murmuring heart, be still!

"Not of all gifts bereft
Even now. How could I say she did not speak?
What real language lights her eye and cheek,
And renders thanks to Him who left

Unto her soul yet open avenues
For joy to enter, and for love to use!

"And God in love doth give
To her defect a beauty of its own,
And we a deeper tenderness have known
Through that for which we grieve;
Yet shall the seal be melted from her ear,—
Yea, and my voice shall fill it—but *not here*.

"When that new sense is given,
What rapture will its first experience be,
That never woke to meaner melody
Than the rich songs of heaven,
To hear the full-toned anthem swelling round,
While angels teach the ecstasies of sound!"

Ah! see we not our spiritual nature here portrayed? The only being in the universe that has not a tongue to speak for God, lips unsealed to praise, a tongue loosed to shew forth His glory and magnify His great name, is the natural man. You have, perhaps, my reader, grown up from infancy to manhood, from manhood you have descended to old age, and to this moment you have remained spiritually dumb! The language of God's children is a strange dialect to you, and you cannot understand what they mean or whereof they affirm. They speak of reconciliation with God, of peace through Christ, of pardon, of justification, of adoption, of the power of indwelling sin, of the desperate depravity of their nature, of the constant alienation of their heart, and yet of an assured hope of endless life in heaven—but you have never learned their language, and cannot understand their speech, because you have never been admitted to their experience. It is an appalling spectacle to meet an individual whose head is blossoming for the tomb, but upon whose lips have never dwelt the heaven-taught accents of a Saviour's love.

But how many of the Lord's own people, especially among young believers, may be said to have a spiritual impediment in their speech,—they open their mouths so seldom or so imperfectly for Christ. They are tongue-tied through fear, or timidity, or shame. They hesitate to own the Lord boldly, to speak unhesitatingly of the great things Jesus has done for them, and to magnify the sovereign grace that has called them to be saints. And even with regard to more matured believers, alas! we understand the language of Canaan but imperfectly. We are "*a people of a stammering tongue.*" The truth of God, the love of Christ, the accents of prayer and praise and thanksgiving—the precious, the endearing name, ABBA, FATHER—do but falter upon the tongue of the most advanced, fluent, and eloquent among us. Alas! that there should be so much fear one of the other, striking dumb each lip when the saints of God meet together. Why should religion be ignored, Christian experience be tabooed, the name of Christ be banished from the social circle where alone the Saviour may be expected to find a welcome and a place? Oh, let us seek to have the heart so replenished with His grace, so glowing with His love, that we may talk of His beauty, and the glory of His kingdom, and the might of His wonderful acts. "*Lord, open Thou my lips, and my mouth shall shew forth Thy praise.*" Let the well-spring of life within my soul be as a gushing fountain; let the beauty of Christ, the glory of His kingdom, the faithfulness and loving-kindness of His dealings, be the themes upon which I dwell.

> "Lord, unloose my stammering tongue:
> Who should louder sing than I?"

We approach now the emotion of Christ. "*And looking up to heaven, He* SIGHED." It may appear, at the first glance, but a commonplace expression of feeling. How many a sigh do we breathe, of which, perchance, we think nothing. The air around us is agitated, like the waves of the sea, with the sadness, the sighs of woe, breathed by our oppressed humanity. We sigh, some from habit, others from sympathy, yet others more from real grief, and the emotion awakens no response. But there was something in the sigh of Christ profoundly significant in its meaning, inexpressibly touching in itscharacter—it possessed an import and a tenderness which no other sigh of our humanity could. Let us not, however, misunderstand it. Christ breathed His sigh over this deaf and dumb man not because He felt unequal to the task of healing him. How frequently do *we* sigh over our conscious inadequacy to meet a case which implores our aid. Not so with Christ. No depression like this forced that sigh from His lips. Well did He know that power ever all flesh was His, that His resources were equal to the demand, and that with a touch He could loose the string, and make those mute lips discourse the sweetest eloquence; and that with a word—"*Be thou opened*"—He could pour into that sealed ear the most delicious melody. Nor did He sigh from anger that they had brought to Him this patient. Never was He known to betray a feeling of displeasure or uneasiness when men appealed to His compassion or solicited His help. Even when His disciples had been more honoured than Himself, and a case which had first been brought to them, had been transferred to Him as incurable, He never uttered a word of upbraiding, but took the child and healed it. Ah, how many of us would have felt our self-complacency wounded that we had not been given the precedence! Blessed Jesus! we will learn of Thee, for Thou wast meek and lowly in heart. No sigh ever breathed from Thy lips the expression of an angered heart, or wounded pride, or disappointed ambition.

And yet why did Christ sigh? In the first place, I would remark, it was an outgush of sympathy bursting from a humanity kindred to our own. It was a sigh of *compassion.* As He benignantly bent over this suffering form, the hidden spring of emotion was moved, and it gave vent in a deep, upbreathed sigh. Ah, beloved! the humanity of your Saviour was really like your own, sin only excepted. That audible emotion expressed an identity with your nature, your infirmities, your weaknesses, unutterably endearing. And when grief, or depression, or anxiety, pent up within your breast, finds an outlet in a sigh

—and for that emotion, perchance, some heartless, unsympathising one harshly chides you—is there no soothing in the thought—"Jesus once sighed as I sigh, and still, in the overflowing of His sympathy and compassion, echoes every sigh that breathes from my lips?"

The sigh of Jesus was awakened, too, by a view of the ravages of *sin.* In that spectacle He beheld the humanity He had originally cast into a perfect, peerless mould, and had pronounced "very good," bruised and crushed—its organs impaired, its beauty marred, its nature tainted—and, Himself lovely and sinless, He could not look upon that wretched, defaced, paralysed specimen of our nature without emotion—without a sigh. Ah, what a glorious truth does this illustrate—the *holiness* of our Lord's emotional nature! Pure and sinless, it is all the more exquisitely tender and touching. The sin which gives birth to our sorrow, the moral taint inseparable from all that we feel and do, impairs not the compassion and sympathy of the Saviour. While on the other hand, so pure and holy is He, He cannot survey the devastating reign of sin, He cannot behold His own image so defaced, a part of His own nature so polluted, without emotion heaving His bosom and breathing from His lips. Beloved! Jesus knew more of the exceeding sinfulness of sin than we shall know through all eternity. There was more of the essence of the sorrow and suffering and fruit of sin in one drop of that cup which could not pass His lips undrank, than we should have known had we been left to drink the wrath of a holy God for ever. Oh, how should this impart to us a holy disgust and loathing of sin! How should we hate the garment spotted by the flesh, and walk humbly and mournfully and softly with God on account of our transgressions, and seek more sympathy with Jesus in His emotion at the ravages and ruin which the fall has produced! Do you sigh for sin—the sin you see in others—the sin yet more visibly and deeply traced in yourself? Ah, there is no calamity that can befall you, were your future pathway to the tomb strewed thick with trials, over which you have more need to sigh than this. And if the deep consciousness of sin heaves your bosom with this emotion, be you assured your holy sigh, as it rises, meets and blends with your Saviour's.

It was a sigh of *practical benevolence.* I have remarked upon the hollow, vapid nature of human pity and compassion. How much of it evaporates in thin air! It is needless, it is heartless, nay, more, it is criminal, to say, "Be ye warmed, be ye clothed, be ye fed, be ye healed," and yet extend not a hand and stir not a foot to help. "*If a brother or sister be naked, and destitute of daily food, and one of you say unto them, Depart in peace, be ye warmed and filled; notwithstanding ye give them not those things which are needful to the body; what doth it profit?*" Oh, let us authenticate our faith by our works; for, "*faith, if it hath not works, is dead, being alone.*" Not so was the emotion of Christ. His was a real, tangible, practical principle. It was always connected with some sorrow comforted, some want supplied, some burden unclasped, some help needed, some blessing bestowed. Oh, we deal with the REAL, the sincere, the true, when we deal with Christ—with facts, not fables; with realities, not fictions; with compassion and sympathy robed with the beautiful garment of real, practical charity.

"The Son of God, in doing good,
Was fain to look to heaven and sigh;
And shall the heirs of sinful blood
Seek joy unmix'd with charity?"

Now trace the marvellous cure, and see how

He blends the power of His deity with the tenderness of His humanity, and illustrates, at each step, the higher healing of the soul. The first move was the *separation*: "*And He took him aside from the multitude.*" He would make it apparent that there was no collusion, no legerdemain, no *finesse* in the cure; but, by making it visible and palpable to all, the miracle should be apparent and the witnesses confounded. What is *real conversion*—the spiritual opening of the mouth and the unstopping of the ear—but a *separation?* When the Lord Jesus converts a sinner, He separates him from the world, from his family, from his former self; takes him apart from the multitude, from his associates, from his worldly, sinful pursuits, and he becomes consecrated to God. "*The Lord hath set apart him that is godly for Himself.*" The religion of Jesus is a *separating* religion. Christ said that He had come to sever the dearest ties of nature, to sunder the closest relations of life, and to divide a house against itself. And often when He is about to work a moral miracle like this—the conversion of the soul—by His providence He takes the subject of it apart from all others, insulates and exiles him, and thus performs the work and secures to Himself the glory. Let Christian, praying parents glean instruction and comfort from this. You have, perhaps, mourned the event that sundered you from your child, that separated him from your influence and your counsels—not your *prayers*—by oceans and continents removing him into exile and loneliness. Ah! many a one can testify that it was not until thus separated, taken thus apart from a loved circle in that strange land, in that solitude and loneliness, on that stormy sea, threading that interminable prairie, crossing that burning desert, or in that distant, quiet, and, perhaps, sick-chamber, the Spirit of God moved upon the heart and led it to Jesus. My beloved reader, has the grace of God SEPARATED *you?*

And then came the *simple means.* Jesus touched his tongue. He did not stand at a distance, like some proud and haughty patron, conscious of superior dignity, of higher sanctity, about to confer a favour which he felt a great obligation to bestow. Oh, no! how unlike Jesus would this posture and air have been! But He placed the Divinity that was about to heal, in an angle with the humanity that was to be healed. The Sinless should be brought into contact with the sinful,—the Divine should heal the human! He inserted His finger into the ear, and He placed it upon the tongue, and the dumb spake and the deaf heard! Oh, how *near* does Jesus bring Himself to us when He would, as with a word or as with a touch, open our ear to hear the voice of life, and loose our tongue to speak the words of love. Christ's plans and modes are simple. A touch—a word—and a work is done, greater, sublimer, holier, and more lasting than when He said, "*Let there be light, and there was light.*" Be not suspicious of sudden conversions, nor afraid of enforcing an immediate repentance and faith. God's ways are not as our ways, nor are His thoughts as our thoughts. In a moment, in the twinkling of an eye,—a touch of His hand, a word from His lips—"*Ephphatha*"—and a new moral creation bursts into existence! a son is given—an heir of glory is born!

And now mark the fulfilment of a beautiful prophecy of Christ—physically and spiritually fulfilled: "*A man shall be a hiding-place from the wind, and a covert from the tempest; as rivers of water in a dry place; as the shadow of a great rock in a weary land. And the eyes of them that see shall not be dim; and the ears of them that hear shall hearken. The heart also of the rash shall understand knowledge, and the tongue of the stammerers shall be ready to speak plainly"* —(margin, "*elegantly.*") And never does the human tongue, in the highest sense, speak "elegantly," until, instructed and sanctified by the Holy Spirit, it speaks of Christ! And the more it discourses of Him,—of the beauties of His person, the perfection of His work, the fulness of His grace, the wonder of His love, the tenderness, compassion and sympathy of His nature—the more eloquent and elegant is its speech. That tongue, untaught by the schools, undisciplined by education and art, may be naturally unlearned and witless—its tones harsh, its language broken, its accents faltering—yet, discoursing of JESUS, there is a softness and mellifluence, an elegance and grace clothing it, which the *belles lettres* of the world could not inspire, which those who dwell in king's houses might envy, and those who occupy university chairs might imitate.

And mark the *attitude* of JESUS as He gave utterance to this emotion. "*He looked up to heaven.*" Oh, how expressive! how replete with significance the picture! It was to His Father

He looked for the present sealing of His Messiahship. His mind and heart and will were in perfect unison with God's, and He could say, "*I came not to do mine own will*, (apart from the Father,) *but the will of Him that sent me.*" And how precious and holy the lessons He would teach the multitude gazing upon the scene! He would thus remind them that "*every good and perfect gift is from above, and cometh down from the Father of lights.*" And when they saw the Son of man, with filial reverence and prayerful reliance, thus gazing into the blue vault of heaven in mystic and close communion with His Father, how deeply would the spectacle impress them with the conviction that it was *by the power of God* the miracle was wrought that broke the silence of those lips and poured delicious sounds into those ears! Learn from this, beloved, what should be your true attitude when the pressure upon your emotional nature forces the deep-drawn sigh from your lips. We sigh, and look *within*—Jesus sighed, and looked *without.* We sigh, and look *down*—Jesus sighed, and looked *up.* We sigh, and look to *earth*—Jesus sighed, and looked to *heaven.* We sigh, and look to *man*—Jesus sighed, and looked to GOD!

Let us glean from this particular view of Christ's emotional nature a few appropriate instructions.

It addresses itself especially to those who are addicted to a like emotion. See how Jesus has recognised and consecrated *the sighs* of His Church. If the Head sighed, surely it is not sinful for the member of the Body to sigh. A *sigh* is often the expression of a holy desire, the utterance of a heart-breathed prayer. It has a meaning and an eloquence understood by, and persuasive with, God.

> "*Sighs* now breathed
> Unutterable, which the spirit of prayer
> Inspired, and wing'd for heaven with speedier flight
> Than loudest oratory."*

Ah, that sigh! what a depth and pathos of meaning has it. You sigh by reason of the body of sin and of death you bear about with you. You sigh over your flaws and failings. You sigh by reason of your infirmities, your domestic, relative, or personal trials. You sigh as you survey the scenes of sickness and suffering and wrong—for all the abominations that surround you. Think not that you are alone—that there are no

* Milton.

responsive echoes awakened by your emotion. Take your sighs to Jesus, and if this is the only language you can command in giving vent to your sorrow or expression to your want, employ it, and wait in hope God's answer.

> "A *sigh* can reach His heart,
> A look can bring Him down from heaven."

We must, however, be cautious lest this emotion should become a physical infirmity. It may grow into a habit—a nervous, morbid habit—and thus, instead of being an outlet of suppressed feeling and a vehicle of sacred intelligence affording unspeakable relief, it may aggravate the suffering it was designed to mitigate. Do not, then, let this emotion be too frequently indulged, lest it degenerate into a meaningless habit. It is only *twice* recorded that Jesus sighed.

Employ your restored and renewed faculties for God. Are you, like Moses, slow of speech and not eloquent? Remember God's words to him—they are equally addressed to you: "*And the Lord said unto him, Who hath made man's mouth? or who maketh the dumb, or deaf, or the seeing, or the blind? have not I, the Lord? Now therefore go, and I will be with thy mouth, and teach thee what thou shalt say.*" Seek, then

Christ's divine and gracious touch, that your tongue may be loosened to vindicate His honour, to defend His truth, to diffuse His gospel, to speak of Him to them that are weary, and to shew forth the praise of your covenant God. "*For with the heart man believeth unto righteousness; and with the* MOUTH *confession is made unto salvation.*" (Rom. x. 10.) And ask Him to unseal your ear—the secret ear of your soul—to the still small voice of His Spirit, the gentle breathings of His love, that you may be skilful to distinguish between truth and error, the law and the gospel, the voice of man and the voice of God. Not only seek the sanctifying touch of Christ, teaching you when to *speak,* but equally do you need it to teach you when to be *silent.* It has been remarked, Better that the feet slip than the tongue. We need as much wisdom, nay, perhaps more, when to be *silent* as when to speak. To be silent when others detract, accuse, and defame; to be silent when reviled, censured, and condemned, displays no little control over the tongue. "Sometimes to unkindness and injustice, *silence* may be safer than even the soft answer that turneth away wrath." The conquest over self under severe provocation by a dignified and holy quietness is a greater victory than his who taketh a city. Oh that our tongue may be Christ's! Oh that it may be employed for the good of our fellows! Oh, that we may be training for the communion and song of the upper skies!

Alas! to what multitudes is life but a "bridge of sighs" to a future of inconceivable and interminable woe! My unconverted reader, *you* are one of this long and melancholy procession, moving slowly, sadly, surely, from the sighs that are temporal to the sighs that are eternal. Life with you is a toilsome journey, a hard struggle, a severe battle, a continuous scene of change and disappointment, of wrong and suffering, of toil and anxiety, of temptation and sin. Your experience has taught you that the world is heartless and insincere, the creature fickle and disappointing, riches unsatisfying and fleeting, ambition a phantom, human hopes illusive, pleasure concealing a sting, sin embittering, and the way of transgressors hard. Truly the sighing of the prisoner is yours. And yet there is a "*Branch*" which maketh the bitter waters of the curse sweet! Jesus made His advent to this world of sin and woe to deliver us from the burden of the curse, to relieve us from the bondage of sin, to transmute our sorrow into joy, our despair into hope, and to make this life-bridge of sighs a radiant, joyful pathway to a world of glory, a land of joy, a home of perfect purity and bliss. "*Christ gave himself for us, a sacrifice and an offering to God.*" Oh, how marvellously changed would be all your present and future being with the sweet forgiving love of God in your heart, and the hope of glory in your soul! With such a Saviour as Christ, with such a salvation as God has provided—a salvation all that your extremest case requires, and that the highest claims of His moral government demands—you need not be the sin-burdened, the sad, the lost, the hopeless despairing one that you are, mournfully exclaiming, as you pass to the tomb, "*My life is spent with grief, and my years with* SIGHING." The Redeemer whom you have hitherto despised, or wilfully rejected, or whose willingness to save you you have doubted, is prepared to receive you as a sinner, to pardon you as a penitent, to reclaim you as a prodigal, and to enroll your name amongst the children of God. "*For the* SIGHING *of the needy will I arise, saith the Lord.*"

Anticipate, child of God, the solemn yet blissful moment when the last gentle sigh will heave your breast. It speedeth on! There awaits us a freedom from sin and grief, a state of perfect purity and happiness, in which will be realised the magnificent picture of the far-seeing prophet, when "*the ransomed of the Lord shall return and come to Zion, with songs and everlasting joy upon their heads: they shall obtain joy and gladness, and sorrow and* SIGHING *shall flee away.*"

And in conclusion, let the sweet words uttered by the wondering spectators of this marvellous and touching display of our Lord's sympathy with man, awaken a deep response within our hearts in all His dealings with us—"*He hath done all things well.*" Yes, from first to last, from our cradle to our grave, from the earliest pang of sin's conviction to the latest thrill of sin's forgiveness, from earth to heaven, this will be our testimony in all the way the Lord our God has led us in the wilderness. In providence and in grace, in every truth of His Word, in every lesson of His love, in every stroke of His rod, in every beam that has shone, and in every cloud that has shaded, in every element that has sweetened, and in every ingredient that has embittered, in all that has been mysterious, inscrutable, painful, and humiliating; in all that He gave, and in all that He took away, this testimony is His just due, and this our grateful acknowledgment through time and through eternity—"*He hath done all things* WELL." Take a survey of His conduct towards you from what stand-point you may,—and it is to His dealings with us in our *individual* history I alone refer, as illustrating and confirming this declaration,—such must be our admiration, and such our testimony of Christ. Has He converted us through grace by a way we had thought the most improbable? Has He torn up all our earthly hopes by the roots? Has He thwarted our schemes, frustrated our plans, disappointed our expectations? Has He taught us in schools most trying, by a discipline most severe, and lessons most humbling to our nature? Has He withered our strength by sickness, reduced us to poverty by loss, crushed our heart by bereavement? And have we been tempted to exclaim, "*All these things are against me?*" Ah! no; faith will yet obtain the ascendency, and sweetly sing—

"I know in all things that befell
My Jesus has done all things well."

Beloved, it *must* be so, for Jesus can do nothing wrong. Study the way of His providence and grace with the microscopic eye of faith, view them in every light, examine them in their minutest detail, as you would the petal of a flower, or the wing of an insect, and, oh, what wonders, what beauty, what marvellous adaptation would you descry in all the varied dealings with you of your glorious Lord! And when the next wave surged, and the next cloud darkened, and the next mystery threw its veil around you, you would hopefully exclaim, "What new truth is He now teaching? what new glory is He now unveiling? what new wonder is He now working to arouse my admiration, to win my confidence, and to deepen my love?"

"I'll sing of Jesus crucified,
The Lamb of God who bled and died,
A healing balm, a crimson tide
Flow'd from His head, His feet, His side.
Above the rest this note shall swell,
'My Jesus hath done all things well.'

"He sought me in the wilderness,
And found me there in deep distress;
He changed and wash'd this heart of mine,
And fill'd me with His love Divine.
Above the rest this note shall swell,
'My Jesus hath done all things well.'

"For what the Lord hath done for me,
For boundless grace so rich and free,
For all His mercies that are past,
I'll praise Him while my life shall last.
Above the rest this note shall swell,
'My Jesus hath done all things well.'

"When sorrow's waves around me roll,
His promises my mind console;
When earth and hell my soul assail,
His grace and mercy never fail.
Above the rest this note shall swell,
'My Jesus hath done all things well.'

"When death shall steal upon my frame,
To damp and quench the vital flame,
I'll look into my Saviour's breast,
And there recline and sweetly rest.
Above the rest this note shall swell,
'My Jesus hath done all things well.'

"And when we join the ransom'd throng,
To chant the sweet immortal song,
With tuneful heart, and voice, and tongue,
We'll roll the lofty note along.
Above the rest this note shall swell,
'My Jesus hath done all things well.'

"To Him who wash'd us in His blood,
And made us kings and priests to God;
Hosanna we will ever sing,
And make the heavenly arches ring.
Above the rest this note shall swell,
'My Jesus hath done all things well.'"

CHAPTER III.

THE TEARS OF CHRIST.

"Jesus wept."—JOHN xi. 35.

IN our inquiry into the emotional nature of our Lord, where shall we find so instructive, consolatory, and touching an exhibition of His sensibility as this? It appeals at once to every heart. Tears are a universal language. The sensibility which they express engirdles the human race. Travel to what nation we may, who cannot interpret the tear of woe—the tear of want—the tear of gratitude—the tear of sympathy—the tear of joy? Now, our Lord could not fully have partaken of our nature, and failing this, He could not have understood the condition of man, apart from this particular emotion. Had He allied Himself only with our joys and smiles, eschewing our sorrows and tears, His fellowship with our humanity had been but partial and defective. He could not in *all* points have been like us.

We are composed of varied emotions, which are inspired and called into play by different objects. And until the finer feelings of our nature have been trained in sorrow, interlaced and edged with suffering, our own humanity is but partially understood. We are unequal to the task of educating and moulding others, until we ourselves have been educated and moulded in the school of human sensibility, which is—the school of *suffering*—the school of *sympathy.* The character that is not reflective, and instinct with sensibility, is incapable of the true condition of natural life, and is inadequate to its high mission. We must be taught by chastening, be purified by trial, be subdued by sorrow and suffering, in order to administer to the condition of man. Thus was our adorable Lord fitted for His great mission. He was born and cradled, educated and trained in the school of suffering. "*Though He was a son, yet learned He obedience by the things which He suffered.*" And all that sorrow and all that suffering was not for Himself alone, but for us. The sensibilities of His human soul were being "*made perfect through suffering.*" He was by this process disciplined to lessen our burdens by participation, to soothe our griefs by sympathy, and to comfort our hearts by the comforts with which His own had been comforted of God. Oh, who would part with this precious truth—Christ, schooled in sorrow, perfected in suffering, a man of grief, with all a man's sensibility, all a man's sympathy, all a man's compassion and yearning! Welcome the affliction, shared, soothed, and sanctified by such a Saviour—such a brother—such a Friend.

We cannot, then, conceive of an incident in our Lord's life which presents Him in a light more truly human than that which now engages our thoughts—*weeping at the grave!* His human sensibilities would now seem to have attained their highest development, and to have found their most exquisite expression. Could He, in touching tenderness, have surpassed it? Does it not in sympathy meet all that we need? Could there be another incident better fitted to elicit the finest feelings of His heart, and to illustrate the noblest traits of His character? Let us examine it more closely.

It was one of the most memorable occasions of His history. Look for a moment at the picture. The first feature that arrests the eye is, the marvellous assemblage, the strange yet perfect blending of opposites, around the lowly grave of Lazarus. Here was bereavement, and the affection that soothed it. Here was death, and the Essential Life that conquered it. Here was the grave, and the Resurrection that emptied it. Here was the melting, weeping sensibility of man, in the closest alliance with the Divine majesty and commanding power of GOD. What a study! The Creator of all worlds, the Author of all beings, the Upholder of the universe, raining tears of human woe and sympathy upon a grave! But why did Jesus weep? Is it possible to analyse those tears? Let us at least attempt it.

The spectacle of *death* would stir to its depths His holy sensibility. No being in the universe could form so vivid a conception of *death*—its pathos as an event, its terribleness as a reality, its ravages as a spoiler, its despotism as a sovereign, and its awful solemnity as a crisis of our being introducing us to the eternal world, as the Son of God! Here stood Essential Life, with Death. To His mind, the fountain of all life,——to His heart, pulsating with all that was tender and benevolent,—to His eye, familiar with all that was bright and beautiful,—what a strange, what a revolting, what a solemn thing must *death* have appeared! More than this—He beheld the ravages of the spoiler! Imagine the feelings of an artist gazing on a work of art upon which he had concentrated all the loftiest powers of his genius and labour—the *chef-d'œuvre* of his chisel or his pencil—lying shattered at his feet! A faint emblem of Jesus! As the Divine Artificer of man bent over that grave, and with eyes that pierced its deep sepulchral gloom, beheld in the shrouded form the destruction of His masterwork, His Father's image defaced, the temple of the Holy Ghost in ruins, and death's pale conquest proudly planted upon the cold, marble brow of one for whom He was about to shed His most precious blood—JESUS WEPT!

The love of bereaved friendship would enter deeply into this expression of Christ's sensibility. His affection for this family, to whom He was now proving Himself the "*Friend that sticketh closer than a brother*," was of the tenderest character. He seemed to have found in them another existence, a second self. If this be a correct definition of true friendship, then Jesus realised it in its fulness. Homeless in a world which He had filled with homes for all but Himself, He loved to steal away from its rudeness and turmoil, and nestle His sad and weary spirit in the warm bosom of the home of Bethany,

> "And share
> The inward fragrance of each other's heart."

Gently lifting its latch, He might say, "No disappointment *here!* no upbraidings *here!* no coldness or unkindness *here!*" And as He entered, Lazarus would advance to welcome Him, Martha would hasten to spread the evening repast, and Mary would quietly take her place at His feet to hear His words. All loved Him, and each testified their affection in their own way. The first, would illustrate the courtesy of the Christian host; the second, the hospitality of the Christian home; the third, the devout earnestness of the Christian disciple. Hallowed home, where Jesus is a guest! happy, happy family, all whose varied gifts and spheres of duty are consecrated to His service! Reader, see that your home has attractions for Jesus. See that He has good entertainment when He comes—the first of your time, the best of your powers, the supremest of your love. He is worthy,—oh, how worthy!—of the highest honour and the sweetest service.

But the home of Bethany was now the scene of mourning. Lazarus was dead! Jesus revisits it, not, as He was wont, to indulge its sunshine, but to share its gloom—not to participate in its joy, but to soothe its grief. It was just the place and the scene where the finest feelings, the deepest sensibilities of His nature would find their freest and their sweetest flow. And as He sat within that house of mourning, and remembered that it was the bereaved home of the friend of His heart, the companion of many a happy hour, the confident of many a sacred feeling, the sharer and the soother of many a lonely, chafing sorrow—JESUS WEPT. Are you deploring a like loss? Are you mourning with a like grief? There is One who has known how *such* a

> "Sorrow wrings the sad soul, and bends it down to earth,"

and is prepared to embosom Himself in it with such a sense of its reality and keenness, and with such a delicacy of feeling and sympathy as no other can. There is a depth of agony and loneliness in the sorrow of bereavement into the secrecy of which the bereaved only can enter. It touches the finest and most hidden springs of the soul. It lies fathoms deep, and seldom passes the lips. The crushed affections — the annihilated hopes—the severed ties of friendship—the grave entombing life's charm, attraction, and sweetener, —quenching the sunbeam that illumined the dreary wilderness—is a grief not always apparent, or that may be known and told, but which yet ploughs the deepest furrows on the brow and silvers the hair with its earliest gray. But, oh, to know that Jesus can enter into its sorrow, is touched with the feeling of this grief, and is prepared to accompany us to the grave and weep with us there, is a solace no language can describe! Precious Jesus! must Thou feel Thy own sorrows thus to enter into ours? Was ever love like Thine!

But not His remembrance alone of the dead, but His affection also for the living, His compassion for the bereaved sisters, would contribute not a little to this outgushing of melting tenderness and grief. They were *the tears of love.* It is a touching parenthesis in the narrative, "*Now Jesus loved Martha, and her sister, and Lazarus.*" *That* love was the secret of His present tears. He knew what a brother Lazarus had been. How like weak and clinging tendrils these sisters had entwined around him for their sunshine and support. And now that he was removed, they were torn from their stay, and lay prostrate and bleeding on the earth. And as He beheld their grief—Martha's impetuous and chiding, Mary's veiled and silent, yet both real, intense, and agonising—JESUS WEPT. Beloved reader, the Lord is acquainted with our domestic ties, and takes an interest in each one. No act of kindness, no breach of faith, no tie tenderly cherished or rudely sundered, no duty faithfully discharged or wilfully neglected, no relation honoured and sanctified, escapes His all-seeing—approving or condemning—eye. And when death enters and sunders a domestic link, and fills the home with mourning and the heart with woe, Jesus comes and makes all grace abound, giving submission to the will, peace to the mind, and consolation to the heart. Oh, there lives not a being in the universe who can enter into our bereavements with the sympathy, the succour, and the soothing of Christ! From this brief glance at some of the probable causes of Christ's tears on this occasion, let us consider the sensibility itself.

The emotions of Christ were perfectly true to nature. The Saviour dissolved in tears, presents a spectacle of apparent effeminacy of character not in keeping with His dignity and greatness. Yet, was it really so? Tears are not always marks of weakness, they are oftener evidences of power. Springing from the depths of the soul, they are sometimes the exponents of great thoughts, of mighty purposes, of manly feelings, and have a language and a meaning more eloquent and effective than ten thousand tongues. Such were the tears of Jesus. In Him they betrayed no cowardice, exhibited no weakness, expressed no softness of character, but were the interpretation of a sensibility in alliance with the omnipotence of power. Let us not, then, give place to the idea that emotions are indices of a feeble faith in God, of a languid hold upon Christ, of a weakness of Christian character. Ah, no! See how close was the sensibility of Christ's manhood with the power of His Godhead. He wept over the dead *like a man*,—He raised the dead to life *like a* GOD! Feeling is an essential element of real religion. A religion that is without feeling, embraces the intellect only, is not true to nature, and is radically and fatally defective. If it enlists but the judgment and not the heart, appeals solely to the intellectual, leaving the emotional of our nature untouched, it is wanting in one of the grand essentials of the religion of Christ. An enlightened perception of sin, a godly contrition springing from the conviction of its existence and guilt, an experience of pardoning love, a sense of God's goodness, nearness to the cross, a faith's view of Jesus crucified—His dying love, His deep sorrow, His unparalleled agonies, His profound abasement, all, all endured for us—will break up the hidden fount of feeling, will stir our sensibilities to their depth, and dissolve the entire soul in tenderness and tears. Oh, deem not a sensibility like that of the Incarnate God unbefitting the strength and greatness of a natural or a gracious character. Affect not to despise a religious experience, the prominent element of which is emotion. The richest and deepest veins of feeling often underlie the incrusted and rugged surface of our nature. The loftiest genius, the profoundest intellect, and the most manly dignity and courage, have been found in union with a woman's delicacy of perception, tenderness, and sensibility of feeling. Condemn not, then, a religious feeling, the prominent feature of which is *tears*. It is equally as essential that the heart should be affected as that the judgment should be enlightened; both are indispensable elements of real religion. Weep on, then, thou mourner for sin and sorrow,—weep!

> "Hide not thy tears, weep boldly, and be found
> To give the flowing virtue manly way:
> 'Tis nature's mark to know an honest heart by,
> Shame on those hearts of stone that cannot melt
> In soft adoption of another's sorrow!"

They were also *tears of sympathy.* We must not omit *the sympathetic* in Christ's present emotion. His heart was not only touched with a sense of His own personal affliction, but it was also touched, deeply touched, with sympathy for the sorrow of others: He wept because the mourning sisters wept. He mingled His tears with theirs. This is true sympathy, "*weeping with those that weep,*" making their sorrow our own. How really our Lord does this with His people. So completely is He our Surety, that He takes our sins and infirmities, our trials and sorrows upon Himself, as if they were all and entirely *His own.* Our sins were so completely laid upon Him, that not one remains charged to the account of those who believe in Jesus. And our present griefs are so entirely absorbed in Him, that, softened by His love, soothed by His sympathy, succoured by His grace, trial is welcome, affliction is sweet, and the rod of a Father's chastening buds and blossoms into delectable fruit. Bereaved mourner! the sympathy of Christ is *yours!* The Saviour who wept at the grave c Bethany, now shares your grief and joins you tears. Deem not your sorrow is lone, or that you tears are forbidden or unseen. You have not a merciful and faithful High Priest who cannot be touched with your present calamity. There exists no sympathy so real, so intelligent, so deep, so tender, so sanctifying as Christ's. And if your heavenly Father has seen it wise and good to remove from you the spring of *human* pity, it is but that He may draw you closer beneath the wing of the God-man's compassion, presence, and love. O child of sorrow! will not *this* suffice, that you possess Christ's sympathy, immeasurable and exhaustless as the ocean, exquisite and changeless as His being? Yield your heart to this rich compassion, and then, "*though ye have lien among the pots, yet shall ye be as the wings of a dove covered with silver and her feathers with yellow gold.*" Learn a lesson from the *practical* sympathy of Jesus. Compassion is as luxurious an emotion of our nature, as it is manly and graceful in him who shews it. "*To him that is afflicted pity should be shewed from his friend.*" (Job vi. 14.) What a sacred privilege to imitate Him "*who went about doing good!*" To visit the widow and the fatherless in their distress, the prisoner in his dungeon, the bereaved in their grief, the sick in their solitude, the poor in their need, the fallen in their self-reproach; in a word, to be an angel of comfort to some child of woe from whose bosom hope has fled—this, oh! *this* is sympathy. Truly,

"No radiant pearl which crested fortune wears,
No gem that, twinkling, hangs from beauty's ears,
Not the bright stars which night's blue arch adorn,
Nor rising suns that gild the vernal morn,
Shine with such lustre as the tear that treaks
For others' woe down virtue's manly cheeks."*

But Christ's emotion was not only in sympathy with grief, but He wept also *in sympathy with souls.* We think no spectacle presents in idea so vividly the moral sympathy of the Saviour—His compassion for the *lost*—as when He wept over Jerusalem. He was on His way, accompanied by His disciples, to the doomed city. As He reached the brow of Olivet, it burst in magnificence upon His sight. Its high encircling walls, its costly edifices, its splendid palaces, its sacred Temple—the central seat of God's chosen people—towering in holy sublimity above them all, was a spectacle

* Darwin.

which might have impressed His mind at any other time with rapt delight. "*But when He was come near, He beheld the city,* AND WEPT OVER IT!" And why those tears? He wept because of its impenitence and unbelief—its rejection and slaying of His prophets—its yet more awful and fearful rejection and slaying of Himself. "*O Jerusalem, Jerusalem, thou that killest the prophets, and stonest them which are sent unto thee, how often would I have gathered thy children together, even as a hen gathereth her chickens under her wings, and ye would not!*" What must have been its sinfulness, its guilt, its doom, to have made Jesus so sad, to have wrung those tears from the Son of God! Christ's tears over Jerusalem!—what a life-like picture of the compassion of Jesus for lost sinners! But more sacred, more precious tears He afterwards shed when He agonised in Gethsemane, and hung upon the cross. Tears of *blood* then gave expression to the deep, tender, loving compassion of His heart for man, *sinful* man. And thinkest thou, O weeper over thy sins, that this weeping, bleeding Saviour will reject you if you come to Him? Never! no, *never!* The tears of Christ, in their mute, persuasive tenderness, bid you come and be saved. What more could Jesus do?

"The Son of God in tears
  The wondering angels see!
Be then astonish'd, O my soul!
  He shed those tears for thee.

"He wept that we might weep,
  Each sin demands a tear;
In heaven alone no sin is found,
  And there 's no weeping there."

We will only further remark, that the tears of Christ were associated *with prayer.* "*Who in the days of His flesh, when He had offered up prayers and supplications, with strong crying and tears.*" (Heb. v. 7.) Christ was a man of *prayer.* He walked with God as man, and as the Mediator He maintained the closest and most continued communion with His Father. His sensibility did not evaporate in mere emotion—in sighs, and groans, and tears. He turned all into *prayer.* So let it be with us! Let us not indulge in mere grief; let our grief take us to prayer, urge us to the throne of grace, prompt us to rise and call upon God. And though we breathe our grief, and our wants, and our sins in no language but that of strong crying and *tears,* yet, He who Himself once so prayed to His Father, will interpret their meaning, and respond to their request.

Deem it not *sinful* to give free scope to the emotions of your nature. The religion of your Saviour encourages not stoicism. It is not the religion of Seneca nor Plato—it is the religion of JESUS—of *Him who wept!* And although, as we shall see in a subsequent chapter, that, holy *joy* and chastened *cheerfulness* are inseparable from the gospel of Christ, that the believer is called upon to *rejoice* all the day long, yet it is not designed to suppress and crush those finer feelings of our humanity which find their suitable expression in tears of penitence and love, of sadness and sympathy. Dost thou water thy couch with thy tears? Are tears thy meat day and night? Do you feel it a relief to the full heart thus to weep? Weep on, Jesus forbids thee not. Only see that your emotions are not in opposition to the mind and dealings of God. Weep, but weep in filial, mute submission to the Divine will. Let not the feeling of rebellion, the emotion of hostility to God, blend with your tears. Then, with David you may pray, "*Put thou my tears into Thy bottle.*"

Be often a weeper at the Saviour's feet. The woman who was a sinner, who followed Jesus into the house of Simon, and stood behind Him weeping, then stooped and bathed His feet with her tears, found her heaven upon earth in that position and in that act. Simon rebuked, but Jesus encouraged her; the one condemned, the other approved. Man may forbid your tears, and when they fall fast and thick, may deem you weak and sentimental; but Jesus invites and will commend them when you lie at His feet a penitent, loving, grateful disciple. Oh, precious tears that flow from a contrite heart for sin, and from a loving, grateful, subdued sense of its full and free pardon!

"Why, O my soul, why weepest thou?
Oh say, from whence arise
Those sacred tears that often flow,
Those groans that pierce the skies?

"Is sin the cause of thy complaint,
Or the chastising rod?
Dost thou departed friends lament,
Or mourn an absent God?

"Lord, let me weep for nought but sin,
And after none but Thee!
And then I would—oh, that I might!—
A constant weeper be!"

Have you long been a weeping suppliant at the mercy-seat? And does the vision tarry? Is there no response? Let me remind you of the promises so appropriate to your case, which, perchance, your intense emotion has vailed from your eyes. "*They that sow in tears shall reap in joy. He that goeth forth and weepeth, bearing precious seed, shall doubtless come again with rejoicing, bringing his sheaves with him.*" "*Weeping may endure for a night, but joy cometh in the morning.*" Humble penitent! earnest, sorrowing seeker of Jesus! tried, afflicted child of God! listen yet again to the promise, "*Thou shalt weep no more: for He will be very gracious unto thee at the voice of thy cry; when He shall hear it, He will answer thee.*" (Isa. xxx. 19.)

When you go to the grave of some loved one to weep and meditate there, *take Jesus with you.* No mourner will bend with you over that tomb with a deeper sympathy, with tears more real, more warm, more soothing than His. Realising His presence, you will indulge in a chastened sorrow, blended with a faith that rises above the scene, with a hope that anticipates heaven, and with a love that adores God for all His dealings.

Honoured grave, bedewed with Christ's tears! It is pleasant to visit it, holding fellowship with the unseen world, and blending the conscious presence of the Saviour with the ideal communion of departed friends. Is it a pious *mother's* grave? Memory loves to make its pilgrimage thither as to the Mecca at whose shrine it kneels, travel where we may. If, of all the graves which bestud the earth, there is one more attractive, more holy, more sacred to Jesus than another, it is *this*—the precious urn which contains the ashes of a once godly, praying mother! And of all the friends who have shared your sorrow, the first to meet you there will be Him who from the cross, and in the agonies of death, bent His last tender look and breathed His latest words of love upon—*His mother!*

Meditate often upon the sensibility of Jesus—it will quicken, sanctify, and soothe your own. If you are an *artist*,—study it. If you are a *poet*—chant it. If you are an *orator*—extol it. If you are a *divine*—preach it. If you are a *disciple*—imitate it. If you are a *mourner*—bring to it your keenest, loneliest, deepest grief. "*Jesus wept!*" "Was there ever a more interesting portrait than what the evangelist has here drawn of the Son of God? If the imagination were to be employed for ever in forming an interesting scene of the miseries of human nature, what could furnish so complete a picture as these words give of Christ at the sight of them—'*Jesus wept!*' Here we have at once the evidence how much the miseries of our nature affected the heart of Jesus, and here we have the most convincing testimony, that He partook of all the sinless infirmities of our nature, and was truly and in all points man, as well as God. We are told by one of the ancient writers,* that some weak and injudicious Christians, in his days, were so rash as to strike this verse out of their Bibles, from an idea that it was unsuitable and unbecoming in the Son of God to weep. But we have cause to bless the overruling providence of God, that though they struck it out of their Bibles, they did not from ours. And why those groans at the grave of Lazarus, if tears were improper? Precious Lord! how refreshing to my soul is the consideration that forasmuch as the children were partakers of flesh and blood, Thou likewise didst take part of the same; that in all things it behoved Thee to be made like to Thy brethren. Hence, when my poor

* Chrysostom.

heart is afflicted, when Satan storms, or the world frowns, or Thy waves and Thy billows go over me, oh, what relief is it to know that Jesus looks on and sympathises! Then do I say, 'Will not Jesus, who wept at the grave of Lazarus, feel for me? Shall I look up to Him, and look in vain? Did Jesus, when upon earth, know what these exercises were, and was His precious soul made sensible of distress even to tears, and will He be regardless of what I feel, and the sorrows under which I groan? Oh no! The sigh that bursts in secret from my heart is not secret to Him; the tear that is my meat day and night, and drops unperceived and unknown, is known and remembered by Him. Though now exalted at the right hand of power, where He hath wiped away all tears from off all faces, yet He himself still retains the feelings and the character of the "Man of sorrows, and of one well acquainted with grief." Help me, Lord, thus to look up to Thee, and thus to remember Thee.'"* Precious and holy is the divine *precept*, illustrated and enforced by so divine an example—"*Weep with them that weep.*" Oh, it is the richest luxury on earth to share by sympathy the sorrow, to soothe by gentleness the

* Hawker.

grief, to wipe away by kindness the tears of another. This Christ did, and we are to prove our discipleship to Him by imitating His example. "*Remember them that are in bonds, as bound with them*"—sharing their chain; "*and them which suffer adversity, as being yourselves also in the body*"—exposed to like weaknesses and assaults, calamities and griefs. Oh, aspire, beloved! to be a drier of human tears; to have a hand always ready to wipe them away! Who can estimate its worth? To have soothed one human sorrow, to have met one pressing want, to have unbound one crushing load, to have dried one tear of grief, to have shed one beam of light upon a dreary path, to have reclaimed one wanderer, to have made the widow's heart to sing for joy, to have befriended and soothed an orphan, oh! it is a work to be measured in its importance and its blessedness only by a life. Again, we repeat, let your life be an outflowing sympathy with the distressed and the needy, the widow and the fatherless. Be Christ-like, "*who went about doing good;*" raise the fallen, strengthen the weak, comfort the feeble-minded; and if tears of compassion and sympathy will soothe and mitigate the tears of penitence and adversity, then be it your mission and your privilege to "*weep with them that weep!*"

In HEAVEN there will be no more tears! It is tearless, because it is sorrowless; it is sorrowless, because it is sinless; it is sinless, because it is the dwelling-place of the holy Lord God and of the "*spirits of just men made perfect.*" How magnificent the description! "*And God shall wipe away all* TEARS *from their eyes; and there shall be no more death, neither sorrow nor* CRYING, *neither shall there be any more pain.*" Such is the condition of the New Jerusalem—the new earth and the new heaven in which the risen and glorified saints will dwell and reign for ever with Jesus at His coming. "*He will swallow up death in victory; and the Lord God will wipe away tears from off all faces.*" (Isa. xxv. 8.) Then there will be no more tears of penitence, for there shall be no more sin. There will be no more tears of parting, for they shall go no more out. There will be no more tears of bereavement, for there will be no more death. "*The Lamb which is in the midst of the throne shall feed them, and shall lead them unto living fountains of waters:* AND GOD SHALL WIPE AWAY ALL TEARS FROM THEIR EYES."

Tears of love! behold them flowing
From the Elder Brother's eye!
See Him as a mourner going
To the grave at Bethany!
He, who through its shadowy portal
Summon'd back the freed immortal,—
He, whose all-commanding word
Sheathed the gloomy victor's sword,—
There, where buried friendship sleeps,
He, our own Immanuel, weeps.

Tears of pity! see them gushing
From their pure and sacred fount!
Angels! your hosannas hushing,
Bend ye from the holy mount.
Stoop to read the wondrous story,
How the "Father's brightest glory"
At a sinner's grave can stand,
Mourner 'mid a mourning band,
With the heart, the voice, the eye
Of a perfect sympathy!

Tears of Jesus! while I ponder,
Blessed comfort let me reap;
"That same Jesus" liveth yonder
Who on earth was wont to weep.
Though His brow the rainbow weareth,
Yet my thorny crown He shareth;
Yet that loving heart Divine
Throbs responsively to mine:
Not a struggling sigh can rise,
But 'tis echo'd in the skies.

Blessed Jesus! in *Thy* sorrow,
Friends and kindred pass'd Thee by;
Thou alone couldst never borrow
The support of sympathy.

When Thy human heart was bursting,
When thy parched lips were thirsting,
When encompass'd with the foe,
Mocking at Thy bitter woe,
Thou, who hadst a heart for all,
Drank *alone* Thy cup of gall.

Now in glory, where Thou dwellest,
  All unknown is sorrow's look,
Yet Thy people's tears Thou tellest,—
  "Are they not within Thy book?"
While my "night of weeping" lasteth,
Ere the morn its brightness casteth,
My blest portion may it be,
That *Thou* weepest, Lord, with *me!*
And one day, with heart and voice,
In *Thy* joy may *I* rejoice! *

* Ellen H. Willis.

CHAPTER IV.

THE EMOTION OF ANGER IN CHRIST.

"And when He had looked round about on them with anger, being grieved for the hardness of their hearts, He saith unto the man, Stretch forth thine hand. And he stretched it out: and his hand was restored whole as the other."—MARK iii. 5.

IT is not in partial light that our Lord's emotional nature must be studied. Like lines radiating to a centre, or the varied hues forming the arch which spans the heavens, His emotions must be considered, not separately and divisibly, but in combination and as a whole, in order to form a correct idea of the portrait. The incident, thus related in His life, presents a feeling differing in its expression, though not in its nature, from any we have as yet considered; and at first sight He appears in a character less lovely and engaging than we have been wont to admire. That the emotion of *anger* should find a place in a heart so loving and gracious would seem discordant with all our tender, holy conceptions of the "*gentleness of Christ.*" But, as we investigate the emotion and the occasion which gave birth to it, we think it will appear consonant with the finest and holiest feelings of His heart, and will develop those qualities of His nature which are necessary to the symmetry and perfection of the portrait. Let it, however, be premised, before we proceed further in this subject, that *anger, wrath, displeasure,* are not the same sinful passions in the Divine that they are in the human. Pure emotions in God, they are expressions of His hatred and punishment of sin, growing out of the holy necessity of His being. God's anger and wrath in punishing the ungodly is nothing less than His holiness and justice in their most awful exercise.

The cross of Calvary was the most august and awful illustration of this truth the universe ever beheld. The spectacle which presents Jesus suffering as the Surety Head of His Church, exhibits Him as enduring the wrath of God to its uttermost, justly due for His people's transgressions. What was the bitter cup our Lord then drained—what the soul-agony He then felt—what the bodily suffering He then experienced—what the ignominious death He then endured, but God's hatred of sin, and the infliction of its penalty in the person of His beloved Son, suffering as the substitute of His Church? "*He was made sin*"—a sin-offering—"*for us, who knew no sin, that we might be made the righteousness of God in Him.*" Child of God! there is no divine wrath, or anger, or displeasure in the bitterest, darkest dispensation of thy God—since Christ, our Divine Surety and Head, endured and exhausted it all for thee. Fear not, then, to enter the dark cloud—tremble not to drink the bitter cup—all, *all* is LOVE.

Proceed we now to view in its spiritual light the Incident and the Emotion.

The first circumstance which arrests our attention is—*the withered hand.* We read, "*And He entered again into the synagogue; and there was a man there which had a withered hand.*" This affliction may be regarded either as a divine judgment, or as a natural infirmity. Instances of both occur in God's Word. As a *judgment* of God, we have an intimation and solemn example in Jeroboam. With unhallowed rashness he put forth his hand to seize the prophet who denounced his idolatrous altar, and God smote and withered it. And so we read, "*His hand, which he put forth against him, was dried up, so that he could not pull it in again to him.*" (1 Kings xiii. 4.) The lesson is solemn and instructive! The hand that would profanely rear idolatrous altars, or that would rashly deal with those who denounce them, JEHOVAH can dry up. The hand that, with unhallowed touch, would assail the truth of God's Word—or which would uphold and advance His kingdom and truth by means human and worldly, distrusting the power and faithfulness of God—He can smite and wither. We have to deal with a God jealous of His honour, who has said, "*My glory will I not give to another,*" and who in regard to His servants has said, "*Touch not mine anointed, and do my prophets no harm.*" In the case of the king of Israel, then, the withered arm was a judgment of God, but in the present instance it appears not to have been a divine punishment, but a natural infirmity, permitted and overruled by God to confirm the mission, and to illustrate the grace and power of Christ. Now let us trace its *spiritual* teaching.

In this withered hand we behold *the emblem of the moral withering of the soul of man.* The moment our first father stretched forth his hand to partake of the forbidden fruit, all his original righteousness, strength, and love withered, decayed, and dried up; and we, his posterity, are the spiritually paralysed and shrivelled limbs of a once stately tree God smote and destroyed. "*It is written, There is none righteous, no, not one: there is none that understandeth, there is none that seeketh after God. They are all gone out of the way, they are together become unprofitable; there is none that doeth good, no, not one.*" (Rom. iii. 10–12.) It is of the utmost moment to our salvation that we should know our nature just as it is. Essentially defective views of original and actual depravity lie at the root of essentially defective views of the Atonement. There floats before the imagination of man an ideal conception of natural goodness and power, which it is of infinite importance we should dislodge and dispel from the mind. The sacrificial work of Christ is built upon the spiritual ruin of the creature—the glory of the divine upon the utter wreck of the human. Nothing of man shall mingle with the work of God. We see the foreshadowing of this in the law given to the children of Israel, "*Thou shalt not sow thy field with mingled seed; neither shall a garment mingled with linen and woollen come upon thee.*" (Lev. xix. 19.) The law, too, defining the construction of an altar, illustrates the same idea, "*If thou wilt make thee an altar of stone, thou shalt not build it of hewn stone: for if thou lift up thy tool upon it, thou hast polluted it.*" (Exod. xx. 25.) God would here teach that the divine garment of Christ's justifying righteousness is not to be interwoven with the fabric of man's righteousness; and that in the uprearing of that one Altar upon which the Atoning Sacrifice of Christ was to be laid, no human weapon was to be employed. In the stupendous matter of our salvation Christ shall be the Alpha and the Omega. With Him the gospel plan originated—by Him it was revealed—by Him it was executed—and in His undivided glory and endless praise it shall for ever terminate. From every tongue in glory, and through the high arches of heaven, the anthem shall peal, "*Worthy is the Lamb!*" Believer in Christ! pants not your soul to join in that song? and exults not your spirit in the truth that salvation, from first to last, is of God? Oh, how precious is this truth in the consciousness of our many failures and defects! Our salvation is all in Christ—our righteousness is all in Christ—our merit is all in Christ—our completeness is all in Christ—in Christ our Covenant Head, our Surety and Mediator; and no flaw in our obedience, no defect in our love, no failure in our service, should so cast us down as to shut our eye to our acceptance in the Beloved. Imperfections we would not overlook, sin we would not allow, disobedience we would not indulge, temptation we would not encourage; nevertheless, we would ever remember, for our encouragement, that, in default of perfection in the most perfect of our own doings, we are fully and eternally *complete in Jesus.*

What a tendency, too, is there in the believer, in consequence of this utter drying up of original holiness and power, to a withering and decay of *grace* in the soul! How many who looked like green fir-trees, tall cedars in Lebanon, have to mourn over spiritual declensions, the loss of vital power, the decay of faith, and the waning of love through indwelling sin, neglect of means of grace, the indulgence and seductions of the world! Thus, the breath of prayer is languid, the fervour of affection is faint, and all the spiritual powers and functions of the soul seem paralysed. How many such withered arms, dried up as to the socket, are found in our Christian synagogues! How are the holiness, beauty, and strength of the Church shaded, marred, and impaired by innumerable cases of dried-up vitality, withered spirituality, decay, and weakness found within her membership. Alas! how few exhibit marks of spiritual healthiness, growing grace, increasing holiness, love, and divine conformity!

But let us turn from the patient to the Physician,—from the sinner to the Saviour. It appears that on entering the synagogue to preach His own gospel, our Lord's quick eye lighted upon one of the auditors who had a withered hand. Moved by the impulse of His own benevolence, He selected him from the multitude and resolved upon his cure. The scribes and Pharisees, ever on the watch to baffle His designs and impeach His sanctity, seized the opportunity suggested by this work of mercy on the Sabbath-day, to accuse Him with the crime of its desecration. Then follows the expression of His displeasure—the emotion which this chapter of our work illustrates. "*He looked round about on them with* ANGER." And what was the nature of this anger which our Lord here expressed? We must acknowledge that never did He appear more unlike Himself than now, and yet never was He more truly so! Had He not exposed the hypocrisy and denounced the malevolence of these whited sepulchres with all the burning, withering, holy indignation of which He was master, then a cloud had shaded some of the brightest beams of His character. Christ was angry, but He did not sin. This could not be the case with us. Let us rebuke sin, let us chide the fall, the error, the inconsistency of a brother faithfully, tenderly, gently as we may, the infirmity and imperfection of our fallen humanity will yet taint and shade it. But this feeling of anger in the heart of Christ was a pure and holy passion, an emotion embodying the deepest hatred of sin with the tenderest compassion for the sinner. Another instance in His life illustrates the same emotion. Entering the temple on one occasion, He discerned men of the same type and mould desecrating the sacred edifice by unholy traffic—turning His Father's house into a mart of merchandise, and converting the place of the Just One into a den of thieves. His righteous soul was moved with holy indignation at the spectacle. "*When He had made a scourge of small cords, He drove them all out of the temple.*" And in what light did His disciples interpret this act? They "*remembered that it was written, The zeal of thine house hath eaten me up.*" Zeal for the glory of His Father self-consumed Him. On another and a memorable occasion, we find our Lord hurling the thunders of His wrath and indignation against the entire Sanhedrim, exposing their false doctrine, unmasking their sanctimoniousness, denouncing their hypocrisy, and branding their unholy lives with the most appalling woes that ever flashed from mortal lips. Never did the emotion of anger stir a bosom more gentle, or yet assume a form or speak in terms more terrific. Never did the Lamb of God seem more unlike Himself, and yet never was He more really Himself as now. Beneath the surface of His demeanour, thus broken into the dark waves of a righteous indignation against sin, flowed the deepest, warmest currents of benevolence, gentleness, and love that ever glided through the channels of our humanity. We see, then, that Christ's *anger* was holiness clad in its judicial vesture—it was the anger of holiness.

The wrath of God, as experienced by the eternally lost, suggests another and yet more awful illustration of this truth. Divine justice, as measured to those who have irretrievably passed the boundaries of hope, and who people the regions of dark and changeless despair, is nothing more than Divine purity in its most appalling and overwhelming exercise. It is Divine justice, unarrested by mercy; it is Divine wrath, unappeased by blood; it is Divine holiness, unclothed with the attribute of grace. Hell is kindled with the untempered, unmixed, unmitigated anger of the holy and righteous Lord God. The day is foreappointed, and it speedeth on, when the awfully sublime scene depicted by John will have its full, its terrible consummation: "*And the heaven departed as a scroll when it is rolled together; and every mountain and island were moved out of their places. And the kings of the earth, and the great men, and the rich men, and the chief captains, and the mighty men, and every bondman, and every free man, hid themselves in the dens and in the rocks of the mountains; and said to the mountains and rocks, Fall on us, and hide us from the face of him that sitteth on the throne, and from the wrath of the Lamb: for the great day of his wrath is come; and who shall be able to stand?*" (Rev. vi. 14–17.) "*The wrath* of the *Lamb!*" What is it? Who can describe, who can fathom, who can stand before it? It can only be conceived or estimated by the glory from which He descended, the humiliation to which He stooped, the sufferings which He endured, and the sacrifice which He offcred in order to save sinners. A wilful, unbelieving, and persisted rejection of such a Redeemer and of such a redemption must enkindle in the bosom whose slighted mercy it wounds, a holy, just, and righteous displeasure as infinite and august as the benevolence that warmed it. It is the wrath of Incarnate Deity—of Him who sorrowed in Gethsemane, who bled on Calvary, and who gave His life a ransom for many. It is the wrath of Him who said, "*Ye will not come unto me that ye might have life.*" "*Him that cometh unto me I will in no wise cast out.*" It is the wrath of Him who pardons the guiltiest, who reclaims the vilest, who saves to the uttermost—who holds out His hand all day long to poor, lost sinners, rushing past it in scorn and madness to swift destruction, choosing death rather than life. Unconverted reader! the judgment is approaching, the great white throne will descend, the books will be opened, the dead will be raised, and all, *all* will confront this gracious or this angered Lamb of God. From His presence there will be no escape. Every eye shall see Him. The mountains will not hide you, the rocks will not shelter you, the grave will not retain you, the sea will not entomb you, but when the trumpet of the archangel sounds, at that bar you must stand, and by that Redeemer you must be judged.

> "But ere the trumpet shakes
> The mansions of the dead,
> Hark, from the gospel's gentle voice
> What joyful tidings spread!
>
> "Ye sinners, seek His grace
> Whose wrath you cannot bear,
> Fly to the shelter of His cross,
> And find salvation there."

Let us proceed to examine the *healing* of the withered hand, and its gospel significance. The first step in the process was the *separation* of the man from the multitude. "*He saith unto the man which had the withered hand, Stand forth.*" Is it not by a like process Jesus initiates our spiritual healing, as we have shewn at length in the preceding chapter? He takes us, by His providence, out of the midst of the world, sets us apart from others, severs us often from our home and kindred and country, and then graciously draws us to Himself. "*The Lord hath set apart him that is godly for Himself.*" Saints are an emphatically separated people, a chosen generation, a church taken out of the world, sanctified or set apart for God. Oh, with what deep emphasis of feeling will you thank the Lord through eternity if the waning of health, or the loss of property, or the vicissitudes of friendship severed the cords, broke the links, that too closely, too inordinately, and too idolatrously bound you to the multitude; and thus alluring you into the desolateness and solitude of the wilderness, there spake graciously, tenderly to your heart. The next step in the curative process was Christ's command to the man, "*Stretch forth thine hand.*" Perchance some beholders of the scene may have thought this a heartless mockery of the poor man's infirmity, or laughed to scorn what appeared an utter impossibility. To extend, by self-effort, a limb shrunk to its socket, all whose sinews and muscles were paralysed and withered, would seem a thriftless, hopeless task. Yet such was the command of the Great Healer. By this act Jesus, the Heavenly Teacher, would instruct us in the mystery of a higher healing: that, spiritual impotency did not destroy moral responsibility in man;—that, though the fall has changed man's original relation to God as a holy being, it has not touched his relation to God as a moral, responsible, and accountable being;—that, what was man's duty and obligation when he wandered through Eden unsullied and happy, is still his duty and obligation now a fugitive from paradise, roaming in misery and woe the face of a sin-blighted and curse-smitten world. "*God commandeth all men everywhere to repent.*" Stricken through with a spiritual paralysis, which has benumbed all your moral powers, dried up the spring of love to God, and withered the right arm of your strength—conclusive and affecting evidence of your moral condition as a fallen being, and of your need of the new birth—Christ commands you to stretch forth the attenuated hand; in other words, to believe in Him to the salvation of your soul. The spiritual hand is withered, but still it is the hand of a reasonable, responsible, and immortal being. The Bible addresses you as endowed with a mind that can examine and feel the force of evidence—with a will that can choose, with a heart that can feel, with a conscience that can dictate; and thus, in the face of evidence the most convincing, of love the most unparalleled, of motives the most overpowering, God commands you to repent and believe—to repent and believe *now.* Stretch forth the withered hand, ground the weapons of your rebellion, cease your hostility, and fall in the dust at His feet. Cease to do evil—learn to do well. Have you no spiritual strength or power, inclination or will? Is the heart insensible, the conscience callous, the mind dark and inert to spiritual and eternal things? This is no excuse for your inactivity and indifference. I admit your moral inability, your utter want of power, of will, and of heart to what is holy and spiritual; and in making this solemn admission, I but confirm the fact of your deep sinfulness, guiltiness, absolute and entire need of the Spirit's quickening, regenerating grace. "*Repent ye therefore, and be converted, that your sins may be blotted out.*"

With the command to extend the withered hand, there went forth the *Divine power* to obey. "*And he stretched it out.*" When Christ had recognised the rationality and responsibility of the man, He then performed *His* part of the cure, which was—*the cure itself.* Man's duty to obey, Christ's prerogative to heal, and the Divine blessing ever attendant upon immediate and unquestioning obedience to God's commands, are lessons of practical truth and wisdom, beautifully and strikingly illustrated and enforced in this part of our narrative. The injunctions, warnings, and invitations of God's Word relax nothing of their authority, and lessen in no degree human obligation, in consequence of moral inability in the creature. Whatever may be our spiritual infirmity, impotency, and disinclination, God remains the same—infinitely holy in His nature, eternal and immutable in His law. Apply this to your present condition as a soul conscious of the spiritual withering, and standing as if in the presence of the healing Saviour. What is the command of Jesus to you? "*Look unto me, and be ye saved.*" "*Believest thou that I am able to do this?*" Simply, then, to BELIEVE in the word of Christ, is tantamount to the command—"*Stretch forth thine hand.*" See! that infirmity is no barrier to your coming. Your heart may be hard, insensible, impure; you may be mournfully conscious of manifold infirmities and impediments; you may turn the eye from the Divine Healer to the poor attenuated limb, looking now at the Saviour, and anon at your sins, wondering if one so weak and sinful, so poor and wretched, so grace-neglecting, so hell-deserving, may venture to touch so divine, so holy, so rejected a Saviour as Jesus is—but this reasoning, this hesitation, need not, must not be. Come, beloved, with the withered limb, approach with the poor, trembling, attenuated hand of faith; with one more effort, one more resolve, a last, a final venture—the crowning one of all—and, oh, you are saved!

"Jesus! full of all compassion,
Hear Thy humble suppliant's cry,
Let me know Thy great salvation:
See! I languish, faint, and die.

"In the world of endless ruin,
Let it never, Lord, be said,
'Here's a soul that perish'd suing
For the boasted Saviour's aid!'

"Saved!—the deed shall spread new glory
Through the shining realms above;
Angels sing the pleasing story,
All enraptured with Thy love."

We are thus conducted to—*the cure.* And now the Saviour appears truly Himself. Now He vindicates His proceedings from all suspicion of unsympathising trifling with the poor man's infirmity, unvails His ineffable benevolence, and manifests His merciful design. It was a perfect cure. "*And his hand was restored whole as the other.*" "*Whole as the other!*" Christ's cures are not half cures. Perfection traces all that He does,—whether He paints a lily or rears an alp, heals the body or redeems the soul, like Himself, all His ways and works are *perfect.* When God justifies the sinner, it is a perfect justification—he is "*justified from all things.*" When He adopts the soul, He fully and inalienably adopts: "*Now are we the sons of God.*" When He pardons the guilty, He entirely and for ever pardons —"*having forgiven you all trespasses.*" The Lord has left nothing in our salvation for us to supply, nothing in the gospel plan for man to supplement. It is on the basis of a FINISHED work the believer stands—his Lord and Surety having done all, suffered all, given all that law and justice demanded for the present redemption and the future glory of His Church. "*When we were without strength, in due time Christ died for the ungodly.*" "*Without strength.*" When the arm was paralysed and withered, Jesus then undertook the cure; and, undertaking, He perfected it. Nothing has He left for us to add—not a tear of repentance to His tears of grief, not a groan of sorrow to His groans of agony, not a drop of blood to His vital stream, not an atom of merit to His infinite and all-sufficient worthiness. Lift up thy heart, then, depressed child of God—rejoice in the Lord greatly. He has perfected the cure of thy soul. All thy salvation is in Christ, and God has pardoned and accepted thee without a work of thine own, rests in His love, and rejoices over thee with singing. Blessed Saviour! put forth the power of Thy grace in our souls, and perfect that which concerneth us. Thou hast completed our justification, complete Thou our sanctification, and mature us fully for glory. Subdue our iniquities, weaken the power of inbred sin, quicken our sensibilities to all that is holy and spiritual, deaden them to all that is earthly and carnal, and bring our souls into a closer communion with the solemn, invisible realities of eternity. "*Heal us, O Lord, and we* SHALL *be healed.*"

In conclusion, let me remark, if Christ is grieved at our unbelief, what must be the joy which our *faith* gives Him! If our hardness of heart shades His countenance, how must that countenance gleam with holy delight over the soul subdued in penitent love at His feet! Think it not presumption, then, to travel to Jesus with the withered hand—with a chilled love, with declension of grace, with weakness of faith, with low frames, and with a tempted, tried, and wounded spirit. Jesus Christ maketh you whole. Christ is for the poor and needy and empty—for them that have *no* helper. It is said of David, the type of Christ, that, there gathered unto him within the cave of Adullam "*every one that was in distress, and every one that was in debt, and every one that was discontented, and he became a captain over them.*" Around the glorious Antitype, Jesus the Son of David, there gathers—received and welcomed—all who are in spiritual distress, who are in debt to the law of God, having nothing to pay, who are discontented with the world, with the creature, with themselves; and, lo, Jesus becomes the Captain of their salvation! We repeat, Christ is for the necessitous, the bruised, the outcast, the bankrupt; and, withered though may be your spiritual strength and beauty,—withered the flower and fruit of holiness and grace,—withered the heart's young springs of love, its gushing streams of sympathy—all its early sensibilities, yearnings, and hopes crushed and withered, blighted and beclouded—the gloom and desolateness of winter mantling and chilling the bright landscape of life, yet JESUS' heart expands, and invites you to the asylum of its warm, fathomless, changeless love.

Be not weary nor discouraged in the Lord's service. Like your Saviour, many will seek to thwart, impeach, and wound you in your work of faith and labour of love for Christ. Heed them not. Rejoice if you are counted worthy to be identified with your Lord and Master in suffering for righteousness' sake. "*Consider Him who endured such contradiction of sinners against Himself, lest ye be weary and faint in your minds.*"

Let us seek grace that the emotion of *anger* in our breasts may more closely assimilate with the emotion of anger in Christ's,—a *holy* anger against sin, blended with a loving, yearning compassion for the sinner. Such is the Divine precept: "*Be ye angry, and sin not: let not the sun go down upon your wrath.*" (Eph. iv. 26.) When this emotion springs from zeal for God, His truth, and worship, and glory, and when it prompts us to seek, in the spirit of meekness, humility, and love, the good of those whose conduct we condemn, it then becomes in us, what it was in Christ, a holy, amiable, God-honouring emotion, unmixed with sin and self, and throwing no shadow of sadness upon the mellow light of evening, when the sun goes down at the hour of prayer.

If, on the contrary, you find this emotion rising in your bosoms, in its sinful, fleshly, and corrupt form, lose not a moment in bringing it to the cross, that by the love, the sufferings, the last prayer for the forgiveness of injury of Him who died upon its wood, that species of anger which dwells alone in the bosom of fools, may be crucified and slain in you. Seek not mercy from thy fellows, and ask not forgiveness from thy Father, whilst unholy anger against a brother or a sister finds a moment's lodgment within thy heart. It has been well remarked, that, "some who profess to bury their wrongs, do but *embalm* them; and a busy and eager memory keeps unbroken all the lineaments of the injury they have received."* But with what sincerity of confession, and with what hope of pardon can such approach suppliantly the Father's footstool, and ask, for sins and wrongs against that Father infinitely more numerous and aggravated, the forgiveness which cancels for ever the guilt and the memory of all? O beloved! imitate Him who overcame *evil* with *good;* and "*let all bitterness, and wrath, and anger, and clamour, and evil-speaking be put away from you, with all malice; and be ye*

* Rev. Dr W. R. Williams, of New York.

kind one to another, tender-hearted, forgiving one another, even as God for Christ's sake hath forgiven you."

Saint of God! in the light of His love interpret the frowns of thy Father's displeasure. The hidings of His face, the rebukes of His word, the smitings of His hand, are but the muffled tones of love. They fall upon your wakeful ear like a dirge; nevertheless they are the deep and solemn utterances of Divine affection, compassion, and sympathy. They are correctives for sin; but they are the correctives of a FATHER, hating your sin, but loving you His child. "*Thou shalt also consider in thine heart, that, as a man chasteneth his son, so the Lord thy God chasteneth thee.*" (Deut. viii. 5.) Humbling yourself under the chastening hand of God, you will rise up instructed, purified, and God-like, exclaiming, as the discipline passes away, leaving nothing but its hallowed effects and its grateful memory—"*O Lord, I will praise thee: though thou wast angry with me, thine anger is turned away, and thou comfortedst me.*" (Isa. xii. 1.)

CHAPTER V.

THE SILENCE OF CHRIST.

"But He answered her not a word."—MATT. xv. 23.

THE *silence* of Christ!—how unlike the winning, glowing conceptions we had been wont to form of His responsive compassion and sympathy! Is it really Christ or some other being of whom these words speak? If it really be Christ whose lips are now so mute to an appeal so touching, how are we to interpret the silence? What are the lessons it conveys?

The reader, conversant with his Bible, will be familiar with the narrative which gave birth to this instructive incident of our Lord's life. It was one of those peculiar and touching instances of our fallen and infirm nature with which humanity alone could sympathise, and which Deity alone could meet. It was a mother eliciting the compassion and invoking the aid of the Saviour on behalf of her daughter, demoniacally possessed. Surely no petitioner ever approached Him with a case more calculated immediately to unseal the deepest, warmest springs of His benevolent, sympathising humanity. How touching, earnest, and irresistible her appeal: "*Have mercy on me, O Lord, thou Son of David; my daughter is grievously vexed with a devil.*" And yet He was silent. "*But He answered her not a word.*" With the depth and tenderness of a mother's love Christ was personally acquainted. He had felt its warm throbbings in infancy; He was subject to its gentle influence in youth; and in manhood, when the sun of His human life was sinking in shame, agony, and death, its last, its latest rays rested in filial affection and solicitude upon his mother.* If, then, there were a request, the tenderness, urgency, and importunity of which it would seem impossible He should resist, it was this mother's. And yet He was *silent!* Not a look expressed His recognition, not a word His sympathy, not an action His response. But oh, what a silence was this! More significant and expressive far its meaning than syllables could utter or deeds embody. Beneath that veil of muteness were con-

* John xix. 26, 27.

cealed some of the most magnificent traits of Christ's character, and some of the tenderest pulsations His heart ever displayed. Nothing can be more evident, from the sequel of the narrative, than that Christ was revolving in his mind thoughts and purposes of love and help towards this woman, —that the largeness of His grace and the outgushings of His compassion were about to weave a diadem for the head of that faith which had now so signally crowned Him. Dropping for a moment the narrative, let us examine the illustration which it affords of a page in God's varied dealings with His saints—*the silence of Christ towards His people.*

There are but few believers who have not passed this stage of Christian experience, or who may not yet add this chapter to the solemn and instructive volume of their own spiritual history. Few trials of faith and prayer are more keen, and few paths in our homeward march more lone and dreary than this. The absence of Christ, in the experience of believers, creates a sadness and a void no other can soothe or supply. For, as the clinging vine cannot be dissevered from its support without laceration and loneliness, so the Christ-loving, Christ-clinging heart cannot part with the Saviour's presence, strength, and communion, without the consciousness of a loss which no created good could remunerate. It is blessed to feel that there is One Being in the universe to whom the heart travels as its centre, reposes in as its rest—that, that Being is *Jesus.* Oh, what dreariness can there be, what sadness and solitude, while the soul, as it ascends from the wilderness, leans upon its Beloved, and travels homeward to His glorified presence! Christ's presence makes a heaven of earth, Christ's absence would make an earth of heaven. And yet there is sometimes this peculiar experience in the history of the saints—*the silence of the Lord.* There may be in prayer no sensible audience, in sorrow no conscious soothing, in difficulty no immediate succour, in appeal no audible response: and this silence of Christ is more painful and discouraging than though every other lip in the universe were eternally mute. Mark how keenly David felt this trial of faith. Listen to his appeal: "*Be not thou* SILENT *unto me, O God, lest if thou be* SILENT *unto me, I become like them who go down into the pit.*" Listen to Job: "*O that God would* SPEAK *unto me.*" But *speak!* Any utterance of His voice that would break the awful silence! Let Him chide, let Him rebuke, let Him refuse me—anything but the *silence* of my God! Oh that He would but *speak* unto me! Let us illustrate, by a few examples, this peculiar phase of Christian experience—the Lord's *silence* towards His people.

There is sometimes a silence *in the Word of God* which to the spiritual mind is deeply significant and instructive. Are there not doctrines and revelations and statements in the Bible around which a solemn silence reigns—a silence which eternity alone will break? In our understanding of these truths, we can advance no further than the voice of God is heard—beyond that, no angel-tongue dare break the mysterious stillness. There is, for example, a solemn silence on the revealed doctrine of the Trinity. We believe, on the authority of the Bible, that there are three Persons in the one Godhead—Father, Son, and Holy Spirit—that these three are personally distinct, yet essentially and indivisibly one. As to the *mode* of their existence, there is a divine and awful silence, to penetrate which we must not, we dare not, venture. There is a silence of Scripture, too, touching the equally revealed yet equally mysterious doctrines of the incarnation of the Son of God,—the substitution and vicarious sacrifice of Christ,—the election and sovereignty of Divine grace, and other cognate doctrines of the Bible, the existence of which in the Inspired Word is as clear as the sunshine bathing the throne of God in heaven. But what is the great and holy lesson the Holy Ghost would convey by this striking feature of revealed truth? It is, to be silent when God is silent! How constantly is the human mind tempted to speculate and philosophise and reason about Divine truth! to attempt to sound that which is unfathomable, to unvail that for which there is no clue, to understand that which baffles speculation, transcends reason, and, like Him whose truth it is, enfolds itself in inexplicable and awful mystery. Enough of God's mind is revealed to shew us how we may be saved, and this must suffice for our present limited range of thought and knowledge. We know but in part. The fall has bedwarfed, and sin has obscured our mental perceptions; and God, in giving a revelation of His mind and will to man, has wisely and consistently withheld such discoveries as would have dazzled and blinded with their excessive light and lustre our feeble and limited powers. Stand in awe, then, of God's Word, and sin not by indulging in vain, speculative attempts to break down the barriers which He has erected around the Sacred Volume. It were impious to tread where God has provided no footing, to tear the vail with which He has encircled the Sacred Ark, to raise the lid and peer into its awful mysteries with a curious, carnal, and forbidden glance. "*Who by searching can find out God? who can understand the Almighty to perfection?*" Leave the *mode* of the Divine existence to the explanation—if, indeed, it ever will be explained—of a higher and more perfect state of knowledge. Cease to speculate respecting the origin of sin,—the permission of evil,—the apparent discrepancies of revealed truth,—the mysteries of the Divine government in the world,—the few that are saved,—the unrevealed details of the future world; leave these questions where God has left them—in solemn, awful, unbroken silence; and let reason give way to faith, and pride to humility, and vain speculation to adoring wonder, gratitude, and love. The only fact necessary for you to know is—*that you are lost.* The only question worthy your research is—*how you may be saved.* And both of these are revealed in the Bible with a distinctness and emphasis unmistakeable and overpowering. You are *lost*—but the "*Son of man came to seek and to save that which was lost.*" You may be *saved*—for "*Christ Jesus came into the world to save sinners.*" You are *guilty*—but "*the blood of God's Son cleanseth us from all sin.*" And to know from experience this, is all that is essential to your salvation to know, until God perfects you in the holiness and knowledge of heaven. Oh, seek to work out this great problem of your life—"Am I saved? am I in Christ? have I Christ in me? shall I be in heaven when I die?" It will essentially aid you in this momentous inquiry if you come to the study of the gospel of Jesus with the lowliness, docility, and trustfulness of a little child. With such a spirit can you alone receive into your soul the kingdom of God. Listen to the words of the Great Teacher come from God—"*Verily I say unto you, Whosoever shall not receive the kingdom of God as a little child, he shall not enter therein.*" (Mark x. 15.) The apostle lays down the same rule—"*If any man among you seemeth to be wise in this world, let him become a fool, that he may be wise.*"

(1 Cor. iii. 18.) Solemn verities are these! Let them sink down into your heart, that the Word of God may be quick and powerful—the word of light, life, and salvation to your soul. Settle it in your mind as a fixed principle guiding your researches into God's Word, that on all subtle questions of speculative theology Jesus Christ, the Eternal Word, is *silent*. Touching the origin and permission of evil—*Christ answers not a word.* Touching the mystery of the incarnation—*Christ answers not a word.* In explanation of the harmony of Divine providence with human freedom, —election and sovereignty,—the eternal Sonship, —the vicarious substitution of the Saviour,—the regeneration of man by the Spirit,—the details of the future relation of the soul—*Christ answers not a word.* When *He* is silent, it behoves *us* to be silent. Presume not, then, to plunge, rashly and profanely, into these profound abysses of Divine mystery, but rather bow before them in faith, love, and obedience, and let both your ignorance and your science be alike docile, receptive, and trustful. The mysteries of Christianity imply no deficiency in revelation; and because you have no line with which to sound its depths, you are not the less saved if you embrace,

in the faith of a humble, penitent, and believing sinner, the great Atonement of the Son of God. Believe and love now, and you will one day know all that God will reveal or you can comprehend.

Conversion, too, is often a work of silence. With what invisible, noiseless power does the kingdom of Christ's grace make its advent into the soul! Real conversion is a marvellous work. No miracle ever wrought approaches it in vastness and wonder. What a mighty moral revolution is passing—what a stupendous work is being wrought—what a magnificent edifice is rising—what a holy temple is forming in the soul! And yet, like that of old—in the construction of which "*there was neither hammer nor axe, nor any tool of iron heard in the house while it was in building*"—not a sound is heard, so gentle, so noiseless, so quiet is the movement of the Spirit upon the heart. Gentle as the day-dawn of light, still as the night-fall of dew, enters Christ's grace into the soul, and lo! as in a moment, a new creation in Christ Jesus bursts into view, and all the sons of God sing together for joy. We trace Christ's silence, too, in the advancing process of sanctification. A great conflict is passing within the soul between the law of the flesh and the law of the mind; the kingdom of God within you is extending its empire of holiness, righteousness, and love; the Divine image is developing its features of beauty and perfection, and the inner man is day by day advancing in its maturity of holiness for heaven, and yet all is so silent! Ah, we often little suspect what is passing within the soul of a child of God. Of his sorrow we are ignorant, and with his joy a stranger intermeddleth not. And because he sounds no note, makes no show, awakens no inquiry, we deem not how, unseen and unheard, Christ is rearing within him a temple which shall reflect His glory through eternity, outshining ten thousand suns.

There is, too, *the silence of Christ's love.* The sense or enjoyment of the Lord's love in the soul may for a season be suspended; the voice of love be still. Jesus answers not a word. There was love in His heart towards the mother suing at His feet on behalf of her daughter, but it was *silent* love. There was love in the heart of Joseph towards his brethren, to whom he spoke roughly, but it was *silent* love. "*He will rest in His love*"—margin, "He will be *silent* in His love." God's love may be silent when it might justly rebuke and chide

—it may be silent when it might be expected to comfort and cheer. And still it is love—not less love because it utters no voice. Oh, deem not that Christ's love has chilled or changed towards you because He answers you not a word! He has loved you, O believer, from everlasting! He loves you still, and will love you unto the end! Wait in faith and patience, Jesus will break the silence—Christ will speak; the tempest shall subside, the clouds shall vanish, and sweet the peace your Father will give.

There is often, too, *the silence of Jesus in prayer.* You approach the throne of grace, you draw near the mercy-seat, but—*He answers you not a word!* Jesus is silent. Around the spot where you had thought His voice would the soonest and the clearest be heard, lo! the stillness of death seems to reign. You have brought a new sorrow, you have come with a new burden, you have repaired with a new want, and Jesus hides Himself. You weep, you cry, you complain, but He answers you not a word. God's answers to prayer are not always immediate and direct. The "vision" has an appointed time, and for that it tarries. But though the Lord is silent in prayer, it does not follow that He hears not the voice, or is indifferent to the appeal of prayer. Oh no! It would seem an utter impossibility that God should be deaf to the voice or disregard the prayers of His people. "*O Thou that hearest prayer, unto Thee shall all flesh come.*" The silence of God in prayer is to be interpreted but as a test of our sincerity, and as a trial of our faith, and as a lesson He would teach us in His own divine sovereignty. His silence in prayer is not indifference. His delays in answer to prayer are not refusals. Were our faith expert and lively, it would take encouragement from silence, and gather hope from delay. Long and silent was the night of the Patriarch's holy wrestlings with the Angel of the Covenant; but when the day dawned it broke the mysterious silence, and Jacob retired from the conflict a prince and a conqueror. The language of the prophet is, "*I will wait upon the Lord, that hideth His face from the house of Israel, and I will seek for Him.*" (Isa. viii. 17.) Faith waits for a silent God, and seeks for a hiding God; believes that He is a God that cannot lie, and so trusts His word of promise even though the silence of death seems to entomb it for ever. Lift up thy heart, then, child of God! thy prayers are heard, thy God will answer. The bright vision may tarry, but it will surely come; the blessing may be delayed, but it will certainly be given. Jesus may answer you not a word, but He knows the thoughts and purposes He has towards you, and beneath the stillness and solemnity of that weary, painful silence there is revolving in His infinite mind and loving heart, responses to your supplications and prayers the most gracious and full, far above all that you had asked or thought.

In the season of trial, affliction, and sorrow, the believer may have much to do with the *silence* of the Lord. He may seem to sit alone in his grief, no one caring for his soul. To the trial of the decay of health, the loss of property, sore and deep bereavement, there may be added darkness of soul, the hidings of God, the silence of Jesus. "*I weep; mine eye, mine eye runneth down with water, because the comforter that should relieve my soul is far from me.*" (Lam. i. 16.) All is gloom and silence. No voice is heard but the resounding billow, no sound save the moans and echoes of the storm. The vessel is tossed amid the waves, the night is dark, and Jesus has not yet come. Such, beloved! is the dreary path travelled by many a home-bound pilgrim. Thou art steering thy bark in the wake of many a gallant vessel—thou art pursuing thy way along a path travelled by many a heaven-enshrined saint. All have experienced the silence of Christ in sorrow. But how is faith to explain and interpret it? Just as the Jews did the silence which sealed the lips of Jesus as He wept in mute grief over the grave of Lazarus. "*Behold how He loved him!*" It is the silence of love! There are some sorrows so deep, so acute, and so delicate, *silence* is the most befitting, touching, and expressive form of soothing and sympathy. We read of the friends of Job who came to mourn with and to comfort him, that when they saw his grief, his sad and changed appearance, "*they sat down with him upon the ground seven days and seven nights, and none spake a word unto him: for that they saw that his grief was very great.*" The silence of a look, the silence of a tear, the silence of a conscious presence in sorrow, oh, who has not felt its magic power and its soothing! Such is the silence of Jesus in grief. He may answer us not a word; He may seem coldly indifferent to the burden that crushes us, to the bereavement that smites us, the cloud that shades us, the temptation that wounds us, the want that presses us, but still it is the silence of a love that once poured forth its utterance of anguish for us on the cross, and now bends down its look of ineffable delight upon us from the throne. If the voice of Christ is mute on earth, it speaks in heaven, and speaks with an authority, power, and tenderness which God cannot resist. The interceding merits of our Saviour intercept our supplications on their way to God, blends them with His own, and bears them to the Father, thus securing the acceptance of every prayer and the bestowment of every blessing.

There is not unfrequently the silence of God *in His dark and afflictive providences.* How often have these dispensations gathered around you in gloom and mystery, the deep, the awful stillness of which not a divine syllable has broken. Your vessel has been tossed amid the waves of grief, night has set in, and gloom enshrouds every object. Yes; the mysteries of providence are for a time totally unexplained, and even unmitigated by a single utterance from Christ. The afflicted one must tread his shady and silent way; must walk through trials and sorrows, confront difficulties and impediments, exclaiming, "Thou art a God that hidest

Thyself! O that Thou wouldest speak, and tell me wherefore thou contendest with me!" Here, again, faith is summoned as the interpreter. And how does it interpret God's silence in afflictive dispensations? Not as the sullen silence of anger, not as the cold silence of indifference, not as the portentous silence of judgment, but as the infinitely wise, holy silence of a Father's love. Afflicted one! God may appear at a great distance from your voice; your cry for succour may not seem to reach His ear, nor your appeal to His compassion touch His heart. You go forward, but He is not there; and backward, but you cannot perceive Him: on the left hand, where He dwelleth, but you cannot behold Him; He hideth Himself on the right hand, that you cannot see Him. Nevertheless, He knows the way you take, and when He hath tried you, you shall come forth as gold. God's silence to you in this overwhelming calamity, in this crushing affliction, in this overshadowing cloud, in this bitter trial, is the silence of infinite and unchangeable *love.* Wait, and He will speak anon, and sweet, assuring, and soothing will be the words that shall break that silence, the stillness of which has filled your mind with forebodings so painful, and with an awe so profound—"*It is I, be not afraid!*" Your bounding heart shall respond, "*It is the voice of my Beloved!*"

And mark the blessing which rewarded the faith of the petitioning parent. From the too impatient disciples, weary of her importunity, she met with an unsympathising repulse. "*Send her away; for she crieth after us.*" Oh, how soon may we come to the end even of a saint's kindness, sympathy, and forbearance! These disciples were dwelling close to the Fountain of boundless compassion, tenderness, and love; and yet how imperfect and shallow their own! how little had they of the heart of Christ! Why marvel we at this? It is but that of a sinful, finite creature, and must of necessity have its end. After another trial of her faith at length she prevailed. "*Then Jesus answered and said unto her, O woman, great is thy faith: be it unto thee even as thou wilt. And her daughter was made whole from that very hour.*" Thus shall faith ever triumph. "*Shall not God avenge His own elect, which cry day and night unto Him, though He bear long with them? I tell you that He will avenge them speedily.*"

The silence of God, both in the kingdom of

nature and in the kingdom of grace, is deeply instructive. We trace the working of the principle in nature, some of whose most genial operations and powerful agencies are the most quiet and noiseless. The sun travels its wondrous path, pouring from its bosom a flood of light bathing the world in glory, and yet not a vibration of his burning wheels is felt. The dew of heaven is distilling by night, and the rain by day, clothing creation with life, verdure, and fruitfulness, and yet so gentle and quiet that not a sound is heard. The whole process of vegetation is going on—the root deepening, the blade shooting, the bud forming, the flower blowing, the fruit maturing—and yet all so still and noiseless. So is it in the kingdom of grace. A deep and powerful work may be going on in your soul, O man! through the agency of the Holy Spirit and the influence of Divine grace, and yet so quiet, unseen, and gentle as scarcely to be perceived. The kingdom of God makes its advent to the heart without observation, grows stronger and stronger, deepens and expands, in solemn and holy stillness. Reflect not, then, against thyself because thou canst not pray fluently, or preach eloquently, or reason profoundly, or open thy lips boldly to speak for Christ. Your Christianity may not be the less true, nor your religion the less sincere, nor your influence the less powerful because it is quiet, gentle, speechless. The silence of a godly, holy life is infinitely more eloquent and effectual in its influence than the most resonant religious zeal in alliance with a dubious profession and an inconsistent walk. It was predicted of the Saviour, "*He shall not strive, nor cry; neither shall any man hear His voice in the streets.*" And yet that government, thus so gentle and meek, shook to its centre the empire of darkness and sin.

We gather, too, from this subject how silent are some of the profoundest and most spiritual emotions of our renewed nature. The *joy* of the Lord, when its inspiration is felt in the heart, often distances all thought and forbids all language—it is "a joy UNSPEAKABLE, *and full of glory.*" The feelings of the soul are too deep for utterance. Could their soundings be measured or their fulness be expressed, could imagery the most rich delineate, or language the most copious interpret them, we might doubt their intensity or question their truthfulness—

> "*Silence* is the perfectest herald of joy:
> I were but little happy, if I could say how much."

Be not, then, distressed if your elevated, and sometimes ecstatic, spiritual feelings are misunderstood or misrepresented by others. Enough that Christ understands you, and has enkindled in your soul a joy so real and deep that a stranger intermeddleth not with it, and which the world cannot take away.

In all your concerns let there be a silent waiting upon and for God. "*Rest in the Lord,*" (marg., "be *silent* to the Lord,") "*and wait patiently for Him.*" (Ps. xxxvii. 7.) "*Truly my soul waiteth upon God,*" (marg., "is *silent* upon God.") (Ps. lxii. 1.) When the Lord speaks it behoves us to hearken; when He smites to hold our peace. Oh, to be silent upon God!—all repining hushed, all murmuring stilled, all disputing mute, the soul behaving and quieting itself as a weaned child. This is no mean attainment in grace, no small triumph of faith. The peace and serenity it will diffuse through the soul passeth understanding. The moment the heart rests from itself, and the mind ceases to reason and the will to dispute, the believer drops his anchor in a tranquil and pleasant haven, unmoved by a breath, unruffled by a wavelet. "BE STILL, *and know that I am God.*"

We may learn a holy, practical lesson from this subject. Is it the wisdom of God to be silent? Surely there are times and circumstances when it were so with us! "*In the multitude of words there wanteth not sin: but he that refraineth his lips is wise.*" (Prov. x. 19.) It has been sagely remarked, that "there are three kinds of silence. Silence from words is good, because inordinate speaking tends to evil. Silence, or rest from desires and passions, is still better, because it promotes quietness of spirit. But the best of all is silence from unnecessary and wandering thoughts, because that is essential to internal recollection, and because it lays a foundation for a proper regulation and silence in other respects." * We need to seek a wisdom higher than our own to know when to speak and when to refrain. Sometimes, when unkindly wounded or unjustly assailed, silence, if it be a committing of our case to Him who pleadeth the causes of His people, and who judgeth righteously, is our best and wisest policy, This may be even safer than the soft answer which turneth away wrath. Study this silence, too, not only in personal provocation and injury, but *in reference to the failings*

* Madame Guyon.

and infirmities of others. Put to confusion all evil-speaking, backbiting, and censoriousness by a becoming, dignified, holy silence. Speak evil of no man. Curb the tongue, seal the lips, be silent touching a brother's or a sister's failings. God is silent of yours; learn you of Him to be silent of your fellow-servants. Go to thy brother and tell him his fault between him and you *alone*, but let no consideration induce you to unvail that fault to another. (Matt. xviii. 15.)

How much of the feuds and heart-burnings, suspicions and wranglings, which mar the happiness of families, and which disturb the peace and impede the prosperity of churches, would be prevented were this sacred, holy silence more strictly observed. Spend a whole night in prayer before you open your lips to utter a sentence or to breathe a word tending to sully the fame, to injure the character, or to wound the happiness of a child of God. Think how dear, how precious, that believer is to Christ, and that in wounding the disciple you wound the Lord. "*Set a watch, O Lord, before my mouth; keep the door of my lips.*"

CHAPTER VI.

THE EMOTION OF LOVE IN CHRIST.

"And to know the love of Christ, which passeth knowledge."
—EPH. iii. 19.

THE mind has often been sensible of a feeling of awe as we have stood upon the shore, and gazed upon the vast expanse of the ocean. With a similar, yet far transcending emotion, we approach the subject which is now to engage our thoughts — *the infinite ocean of Christ's love.* Of all the sympathetic emotions of our Lord's humanity, the emotion of Love must be regarded as the parent source. We should have known nothing of Christ, or of His redemption, but for *love.* The stupendous fact that Christ loves us — loves man, sinful man—admits us to the secret of all that He has done, and is still doing, for man. There is no other solution to the marvellous mysteries of His Incarnation and Sacrificial Death but this—Christ hath *loved* us. Love originated all, explains all, illustrates all,—love is the interpreter of every Divine mystery. There is not a circumstance of our Lord's history which is not another form or manifestation of love. His incarnation, is love stooping; His sympathy, is love weeping; His compassion, is love succouring; His grace, is love acting. His teaching, is the voice of love; His silence, is the repose of love; His patience, is the restraint of love; His obedience, is the labour of love; His suffering, is the travail of love; His cross, is the altar of love; His death is the burnt-offering of love; His resurrection, is the triumph of love; His ascension into heaven, and His sitting down at the right hand of God, is the enthronement and the intercession of love. Such is the deep, the vast, the boundless ocean upon which our thoughts are now about to launch. The soul muses in silent awe as it gazes upon this fathomless, illimitable sea. Like the eternity of God, we know not where it begins, or where it terminates. It has neither beginning nor ending. Like the peace of God, "*it passeth all understanding;*" like itself, "*it passeth all knowledge.*" And yet there exists not an emotion of Christ of which the saints of God have a more truly blessed experience. Christianity is the experience, as it is the embodiment, of love. A religion destitute of the love of God in the heart is a vain religion. A religion without love, is a religion without soul, without life. All real, vital, saving religion resolves itself into love—love to God in Christ, and love to man. Your religion, beloved, may be wanting in some of the more visible attributes of profound knowledge, brilliant gifts, costly offerings; yet, is there in that heart of yours the deep, silent, gentle, throbbing of a true and sincere love to Christ?—then your religion is real. You have no eloquence, perhaps, to speak for Christ, and you have no power to do for Christ; but you have love enough to suffer for Christ, yea, if need be, to die for Christ. Enough! "*Lord, thou knowest all things, thou knowest that I* LOVE *thee.*" "Enough, my disciple," says your Lord; "go and feed my lambs." Lord! I go; Thy love constrains me to the lowliest service in Thy Church! Let us now descend from the shore and dip our line of faith into the depths, and endeavour to "*comprehend with all saints what is the breadth, and length, and depth, and height*" of this infinite ocean of love which has flowed down to us from God through Christ,—an ocean which has its *shallows* for the babe, and its *depths* for the perfect man in Christ Jesus.

The love of Christ is a *divine* emotion. Were it the most exquisite, profound, and pure that could possibly find a home in the human heart, and yet were created, it would still be but a finite affection; and a mere finite love could not have met the requirements of God's moral government, by the perfect satisfaction and honouring of which sinful man is saved. Why is it a love that passeth knowledge? Why cannot the deep line sound it—the swift wing reach it—the eagle eye pierce it—the eloquent tongue describe it? Why are there depths and heights, lengths and breadths, which distance all thought, imagination, and measurement? Because it is the love of DEITY. The love of Christ is the love of GOD. We employ no rhetorical exaggeration, we speak not in hyperbole, but the words of truth and soberness, when we declare, on the authority of revealed truth, Christ to be the eternal and essential Son of God—"GOD *over all, blessed for evermore.*" Listen to the argument. "*God hath in these last days spoken unto us by* HIS SON—*the brightness of His glory, and the express image of His person.*" (Heb. i. 2, 3.) "*Unto* THE SON *he saith,*

Thy throne, O God, *is for ever and ever: a sceptre of righteousness is the sceptre of Thy kingdom.*" (Heb. i. 8.) All the names, attributes, and works predicated of Deity are ascribed to Him, which, were He not God, essential, absolute God, were blasphemy the purest and most sublimated. Hear the voice of prophecy: "*His name shall be called Wonderful, Counsellor, The mighty God, The everlasting Father, The Prince of Peace.*" (Isa. ix. 6.) Speak we of *Creation?* "*By Him were all things created, that are in heaven, and that are in earth, visible and invisible, whether they be thrones, or dominions, or principalities, or powers: all things were created by Him, and for Him.*" (Col. i. 16.) Speak we of *Providence?* "*By Him all things consist.*" (Col. i. 17.) Speak we of *Universal Dominion?* "*He is Lord of all.*" (Acts x. 36.) Claim we for the Scriptures of truth *Divine Inspiration?* "*The words that I speak unto you, they are spirit, and they are life.*" (John vi. 63.) "*Then opened He their understanding, that they might understand the scriptures.*" (Luke xxiv. 45.) Speak we of *Omniscience?* "*All the churches shall know that I am he which searcheth the reins and hearts.*" (Rev. ii. 23.) Of *Omnipotence?* "*Christ the power of God.*" (1 Cor. i. 24.) Of *Omnipresence?* "*Where two or three are gathered together in my name, there am I in the midst of them.*" (Matt. xviii. 20.) Of *Immutability?* "*Jesus Christ the same yesterday, and to-day, and for ever.*" (Heb. xiii. 8.) Is it the office and power of *Judge?* "*We must all appear before the judgment-seat of Christ.*" (2 Cor. v. 10.) Is He to be loved with a love belonging only to Deity? "*If any man love not the Lord Jesus Christ, let him be Anathema Maran-atha.*" (1 Cor. xvi. 22.) But enough! It is not the accumulation of Scripture proof woven around a doctrine that establishes its truth. One text of Scripture, or single declaration of God's Word taken in its connexion, simple in its meaning, grammatical in its construction, and correct in its rendering, should be sufficient to command our unquestioning faith, win our deepest affection and purest homage, when so essential and vital a doctrine as the DEITY of Christ is taught us in the Bible; such should be our full belief in, and profound reverence for the revealed Word of God.

In addition to the direct and positive evidence, there are collateral proofs of the Deity of Christ equally as strong and conclusive. Our Lord is beautifully styled the "*forth-beaming of the Father's glory.*" (Heb. i. 3.) Could this be affirmed of a mere creature? Light flows from the sun. The ray that trembles in the eastern sky at day-dawn, and the light that glows in noon-tide effulgence, equally emanate from the majestic orb, and alike partake of its nature and reflect its beauty. Were it possible to exhaust the sun of its light, you would not merely exterminate the light, but you would inevitably destroy the source of light—the sun itself. We cannot separate Christ from the essence of the Godhead without destroying the Godhead. To destroy the Deity of Christ, we must first destroy Deity itself. A denial of the Divinity of the Son, is a denial of the Divinity of the Father. "*He is antichrist, that denieth the Father and the Son. Whosoever denieth the Son, the same hath not the Father.*" (1 John ii. 22, 23.) Prostrate thyself, my soul, before this great mystery of godliness—"GOD *manifest in the flesh.*" Angels study it—seraphim and cherubim adore it—the spirits of just men made perfect magnify it—do thou believe it, rest in it, entwine it with every fibre of thy heart, blend it with thy sweetest song, O my soul, for thy Saviour is DIVINE, thy Redeemer is GOD! Nothing short of a *divine* love could or would have borne our *sins*, and the *punishment* of our sins. The weight of the one and the terribleness of the other would have crushed and annihilated a mere created affection. There existed no love but the love of DEITY equal to the work of salvation. Who was willing, who was able, to bear that heavy load, to endure that overwhelming curse, but the eternal Son of the Father? Oh, think, beloved reader, what the love of Christ has done and suffered—the burden it bore, the sorrow it felt, the humiliation it underwent, the insults, ignominy, and privation through which it travelled—its groans, its sighs, its tears, its darkness—how inconceivably it agonised, how freely it bled, how voluntarily it died,—think of the sins it has pardoned, the guilt it has cleansed, the declensions it has restored, the backslidings it has healed, the sorrows it has soothed, the patience it has exercised, the gentleness it has exhibited, and then ask, could any other but a *divine* affection have done all this and endured all this? Yet all this was exhibited in the love of Christ which passeth knowledge. Love less divine, less strong, less gentle, had never won thy heart, uprooted thy enmity, tore thee from thy idols, enthroning Christ—Christ all, Christ only, Christ supremely, Christ for ever!

> "Love divine
> Constrains me: I am thine. Incarnate love
> Has seized me, and holds me in Almighty arms.
> Here's my salvation, my eternal hope—
> Amidst the wreck of worlds and dying nature,
> I am the Lord's, and He for ever mine."

It follows from this statement that *the love of Christ is* ETERNAL. There is no reasoning, no philosophy so correct as that of God's Word. Did men—theologians—employ the same rules of interpretation, or the same process of reasoning in the study of the Bible that they do in their scientific researches and inquiries, there would be less false doctrine, crude, blind, erroneous teaching in the pulpit and from the press. Why should the doctrine of Christ's eternal, electing love be thought a thing incredible? Admit His Deity, and you acknowledge His eternity. Acknowledge His eternity, and you must accept the truth of His *everlasting* love.

We have proved from Scripture His Deity, and, of necessity, His eternity; and yet there is so direct a declaration of this doctrine in the book of Proverbs we would place it before the reader.

"The Lord possessed me in the beginning of His way, before His works of old. I was set up from everlasting, from the beginning, or ever the earth was. When there were no depths, I was brought forth; when there were no fountains abounding with water. Before the mountains were settled, before the hills was I brought forth. While as yet He had not made the earth, nor the fields, nor the highest part of the dust of the world. When He prepared the heavens, I was there: when He set a compass upon the face of the depth: When He established the clouds above: when He strengthened the fountains of the deep: when He gave to the sea His decree, that the waters should not pass His commandment: when He appointed the foundations of the earth: then I was by Him, as one brought up with Him: and I was daily His delight, rejoicing always before Him; and my delights were with the children of men." (Prov. viii. 22–31.) Of what could this be predicated but of a *Person*, and of whom but of the Eternal Son of God, even Him who is the "*Wisdom of God*," the hidden Wisdom? Such is the antiquity of the love of Christ! And what a glorious and precious truth is it to the spiritually-taught soul; sweeter than the honey in the honey-

comb to them who have tasted the bitterness of sin, and have felt the plague of their own heart! "*I have loved thee with an everlasting love,*" is the Divine declaration which places the antiquity of Christ's love beyond a doubt. Christ is the Covenant Head of His people, the "*Head over all things to the Church.*" In Christ we are chosen, through Christ the covenant is made with us by the Father—in Christ we are blessed with all spiritual blessings—in Christ we are called—and in Christ we are pardoned, justified, sanctified, and glorified. Every blessing that appertains to our salvation from first to last is interwoven with Christ—in His hand, and through His relation to the Father and to us. Well may the apostle give utterance to that magnificent doxology: "*Blessed be the God and Father of our Lord Jesus Christ, who hath blessed us with all spiritual blessings in heavenly places in Christ; according as He hath chosen us in Him before the foundation of the world, that we should be holy and without blame before Him in love: having predestinated us unto the adoption of children by Jesus Christ to Himself, according to the good pleasure of His will, to the praise of the glory of His grace, wherein He hath made us accepted in the Beloved.*" Such is the eternal ocean from whence flows this river, these rivulets and springs, which, bearing on their bosom innumerable blessings of grace, glide through the Church of God—Christ's garden—clothing it with living verdure, enriching it with divine fruit, adorning it with unfading bloom, and breathing over it the fragrance of a "*field which the Lord hath blest.*" Thou everlasting love of Christ!—divine source of my eternal redemption—fontal spring-head of my sweet refreshment in this weary land where no water is—pledge and earnest of all which my faith believes, which my hope expects, and for which my panting spirit longs, enthrone thyself upon my heart, and under thy gentle, yet all-commanding, all-constraining power may my consecrated being, my surrendered life evince

"How much I owe, how much I love!"

The love of Christ is *condescending.* We measure an act of condescension by the position, rank, or power of the individual from whom it emanates. Forming our view of Christ's love upon this principle—sounding its depth and testing its greatness and intensity by this criterion, even our profoundest conception of the self-abasement and humiliation to which it descended will be at an infinite remove from the reality. The stoop of the Son of God to our humanity—the Incarnation of Deity—was an event so unheard of, a fact so stupendous, marvellous, and transcendent, that it stands in the history of the universe like an orb in its own solitary, unapproachable grandeur, and will be the wonder, the study, and the song of all pure, holy intelligences through eternity. Such was the love of Christ! It drew Him from heaven, brought Him down to earth, to live and labour, suffer and die, robed in the humanity which He stooped so low to save. "*Forasmuch then as the children are partakers of flesh and blood, He also Himself likewise took part of the same. . . . . For verily He took not on Him the nature of angels; but He took on Him the seed of Abraham.*" (Heb. ii. 14, 16, 17.) "*The* WORD *was made flesh, and dwelt among men.*" "GOD *manifest in the flesh.*" Not only—as if this did not suffice to demonstrate the lowliness of His love—did He consent to wear our nature, but He linked Himself in that nature with meanness and poverty, with obscurity and privation, with toil, weariness, and want! In addition to this, He was spit upon, scourged, reviled, maligned, denied; was the "rich man's scorn, the poor man's contumely;" bowed His dear, devoted head meekly, uncomplainingly to the storms of human insult, contempt, and derision which broke over Him. Oh! was ever love like unto this? And such, beloved, is still the condescension of Christ's love. Having stooped so low, it would seem as if there were no deeper depths to which it could not sink. Ah! perhaps, in your personal history there are circumstances of woe, of scorn, of humiliation, from which you imagine the Son of God must shrink,—an abyss which He cannot fathom,—physical and mental prostrations with which He has no sympathy—to elevate which He has no power. But judge Him not thus. His thoughts are not your thoughts. The love of Christ is prepared to entwine itself with every event and circumstance of your being and history. Having taken into union with His divinity your nature, all prostrate, and bruised, and crushed beneath the curse, think you that there can be a position in which your fallen humanity is placed beyond the pale of His compassion, or the reach of His arm? Ah, no! Love made the God willing to unite Himself with the man; and love made the God-man willing to unite Himself with all the lowliness, degradation, and suffering of the human. And the same love of Christ that stooped to all this is prepared to descend with you into the vale of poverty, to enter with your trembling spirit into the cloud of adversity, to divide with you the cup of sorrow, to cheer your exile, and share the ignominy, insult, and neglect to which you may be exposed. Will Incarnate Love, which once stooped to wash the disciples' feet, shrink from any office or service with which your happiness, honour, or wellbeing is entwined? "*Lord! Thou shalt never wash my feet,*" says your resisting spirit. "*Suffer it to be so now,*" replies your condescending Lord. I am that Friend that loveth at *all times,* a Brother *born for adversity.* Having stooped to the vesture of your nature, think you that I have not love, and grace, and lowliness enough to sink with that nature to its lowest condition of necessity and woe? Though others, recoiling from your position, deaf to your entreaty, and ashamed of your bruise, may pass you by on the other side, I am prepared to identify myself with your case, to rouse your sinking pulse with the wine of my love, to heal your wound with the soothing oil of my compassionate sympathy; and, amid the strife and clamour of tongues, to spread around you the invincible shield of my power. Truly may we say, "*In the time of trouble He shall hide me in His pavilion: in the secret of His tabernacle shall He hide me; He shall set me up upon a rock. And now shall mine head be lifted up above mine enemies round about me.*" It is the pavilion of LOVE.

Labour is another characteristic of the love of Christ. The apostles speak of the saints' "*labour of love,*" or loving labour. In a sense infinitely transcending this do we speak of Christ's labour of love. His first, His chief labour was not in sharing the sorrows, bearing the infirmities, or in healing the sicknesses of our humanity, but it was in the *perfect obedience* to the precepts of the law which His holy, fervent, toilsome life rendered. This was His highest, holiest, divinest labour of love. "*If by the disobedience of one many were made sinners, by the obedience of one many are made righteous.*" He found His own law broken, desecrated, dishonoured. He consented to be made under the law, that He might redeem them that were under the law. He could only be held responsible by the law for obedience, as He placed Himself under its power, precept, and authority.

He, the Lawgiver, and the Administrator of the law, consented thus to humble Himself. There was but one Being in the universe who could magnify that law and make it honourable by a full recognition of its authority, and a perfect deference to its just and holy requirements;—it was God's co-equal and eternal Son. His God-head gave dignity, His sinlessness imparted perfection, His love clothed with voluntariness the obedience and honour which He rendered to God's moral government, from which man had plucked the diadem of glory, trailing and trampling it in the dust. And now, this obedience, thus deriving its sanction, perfection, and acceptance from the dignity and sinlessness of His nature, is the "*righteousness of God*," finished and imparted, which justifies the believing sinner, and which exalts and glorifies the accepted saint. "*He hath made Him to be sin for us who knew no sin, that we might be made the righteousness of God in Him.*" "*Blessed are the people who know the joyful sound; they shall walk, O Lord, in the light of Thy countenance, and in Thy righteousness shall they be exalted.*" The life of our Lord was one continuous, unswerving, unbroken act of homage and obedience to His

Father's law. He alone of all others could say, "*My meat and my drink is to do the will of Him that sent me, and to finish His work.*" The two objects He had in view in this labour of love were—the offering of such an obedience as would constitute our righteousness, and thus secure our perfect and free justification; and the second was the honouring and magnifying of the law in its divine authority and holiness, thus winning back to the Father the glory He had lost by the violation of that law. With these objects before Him, and impelled onward by the irresistible force of His own love, He faltered not, swerved not, deviated not an hair's-breadth from His sublime and holy purpose. His was the true battle of life. The world sought to allure, men sought to entrap, Satan sought to tempt Him; but He passed through the fiery ordeal untouched and unscathed—observing every requirement, and keeping every precept. To what shall we ascribe this unswerving, unfaltering obedience, this pure and perfect compliance with the law's stern and righteous demands, but to His divine dignity and perfect sinlessness? And all this was the labour of love! Well knowing that the salvation of His Church was based upon the law's fulfilment, and that that salvation was confided to His hand, it was His meat and His drink to entwine with every word, and thought, and deed the perfect doing of the will of God with His everlasting love to His saints—zeal for God's glory with fidelity for His people's cause. Behold the groundwork of our full justification!—justified on the basis of a repaired, restored, honoured law—a law upon which, divine and glorious though it was, the obedience of the SON OF GOD shed a new and ineffable lustre. "*He hath magnified the law, and made it honourable.*" Behold the ground and channel of *peace* with God!—peace through faith in a righteousness which renders it illustrious in God to justify the sinner. "*Being justified by faith, we have peace with God through our Lord Jesus Christ.*" Is *this* not true, assured, and perfect peace? To know that the indictment against us is quashed, the sentence is cancelled, the condemnation is removed, and that we are reinstated in a Paradise, forfeited, but restored; lost, but regained—a Paradise amid whose sylvan bowers no tempter lurks, upon whose sunny banks no shadow reposes, whose vernal bloom no curse blights, whose perfumed air no sin taints; into which nor sickness, nor suffering, nor death, nor parting ever enters; where is neither sorrow nor crying, neither shall be any more pain—surely, "*the work of righteousness is peace, and the effect of righteousness, quietness, and assurance for ever.*" We return to the statement that all this is ours through the obedience of the "*Lord our Righteousness.*" Heaven, the coming paradise of the saints, is won by no creature-merit. Not a grain of human worthiness mingles with the merit that justifies the sinner before God. Not a filament of creature-obedience is woven into the wedding-robe that will give us a place at the "*marriage-supper of the Lamb*"—all, *all* must be the worthiness, the merit, the obedience of GOD in our nature. Gracious soul! brought to the end of all thine own duties, doings, and sacrifices—seeing all to be but as dross and chaff, nay, more, but so much gilded, splendid sin—bowed down to the earth beneath thy load of guilt—shut up to the condemnation of the law, with not a ray of hope trembling upon the thunder-cloud of divine wrath which enshrouds thee—oh, look up! in the LORD you have righteousness and strength. The Eternal Spirit is now graciously and effectually teaching you this glorious, precious truth in the school of your own utter emptiness, vileness, and poverty. Be not, therefore, hopeless and despairing. In Christ Jesus there is pardon, acceptance, grace, sanctification, salvation for the vilest, the most hell-deserving penitent that earth ever saw, or that heaven ever received. Oh, what a glorious gospel is ours! What a marvellous truth is this which it reveals—a justifying righteousness divinely provided, freely given, believingly received, which exchanges our filthy rags for a spotless robe, our condemnation for hope, our hell for heaven, an eternity of woe for an eternity of bliss! What divine peace should this truth impart, what fervent love should it inspire, what holy, unreserved surrender should it induce! How precious to our hearts should be this gracious Saviour, how welcome His yoke, how delightsome His service, how pleasant and sweet His cross. And, oh! how will the challenge, bursting from countless tongues, awaken the deep, undying echoes of eternity—"*Who is he that condemneth? it is* GOD *that justifieth!*"

> "And lest the shadow of a spot
> Should on my soul be found,
> He took the robe the Saviour wrought
> And cast it all around."

The reception of Christ's obedience as our justification *by faith* is a kindred and equally essential and precious truth. Oh, it is a wondrous fact that God has made our salvation entirely independent of ourselves, in making it to rest upon our *believing*, and not our doing! "*It is of faith, that it might be by grace.*" "*By grace are ye saved, through faith, and that not of yourselves; it is the gift of God.*" It is not our penitence, nor our love, nor our knowledge that looks to the cross and lives,—it is our *faith*. It was not the hand, nor the foot, nor the tongue, nor the ear which availed to the poor bitten Israelite, stung with the fiery flying serpent,—it was the *eye*. He travelled not, he spake not, he handled not, but simply raised himself, or, perchance too feeble, was uplifted in the arms of another, and rested his eye upon the serpent of brass, looked, and was healed. How much more facile an effort was this! It was easier, more simple, and effectual to *look*, than to perform a tedious task with the hands, or to utter long sentences with the tongue, or to take a wearisome pilgrimage with the feet. Thus simple and easy is the divine instrument God has appointed for your salvation! Faith *beholds* the Lamb of

God; faith *looks* upon Him whom our sins have pierced; faith *sees* Jesus, and the simple "looking unto Jesus" crucified heals the wounded conscience, unbinds our burden of guilt, and the Sun of Righteousness arises in the soul with healing in His wings. But while thus we insist upon *faith* as the instrument of your justification, and consequent peace with God, as earnestly would we remind you that faith is *but an instrument.* It is not the *object* that is to engage your thought, awaken your interest, or arrest and fix your gaze. That object is Christ, and Christ alone. And now we would have you for a moment forget all that we have said upon faith, and think of JESUS, and of JESUS only. It was not the eye that healed the bitten Israelite,—it was the eye in contact with its distant, and, perhaps, dim and obscure object, reposing upon which, in obedience to the Divine command, instantaneous life was the consequence. Suppose the dying man had argued, "I cannot see, by reason of my wound. The shadow of death is upon me. The film of death is on my eyes,—darkness dims my sight, and I cannot see." Still, the command was—"*Look* to the uplifted serpent;" and, looking, the dying lived. No objection lay against the feebleness and dimness of the sight; his refusal to raise and open that eye, dim and dizzy though it was, and rest it upon the pole, was *death.* Oh, I beseech you, deal less with faith, and more with Christ, the object of faith. Your weak faith, your little faith, your obscure faith, your tried faith, your sinking faith, is no reason why you should not look to, cleave to, and rejoice in Christ Jesus, knowing of a truth that your sins are forgiven, and that your person is accepted in the Beloved. One believing *blink* of Christ, as the holy Rutherford expresses it, and you are saved. Or, to quote the lively picture of faith presented by another worthy, one of the early Reformers of Scotland:—"It is not the quantity of faith that shall save thee. A drop of water is as true water as the whole ocean. So a little faith is as true faith as the greatest. A child eight days old is as really a man as one of sixty years; a spark of fire is as true fire as a great flame; a sickly man is as truly living as a well man. So it is not the measure of thy faith that saves thee; it is the blood that it grips to that saves thee. As the weak hand of a child that leads the spoon to the mouth will feed as well as the strongest arm of a man,—for it is not the hand that feeds thee, albeit it puts the meat into thy mouth, but it is the meat carried into the stomach that feeds thee, —so if thou canst grip Christ ever so weakly, He will not let thee perish. All that looked to the brazen serpent, never so far off, they were healed of the sting of the fiery serpent; yet all saw not alike clearly, for some were near at hand, and some were far off. Those that were near at hand might see more clearly than those that were far off; nevertheless, those that were far off were as soon healed of the sting when they looked to the serpent as those that were near at hand; for it was not their look that made them whole, but He whom the serpent did represent. So if thou canst look to Christ ever so meanly, He can take away the sting of thy conscience if thou believest. The weakest hand can take a gift as well as the strongest. Now Christ is the gift, and weak faith may grip Him as well as strong faith; and Christ is as truly thine when thou hast weak faith, as when thou hast come to these triumphant joys through the strength of faith."*

Another and more modern writer, speaking of Christ and faith, thus forcibly testifies to the

* John Welsh.

same truth:—"The less that is said about faith,—the mere act we mean—and the more that is said about its object, the Saviour, all the better; and the less people think about faith, and the more they think, and hear, and read about the Saviour himself, and His work, and His great salvation, all the better. There is a discoursing about the mere belief, and an exhorting to the mere belief, the only effect of which is to leave the impression on the mind that it is some 'great thing' which people have to do in order to their acceptance with God. Whereas, saying nothing, or as little, at least, as the Bible says, about the act and the duty, and all about Jesus himself, His cross, and His crown; faith, through the Spirit's use of this, will spring up as a thing of course. There is a dry arguing in behalf of the belief, and a setting forth of reasons and motives for exercising it, as if the thing could ever go into the heart by mere force, or dint of argument, or bribes, or terrors, or any way else whatever, but by the truth itself being exhibited and seen. The consequence is that some, through an excitement from without, or by a direct force on their feelings, persuade themselves that they have done this 'great thing'—that they have believed, and they are forthwith glad; but glad in it, their fancied faith—not in the Lord himself. It is the gladness and joy, if not of the hypocrite, at least of the self-righteous and the self-deceived; while others are kept labouring and labouring after this thing in legal miserable bondage all their lifetime, and never advance an inch nearer the object of their wishes. Oh that we all, ministers and people, took the wiser and scriptural course!—the one making the facts of the gospel their meaning, their glory, their grace, their truth, the constant burden of their ministry; the other making these same facts the grand and sole objects of their regard. Then would faith, which, like our shadow, only flees from us if we follow it, arise without our seeking or labouring for it at all; because the things, the realities which give it being, the substance, which, with the light of the Spirit, always casts it, would be there."*

The same reasoning will conduct us to a like conclusion respecting faith's dealing with the *promises* of God. If our faith can lay hold of but *one* divine promise of the gospel, then *all* the promises are ours. It is not our faith that gives us a warrant to receive the promise, or

* Purves.

upon which the efficacy of the promise depends; it is the word, power, and faithfulness of the Divine Promiser. If, then, beloved reader, your faith can rest in any one of these promises, "*Him that cometh unto me I will in no wise cast out;*" "*Come unto me, all ye that labour and are heavy laden, and I will give you rest;*" "*Call upon me in the day of trouble, and I will answer thee and deliver thee,*"—then you may put in your claim to every precious promise in the Bible, and say, "It is *mine.*" "The promises can be no more divided than Christ can be divided, or than heaven can be divided; the promises are not like loose pearls, but as pearls made into one entire chain. He that can lay his hand upon that promise in Matt. v. 6, 'Blessed are they which do thirst after righteousness, for they shall be filled,' and truly say, This promise is mine, may safely lay his hand upon that promise, ver. 8, 'Blessed are the pure in heart, for they shall see God,' and say, This promise is mine; and the same he may say of the rest of the precious promises of that chapter. He that can lay his hand upon any one promise that God has made for them that love Him, and truly say, This promise is mine, may safely lay his hand upon every promise that God has made to them that love him, and say, These are mine. He that can lay his hand upon any one promise that God has made to them that fear Him, and truly say, This promise is mine, may assuredly lay his hand upon every promise that God has made to them that fear Him, and say, These are all mine. He that can lay his hand upon any one promise that God has made to faith in Christ, to believing in Christ, and truly say, This promise is mine, may safely lay his hand upon every promise that God has made to faith in Christ, to believing in Christ, and say, All these promises are mine. He that can lay his hand upon any one promise that God has made to the returning sinner, and truly say, This promise is mine, may securely lay his hand upon every promise that God has made to the returning sinner, and say, All these are mine. He that can lay his hand upon any one promise that God has made to the waiting soul, and truly say, This promise is mine, may without peradventure lay his hand upon every promise that God has made to the waiting soul, and say, All these are mine. Prove but your right in one, and you may safely infer your right to all." *

* Brookes.

But Christ's love possesses yet another and more touching feature, one that has never failed to dissolve and win the heart wherever it has effected a believing entrance, and will be as potent to the end of time—*the suffering, dying love of Jesus.* It travelled its wearisome, law-fulfilling path until it confronted the cross. Could it pass the instrument of torture and of death? Must it be crucified, bleed, and die? Ah, yes! what significance, unmeant by His enemies, in the taunt which they cast at His dying agonies, "*He saved others, Himself He cannot save!*" Yes; He saved others, and He *could* have saved Himself. It was voluntary on His part to die, or not to die.* As easily could He have descended from the cross as He ascended from the grave. But the same love to poor sinners which emancipated Him from the one, kept Him impaled upon the other. Love could not regard its mission accomplished, its purpose fulfilled, until it had sacrificed itself; it must be baptized in suffering, be clothed in a vesture dipped in blood—its *own* blood. And why this suffering, sacrifice, and death? The answer shall be in the words of the Holy Ghost: "*Christ hath* LOVED *us, and hath*

* John x. 17, 18.

given Himself for us an offering and a sacrifice to God for a sweet-smelling savour." We can find no proper solution to the mystery of Christ's sufferings and death but that supplied by this fact, that He died as a SACRIFICE for our SINS, to offer an ATONEMENT to the justice of God for our TRANSGRESSIONS. "*An* OFFERING *and a* SACRIFICE"—a sin-offering, an expiatory sacrifice, a justice-satisfying oblation. How sacred and precious are the sufferings of His love, viewed in this light! What love they inspire, what joy they create, what comfort they impart, what hope they shed upon the dark, the solemn future! Christ has *died,* thereby condemning sin in the flesh. Christ has *died,* thereby freeing us from the curse of the law, being made a curse for us. Christ has *died,* thereby washing out and effacing all our guilt—His own most precious blood cleansing us from all sin. Christ has *died,* therefore the believing sinner that accepts that death as his one and only sacrifice, his sole and complete salvation, shall never die. Such is the love of Christ! Was it ever equalled? Where shall we find its parallel? To have accepted the mission of our salvation upon such terms—a stoop so low, a humiliation so profound, a labour so immense, mental anguish so acute, bodily suffering so agonising, a death so ignominious—was ever love like this? There was nothing coercive or compulsory, ignorant or blind, in the marvellous step. Christ well understood the work He was to accomplish, and had counted well the price He was to pay. He knew the nature of the burden He was to bear, the ingredients of the cup He was to drink, the terribleness of the death He was to die. Never was love so intelligent and far-seeing as His. The grim, dread instrument of torture and of death was vivid to His mind; and yet He was willing to endure it all. Two wills consented to the issue—the will of the Divine, and the will of the human nature of our Lord. And although, like streams from opposite sources, these two wills met, they yet met in perfect harmony and conjunction, forming one confluent tide of love, which bore Him onward upon its bosom, until He reached the cross, and expired. Blessed Jesus! Thy love, like Thine agonies, is an unknown and unfathomable depth—it passeth knowledge. Let it rise and expand before me, until it fill the entire scope of my soul's vision, occupy every niche of my heart, and bear me onward by its all-commanding, all-constraining influence in the path of a holy loving obedience and surrender.

But there are some *characteristics* of the love of Christ which bring it more home to our bosoms, forming a perfect and holy model for our imitation.

The believing mind delights to dwell upon the *filial element* of our Lord's love. Both the Divine and natural Sonship of Christ are mysteries; and yet the mind accepts, and faith believes them. As the Son of God and the Son of man, His love was the most perfectly *filial* that ever existed. His love to God the Father was the affection of a reverential, obedient son. He could say, "*I do always those things which please Him.*" It was this filial love which made Him willing to uphold the honour of His Father's name, the glory of His Father's government, at the costly expense of the sacrifice of Himself. "*Wist ye not that I must be about My* FATHER'S *business?*" Then glance at His filial love to His earthly parents. It is said that, "*He was subject unto them,*"—that is, He reverenced their parental authority, manifested towards them all dutiful respect, yielded an unquestioning and cheerful obedience to their wishes and commands, lived with them, laboured for them, and clung to them until He reached the period of manhood. Nor did His filial love terminate here. He bore it with Him to the death—breathed it in touching expressions from the cross. In that hour of woe, when the throes and throbs of agony were upon Him, and His soul was travailing in sorrow beneath the weight of His people's sins and the inflictions of Divine wrath, He beheld His mother! Forgetful of Himself, He thought only of her; and bending upon her a look of filial affection, He commended her to the care of the disciple whom He loved, who from that hour adopted her as his own. How holy and touching this example of filial love! What an illustrious and impressive enforcement of the Divine precept—"*Children, obey your parents in the Lord: for this is right. Honour thy father and mother.*" Would you be Christ-like?—then cherish the deepest affection for your parents, the profoundest reverence for their authority, and regard for their wishes. And when bereavement and sorrow, age and infirmity, poverty and sickness overtake them, cherish them as the most costly and precious of earth's treasures. Rock the cradle of their old age as gently and watchfully as they rocked yours in infancy, through the silent vigils of many sleepless, weary hours by day and by night.

The love of Christ is also *fraternal.* It is the love of a BROTHER. He calls us brethren, and Himself our Elder Brother. Listen to His words: "*Whosoever shall do the will of God, the same is my* BROTHER;" "*Go to my* BRETHREN." And oh, what a tender, loving, faithful Brother is He! Truly and emphatically is He a "*Brother born for adversity.*" Oh, never forget that the love of Christ to you is the love of—Joseph! Go to Him in want, go to Him in difficulty, go to Him in sorrow,—take to Him the empty vessel; and, though to test your sincerity, to try your faith, to prove your love, and make His own all the more precious and resplendent, He may speak roughly to you in His dealings, yet a Joseph's heart, a Brother's love beats deeply and warmly beneath it all; and, ere long, He will throw off the disguise, and exclaim, in tones of melting tenderness, "*I am Christ your* BROTHER." Let your love to the brethren assimilate to this fraternal love of Christ Jesus. Love them because they are brethren in Christ Jesus, irrespective of national, ecclesiastical, or social distinctions. Love them for the Father's sake,—love them for the

Elder Brother's sake,—love them for their own sake; not because their creed chimes with yours, or that you kneel at the same altar with them in the outward rites of worship, but because they are Christ's brethren, and your brethren in Christ Jesus. Act towards them the part of a loving, sympathising, helping brother, and so you will please and resemble Him who, when He acknowledges it at the last day, will say, "*Inasmuch as ye have done it unto the least of these* MY BRETHREN, *ye have done it unto Me.*"

The love of Christ is the love of a *Friend.* How touchingly and pointedly did He delight to speak of this: "*Greater love hath no man than this, that a man lay down his life for his* FRIENDS. *Ye are* MY FRIENDS, *if ye do whatsoever I command you. Henceforth I call you not servants; . . . . but I have called you* FRIENDS." (John xv. 13–15.) God has created in the human heart the desire for friendship. The sunflower turns not more instinctively to its orb, drinking in the golden beams of light and warmth, and returning its grateful smile, than turns the human heart to the friend it loves. The religion of Jesus is not indifferent to any noble sentiment of our humanity, but teaches us to cultivate that sentiment to its highest degree of development, and of consecration to God. Thus, so far from ignoring or trampling upon the fine sensibilities and affections of our nature, the gospel of Christ recognises them, and instructs us in the holy art of their sacred culture and supreme dedication to the Divine glory. The disciple of the Lord affects not, therefore, to look coldly upon those noble, generous specimens of affection which adorn our humanity, or to be insensible to the touching beauty with which some pens have portrayed the love of an ardent and sacred friendship. Among the most glowing is, perhaps, that of one of our own poets:—

> "I had a friend that loved me;
> I was his soul: he lived not but in me.
> We were so closed within each other's breast,
> The rivets were not forged that join'd us first,
> That do not reach us yet: we were so mix'd,
> As meeting streams; both to ourselves were lost:
> We were one mass; we could not give or take
> But from the same; for he was I, I he.
> Return, my better half, and give me all myself,
> For thou art all!
> If I have any joy when thou art absent,
> I grudge it to myself: methinks I rob
> Thee of thy part." *

* Dryden.

But the renewed heart, vivified with spiritual life, glowing with Divine love, and breathing with heavenly aspirations, yearns for a diviner, purer, and more lasting friendship than this lovely picture portrays,—such as earth yields not—such as heaven only can give. Jesus meets this holy yearning of our renewed nature; He reveals Himself as our FRIEND,—the Friend who loved us from eternity, who shed His blood for us, sacrificed His life for us, paid our great debt, delivered us from captivity, and has enfranchised us with the title, freedom, and wealth of a heavenly citizenship, henceforth calling us friends. Oh, what a Friend is Jesus! Truly may we say of Him,—

> "He loved me well; so well He could but die
> To shew He loved me better than His life:
> He lost it for me."

Cultivate Christ's friendship,—love Him as your Friend,—confide in Him as your Friend,—confess Him as your Friend,—consult Him as your Friend,—be faithful to Him as your Friend,—ever repair to Him as your Friend. Your love delights Him, your faith honours Him, your service glorifies Him; and every want and trial, every sin and infirmity, that brings you to Him, but tests His friendship, and endears Him to your heart, and makes you better acquainted with your best, your only Friend. You may be called to learn this precious truth—the friendship of Christ—by a painful discipline,—amid the fading of earthly friendships,—by the rupture of ties once so close, sacred, and endeared, —distance separating you, misunderstanding alienating you, death sundering you from the friend your heart enshrined as God's most precious earthly gift;—be it so, if *this* the result—your closer intimacy with Jesus, the "*Friend who loveth at all times,*" and who, in all the changeful, chequered scenes and circumstances of life, will "*shew Himself friendly.*" Seek to mould your earthly friendships like unto Christ's. Let His friends be your friends, and your friends the most spiritual, unworldly, and Christ-like.

But this chapter, which has grown with its subject, must close with one or two exhortations. Seek to *know* this love of Christ, though it is so vast that it "passeth knowledge." Infinite though it is, you may experience its reality, taste its sweetness, and be influenced by its all-commanding, all-constraining power. "*The love of Christ constraineth us.*" Let it constrain you to a loving, unreserved obedience, to a cheerful bearing of His cross, to a manly vindication of His truth, to a close imitation of His spirit, and to "deny all ungodliness and worldly lusts, and to live righteously, godly, and soberly in this present evil world."

Confide in the unchangeableness of Christ's love. Nothing shall take it from you, or separate you from it. It ebbs not with the ebbing of your feelings; it chills not with the chill of your affections; it changes not with the changing scenes and circumstances of your life. A love that "passeth knowledge" must have depths we cannot sound, heights we cannot explore, an infinite fulness and freeness tiding over all the sins, infirmities, and sorrows of its blessed and favoured objects.

"Nothing for us remains—
Nothing but love;
Love that no tongue can teach,
Love that no thought can reach,
No love like His.

"God is its blessed source,
Death ne'er can stop its course,
Nothing can stay its force,
Matchless it is."

Do not limit your *heart-experience* of Christ's love, for it is infinite in its nature and boundless in its extent. The prayer of the apostle for the

Ephesian saints was, that they might "KNOW *the love of Christ which passeth knowledge.*" As yet, how many of us stand but upon the shore of this ocean! How little do we know, *experimentally,* of the love of Christ in our souls, dislodging slavish fear, a bondage spirit, unbelieving doubt, and so enlarging our hearts that we may run the way of the Lord's commandments. Bring your heart with its profoundest emptiness, its most startling discovery of sin, its lowest frame, its deepest sorrow, and sink it into the depths of the Saviour's love. That infinite sea will flow over all, erase all, absorb all, and your soul shall swim and sport amid its gentle waves, exclaiming in your joy and transport, "Oh, the depths!" The Lord direct your heart into the love of God!—just as it is, hard, cold, fickle, sinful, sad and sorrowful. Christ's love touching your hard heart, will dissolve it; touching your cold heart, will warm it; touching your sinful heart, will purify it; touching your sorrowful heart, will soothe it; touching your wandering heart, will draw it back to Jesus. Only bring your heart to Christ's love. Believe in its existence, its reality, its fulness, and its freeness. Believe that He loves you, and just as love begets love, so the simple belief in the love of Jesus will inspire you with a reflected, responsive affection; and your soul, like the chrysalis, will burst from its captivity and gloom, and, soaring in life, liberty, and beauty, will float in the sunbeams of God's full, free, and eternal love, and, in a little while, will find itself in heaven,—where all is LOVE!

"LOVE DIVINE! 'neath human feature
Thou Thy glory hast conceal'd:
Love! to me, a fallen creature,
Thou Thy fulness hast reveal'd.
Love! I give myself to Thee,
Thine to be eternally.

"Love! before my soul's creation,
Thou my ransom didst decree:
Love! to purchase my salvation,
Thou becamest a man like me.
Love! I give myself to Thee,
Thine to be eternally.

"Love! the shameful cross enduring,
Thou Thyself to death didst give:
Love! eternal bliss securing,
Thou dost bid the sinner live.
Love! I give myself to Thee
Thine to be eternally.

"Love! at once both strength and being,
Word and Spirit, truth and light;
Love! since I, for refuge fleeing,
Find deliverance through Thy might;
Love! I give myself to Thee,
Thine to be eternally.

"Love! thine easy yoke upon me,
All my powers shall cheerful own;
Love! the sovereign grace which won me,
Reigneth in my heart alone.
Love! I give myself to Thee,
Thine to be eternally.

"Love! which changeless, ever-living,
Step by step, me onwards leads;
Love! which peace unbroken giving,
Prevalently intercedes.
Love! I give myself to Thee,
Thine to be eternally.

"GOD IS LOVE; AND HE THAT DWELLETH IN LOVE DWELLETH IN GOD, AND GOD IN HIM."—1 JOHN IV. 16.

CHAPTER VII.

THE SENSITIVENESS OF CHRIST TO SUFFERING.

"O my Father, if it be possible, let this cup pass from me."
—MATT. xxvi. 39.

THERE is no point of light in which Christ is viewed so appropriate and soothing to our present condition of sorrow as that of our *Fellow-sufferer*. In suffering, we naturally seek for companionship; we instinctively yearn for sympathy. And if we but meet the individual whose history bears some resemblance to our own,—who has suffered as we suffer, has sorrowed as we sorrow, and who in both has betrayed like human feelings, infirmities, and weakness with ourselves—we are at once conscious of a support the most sustaining, and of a sympathy the most grateful and soothing. It is just in this particular that Christ meets our case, and meets it as no other being can.

The absence of personal suffering in the experience of our Lord, would have been the absence of one of the strongest characteristics of our present condition; and the absence of that sensitiveness which shrinks from sorrow, which recoils from pain, to which we cannot teach human nature to be wholly indifferent, would have been the absence of one of the most essential elements of His sympathy with man. When, therefore, we contemplate our Lord as a sufferer, and as betraying in suffering the sensibility, the sensitiveness, and the trembling, proper to our nature, and of which we are so constantly the subjects, we have truly found in Him a Fellow-sufferer in all points like us, save in that which must ever be the one grand exception—*our sinfulness.* How full of strong consolation, then, to the Christian, is the subject which is about to engage our study,—Christ's instinctive dread of suffering! How close it brings Him to us! How real, how truly man, how essentially human, how like ourselves does He appear! This is just the one attribute in suffering we feel the most replete with soothing and sympathy. It is not merely that Christ was a Sufferer, but that He betrayed in suffering that human sensitiveness, that shrinking from pain, and that deprecation of sorrow, which sued for exemption from the cup, which, perhaps, in our own case, we have often thought unbecoming our dignity as men, our piety as Christians, and our filial submission as children of God. But before we embark upon the leading subject of this chapter, it will be proper briefly to view our dear Lord in the light of His own sufferings. We can only understand in some measure what that human sensitiveness to suffering was which He betrayed, by forming some faint conception of the nature of the suffering from which His spirit shrank. And, although we institute no comparison whatever between the expiatory sufferings which our Lord endured and our own, we may yet trace sufficient resemblance between His human nature and ours in suffering, as to establish a bond of sympathy the most sustaining, comforting, and precious. Let us, then, address ourselves briefly to the task of ascertaining the nature of those ingredients which composed the cup of sorrow from which now His sensitive spirit recoiled. "*O my Father, if it be possible, let this cup pass from me.*"

The language is figurative. The suffering upon which the Lord now entered in the garden of

Gethsemane, into whose central horrors, and towards whose dark climax on Calvary each step was conducting Him, He compares to the drinking of a "cup." "*This cup.*" And what was this cup from which His sensitive spirit shrank in terror and dismay? Surely it must have been a chalice of which none other had ever tasted—and which none but the Divine-Man could taste. And truly it was so. Lose sight of the fact that Christ suffered in His representative character as the Surety and Mediator of His Church,—that His obedience was preceptive, and His death expiatory,—the one honouring Divine law, the other satisfying Divine justice,—and you have lost all clue to the otherwise profound and inexplicable mystery of His sacrifice. Upon no other hypothesis can we arrive at a satisfactory, or even intelligent solution of this strange, this anomalous fact—the Innocent suffering for the guilty, the Righteous dying instead of the unrighteous, as it is written, "*Christ also hath once suffered for sins, the just for the unjust, that he might bring us to God.*" But the Bible is interwoven with this truth as by a thread of gold, not simply running through its centre, but ramifying every part, linking and interlacing itself with each doctrine, precept, promise, and statement,—every revealed truth vivified and tinted with—ATONING BLOOD. Yes, let the denier of Christ's sacrifice remove from the Bible this essential, fundamental doctrine of faith, and it is as though he had blotted the sun from the heavens, wrenched the soul from the body, sapped the foundation of the building; he has robbed Christianity of Christ, the sinner of salvation, the dying of hope, the saint of heaven. "*There remaineth no more sacrifice for sin, but a fearful looking for of judgment and fiery indignation, which shall devour the adversaries.*" Saint of God! it is written,—and it standeth until the end of the world, the salvation and hope of the last sinner that shall be saved—'*He was wounded for our transgressions; he was bruised for our iniquities.*" Behold your *Sin-bearer*, and rejoice! The work is all complete; the debt is all cancelled. Christ has died, rather, is risen again; and His resurrection from the dead is the Father's acceptance of the Saviour's work, and the pledge and earnest of your resurrection to life eternal. Oh, with what melody should you make the mountains and the valleys ring and echo with your song!—Jesus, my Sin-bearer, has died for me, and I am saved!

"Thy works, not mine, O Christ,
Speak gladness to this heart;
They tell me all is done;
They bid my fear depart.
To whom, save Thee,
Who can alone
For sin atone,
Lord, shall I flee!

"Thy pains, not mine, O Christ,
Upon the shameful tree,
Have paid the law's full price
And purchased peace for me.

"Thy tears, not mine, O Christ,
Have wept my guilt away;
And turn'd this night of mine
Into a blessed day.

"Thy bonds, not mine, O Christ,
Unbind me of my chain,
And break my prison-doors,
Ne'er to be barr'd again.

"Thy wounds, not mine, O Christ,
Can heal my bruised soul,
Thy stripes, not mine, contain
The balm that makes me whole.

"Thy blood, not mine, O Christ,
Thy blood so freely spilt,
Can blanch my blackest stains,
And purge away my guilt.

"Thy Cross, not mine, O Christ,
Has borne the awful load
Of sins that none in heaven
Or earth could bear, but God.

"Thy death, not mine, O Christ,
Has paid the ransom due;
Ten thousand deaths like mine
Would have been all too few.

"Thy righteousness, O Christ,
Alone can cover me;
No righteousness will do
Save that which is of Thee.

"Thy righteousness alone
Can clothe and beautify;
I wrap it round my soul;
In this I'll live and die."

But it is a specific view of this subject which now engages our attention—our Lord's sensitiveness to suffering; and the consideration of this will yet more fully unfold the depth and keenness of His sufferings. It would seem impossible that as man Christ should be indifferent or insensible to suffering. Had sorrow lighted upon Him as the snow-flake falls on the ocean, or as the arrow flies through the air, untraceable by a single impression, then we might justly have questioned the perfect identity of His nature with ours. But when we mark the surging of the soul, the quivering of the lip, the trembling of the hand, the plaintive cry of pain, and the uplifted prayer for deliverance, we see in Jesus our Fellow-sufferer, bone of our bone, and flesh of our flesh.

Let us cite a few examples of our Lord's sensibility to suffering.

Select, as the first and chiefest, that which is placed at the head of this chapter—the cup of wrath now trembling in His hand. "*And he went a little farther, and fell on his face, and prayed, saying, O my Father, if it be possible, let this cup pass from me.*" How perfectly true to nature the affecting prayer, the touching ejaculation, thus breathing from the Saviour's lips! There was nothing in it wild, enthusiastic, extravagant,—no coveting of death, no choosing of pain, no stoical indifference to agony. Unlike some martyrs who have rushed to the stake with maddened joy, goaded by a blinded, excited, intoxicated nature, a high excitation of feeling blunting the apprehension of a coming woe, He entered into this dark cloud of sorrow and suffering with fear and trembling! And why? Because He was bearing sin, exhausting the curse, and drinking the wrath of God for us. This makes all the difference between Christ's sufferings and those of the noble army of martyrs whom we reverence. He went to the cross laden with all sin,—they went to the stake with all sin forgiven. He lifted to His lips and drank the cup of pain and of suffering, embittered with all the strength of the curse, and brimmed with the unmitigated wrath of God,—they drank their cup of suffering, as we drink ours, sweetened and alleviated with Divine love, sympathy, and soothing.

But look at His sensibility. "*Let this cup psss from me.*" It was from soul-agony, from mental grief, that He now shrunk. "*Now is my soul troubled.*" He had reached the crisis of His mission, the goal of His passion; and as the dark hour drew on,—His enemies watching, His disciples sleeping, His blood-impurpled brow pressing the damp soil of the garden,—the midnight stillness is broken with His cry of agony,—His prayer for deliverance—"*O my Father, if it be possible, let this cup pass from me.*" Beloved reader, is your spirit troubled? is your mind disquieted? and do you shrink from the cup your heavenly Father has given you to drink? Oh, behold the source of your true sympathy,—the lessons and the consolations flowing from Him, "*Who in the days of his flesh, when he had offered up prayers and supplications, with strong crying and tears, unto him that was able to save him from death, and was heard in that he feared; though he were a Son, yet learned he obedience by the things which he suffered; and being made perfect, he became the author of eternal salvation unto all them that obey him."* Your Saviour was sensitive to soul-sorrow, and think you that He will chide or be indifferent to yours? Ah, no! He knows your spirit's grief, and will comfort it. He has passed through your mental sorrow, and will soothe it. He has felt your soul-darkness, and will cheer it. You are, perhaps, suffering from a present, or are shrinking from an anticipated, sorrow. The cup is in your trembling hand. You pray, "O my Father, if it be possible—*if it be possible*—let it pass from me. Sustain me in this calamity beneath which my wounded spirit sinks. Spare me the impending blow from which my sensitive spirit recoils."—— Oh, think you that the sympathy of Christ is not with you now? Can He not enter with you into that cloud, share with you that cup, understand that recoil of feeling, and make all allowance for these keen, wounded, crushed sensibilities. "Father, if it be possible——." Who will forbid that prayer?—*not Jesus!*

Our Lord was equally sensitive to *bodily pain.* This was, doubtless, one of the ingredients of the cup Christ was now about to drink to its dregs. The body was involved in the fall of man—the inlet to the sin of the soul. In the working out of an atonement for sin it must also suffer. Our dear Lord's entire exemption from a sinful nature did not exempt Him from a sensitive nature—a nature sensitive to *physical* suffering. The absence of sensibility to pain of body would have compromised the fact of His actual humanity. What an essential defect in His sympathy would have been His freedom from bodily pain! How could the Head then have sympathised with the members? The diseases which assail our frame, it is true, found no counterpart in Him; yet, was He not the less exempt from suffering of body. Oh, was there no bodily agony in the laceration of the scourge, in the heavy blows of the clenched fist, in the plucking off the hair, in the thorn-crown, in the spikes impelled through the hands and the feet, in the thrust of the spear entering the side and piercing the heart of Jesus? Was there no torture in the long, lingering agony of the cross, the blood oozing from the wounds by drops, and life ebbing slowly by inches? How literally was verified His own prophetic words, "*I gave my back to the smiters, and my cheek to them that plucked off the hair!"* Hear His cry, "*Father, if it be possible, let* THIS *cup pass from me*"—this cup of mortal agony. You, too, may thus be shrinking from bodily suffering. Does the weak flesh recoil from those agonies which no tongue can describe, which no skill can baffle, which no anodyne can soothe, and which no affection can prevent? Jesus can sympathise with you. Think you that He will desert you in this trial of your humanity, or make no allowance for the weakness of the flesh, the pain and nervousness, the agony and languor, the fainting and swooning which so much interferes with your soul's enjoyment, beclouds your mental powers, and prevents those spiritual exercises of reading, meditation, and prayer in which you have been wont so happily to indulge? Ah, no! He is your fellow-sufferer! and when, in anticipation of the throes, the agonies, and the convulsions which rack the body with pain, the spirit fails, the flesh shrinks, and your trembling heart breathes to heaven its earnest, plaintive cry, "Father, if it be possible,"—you are at once in the closest sympathy with your Saviour's sensitiveness to bodily suffering, and He in sympathy with yours. Who will arrest that prayer?—*not Jesus.*

Our Lord was sensitive to the pain of *domestic slight.* It is marvellous to trace the perfect assimilation of His humanity to all the natural circumstances of ours. Was there no betrayal of sensitiveness to this peculiar form of suffering when He quoted the proverb as applicable to Himself,—"*A prophet is not without honour, save in his own country, and in his own house?*" He was as a stranger among His brethren, an alien in His Father's house. They doubted Him—slighted Him—insulted Him. Jesus felt the neglect—and felt it keenly. His sensitive spirit was wounded. How many of the Lord's people are drinking *this* cup of sadness, are enduring this form of suffering! The icy coldness, the studied slight, the marked neglect of those of your own house, whose confidence, affection, and sympathy you had not forfeited and had a right to possess, is a daily cross, chafing, wounding, fretting the spirit sore. But your Lord and Master prepared you for this—teaching you the precept, and then enforcing it by His example: "*Suppose ye that I am come to give peace on earth? I tell you, Nay; but rather division: for from henceforth there shall be five in one house divided, three against two, and two against three.*" "*And a man's foes shall be they of his own household.*" How faithfully does our Lord here forewarn His disciples, that love to Him and a profession of His gospel would, in many instances, involve the weakening, if not the entire rupture, of those ties, the closest and the dearest, which bind us to earth's kindred. The religion of Jesus is a *separating* religion; it has done but little for us if it has not severed us from the world, and quenched in us the spirit of the world, and separated us from all worldly association, and sympathy with the world's followers, bound to us though they are by ties which we cannot and may not entirely sunder. Oh, how marvellous and subtle a snare is *the world* to a disciple of Jesus—to one desirous of living for eternity! Our relations are snares—our friendships are snares—our alliances are snares—our business transactions are snares—our necessary recreations of intellect and taste are snares—and our social and domestic enjoyments are often but elysian bowers within whose foliage lurks the tempter. If, then, beloved reader, the Lord has given you grace to tread the narrow path of separation—shaded and secluded though it be; if you are called to witness for Jesus and His gospel against the world, error, and sin, surrounded by those with whom you sported in childhood, among whom your youth was trained, who are entwined with associations of later life the sweetest, and with memories of earlier life the most sacred and dear, and yet you are the object of alienated affection, frigid neglect, doubt, and scorn, because you love the Saviour,—oh, be not cast down as though some strange thing had happened to you. Your Lord and Master, for whom you suffer, suffered all this, and infinitely more, for you; and in sympathy and in love soothes and succours and suffers with you now.

Having given prominence to this feeling of our Lord, as man—His sensitiveness to suffering—let us briefly draw from it some holy, practical deductions.

We learn how completely Christ could be our fellow-sufferer, without the slightest compromise of His essential dignity and greatness. It betrayed no defect in our Lord's character that He should rather have repelled than coveted suffering. We seek the evidence of *real* humanity—we have it here! Taken into alliance with His absolute Deity, there could be no element in it not in harmony with His higher and superior nature. When, therefore, we find our Lord in the days of His flesh shrinking from pain, as we now do, we find nothing in it to disturb the perfect equipoise of a well-balanced mind, or to cast a shadow upon the lustre of a strong and a great One. A great and holy mind may be so sustained in the endurance of suffering, loss, shame, or death, as to rise superior to them; but it is no mark of real greatness to affect to despise or to be indifferent to them absolutely and unconditionally. A man of God would willingly accept them as alternatives, but thankfully would he escape them, if by so doing he did not compromise his own honour and self-respect, and, above all, his allegiance to Christ and truth. Behold, then, beloved, your Lord as in all respects your fellow-sufferer. He sympathises with you when you shrink from pain; for there was an hour when He shrunk from it Himself; and in that hour of extreme distress, every nerve quivering, and the sweat like blood dropping from His sacred body, He prayed that the cup might be taken away. Oh, think not that you betray an improper weakness, or prefer an undutiful petition, when the poor frail flesh dreads the pang, and the spirit cries—Let this cup pass from me!

But not only may this tender susceptibility to pain be perfectly consistent with true greatness and dignity of character, but equally so with the perfect submission of the will to God. An intense desire to be saved from suffering may be in strict harmony with the holiest resignation, fortitude, and courage in suffering. What a page in the history of our Lord is here! "*If this cup may not pass from me except I drink it, thy will be done.*" It was not possible that that cup should pass His lips undrank. The salvation of His elect Church hung upon it—the glory of His Father was involved in it—the interests of the universe were bound up in it—it was *not possible!* But not less did His own love constrain Him to exhaust that cup, than the necessity imposed by the eternal purpose and will of the Father. Oh, deem not that that sensitiveness to pain, that shrinking from suffering, betrayed in the plaintive cry, "*If it be possible,*"—augured the slightest veering of love, the remotest vacillation of mind, the least hesitancy on the part of Christ to offer Himself as a voluntary sacrifice for our sins. Oh, no! Light flows not from the sun more spontaneously, the winds blow not more freely, nor does the mountain stream rush on to the ocean more impetuously, than went our blessed sacrificial Lamb of God to the altar of atonement. And yet we thank, we bless, we laud Him for this plaintive ejaculation—"*If it be possible.*" This is nature, and this is truth. I need not pause to inquire what nature—it is enough that it harmonises with *my* nature, that it is true to all the instincts of my manhood, and pours a deeper, richer, sweeter tide of sympathy and soothing into my troubled spirit than the most stoical nature foreign from my own could have done. Oh, how much more deeply and tenderly does that cry of weakness and of suffering touch my sad heart, than the sublimest words of excited heroism! It assures me that my feebleness, my sensitiveness, my prayer for exemption from pain, is not sinful, is not wrong, is not unmanly and undignified, and will meet with no check nor rebuke from Him who in the days of His flesh offered up prayers and supplications, with strong crying and tears, unto Him that was able to save Him from death. Before this loving, sympathising Saviour I am subdued and melted. Oh, how my love is awakened! I love Him, because that He, though GOD, is near to me, near in the valley of tears and suffering, not chiding but sharing, not crushing but sustaining, not repelling but sanctifying my infirmities, feebleness, and sorrow. I love Him for the sympathy that soothes, and for the power that succours me. I love Him who, while He sighs with me, weeps with me, sorrows with me, encircles me with His omnipotent arms, upholds me with His Divine grace, and perfects His strength in my weakness. *"I love the Lord, because he hath heard my voice and my supplications. Because he hath inclined his ear unto me, therefore will I call upon him as long as I live."*

We recur again to the thought that we must not only claim Christ's alliance with us in our cup of suffering, but if we would experience all the advantage of His sympathy, we must conclude His prayer—"*Nevertheless, not as I will, but as Thou wilt.*" While our Saviour would stoop to our human sorrow, He would raise us to His Divine resignation. He seems to say to us—"Ye shall indeed drink of the cup that I drink of, and in the same spirit of filial submission to your Father's will." Yes, child of suffering and of sorrow! it may *not* be the will of God that your request should be granted

That cup from which you shrink—it is not possible should pass. It becomes you to drink and drain it, as did He—but His words shall strengthen and aid you, "*Thy will, not mine, be done.*" It is in cleaving by faith the deep waters, and in climbing the difficult ascent, we reach the firmest footing, and the highest, brightest, holiest elevation in our Christianity—the complete absorption of our will in God's will. Great trials make great saints. The most deeply afflicted are the most deeply sanctified. It was not until our blessed Lord first pressed that cup to His lips that the conflict and the triumph of will took place. "Let this cup pass from me—Thy will be done." Oh, it were worth any cup our Father mingled to be able to bow our head to the earth and say—

> "Let me never choose—or to live or die,
> Bind or bruise, in Thy hands I lie."

What a holy, practical lesson may we here learn! Does Christ thus sympathise with us? does the Lord know our weak frames and remember that we are dust? Then let us go forth in perfect sympathy with Christ in everything that relates to His truth, His kingdom,

His people. He is unworthy of a love so self-sacrificing, of a sympathy so engirdling, who feels not himself one and identified with Christ in everything that relates to the honour of that name at which every knee shall bow. Embraced by such a love, and interested in such a sympathy, let us melt into the profoundest sensibility at the thought that it was for *us* Christ sighed and wept, bled and suffered; and, standing before that awful spectacle—the wonder and marvel of the universe—let us resolve that the sins which crucified Him once shall not crucify Him again; but that the death our Saviour died *for* sins, shall be our death *unto* sin, and that henceforth we will be Christ's true disciples, Christ's faithful followers. You will learn, too, to sympathise with the suffering members of Christ's body. Soothed by such a sympathy as His, your own will flow forth in its tenderness toward all who through the weakness and infirmity of the flesh are shrinking from or are drinking the cup of suffering. Catching the spirit, imbibing the gentleness and tenderness of Jesus, in imitation of Him, you will, by your compassion, prayers, and substance, seek to alleviate the pain, soothe the grief, and supply the need of those, the companions and representatives of your Lord, in whom are filled up the afflictions of Christ, which are behind. Recognise a suffering Christ in His suffering members, a persecuted Christ in His persecuted members, a poor Christ in His poor members, a despised Christ in His down-trodden members, an imprisoned Christ in His imprisoned members; a sick, a naked, a hungry Christ in those whom worldly adversity, penury, and want have smitten and laid low. "*Inasmuch as ye have done it unto one of the least of these my brethren, ye have done it unto me.*"

Whatever may be the cup your heavenly Father prepares for you, keep firm hold of this truth, that He will never forsake you. "*He forsaketh not His saints.*" Shrink not from the suffering that seems inevitable, the cup which may not pass your lips untouched—God will be with you. You are, perhaps, anticipating a fiery ordeal, a dread crisis of your case; the flesh shrinks from the knife, the heart dies within you at the thought of that hour of silent agony which approaches. Oh, have faith now in your heavenly Father. Think you that He will leave you to drink that cup alone? to endure that pain alone? to pass through that hour alone? Oh, no! He will be with you, Christ will be with you, the Comforter will be with you, and, as "*thy day, so shall thy strength be.*" Has God ever yet been to you a wilderness? Has His promise ever failed? Has Jesus ever stood aloof from your sore, leaving your wound untouched, unsoothed, unhealed? Has not the Lord always been better than all your trembling anticipations, quelling your fears, reassuring your doubting mind, and bearing you gently and safely through the hour of suffering which you dreaded? Then trust Him *now!* Never, *never* will He forsake you! Let His will be done in you, and by you—and thus, both in doing and suffering, you may sweetly sing—

"My Father, choose the path I tread,
Midst drooping hopes and pleasures fled,
Or with bright sunshine round me spread,
But never let me go!

"My Father, choose the rank I fill,
To rule a nation at my will,
Or lowliest services fulfil,
But never let me go!

"My Father, choose my lot in life,
A peaceful home, unvex'd by strife,
Or stormy scenes, with danger rife,
But never let me go!

"My Father, choose my work for Thee,
To toil in bright activity,
Or pause and wait on bended knee,
But never let me go!

"My Father, choose my dying day,
In prime of life to pass away,
Or sink in age's slow decay,
But never let me go!

"Yes, Lord, Thy wisdom, love, and power
Are my strong rock, my sheltering tower,
And this shall soothe life's darkest hour,
Thou wilt not let me go!"

CHAPTER VIII.

THE SYMPATHY OF CHRIST WITH TRUE SHAME.

"And Jesus answered and said unto them, Are ye come out, as against a thief, with swords and with staves to take me?"—MARK xiv. 48.

OUR LORD'S nature, from its essential sinlessness, was at an infinite remove from every sentiment and feeling of littleness. There was in His character no admixture of meanness with majesty, of baseness with dignity, of littleness with greatness. No thought lodged in His mind, no emotion stirred His bosom, no motive swayed His conduct, no act traced His life that towered not in its loftiness and splendour above the taint and shadow of suspicion. More than this. There was not only the actual existence in Christ of the most perfect honour and rectitude, but, superadded to this, there was a holy sensitiveness to and shrinking from, the least *appear-*

ance of the opposite. He not only was not a thief, but He refused to be dealt with as a thief. He was not only free from crime, but He would also be free from the suspicion of criminality. He possessed in the highest degree the element of *true shame.* It was an element of His being, a characteristic of His nature: His delicacy of feeling was remarkable; His sensibility exquisitely acute; His sensitiveness shrinking from the slightest breath. Our Lord possessed the most perfect sympathy with true shame. It was an essential feature and evidence of His greatness. A remarkable and touching illustration of this characteristic is before us. The scene, is the garden of Gethsemane; the time, is midnight; and the occasion, His arrest. Look at one particular of the scene—*His arrest.* It was by Judas, one of the twelve, attended by circumstances which must have been exquisitely torturing to the feelings of Christ. He had committed no wrong, had done no violence, had sought no concealment, had attempted no escape; and yet the betrayer hunted Him as a fugitive from justice, and arrested Him as a criminal fit only to die. There was a degree of dishonour and degradation attached to the mode of His apprehension from which His native dignity, and conscious innocence, and human sensitiveness to shame instinctively and painfully recoiled. Shrinking from their touch, while awe-struck they stood motionless in His presence, He exclaimed, in tones of conscious dignity and integrity, which must have sent the keen rebuke deep into the breast of His betrayer, "*Are ye come out,* AS AGAINST A THIEF, *with swords and with staves to take me?*" There was nothing exaggerated, nothing untrue to nature in this. It was precisely the sentiment, the feeling, and the words to which conscious integrity and superiority would give birth. He was upright, and He would not be arraigned as a felon. He was innocent, and He would not be prejudged as guilty. He was willing to die, the just for the unjust, expiating, by a voluntary offering of Himself to Divine justice, the sins of His people; but there shall be no physical force, no human impeachment of His sanctity, no act in the mode of His arrest, which, by implication, should incriminate His conduct, shade His holiness, or brand Him in the eyes of men as a sinner and a culprit. He had a character to maintain, a mission to perform, which demanded an integrity and uprightness which should stand out before the world unimpeached and unimpeachable, at an infinite remove even from the appearance of evil. Willing to be "*numbered with transgressors,*" and to "*make His grave with the wicked in His death,*" He yet refused to be arrested by an armed force, and to be haled to the judgment as a felon and an outlaw. "Then Jesus answered and said unto them, Are ye come out, as against a thief, with swords and with staves to take me?"

In all this we discern a perfect identity of our Lord with our nature—the truest sympathy with one of its most peculiar and deeply-veiled features — the believer's holy regard to true shame. There is a *false* shame, which we are prayerfully to avoid; and there is a *true* shame, which we are studiously to cherish. False shame deprecates the good, true shame deprecates the evil;—the one is ashamed of being found doing right, the other is ashamed of being found doing wrong. There is a spurious feeling of shame attaching itself to our nature, with which true greatness of character and high moral bearing in the saints of God would ever lead them to combat. Our Lord abjured it, as we shall presently see. His life was one unbroken testimony to the fact that this false sentiment never found a moment's lodgment within His breast. And this fact furnishes another and no slight evidence of His perfect sinlessness. If sin were utterly extirpated from our heart, our cheek would never be suffused with a blush when doing right, as though there was a consciousness of doing wrong. We might blush to find our good, done by stealth, had become fame; or we might be annoyed to find that good evil spoken of, but for the good itself we should never be ashamed. Having said thus much in explanation of the false and the true shame, in the further prosecution of this subject we shall notice Christ's sympathy with true shame, and the instruction and comfort we are permitted to derive from it.

In the first place, our Lord was not ashamed of assuming a nature lower and inferior to His own. "*The Word was made flesh, and dwelt among us.*" "*Forasmuch as the children are partakers of flesh and blood, he also took part of the same.*" "*He that sanctifieth, and they who are sanctified, are all of one: for which cause he is not ashamed to call them brethren.*" Such are the declarations affirming this truth. Here was an example of freedom from false shame worthy our profoundest study and closest imitation. That it was a stoop, a descent, a lowering of Himself, who can doubt? It involved a humiliation in the sight of holy intelligence the deepest to which an infinite Being could stoop. It was not the created sinking in the scale of creation: it was the Infinite descending to the finite. It was the Divine invested with the human. And yet, conscious that He was doing no wrong, conscious of the perfect rectitude and purity of His doing, He lifted His brow to heaven untinged with a blush of shame. What a precious truth is this! Repair, O believer, to Christ, with your nature laden with infirmity, sorrow, and want. Christ will not turn away from His own flesh: He will own you as a brother, for He is not ashamed to call us brethren.

Nor was Christ ashamed *of low and obscure birth.* Had He so willed it, He might have been born in a palace rather than in a stable; the son of a prince rather than of a carpenter; his mother a king's daughter rather than the wife of a mechanic. But no! He was born to humiliation, and He eschewed not meanness and obscurity of birth. Let no child of God be ashamed of the circumstance of his parentage and birth, for God has appointed both. Low birth entails no dishonour, and mean parentage is no disgrace. The greatest and the holiest have traced their earthly origin to this. But if our Lord could not boast of noble birth, He could boast of Christian birth. Obscure and mean as were His earthly parents, they were holy, God-fearing parents. Are we like favoured? Did God give us pious, holy, praying parents? Then the patent of true nobility was theirs. And although Divine grace is not hereditary, for the new birth cometh not by the will of the flesh nor of the will of man, but of God, nevertheless, we may be thankful for a God-fearing father and for a praying mother, as among God's most sacred and precious gifts.

Nor was our Lord ashamed of *earthly poverty and toil.* His parents were poor in this world, and toiled with their own hands for daily sustenance. That He shared their poverty and toil, there can be no doubt. He was not merely the reputed son of a mechanic, but, doubtless, He himself plied at the same lowly craft. He was the son of a carpenter, and Himself a carpenter. Nor was he ashamed of this. Why should He be? There is no discredit in honest poverty; there is no disgrace in industrious toil. He who earns his bread by the sweat of his brow, who labours with his own hands for himself and for those who cannot thus toil, is pursuing an honourable and dignified course; and, however lowly may be his calling, however mean his craft, poverty is to him no crime, and labour no disgrace; and he may walk among his fellows without opprobrium, and lift his countenance unmantled with a tinge of shame.

Our Lord was not ashamed of *the opinion of the world.* It had its views of Christ, its opinion of His character and conduct. And although there were occasions when Christ manifested an interest in the popular sentiment concerning Himself, "*Whom do men say that I am?*"—thus teaching that there is a sense in which His disciples may not be wholly indifferent to the sentiment of others,—yet, whatever that opinion was, favourable or unfavourable, He never for one moment allowed it so to influence or control Him as to swerve one hair's-breadth from the strictest, straitest line of duty, integrity, and love. Every believer, however limited and veiled from human eye his sphere of life, will create a public sentiment respecting his individual self. His relations, his friends, his neighbours, will form their opinion of his character, doings, and life. Few pass through life incognito to eternity; few glide through society unseen, unnoticed, unfelt. To this we cannot be, nor ought we to be, wholly indifferent. Each individual Christian especially should live for an object. He should so live as to make his talents, influence, and example tell upon the present and eternal well-being of all with whom he comes in contact. "*No man liveth to himself.*" As a "light," he is to shine; as "salt," he is to influence; as a "witness," he is to testify for Christ. In a world like this, where there is so much evil to correct, so much temptation to resist, so much sorrow to soothe, so much want to supply, so much misery to counteract, so much ignorance to instruct, so much good to be done, none need be all the day idle, dreaming away existence, vegetating in selfishness, not living for man or labouring for God. Oh, be an earnest, active Christian! Be up and doing. Life is too real, too solemn, too responsible, for sluggishness, inactivity, and selfishness. We are gliding down the stream onward to eternity. Shall we spend our fleeting moments in grasping at the floating straw, when for every moment and act of our present course we shall soon be cited at Christ's bar for scrutiny and judgment? Souls are perishing—ignorance of the gospel is prevailing—iniquity is abounding—Satan is unslumbering—death plies its scythe, and the grave yawns each moment, and an eternity of bliss or of woe is gathering, at every stroke of the pendulum, deathless beings to its bosom. Shall we not, then, be active and earnest in a world like this? But in so doing we must learn, like our Divine Master, to live above the world's opinion. We must not blush, nor cower, nor bend before it. The world hates us because we are not of the world, but testify of its works that they are evil. We must, therefore, set our face as a flint against its opinion, its opposition, its malice, and its hate, not ashamed of the evil report from which none are entirely exempt who, like Jesus, go about doing good. Oh for more of this dignified, holy freedom from the opinion of men! If we are carrying out our Christian principles, reducing to practice the great and glorious truths of Christ's gospel,—meekly, humbly pursuing that course which truth and conscience and love dictate, however opposed by human opinion, and the principles and the spirit and the customs of the world,—we may indeed confront the frowns and scorn the censure of man, but we shall walk with an approving conscience, and beneath the smile of a favouring and sustaining God.

Another illustration of our Lord's freedom from false shame was the avowal, everywhere and on all occasions, *that His life was ruled by the fear and terminated in the glory of God.* He could say, as none other could—"*I do always those things which please Him.*" And why should the child of God, the disciple of Christ, blush to acknowledge that the fear of God is his governing principle, and the glory of God the great end of his being? Why should we shrink to answer—"I cannot pursue that course; I cannot adopt that mode; I dare not conduct my business on those principles; I cannot descend to those questionable arts and subterfuges, because I am a follower of Christ. Others may stoop to the tricks of trade, its artifice and fraud and commercial immorality; so do not I because of the fear of the Lord." Oh, let no false shame turn you from this course. The world may laugh the false religious professor may scorn, the infidel may scoff, friends may censure, but yours is the honour, the dignity, and the reward of having lived and walked and acted as in the fear of God.

Nor was our Lord ashamed of *the death which He died.* It was the death of a Roman felon, the most ignominious, tortuous, and accursed death He could die—the death of the cross. And yet we read—"*Who for the joy that was set before him endured the cross, despising the shame, and is set down at the right hand of the throne of God.*" Oh, never did His real greatness, true dignity, rise to such an altitude as now! See Him impaled upon that tree, stretched upon that wood, scourged, spit upon, insulted, mocked, derided, taunted, wounded, then left to linger and die; and yet, oh, what glory gathered round that scene of humiliation, suffering, and death! Jesus rose superior to it all, enduring the cross with all its unknown horrors, despising the shame with all its unfathomable depths, all endured, all suffered, all despised, for the love He bore us!

This subject has its practical lessons as well as its rich consolations. Let us glean a few in conducting the chapter to a close.

It is a *false* shame to be ashamed of Christ and of His gospel. That there is a tendency to this, even in the renewed heart, is clear from the meaning and instruction of Christ himself. "*Whosoever shall be ashamed of me and of my words, of him shall the Son of man be ashamed, when he shall come in his own glory, and in his Father's, and of the holy angels."* True Christian discipleship demands an uncompromising avowal of attachment to Christ, of adhesion to His people, and of adherence to His truth. The offence of the cross is not ceased. A real decision for the Redeemer cannot exist without some sacrifice, demanded and made, as a term of discipleship. "*If any man will come after me, let him deny himself, and take up his cross and follow me."* The sacrifices thus expected and thus endured are various. Some are called to assert their conscientious decisions confronted by hostility from quarters the most loved, venerated, and cherished, but all the keener and the more overwhelming. Arrayed against him are father, mother, brother, sister, wife, husband, child,—ties of affection which bind the heart so closely to the family altar and the hearth. The pang of separation from these, who can estimate? The deep, lone grief, who can describe? Yet the Saviour has said—"*He that loveth father or mother more than me, is not worthy of me; and he that loveth son or daughter more than me, is not worthy of me."* Other saints are called to abandon their worldly interests, to renounce their earthly property, to exclude themselves from the means of acquiring distinction, rank, honour, wealth, and to link them with poverty and toil and want, encountering the reproach of friends, blighted hopes, disappointed wishes, ruined expectations. Be it so. This is nothing more than Jesus foretold and forewarned: "*Let us go forth, therefore, unto Him without the camp, bearing His reproach.*"

But for whom are you enduring and suffering and sacrificing all this? For Jesus! For Him who, though He was rich, for your sakes became poor, that you through His poverty might be rich. For Him who was not ashamed to call you His brother, but bowed His Godhead to your nature, and on your behalf became a man of sorrows and acquainted with grief. For Him who, while working out your righteousness by His life of unwearied and perfect obedience, could say—"*Foxes have holes, and birds of the air have nests; but the Son of man hath not where to lay his head.*" For Him who gave His back to the smiter, and His cheek to them that plucked off the hair; who sorrowed in Gethsemane, clad in a purple robe of blood; who was mocked and buffeted and spit upon in the judgment-hall;

who bore the full weight of sin and the curse, and the suffering and the desertion upon the cross, and then bowed His head and died. Before this stupendous spectacle, this amazing sacrifice, we exclaim, in the language of an inspired apostle, "*I am* NOT ASHAMED *of the gospel of Christ; for it is the power of God unto salvation to every one that believeth.*" And, in the words of a Christian poet—

> "Were the whole realm of nature mine,
> That were a present far too small;
> Love so amazing, so divine,
> Demands my soul, my life, my all."

Be sensible to *true* shame. This was the shame our Lord felt. "*Jesus answered and said unto them, Are ye come out,* AS AGAINST A THIEF, *with swords and with staves to take me?*" I marvel not at this holy indignation and recoil of my Saviour! The mode of His arrest was repulsive to every high, honourable feeling of His nature. It was a reflection upon the purity of His character. It was an imputation of His loyalty and honesty in His civil relation to the State. It was a slight upon the pacific nature of His religion and kingdom. It was a denial of the voluntariness of His sacrifice. And it was an impeachment of the sincerity and integrity of His whole career. We marvel not that with holy shame He indignantly repelled the armed force that would arrest and hale Him as a criminal to the judgment. Imitate Christ in this! Be sensible to *true* shame. Whatever would place you in a *false* position before the world—whatever would reflect unjustly upon your Christian character, meekly but firmly repell;—silence the slander, vindicate your integrity, and then commit your case to Him that judgeth righteously. So acted the noble and magnanimous apostle. He and his companions had been unjustly arrested and cast into prison. An earthquake ensued. The magistrates, filled with fear, sent the sergeants, saying, "Let these men go." No, exclaimed Paul,—"*They have beaten us openly uncondemned, being Romans, and have cast us into prison; and now do they thrust us out privily? nay verily, but let them come themselves and fetch us out.*" And so they did. The religion of Jesus ignores not our civil rights, tramples not upon our natural privileges, nor forbids us to vindicate, before magistrates and rulers, our innocence, uprightness, and integrity against falsity, malice, and injustice.

Like your Master, and like our "beloved brother Paul," we must expect to be maligned, falsely accused and condemned, traduced, slandered, and evil spoken of. We must expect to have our doings censured, our motives impugned, our principles scorned, our ends questioned. Nevertheless, "*let us consider Him that endured such contradiction of sinners against Himself, lest we be weary and faint in our minds.*"

There is much indeed in ourselves of which we have reason truly to be ashamed and to be filled with profound self-abhorrence. We have need to be ashamed of our unbelief—of our low thoughts of the Saviour—of our little love to God—of our slow advance in the divine life—of our imperfect conformity to Christ—of the power of indwelling sin—and of our slender spiritual attainments in knowledge, personal holiness, and heavenly meetness. What shamefacedness should cover us that we are so ready to compromise, to falter, and to halt. How deeply humbled should we be that there still exists in us so much carnality, love of the world, and conformity to the world — so little of the crucified spirit, of a cross-bearing Saviour! What cause of shame that, with all our profession, the pulse of spiritual life beats in our souls so faintly, the spirit of prayer breathes in us so feebly, that we possess so little real, vital religion, and follow Christ at so great a distance. Filled with self-abasement should we be that the fruits and graces of the Spirit are in us so sickly, drooping, and bedwarfed—that we have so limited a measure of faith, love, and humility, are so defective in our patience and meekness, wisdom, and gentleness—that, with all our blossom and foliage, there is so little real fruit to the glory of our Father. May we not, in view of all this, exclaim with Ezra, in his deep grief and humiliation for the sins of the people, "*O my God, I am ashamed, and blush to lift up my face to thee, my God: for our iniquities are increased over our head, and our trespass is grown up unto the heavens?*" Oh, whither shall we fly, where hide our blushing face but in the blood of atonement! sprinkled afresh with which, we may lift up our heads and not be ashamed.

My dear reader, look well to your foundation, to your religion, to your hope, to your daily walk. Be this your constant prayer, mixed with a constant self-examination and faithful dealing with conscience—"*Let me not be ashamed of my* *hope.*" If you are justified by faith, you will know what peace with God through our Lord Jesus Christ is; and then you will experience that hope that maketh not ashamed, because the love of God will be shed abroad in your heart by the Holy Ghost which is given unto you.* And, oh, may we live in the believing, hopeful expectation of *our Lord's coming* to roll away our shame and reproach, and to exalt us to glory, honour, and immortality. May we not be ashamed at His coming! But, owning and serving Him now, may we then hear Him say—"Come, ye blessed! ye who have continued with me in my temptations, confessed my name, borne my cross, suffered for me on earth, I appoint unto you a kingdom, as my Father hath appointed unto me. Enter ye into the joy of your Lord."

> "Then will He own my worthless name
> Before His Father's face,
> And in the New Jerusalem
> Appoint my soul a place."

Go, dear reader, from the perusal of this chapter, to the solitude of your closet, there to beseech the Lord to give you grace henceforth, Caleb-like, wholly and unreservedly to follow

* Rom. v. 1–5.

Him without the camp, bearing His reproach. We read of the first disciples of the Lord,—"*And they forsook all and followed Him.*" The solemn confession of Christ you have made before the world pledges you to the offence, the shame, the crucifixion, and the self-denial of the cross of Jesus. You have bound that cross around your heart, you have identified yourself with its reproach and its boast, its defeats and its victories, its humiliation and its glory; onward you must bear it through flood and flame, through good and through evil report, glorying in its doctrine, despising its shame, enduring its crucifixion, until the Master bids you exchange your sword for a sceptre, your cross for a crown, which His own hands will place upon your head. Blessed, thrice blessed, ye who, when that blessed moment arrives, will be enabled calmly, exultingly to exclaim, "I AM NOW READY TO BE OFFERED, AND THE TIME OF MY DEPARTURE IS AT HAND. I HAVE FOUGHT A GOOD FIGHT, I HAVE FINISHED MY COURSE, I HAVE KEPT THE FAITH. HENCEFORTH THERE IS LAID UP FOR ME A CROWN OF RIGHTEOUSNESS, WHICH THE LORD, THE RIGHTEOUS JUDGE, SHALL GIVE ME AT THAT DAY: AND NOT TO ME ONLY, BUT UNTO ALL THEM ALSO THAT LOVE HIS APPEARING."

"Jesus, I my cross have taken,
All to leave, and follow Thee;
Naked, poor, despised, forsaken,
Thou from hence my all shalt be.
Perish every fond ambition,
All I've sought, or hoped, or known;
Yet how rich is my condition,
God and heaven are still my own!

"Let the world despise and leave me;
They have left my Saviour too;
Human hearts and looks deceive me,—
Thou art not, like them, untrue;
And whilst Thou shalt smile upon me,
God of wisdom, love, and might,
Foes may hate, and friends disown me,—
Shew Thy face, and all is bright.

"Go, then, earthly fame and treasure,
Come, disaster, scorn, and pain;
In Thy service praise is pleasure,
With Thy favour loss is gain.
I have call'd Thee, Abba, Father;
I have set my heart on Thee;
Storms may howl, and clouds may gather,
All must work for good to me.

"Man may trouble and distress me,
'Twill but drive me to Thy breast;
Life with trials hard may press me,
Heaven will briug me sweeter rest.
Oh, 'tis not in grief to harm me,
While Thy love is left to me;
Oh, 'twere not in joy to charm me,
Were that joy unmix'd with Thee.

"Soul, then know thy full salvation;
  Rise o'er sin, and fear, and care;
Joy to find in every station
  Something still to do or bear.
Think what Spirit dwells within thee;
  Think what Father's smiles are thine;
Think that Jesus died to win thee,—
  Child of heaven, canst thou repine?

"Haste thee on from grace to glory,
  Arm'd by faith and wing'd with prayer;
Heaven's eternal days before thee,
  God's own hand shall guide thee there.
Soon shall close thy earthly mission;
  Soon shall pass thy pilgrim days;
Hope shall change to glad fruition,
  Faith to sight, and prayer to praise."

CHAPTER IX.

THE SYMPATHY OF CHRIST WITH SPIRITUAL JOY.

"In that hour Jesus rejoiced in spirit."—LUKE x. 21.

IT is a frequently-quoted remark of one of the fathers, that Christ was often seen to *weep*, but never once to *smile*. We doubt both the correctness and the wisdom of the statement. Our Lord was a man of joy as well as a man of sorrow. He must, in the fathomless depths of His holy soul, have been as intimately acquainted with gladness as with grief—with the emotion of joy as with the feeling of sorrow. And can we picture Him to our mind thus rejoicing in spirit, the oil of gladness poured upon Him without measure, and insinuating itself into the innermost depths of His being, without a gleam, a smile of joy lighting up that benign, placid, and expressive countenance which more than all others must have been a perfect index of the soul's hidden varied, and profound emotions? Impossible! A portrait of Christ, with nought but shadows, —shadows of grief and sorrow darkening the entire picture,—would be wanting in one of its most essential and life-like features. That a pure and deep joy never found a home in the Saviour's breast, we cannot, then, for a moment credit. That His heart was the seat of grief unmitigated, of sorrow unmixed—that, from that harp breathed no sounds but woe—that from that fount of sensibility welled up no emotions but found their utterance in sighs and groans and tears, is far, very far from our conceptions of the Saviour. And that, when the emotion of joy did for a moment glow in the human soul of Christ, there was no corresponding glow lighting up and illuming every feature of that wonderful countenance, and for a while clothing it with the warm sunshine and radiance of a holy *smile*, we cannot believe.

Again,—Is the statement of Christ's joyless expression wise? We think not. It gives a wrong, distorted, gloomy portrait of His holy religion. The religion of Christ is the religion of JOY. Christ came to take away our sins, to roll off our curse, to unbind our chains, to open our prison-house, to cancel our debt; in a word, to give us the oil of joy for mourning, the garment of praise for the spirit of heaviness. Is not *this* joy? Where can we find a joy so real, so deep, so pure, so lasting? There is every element of joy—deep, ecstatic, satisfying, sanctifying joy—in the gospel of Christ. The believer in Jesus is essentially a happy man. The child of God is, from necessity, a joyful man. His sins are forgiven, his soul is justified, his person is adopted, his trials are blessings, his conflicts are victories, his death is immortality, his future is a heaven of inconceivable, unthought-of, untold, and endless blessedness—with such a God, such a Saviour, and such a hope, is he not, ought he not, to be a *joyful* man?

We propose, in the further unfolding of this subject, to state the grounds of the Lord's joy, and the corresponding grounds of the spiritual joy of the Lord's people; thus illustrating the perfect sympathy of Christ with His saints in this holy, elevated element of Christian experience.

We have already remarked in this volume, that the varied emotions of Christ never resolved themselves into empty sentiment, or evaporated into mere feeling—which, alas! is so much the case with many of His professed disciples—but that they were always in harmony with the occasions which gave them birth: that they were either an embodiment of some Divine principle or in illustration of some important truth, or in connexion with some beneficent act—a doctrine of the gospel propounded, or a miracle of mercy wrought. In the present instance, the joy of Christ is in connexion with the enunciation of one of the most important doctrines of the Bible—the gospel, hidden to the worldly-wise, revealed to the spiritually enlightened and taught. "*In that hour Jesus rejoiced in spirit, and said, I thank thee, O Father, Lord of heaven and earth, that thou hast hid these things from the wise and prudent, and hast revealed them unto babes: even so, Father; for so it seemed good in thy sight.*" In tracing our Lord's joy to some of its causes, let us place this one in the foreground—His joy at the sovereign revelation of His gospel to His disciples.

What a solemn, and equally true, statement of our great Teacher is this—the gospel a hidden, concealed thing to the carnal mind! "*Thou hast hid these things from the wise and prudent.*" The "wise and prudent," in the general acceptation of the title, include the great men of the unregenerate; all those to whom the mysteries of the kingdom are not revealed; but, doubtless, our Lord had a special reference to the carnally-wise, the lettered philosophers of the world, who, wise and prudent in the learning and science and arts of this life, were yet profoundly ignorant of the things of the Spirit of God. Now, this arises from no defect either in the nature of the gospel, or in the evidence of its divinity, or in the simplicity of its statements. There is everything in the gospel to awaken the intellect, to incite the imagination, to gratify the taste, to enlist the sympathies and sensibilities of the finest and most cultivated minds. Its themes of thought, its touches of beauty, its unveilings of grandeur, its history, its philosophy, its poetry, its science, are such as to charm and feast the noblest intellect that ever shone in the world of mind. And when the soul at first wakes up to the sublimity and power of the gospel of Christ, it marvels and it wonders that all this magnificence and beauty and tenderness, all these sources of the highest thought and purest feeling, should have been so long and so deeply veiled from its view.

Nor does this ignorance of the gospel, and lack of interest in its revelations, arise from any deficiency of evidence. God has made nothing more demonstrably true than His gospel. If ever proof, self-evident and overwhelming, accumulated around an object, that object is the glorious gospel of the blessed God. Internal and external, immediate and collateral, positive and presumptive, the evidences of the truth of the gospel are many and mighty, convincing and conclusive; leaving the sceptic, unbelieving mind without one excuse to justify or palliate at Christ's tribunal the fearful crime of its rejection. If you, my reader, are rejecting the Bible on the ground of its unsatisfactory proof, on the plea of its lack of evidence, and at the same time, it may be, giving the fullest credence to some old wives' fable unsupported by one shadow of evidence, I bid you pause before you advance one step further, and ponder these solemn, searching words of Christ—"*This is the condemnation, that light is come into the world, and men love darkness rather than light, because their deeds are evil.*" Light is come—the light of Christ, the light of revelation and the light of evidence. Not for want of light, then, will you finally be condemned. Then, for what? For your wilful rejection of that light. And why this rejection of the light? Because you love the darkness of sin! Examine yourself honestly, and ascertain if your infidelity, your scepticism, your unbelief, your quibbling and cavilling at the truth of the Bible, has not its seat, not in a mind that cannot be convinced, but in a heart that will not! Infidelity is not the child of reason; it is the deformed offspring of a depraved heart. There is a love of sin—of some master, dominant sin—underlying all scepticism. The light is rejected, because the darkness is loved; the truth is renounced, because the sin is preferred. The Bible is hated and ignored, because it is against sin, and testifies of the world that the works thereof are evil. We reiterate the statement, that atheism and infidelity are not the beauteous flowers of intellect, as some affirm, but the indigenous plants of a sinful and sin-loving heart. "*The fool hath said in his* HEART"—not in his *head;* the intellect could not affirm that—"*there is no God.*" The words, "*there is,*" are in italic, denoting that our translators have supplied them, needlessly we think, so that, viewing the passage as in the original, it would read—"*The fool hath said in his heart*—NO GOD"—*i. e.*, "No God for me I want no God, though in my judgment I know that there is one." Such is the wisdom of the worldly-wise and prudent. Truly may the apostle affirm, "*the wisdom of this world is foolishness with God*," and "*the wisdom of God is foolishness with men*."

Nor does this blindness of the unrenewed mind to the glorious gospel of the blessed God arise from any want of *simplicity* in the gospel. Inconceivably great, indescribably grand, transcendently sublime as is the gospel of Christ, it is the very essence of simplicity—as all God's works and ways are. Was ever any scheme, any plan, any command so simple as this, "*Believe in the Lord Jesus Christ, and thou shalt be saved?*" And yet, this is the whole gospel! This is the sum and substance of salvation! The first principles of Christianity, the elements of the gospel, are few and simple. And this forms the stumblingblock—the naked simplicity of "the truth as it is in Jesus." The "wise and the prudent" stumble, not at the profoundness, not at the grandeur, not at the difficulties of the gospel, but at its severe, its pure, its perfect simplicity. And because it submits its mysteries to faith, and not to reason; appeals to the heart, and not to the intellect; demands the evidence of the child, and not the understanding of the philosopher; the silent, lowly, believing homage of the soul, and not the haughty, towering reasoning of the mind, the philosophising, pharasaical, and proud of this world instantly, scornfully, and totally reject it.

Such is the solemn truth our Lord affirmed; and the entire analogy of Scripture maintains the fact. The gospel is a hidden glory to the unrenewed man. The apostle thus confirms the statement—"*The natural man receiveth not the things of the Spirit of God: for they are foolishness unto him: neither can he know them, because they are spiritually discerned.*" The Greek is more emphatic—"he is not able to know them"—his spiritual organs are impaired; he has eyes, but the transcendent wisdom and sublimity of the gospel he sees not; he has ears, but the thunders of its threatenings and the soft-breathing music of its doctrines he hears not. With all his human acumen—his attainments in philosophy, his discoveries in science, his perfection in art, his power to sound the depths of human mystery, the Bible is to him—unenlightened, untaught, unregenerated by the

Spirit—a book seven times sealed—he is not *able* to know it. And the poor, uneducated peasant, dwelling in some lowly cottage, with nought but his Bible and its Divine Author to enlighten and instruct him, shall travel far into the depths of revelation and sound their wonders; shall grasp the truths of the Bible, understand their meaning, feel their power, receive their comfort, and explain the mind of the Spirit with a lucidity, beauty, and power which might put to the blush many an acknowledged champion of literature and many a professed college divine. And what causes the difference? The cottage expositor of God's Word is taught by the Divine Spirit: the learned expositor of the schools still belongs to the worldly-"wise and prudent," to whom the gospel is a *hidden* thing! My reader, become a disciple of Jesus! Quit the schools and the teaching of men for the school and the teaching of Christ. Receive the gospel as a little child. Become a fool that you may be wise. Lay your human learning and philosophy, your pride of intellect and of merit, beneath the cross, and take your place at the Saviour's feet, and learn of Him, and be taught by Him the truth as it is in Jesus. Be this your petition, urged importunately until the Spirit responds—"*Open mine eyes that I may behold wondrous things out of Thy law.*"

Turn we now to one of the causes of the Saviour's joy. "In that hour Jesus rejoiced in spirit and said, I thank thee, O Father, Lord of heaven and earth, that thou hast hid these things from the wise and prudent, and HAST REVEALED THEM UNTO BABES." This was His joy—that His Father, in the exercise of His electing love and sovereign grace and Divine power, had passed by the worldly-wise and prudent, and had revealed the glorious things of the gospel to those whom the world regarded as "babes" in intellect, in power, and in knowledge. These "babes," then, are not children of tender years, but children in docility, humility, and simplicity; those who not only "from a child have known the Holy Scriptures," but who, *as a child*, have received them into their understandings and hearts. Now let us pause and press the inquiry—Has the gospel been *revealed* to you? Has it pleased God to *reveal* His Son in you? Has the spirituality of the Divine law been revealed to you? Has your condemnation under the law been revealed to you? Has the plague of your own heart been revealed to you? Has the salvation of Christ been revealed to you? In a word, has God in Christ, and Christ Himself, the sent of God, the gift of God, the Son of God, been revealed by the Holy Ghost to your soul? Take nothing for granted in ascertaining this momentous matter. Assume nothing as true, unauthenticated, unconfirmed, unsealed by the Holy Spirit. "*The Spirit beareth witness with our spirit, that we are the children of God.*" Oh, what an unspeakable mercy—the greatness, the grandeur, the blessedness of it, who can describe?—of having a revealed Christ to our souls! To have the Divine truths, the precious promises, the glorious revelations, the sublime hopes of the glorious gospel of the blessed God made known to our minds, sealed upon our hearts, ingrafted upon our souls, is to be the partakers of a joy such as glowed in the breast and lighted up the countenance of Jesus in that hour when He looked up to heaven, and said, "*I thank thee, O Father, Lord of heaven and earth, that thou hast revealed these things unto babes.*" Rest not short of this revelation by the Spirit of Jesus to your soul. Without it you are lost—your religion is vain, your evidences are spurious, your conversion is false, and your hope will make you ashamed.

Another ground of the Lord's joy was, *the sovereignty of God* thus displayed. Seeing that the gospel, hidden from the wise, was revealed unto babes, and resolving this into the sovereign will and discriminating grace of God, He rejoiced in spirit, and said, "*Even so, Father, for so it seemeth good in thy sight.*" And here it is we must find a solution to what would else, in our poor ken, appear partial, unjust, and inexplicable in God's testimony of His grace—why the gospel should be a hidden thing to one, a revealed thing to another; why one should be called and another left, we can only explain and understand in the exercise of that Divine sovereignty which belongs essentially to God. "*He giveth no account of any of His matters.*" Who art thou, then, O man, that repliest against God? Shall not He, the Judge of all the earth, do right? Has He not a right to do with His own as He will? And in the merciful decisions of His grace, and in the awful decisions of His providence, and in the yet more tremendous decisions of His judgment, He, the Most Upright, will be guided by the eternal principles of righteousness, rectitude, and wisdom. Beware, then, how you quarrel with God's sovereignty! You touch one of the most righteous principles of His administration, you shade one of the brightest perfections of His being, you pluck one of the costliest gems from His crown, when you attempt to arrest the sovereign exercise of His own will. How clearly and emphatically is this set forth by the Holy Ghost! "*Who worketh all things after the counsel of His will.*" "*Of His own will begat he us by the word of truth.*" "*Having predestinated us unto the adoption of children by Jesus Christ to himself, according to the good pleasure of his will.*" "*Therefore hath he mercy on whom he will have mercy, and whom he will he hardeneth.*" "*Hath not the potter power over the clay, of the same lump to make one vessel unto honour and another unto dishonour?*" Let your whole soul, amid the mysteries and shadows of the Divine administration of grace, bow down to this glorious doctrine, exclaiming, "*Even so, Father, for so it seemeth good in thy sight.*" This interpretation, too, of what is dark, inexplicable, and painful in the providential dealings of God with you, will infuse joy and create repose throughout your tried and agitated mind. God will have you meekly, truthfully resolve all the mysteries, enigmas, problems of His divine dispensations into this—"*Even so, Father, for so it seemeth good in thy sight.*" And the moment you are brought to acquiesce in the sovereignty, equity, and love of God's trying, afflictive, correcting dealings with you—to feel that it is all right, all wise, all good, all faithful—your storm-tossed, agitated barque is at anchor in the roads of perfect security and peace. Truly, this is joy!

Here, then, is our Model—the joy of the Lord. Surely if Christ was a man of joy, we, who are Christ's, should be joyful too. And yet how much this Christian grace is overlooked! How few aspire to this attainment in the divine life! Joy is as much a fruit of the Spirit as any other. "*The fruit of the Spirit is*—JOY." And the Divine precept is, "REJOICE *in the Lord alway. And again, I say,* REJOICE." And was not this one of the distinct blessings sought for His disciples in our Lord's intercessory prayer, "*That they might have my joy fulfilled in themselves?*" He here prays His Father that His own personal joy—the joy of which He was the subject—and the disciples' joy—the joy of which He was the object—might be realised in their experience. Did Christ thus care and pray for our joy? Oh, then, let us not deem this too lofty, too holy an attainment in our Christianity to aspire to. To stimulate your aspirations after it, to aid your endeavours to climb this sun-lit height in your Christian experience, let me suggest the grounds you have for holy, spiritual rejoicing in the Lord—and then remind you how closely Christ sympathises with you in your joy.

What a ground of joy is *your possession of Christ!* There is everything in Christ, and in the knowledge and possession of Christ, to make the believing heart joyful. You may have strong corruptions, powerful inbred sins, sore temptations, deep trials, heavy afflictions, yet if you know Christ, and have Christ in the midst of all, you have ground for the deepest, holiest joy. All joy apart from Christ is but the inspiration of the wind. The man who seeks the element of joy in his baptism, in his sacraments, in his church, in his religious duties, in his zeal, in his usefulness, yea, in anything out of Christ, is building upon that which hath no foundation. It is a false, a spurious, a fatal joy, a joy which will prove but as the crackling of thorns under a pot. But, beloved, we hope and speak better things of you. You have found Christ, or rather, Christ has found you, and you have in Him the substance, the essence, the fulness of all holy joy. You possess in Christ a Divine Redeemer, a loving Friend, a sympathising Brother, an ever-interceding Intercessor, a powerful Advocate; One whose presence is with you always, encircling you as an atmosphere in all places and under all circumstances—truly this is a ground of the deepest, holiest joy. Oh, what a portion is Jesus in a portionless world! What a rest is Jesus in a restless world! What a joy is Jesus in a joyless world! What a hope is Jesus in a hopeless world! Beloved, we too little and too imperfectly realise what we possess in possessing Christ. Throw into one scale all the good of the world, its rank, its honours, its wealth, its pleasures—all the love, the kindness, the sympathy, the power of the creature and of all creatures; and place in the other scale, CHRIST—Christ as your Saviour, Christ as your Friend, Christ as your Portion, and Christ as your all,—which kicks the beam? which sinks, and which rises? Nay, more—cast into one scale poverty, and sickness, and affliction of every kind, and sorrow of every form—the adversity that swept from you affluence, or the bereavement that tore from you the creature—and place JESUS in the other—Jesus in His deathless love, Jesus in His human sympathy, Jesus in His boundless fulness, Jesus bearing you upon His heart in heaven, and receiving you into His grace on earth,—and then decide what should be the nature, the depth, the music of your joy. "*This is my Friend, and this is my Beloved.*" Oh, be joyful, then, believer in Jesus! There breathes not a being in the universe—tried, tempted, sad though you are—who has greater reason to be of a gladsome spirit than you. Rejoice, then, in what Christ is in Himself—in His preciousness and fulness; rejoice in what Christ is to you, and rejoice in what you are to Christ. Truly, "*we rejoice in Christ Jesus, and have no confidence in the flesh.*"

The work of Christ is also a ground of joy to the Lord's people. There is everything in the salvation of the Lord to meet the necessities of our soul, and therefore to inspire the emotion of joy. What a source of the truest, purest, deepest joy is the blood and righteousness of Christ—the finished work of Christ—the revealed, accepted sacrifice of Christ — the infinite suffering of

Christ — the resurrection of Christ from the grave—and the present advocacy of Christ at the right hand of God! Truly may "*we joy in God through our Lord Jesus Christ, by whom we have now received the atonement.*" Is not the forgiveness of all your sins—the full justification of your person—your inalienable adoption into God's family—the complete payment of all that great debt you owed, and the assured and certain prospect of being where Christ is, and with Christ, beholding His glory for ever, a well-grounded source of joy? Most truly! Why, then, are you not a more joyful believer? Why go you mourning all your days, without one gleam of sunshine, one thrill of joy, one ray of hope, one note of praise? Is it not because you are looking to yourself and within yourself, to the almost entire exclusion of Christ and of the great and complete salvation wrought for you in and by Christ? No material for joy and gladness, beloved, will you find within yourself. It is all sin there—all corruption there—all gloom there. Its chamber of imagery is all dark, and repulsive, and depressing. Oh, turn the eye of faith to Christ, look simply, and fully, and exclusively at Him, and every chord of your soul will thrill and resound with the joy of the Lord's salvation. "*I will greatly rejoice in the Lord, my soul shall be joyful in my God; for he hath clothed me with the garments of salvation, he hath covered me with the robe of righteousness.*"

And what a God and Father have you to rejoice in! Truly, here is a source of spiritual joy the divinest and surest. To have a God to go to in all difficulties, troubles, and fears; a Father to fly to with every pressure, every sorrow, every want, His ear ever hearkening, His hand ever outstretched, His power equal to His goodness, His ability to aid equal to His readiness to aid, surely—with such a covenant God and such a loving Father as ours—our spirit ought to rejoice more in "*God our exceeding joy.*" There is everything in God to make us joyful all the day long. All His perfections smile upon us in Christ, and all are pledged to defend us, to provide for us, to supply us, and to bring us through all and out of all the vicissitudes, trials, temptations, and sins of this present life into life eternal. We rejoice so faintly in God, because we are so imperfectly acquainted with Him. And we are so little acquainted with Him, because we have so few close transactions with Him. We run to the creature—we rest in the creature—we rejoice in the creature, until the Lord empties, embitters, or removes the creature; and then we learn that "*men of low degree are a vanity, and men of high degree are a lie*," and that it is better to put confidence in God, even our own God, than in earth's mightiest potentates. And, oh, what a new-born joy do we then find God to be! It would seem as if we had never known, had never trusted, had never loved, had never fled to Him before. The newly-broken cistern has given us a new, a more vivid view of the Divine, the never-failing Fountain. The paralysing of the human arm has thrown us more entirely on the strength of the Divine arm. The utter vanity and disappointment we have found in the creature has brought God more really, fully, and blessedly into our soul; and we have learnt more of Him as our trust, our hope, our joy, more of His condescension, His faithfulness and love, more of Him as our Father and our God, in that one, that earthly disappointment, than we ever learnt in all the fulness of the world's sufficiency. Child of God! rouse you to the truth that, be the depths of your soul's distress, or mental despondency, or temporal embarrassments never so profound—too deep for human power to sound, soothe, or relieve—yet you may hope and joy in God. "*I am the Almighty God*"—God all-sufficient. God can, God will, God has promised to help you. Let your faith reason thus—"*Why art thou cast down, O my soul? and why art thou disquieted within me? Hope thou in God; for I shall yet praise him, who is the health of my countenance, and my God.*" God can make you joyful amid the circumstances which else would make you sad. All things may seem against you but the promises of God, all beings but the God of the promises. Divine providences are dark, but the Divine promises are light. And the very billows that swell, and foam, and surge around you, shall but uplift and cast your soul more entirely upon the Rock that is higher than you. Oh, I desire you to see what a source of joy you have in JEHOVAH amid the joyless, sorrowful path you tread. There is everything in Him to make you happy. Everything to win your confidence, to inspire your love, to awaken your joy. Creatures shall fail, resources shall fail, hopes shall fail, but GOD will never fail you. His love is as changeless, His power is as omnipotent, His faithfulness is as firm, His resources are as boundless, as infinite as His being. Listen to the song of faith, sung by saints who have gone to glory, once as tried, as tempted, as sorrowful as you, —"*My soul, wait thou only upon God; for my expectation is from him.*" "*I had fainted, unless I had believed to see the goodness of the Lord in the land of the living. Wait on the Lord; be of good courage, and he shall strengthen thine heart; wait, I say, on the Lord.*" "*Although the fig-tree shall not blossom, neither shall fruit be in the vines; the labour of the olive shall fail, and the fields shall yield no meat; the flock shall be cut off from the field, and there shall be no herd in the stalls:*" (what condition could be more barren and desolate?) "*yet I will rejoice in the* LORD, *I will joy in the God of my salvation,*" (Hab. iii. 17, 18.) See how the believing soul may experience GOD its exceeding joy in the depth of its exceeding trial. And all that He now asks at your hands is that you will trust in Him. What though He has written you a widow, what though He has made you fatherless, what though He has blown upon riches, blighted health, bereaved you of friends, yet still He is your God, and your Father, and your exceeding joy. Not one spring of His own love, and compassion, and grace, and power is dried, whatever others have may have passed for ever away. "*Come, let us return unto the* LORD; *for he hath torn, and he will heal us; he hath smitten, and he will bind us up.*" Again, we find two notable instances of deep joy in the midst of deep tribulation in the experience of David, worthy of our study. For a moment the popular idol had become a subject of popular hate. The people spake of stoning David: "*David was greatly distressed; for the people spake of stoning him, because the soul of all the people was grieved; but* DAVID ENCOURAGED HIMSELF IN THE LORD HIS GOD," (1 Sam. xxx. 6.) Has the creature turned against you? Have you found popular favour but a floating bubble—the fickle wind? Are those now against you who once rent the air with your acclaim? Oh, see what a source of joy you have in God, and in the Lord your God encourage yourself. The other example is taken from a yet more tender, affecting page in David's history—the treason of Absalom. And yet, listen to his language in that the deepest of a parent's grief:—"*Although my house be not so with God; yet he hath made with me an everlasting covenant, ordered in all things, and sure: for this is all my salvation, and all my desire."* Beloved, take hold of this covenant in this the dark stage of your journey. Be the cloud what it may that enshrouds your path, be the sorrow what it may that wounds your heart, be the hand what it may that wings the dart that pierces your soul, to this everlasting covenant of grace, well-ordered and sure, take a firm grasp of faith, and your soul shall rejoice with joy unspeakable and full of glory.

"My God, the covenant of Thy love
Abides for ever sure;
And in its matchless grace I feel
My happiness secure.

"Since Thou, the everlasting God,
My Father art become;
Jesus my Guardian and my Friend
And heaven my final home:

"I welcome all Thy sovereign will,
For all that will is love:
And, when I know not what Thou dost,
I wait the light above."

And overlook not the ever fresh, ever perennial spring of spiritual joy that flows *from the throne of grace.* Who can fully describe the joy which *prayer* brings into the soul? God has graciously appointed this medium of communication with Himself. Prayer is the soul's safety-valve, and God's channel. This is the outlet of the soul's deep overcharged feelings which, but for this escape, would serve to rend it in twain. And it is the channel through which the God of all comfort, who comforteth those that are cast down, conveys into the heart of His child the strong consolations of His love. Oh, then, seek to enkindle your holy, spiritual joy at this blessed altar—a throne of grace, accessible through Jesus, sprinkled with His blood, encircled by every assurance and promise of acceptance and response, from which none are debarred but those who debar themselves. Arise, and give yourself to prayer. Prayer will turn your night of weeping into a morning of joy. Prayer will dissipate the sadness, dissolve the cloud, quell the fear, and calm the tempest of your soul. Prayer will restring and retune the broken and silent chords of your heart, and you shall sing, "*Blessed be the* LORD, *because he hath heard the voice of my supplications. The* LORD *is my strength and my shield; my heart trusted in him, and I am helped: therefore my heart greatly rejoiceth; and with my song will I praise him.*" Betake yourself, then, to the throne of grace, and, however sad and heavy be the heart you bear to this hallowed spot, you shall return rejoicing in Christ Jesus.

And what holy, spiritual, deep joy should fill your soul in the assured prospect of your being in heaven! Believers rejoice too little in hope of the coming glory. And yet what rich material for joy have we in the anticipation of being for ever with Jesus! Heaven should have a more direct, powerful influence upon our minds than it has. It should be more exclusively the centre of our soul's moral gravitation. Our affections, our meditations, our aspirations, our longings should be oftener and more supremely there. Heaven has every attraction to win, every prospect to soothe, every motive to stimulate, every aspect to sanctify us in our homeward journey. Rejoice, then, in the anticipation of glory. Let sick and suffering saints be joyful on their beds let afflicted saints be joyful in their tribulations; let the labouring servants of Christ rejoice amid their toilsome, arduous, self-denying service; let all rejoice in hope of the glory that is to be revealed, when Christ shall say, "Come up hither." "*Whom not having seen, we love; whom though now we see him not, yet believing, we rejoice with joy unspeakable and full of glory.*"

And should not *the coming of the Lord* be to us a cause of longing, spiritual, unutterable joy? Most assuredly! What theme more holy, what prospect more comforting, what hope more blessed, what truth more sanctifying than—the glorious appearing of our Lord! The Word of God speaks of those who "*love His* APPEARING." It exhorts the saints to be "*looking for and hasting unto the* COMING *of the day of God.*" It comforts those who are bereaved of holy ones by the assurance that, "*those also that sleep in Jesus will God bring with him.*" And it supplies us with one of the most powerful, most solemn, most winning motives to *personal holiness,*—"*The very God of peace sanctify you wholly; and I pray God your whole spirit and soul and body be preserved blameless* UNTO THE COMING OF OUR LORD JESUS CHRIST." And, oh, what links of blessing bind us to this "*blessed hope, the* GLORIOUS APPEARING *of the great God our Saviour!*" What are some of them? We shall see Him as He is—we shall be like Him—we shall appear with Him in glory—we shall not be ashamed at His coming—we shall be blameless—we shall have part in the first resurrection—we shall be reunited with those who died in the Lord—we shall receive a crown of life—we shall reign with Him for ever—and we shall be with the New Jerusalem saints in the new heavens and the new earth—"*And God shall wipe away all tears from their eyes; and there shall be no more death, neither sorrow, nor crying, neither shall there be any more pain: for the former things are passed away.*" Let the second coming of the Lord, then, be more a theme of your devout meditation, a subject of more prayerful study, an event of more ardent longing, and more believing, hopeful, joyful expectation. "*Wherefore, beloved, seeing that ye look for such things, be diligent that ye be found of Him in peace, without spot, and blameless.*"

Did Christ rejoice in spirit? Then He will sympathise with your gospel joy. Do you rejoice that He came to save sinners—that He died for sinners—that He receives sinners—the poorest, the weakest, the vilest? Then with this holy joy trembling within your heart, Jesus your Saviour warmly, tenderly sympathises. Think not that He will forbid, repress, or discourage it. Oh no! He will rather mend the bruised reed and fan the smoking flax; He will rather heal the broken bones that they may rejoice in His salvation. Christ delights in your joy, loves your joy, is glorified by your joy; and when He sees you resting in His blood and righteousness, coming in your poverty to the unsearchable riches of His grace, in your emptiness to His infinite fulness, in your guiltiness to His atoning blood, "*He will rejoice over thee with joy; he will rest in his love; he will joy over thee with singing.*"

Spiritual joy is a holy, sensitive plant—it shrinks from the rude, ungentle touch—from every influence uncongenial with its heaven-born nature. Watch it with sleepless vigilance—shield it with every hallowed defence. There are many hostile influences to which it is exposed, any one of which will seriously injure it. Temptation courted, sin tampered with, worldliness indulged, the creature idolised, means of grace slighted, Christ undervalued,—any one of these things will damp your joy, cause it to shrink, and compel it to retire. But nothing will sooner or more effectually do this than looking away from the Object and Source of joy—the Lord Jesus Christ. Your joy is not only *of* the Lord, but it is a joy *in* the Lord. That which caused the Ethiopian eunuch to go on his way rejoicing was, not his baptism—Christ-like as it was—it was CHRIST Himself. He had found Christ the Messiah—Christ the Sin-Bearer, Christ the sin-atoning Lamb, as preached by Isaiah in the fifty-third chapter of his evangelical prophecy, and *this* it was that sent him on his way rejoicing! Oh, there is everything in Jesus to inspire and increase your spiritual joy—and He who first awakened in your soul the celestial emotion must sustain and nourish it. As there is no music in the Æolian until the wind breathes upon it—as there is no perfume in the flower until the sun warms it—as there is no verdure in the grass until the rain and the dew moisten it, so there is no melody, no fragrance, no fruitfulness in the soul until it is brought into close believing relation with Christ. Again, I remark, there is everything in Christ to make you a joyful Christian. There is all redundance of grace to subdue your corruptions, an overflowing sympathy to soothe your sorrows, a sovereign efficacy in His blood to cleanse your guilt, infinite resources to meet all your wants, His ever-encircling presence around your path, His ceaseless intercession on your behalf in heaven. His loving cognisance of all you feel, and fear, and need,—oh, is *this* not enough to make your heart a constant sunshine, and your life a pleasant psalm?

But be not discouraged, however, if you seldom reach this high attainment in Christian experience. Many an eminent saint of God passes to the land of light and song with little or no spiritual *joy* in his soul. It is not a grace *essential* to salvation. It is but seldom remarked of our Lord that He rejoiced in spirit—often that He sighed, and groaned, and wept. He seemed more intwined with sorrow than with joy—better acquainted with grief than with gladness. There may be many disturbing causes affecting and preventing your spiritual joy. You may be constitutionally of a sad, nervous, and pensive nature,—you may be the subject of constant mental depression, imparting its complexion of sadness and gloom to every bright view of the present and hopeful expectation of the future. There may be in your Christianity a tendency to look more to self than to Christ; to dwell in contemplation more upon the interior of your own heart than the interior of the Lord's heart; to a microscopic view of your varied and ever-fitful feelings, to a too close and minute analysing of Christian experience; or, your path may be one continuity of shade flung upon it by the pressure of a daily cross, a home sorrow, a lone grief, a physical frame unstrung and shattered by disease; all, or any, of these causes may contribute to the absence of spirtual *joy* in your soul. But, yield not yourself, in consequence, to despondency and despair. It is not spiritual joy that saves you—you are saved by faith in Christ, by Christ, and with Christ. And in the absence of joy thrilling your soul, illumining your countenance, and waking the echoes of the wilderness with its melody, there is, perhaps, the quiet, simple recumbance of your faith on Christ as all your salvation and all your desire, ever and anon giving vent to this its Christ-sent breathing —"*Whom have I in heaven but thee? and there is none upon earth that I desire besides thee.*" Then, be still, trustful, assured that you are Christ's, and that where Christ is, there you also will be.

Let us seek more personal identity with the joy of the Lord in the progress of His kingdom in the world. What emotion in Christ's soul was deeper and superior to every other? What caused Him to long for the garments rolled in blood, to pant for His baptism of suffering, to press the cold earth of Gethsemane, to embrace the rude cross of Calvary, and to confront the serried ranks of His enemies in that fatal hour? Oh, it was this—"*Who for the* JOY *that was set before Him, endured the cross, despising the shame.*" It was the joy of saving sinners—the joy of ransoming His Church—the joy of supplanting earth's sin, and woe, and curse, with the holiness, the happiness, the blessing of His gospel. Identify yourself—your intellect, your wealth, your influence, your time—with this joy of your Lord! Then shall Christ's joy be fulfilled in you. Oh, hallowed and ecstatic the joy of saving a soul from death—of reclaiming a wanderer to the fold—of planting a jewel in Christ's crown! How touching the picture of Christ's joy—"*And when he hath found it, he layeth it on his shoulder,* REJOICING. *And when he cometh home, he calleth together his friends and neighbours, saying unto them,* REJOICE *with me: for I have found my sheep which was lost.*" Be this, beloved reader, *your* joy, then, indeed, will you now enter into the joy of your Lord—the joy of saving *one* soul! It will give to your life a brighter sunshine—to your death a more hallowed memory—it will heighten the glory and sweeten the music of heaven

Remember that Christ's joy and your joy are *one*—His joy is fulfilled in you, and your joy flows from Him—and this brings Christ and you into the closest sympathy. You belong to Christ, and therefore Christ admits you to a partnership in His own joy. He shares it with you. He takes your sorrow, and gives you His joy; and thus you become mighty, yea, almighty in your weakness, because "*the joy of the Lord is your* STRENGTH." This reciprocity of joy should deepen the realisation of your being Christ's. And if you are Christ's He will guard and increase your joy, and will share and lessen your sorrow, and you shall dwell in safety by Him,—"*because you belong to Christ.*"

Live much in anticipation of the fulness of joy that awaits you in heaven. If our present is blended with sighing and weeping, with toil and temptation, with the sword and the cross, our future will be a pure, simple, unmixed joy, truly and emphatically "*a joy* UNSPEAKABLE *and* FULL OF GLORY." And if now the joy of the Lord in your soul is at times so overpowering as to compel you to exclaim, "Lord, stay Thy hand, or.

enlarge my capacity," oh, what will be the FULNESS OF JOY THAT IS AT HIS RIGHT HAND, AND THE PLEASURES THAT ARE FOR EVER MORE? Blessed Jesus! Thou art my joy now—and to see Thee then, will be joy, full, perfected, and eternal. Until then, keep me very near Thy side—Thou my joy, my hope, my all! "*The beloved of the Lord shall dwell in safety by him; and the Lord shall cover him all the day long.*"

"Since I belong to Thee, my Saviour-God,
All must be well, however rough my road;
However dark my way or prospects be,
All, all is right, since overruled by Thee.

"Safely in Thee shall Thy beloved dwell,
Though storms may rage, and angry tempests swell;
'All the day long,' their covering Thou shalt be,
What then can harm those, Lord, kept by Thee?

"Feeblest of all Thy flock, Thou knowst me, Lord,
Helpless and weak, I stay upon Thy Word;
In all my weakness, this is still my plea—
That Thou art mine, and I belong to Thee.

"Then come whatever may, I am secure;
Thy love unchanged shall to the end endure,
Frail though I am, Thine everlasting arm
Shall shield Thy child from every breath of harm.

"Thy loving eye shall guide where'er I roam;
Thy Holy Spirit lead me to my home.
Thou wilt not let Thy feeble frail one stray,
Though dark temptations oft may crowd my way.

"In sorrow's saddest hour, Thy strength my stay;
My darkest night, Lord, Thou canst turn to day.
The most loved here may sometimes changeful be;
Thou changest not—and I belong to Thee.

"Then may the life, which now on earth I live,
Be spent for Him, who His for me did give.
Oh! make me, Lord, in all I will and do,
Ever to keep Thy glory in my view.

"And when my course is run, and fought the fight,
Life's struggles o'er, and faith is changed to sight,
Then all triumphant I shall ever be,
Safe in Thy Home, for I belong to Thee.

"'Fulness of joy' with all Thy ransom'd there,
In Thy loved presence I shall ever share;
With them I'll sing the love that made us free,
The grace that taught us we belong'd to Thee."

C. H. I.

CHAPTER X.

CHRIST'S SENSITIVENESS TO DESERTION.

"My God, my God, why hast thou forsaken me?"—
MATT. xxvii. 46.

HOW really and perfectly did every shade of our life's picture meet and blend in the life of Jesus! Conducted along no avenue of our existence shall we be by the invisible yet ever-guiding hand of our God, in which faith shall not descry some trace of Him who, "*when He putteth forth His own sheep, goeth before them, and the sheep follow Him.*" Take the touching illustration of this fact presented in the subject of the present chapter. Our Lord loved solitude, yet was sensitive to desertion. For the one He pined, from the other He shrank. His sad and pensive spirit led Him frequently to the mountain's solitude to spend long hours amid its calm stillness in devout meditation and prayer.

These hours of separation and solitude must have been as essential to His mission as it was in harmony with His nature. There could not but have been the consciousness of the necessity of privacy and prayer in order to the bracing of His spirit for the countless demands made upon His compassion, sympathy, and power. Always giving out—for He was *man* as well as GOD—His weary, jaded, saddened spirit needed the reviving and recruiting found only in periods of entire separation from man and close communion with God. Our Lord, therefore, often coveted and sought—

"The calm retreat, the silent shade,"

that He might replenish His resources, plume His spirit, refresh and gird His mind for the work and the battle of His life.

But the feeling of which He now so mournfully complains differed essentially from the solitude which He loved and courted. It was not solitude nor loneliness, it was DESERTION which wrung from His sad spirit this dolorous cry—"*My God, my God, why hast thou* FORSAKEN *me?*" There was more than a sense of loneliness, more than the sadness of solitude—there was the keen, painful feeling of *abandonment*—of abandonment, too, at a moment and under circumstances which must have imparted a peculiar pang and unlocked an additional source of suffering, to the sensitive spirit of our Lord. Ah! is there a sword that penetrates the heart more surely, more deeply than this—deserted by those we trusted in—forsaken by those we loved? Such was now the Saviour's position. Thus is our Lord brought into personal sympathy with one of the most delicate forms of human grief, with one of the most lonely sorrows of the heart—*the sorrow of the forsaken.* Before we proceed to claim His sympathy, let us follow Him a few steps in this gloomy path, and study His character amid the deep shadows now darkling around Him.

That our Lord should ever have been subjected to such a discipline, that He should have known the sorrow of one forsaken and abandoned by those in whom He trusted, and to whom He clung with more than a woman's confiding love, seems a wonder and a marvel. He had now reached the darkest hour of His sorrow—it was the total eclipse of the Sun of righteousness—the concentration, in their focal power, of all the physical, mental, and soul sufferings to which He was subjected. He was now exhausting that cup we have just seen could not pass His lips. He was wringing out the dregs of that chalice of woe, the bitterest draught of which was reserved for the hour of His impalement upon the tree. He was now treading the wine-press of Divine wrath alone—forsaken of man, abandoned by God. "*About the ninth hour Jesus cried with a loud voice, saying, Eli, Eli, lama sabachthani? that is to say, My God, my God, why hast thou forsaken me?*" That hour was about three o'clock in the afternoon, at which time the daily sacrifice was being offered in the temple; and just at the moment that that sacrifice was typifying Him, He, its great Antitype, was laying upon the altar of Justice a more Divine, glorious, and efficacious sacrifice for sins,—"*giving Himself for us an offering and a sacrifice to God for a sweet-smelling savour.*"

In considering our Lord's abandonment by the Father on the cross, there are two or three preliminary views we must keep before the mind, or we may be beguiled, unconsciously, into perplexity and error. In the first place, let it be premised that in this hour of darkness and desertion through which our Lord was passing, there was no separation, not the slightest loosening of the tie that bound them, of Christ's Divinity from His humanity. The fulness of the Godhead still dwelt in Jesus bodily; He was not the less Divine now that, in His extreme anguish and suffering, He appeared all the more human. As it was from His Divinity that the atoning sacrifice of Christ derived its virtue, it was not probable, nor was it possible, that, at the awful crisis of His atoning death, there should be the slightest separation between the complex natures of our Lord. His Deity was in union with the humanity at the moment He uttered the cry of desertion, now the subject of our study. To the fact of the existence of a *Divine* Sufferer, all nature, in her marvellous prodigies, now bore testimony. The earth trembled on its axis—the sun veiled its light—the rock was rent in twain—hades gave back its population—the grave yielded up its dead—all nature was robed in mourning because He who formed the earth created that sun, piled those rocks, and wore in His girdle the keys of hades and the grave, was, as man, and for man, expiring upon the tree. It was nature's testimony to the Godhead of its Maker.

To a like conclusion we may come, beloved, in

all our reasoning in seasons of soul-darkness and distress. Through whatever mental or spiritual exercises the children of God may pass, there is not the slightest change in their divine and heavenly nature. The child of God is born again of incorruptible seed; he is a partaker of the Divine nature; and no deeper discovery of the principle of corruption in his heart, no veiling of the light of God's countenance, touches the spiritual principle, or affects the divine nature. The soul may pass through various eclipses, sometimes partial, at other times total, nevertheless, like our blessed Lord, the profoundest gloom which enshrouds it but shades, not extinguishes, the divine sun within. Rejoice, then, O believer, in the immortality of your divine relationship to God, in the indestructible nature of your spiritual life,—once His adopted child, remember that you are His child for ever.

Nor are we to imagine, as included in this desertion of Christ on the cross, any, the slightest, variation in the love of the Father to His Son. This hiding of God from Jesus was a suspended manifestation, a veiled light, a concealed presence. If ever the Father loved His Son with an intense, approving, unchanged affection, it was at that moment that the "darling"* of His soul was enduring all this anguish, desertion, and horror to uphold the honour and win back the glory of the Divine government. In like manner may the saints of God argue respecting God's love to them in their darkest desertions and deepest sorrows. There is not the slightest veering in God's love to us in the discipline of the covenant. He may seem to frown, darkness may conceal the light of His countenance, and in His profoundly mysterious dispensations we may be led to exclaim, "Verily, thou art a God that HIDEST thyself," nevertheless, He loves us still — loves us with a love changeless as His being,—from everlasting to everlasting. Oh, argue no change or chill in the love your heavenly Father cherishes towards you from the severity of His dealings; but rather from the very severity of the chastening and the rebuke by which He seeks to make you a partaker of His holiness, infer the realitv and tenderness of His love.

With this explanation, we proceed to consider the nature of the trial through which our Lord was now passing. In one word, it was—DESERTION. "*My God, my God, why hast thou*

* Psalm xxii. 20.

FORSAKEN *me?"* This forsaking of Christ was the withdrawment of the sensible presence of God from the human soul of Jesus. And why this withdrawment, this hiding, this abandonment by the Father? The suffering Son of God himself asks the question—"WHY *hast thou forsaken me?"—why* this darkness?—*why* this forsaking? It was an act so new, so strange, so appalling, that, in the depth of His soul-agony Jesus uplifts His eyes to heaven and asks the cause—*why, for what,* hast Thou withdrawn Thyself from me? Beloved, there is but one answer to this question, but one solution to this mystery Jesus, our Surety, was now bearing all the sins of His whole Church by imputation; and it was from that tremendous load, it was in view of those accumulated transgressions that the Holy One, "who is of purer eyes than to behold iniquity," turned away—the sun of His glorious presence fading into the deepest, profoundest gloom. There was darkness on the whole earth from the sixth hour until the ninth; but what was *that* darkness in comparison with the darkness in which the holy soul of Jesus was enshrouded? But think not, howev[illegible] that, in this abandonment of Christ by the Fath[illegible] to loneli ness, darkness, and horror, there was any, the slightest, withdrawment of His love to, or of His interest in, His Son. Nor let it be imagined that in this forsaking there was any, the least, suspension of His upholding, sustaining power. Far from this. It was but the *sensible*, not the actual, withdrawment of God in this the darkest, direst hour of the Saviour's passion. But Jesus was now the antitypical Scapegoat on whose head Israel's sins were placed—Jesus was now the true SIN-BEARER, on whom the Father had laid the iniquities of His people; and it was proper that, in the eyes of all holy and unholy intelligences, God should, in that hour of accumulated, concentrated sin, demonstrate to the universe that He was a God of purer eyes than to *look* upon iniquity. Studied in the light of this truth, who can deny and reject the expiatory nature of Christ's death with reason or impunity?

But let it not be supposed—as some modern theologians have most erroneously affirmed—that this was the first and only period in our Lord's life in which He officiated as the SIN-BEARER of His people. No statement could be more unscriptural. His relation to the Church as her Sin-bearer commenced with the first pressure of His foot upon our sin-tainted earth,—the moment He touched its horizon, that moment commenced the bearing of sin and the work of its removal. The manger of Bethlehem was the starting-point, the cross of Calvary was the goal, in His career of working out the salvation, accomplishing the redemption of His people. He had known nothing of the curse when He came under the broken law of God,—the first drop of which moistened His infant lips,—had not sin by imputation been laid upon Him. If I reject the fact of the sin-bearing commencing with His life, I must necessarily reject the fact of His obedience to the law commencing with His life, which obedience becomes the "*righteousness of God unto all and upon all those that believe.*" But it is written—written by the pen of the Holy Ghost—"*Who his own self bare our sins in his own body on the tree,*"—in the original—TO *the tree.* *To* the tree, as the final stage, *to* the tree, as the end of sin, He bore, step by step, the tremendous load. That, in the great truth of His Suretyship He was a learner—learning something more and more of sin, and of the consequences of sin, and of the penalty of sin—who can doubt? The pressure increased upon Him by degrees, the load augmented in weight as He advanced, the storm thickened in darkness and deepened in intensity as He pressed forward to the goal. "*Though He were a Son, yet* LEARNED *He obedience by the things which He suffered.*" "*The Captain of our salvation was made perfect through suffering.*" And the great lesson He learned in this school of suffering was—OBEDIENCE. And how could He learn obedience but under the growing burden of His people's accumulated, concentrated sin and curse? Each step deepened His knowledge of what sin was—and this only could be as the sin was imputed. It was by suffering He was perfected in obedience, and His suffering commenced with the commencement of His life. It was not physical suffering alone by which our Lord was thus instructed. He suffered mentally, He suffered spiritually; and this school of suffering began from the moment that Herod sought His infant life, and virtually slew Him when he "slew all the children that were in Bethlehem, and in all the coasts thereof, from two years old and under," and terminated when He breathed these wondrous words—"*It is finished!*" Then it was our Lord began to learn what sin was, and what the suffering for sin. The more He came to learn the nature, the evil, the exceeding sinfulness of sin, the more must He have learned, not only the necessity of an expiation, but that *He* was the Expiator. And as He grew in stature, He grew in acquaintance with sin. Its monster form dilated before Him in gigantic proportions,—the tornado of the curse grew thicker and darker,—the wrath-cup became fuller and fuller as He advanced to meet the central horrors of the last, the latest hour of His passion. And how could this be but as, from His cradle to His cross, our adorable Emmanuel was our Divine, glorious—SIN-BEARER? But let us not, in this refutation of an error, lose sight of the truth we are unfolding—the darkness of Christ's soul upon the cross. Now indeed was the hour of darkness! Now was the Sun of righteousness in total eclipse—an eclipse which extinguished every ray of light, dried up every spring of joy, silenced every expression of sympathy and every word of comfort. Hear Him again exclaim, in the prophetic language of His prototype, "*My God, my God, why hast thou forsaken me? why art thou far from helping me, and from the words of my roaring? O my God, I cry in the day-time, but thou hearest not; and in the night-season, and am not silent. But thou art holy.*" Oh, love of Christ! unsurpassed, unparalleled! My soul, all this darkness, all this desertion, all this love was for thee!

Contrast this, your Lord and Master's condition, with the light of God's reconciled countenance by which you walk in darkness. Such was the testimony of Job—"*By His light I walked in darkness.*" Ah, beloved reader, in your gloomiest hour you experience no such darkness as the soul of Jesus now did. Your spiritual eclipse is never total. And even when, though a child of the light, God leads you by a way that is dark, a path that is lone and dreary, there is no punitive justice, no Divine wrath, no darkness of hell in the cloud that shades your soul. Nor are you forsaken. Christ is with you—unknown, unseen, unfelt it may be, still not the less really is He treading that lone and gloomsome way side by side with you. "*When I pass through the valley of the shadow of death,*" (which the path of sorrow is sometimes termed,) "*I will fear no evil, for Thou art with me.*"

"My God, the spring of all my joys,
The life of my delights,
The glory of my brightest days,
The comfort of my nights.

"In darkest shades if He appear,
My dawning is begun;
He is my soul's sweet Morning Star,
And He my rising Sun.

"The opening heavens around me shine,
With beams of sacred bliss,
While Jesus shews His heart is mine,
And whispers, I am His."

Our Lord was also *forsaken by man*. As man, He felt this sword to enter deeply into His soul. For as man, He clung to man—to the companionship, the solace, and the sympathy of man,—as we shall more fully shew in a subsequent part of this work. But He, like many of His followers, was destined to learn how vain was human help, how fickle was human love, how changeful was human friendship. He was forsaken by man, by the very men whom He had constituted His College of Apostles, whom He had admitted to His confidence, who had shared His love, and who had sworn eternal fealty to Him their Lord and Master. But now, in His deepest sorrow, "*they all* FORSOOK *Him and fled.*" But in this His prophecy was fulfilled which said, "*I have trodden the winepress alone; and of the people there was none with me.*" There was a fitness, a propriety in this that our Lord should accomplish the work of our salvation unaided by creature power, uncheered by human sympathy. Oh, how different it is with us! There are few of God's people who taste the cup of human sorrow unsweetened by the element of Christian compassion and sympathy. The Lord gives us, what He denied Himself, the clinging, soothing, cheering presence and affection of Christian friends and fellow-disciples. He was utterly forsaken; we are not so. Few believers there are who tread the shaded valley, confront the sweeping tempest, unaccompanied, uncheered by one loving heart, one sympathising spirit, one second self. Jesus, insulated from heaven and earth, was alone!

And, as if to complete the picture, nature seemed to conspire against Him. The sun forsook Him on the cross, withdrawing its cheering light, and leaving Him to the deep, sepulchral gloom of a total and protracted eclipse. Who has not, in deep sorrow, felt his heart ascend in thanksgiving to God for the pleasant sunshine? "*Truly the light is sweet, and a pleasant thing it is for the eyes to behold the sun.*" "Draw the curtain, raise the blind, let me see the sweet sun," is the languid request of many a sick and fading one. And what a glow have those golden beams imparted to the pallor of sickness! what solace to suffering! what cheering to the gloomy and lone chamber! But all this was denied our blessed Lord in the hour of His dissolution. The sun veiled its splendour, the light paled into darkness,—the darkness without only surpassed by the deeper darkness within His holy soul. Thus was our adorable Saviour forsaken by God —by man—by nature.

The remainder of this chapter will be devoted to the tracing of some analogy between this experience of Christ and that of many of His saints. It enters deeply into the moral discipline of the child of God that *loneliness* should occupy a large portion of his experience. It may be one of the most painful, yet is it one of the most wholesome and prolific causes of spiritual growth. Let us trace this feeling of desertion and loneliness to a few of its causes.

It is sometimes produced by a deeper self-acquaintance. The more thoroughly we come to know our own selves—the inner world, the life within life, the heart with its deep-rooted and deep-veiled sinfulness, the mind with its perplexities of thought, the will with its marvellous counter-workings,—the more deeply we seem drawn into the profoundest isolation and solitude. The very discovery we have made of ourselves, seems to isolate us from all others, and to shut us up to ourselves. With such conscious impurity and defect we shrink from the society and fellowship of the holy, as though others read our heart as we read it, and knew our unworthiness as we know it. And, as the leper, shrinking from the haunts of men, retired to his separation and loneliness, a like moral instinct often would force us to wander in solitary places, bemoaning our sinfulness, and holding intercourse only with Him from whose gracious presence no unworthiness shall exclude, and from whose loving eye no sorrow shall shade, nor solitude shall hide us. Still, we must guard against an extreme of feeling here. No intimacy with ourselves, no consciousness of infirmity, failure, and dereliction should be allowed such influence and mastery as to force us, by self-isolation, from the society of our fellow-Christians, or drive us from the scene of influence, service, and battle, into slothful inaction and ignoble solitude.

Our religious profession, too, may separate us from others. In addition to what we have already advanced on this head, we may remark that religious principles, character, and profession necessarily involve *separation.* The Church of God and the world are two distinct, opposite, and antagonistic corporate bodies. We cannot in our Christian character belong in part to the one and in part to the other. There can be no compromise, no truce, no uniting the two in a Christ-witnessing profession of love to the Saviour. There, then, is separation. But, added to this, we shall often find that even the bosom of the family circle is to us a lone desert. There shall be chilled affection, alienated interest, suspended sympathy, shunned intercourse, on the part of near and dear ones from whose principles and spirit, from whose worldliness, and even from whose religion, we feel compelled, by all that is dear, and sacred in the name, the religion, and profession of Christ, decidedly and entirely to separate ourselves. Oh, what a desert may a parent's home be—what isolation and solitude, among life's nearest and dearest! But Jesus trod this path before us—penetrated these solitudes far more deeply than we. He *was* all alone;

we never can be. The echoes of the mountains and the vales, to which He repaired, were the only responses to His sighs, groans, and prayers; —ours are in unison with voices of kindness, affection and sympathy uttered by a thousand Christ-loving and saint-loving hearts. Still, the desertion is bitter, the solitude irksome, and the discipline, though needful and wholesome, is unspeakably humiliating and painful.

The saints, too, will often experience *the truth* of God to be a separating element. There are many who desert our communion because of the doctrines of grace. It is a narrow path, the path of Christ's truth, and there are but few who walk in it. Doctrines separate—differences of judgment separate—varieties of interpretation separate—and thus those who really love the same Lord, and are travelling to the same inheritance, are divided in fellowship and sympathy the one from the other on this very ground. There are but few who love, delight in, and preach the distinguishing doctrines of grace, or who have much sympathy and fellowship with those who do. And because this path is so narrow, few walk in it together. When our Lord, the great Teacher from heaven, propounded the doctrine of Divine sovereignty, we are told that "*many went back, and walked no more with Him.*"

Worship is often another separating element in the Church of God. The question which divided the opinions and sundered the fellowship of the two great sections of the Jews—"where ought men to worship?"—still exists. *Where* shall we worship—in this sanctuary or in that? *How* shall we worship—with a liturgy or without? are questions which still separate multitudes of God's people,—some of whom are united by the closest ties of nature, and dwell beneath the same roof—the one from the other. Alas! that it should be so! Nor would it thus be, at least to so great and so bitter an extent, did we more deeply enter into our Lord's definition of true worship. "*The hour cometh, and now is, when the true worshippers shall worship the Father in spirit and in truth: for the Father seeketh such to worship Him.*" "*God is a spirit; and they that worship him must worship him in spirit and in truth.*" Realising this idea of true worship, it will be to us of but trivial moment where we worship our heavenly Father—whether in mount *Gerizim* or in *Jerusalem*—or how we worship Him—whether with or without a ritual—so that we worship

Him in spirit and in truth. It is the *heart* at which He looks, with which He has to do—the sincere, lowly, loving heart; and if *that* be true, I see not why differences of judgment as to a liturgical or a non-liturgical service should separate the saints of God in worship, create in them suspicion and distrust, still more alienation and bitterness. The more deeply we imbibe the true spirit of worship, the less formal and cold shall we be in the use of a prescribed form; and the more orderly, reverential, and devout shall we be without it. God has His eye and His heart upon all such true and humble worshippers. Listen to His gracious words of recognition,—"*Who is this that engaged his heart to approach unto me? saith the Lord.*" Truly may we respond, "*Blessed is the man whom thou choosest, and causest to approach unto thee, that he may dwell in thy courts: we shall be satisfied with the goodness of thy house, even of thy holy temple.*"

The ways of Divine providence, too, often bring us into this feeling of desertion and loneliness. As in grace, so in providence, the dealings of our God with us individually are frequently such as to lead us into paths diverse and separate from all others—paths sequestered, solitary, and lone;

awakening no observation, constraining no sympathy, inviting no intercourse, unsoothed, unnoticed, and unknown. And by how sudden, unlooked-for, and painful a process are we often led into this shaded way of the Lord! A removal by death—a reverse of fortune—the change of place or relation in life—the breaking up of a centre of affection and union, has plunged us into the depths of solitude, and henceforth life's lonesome journey brings us into closer assimilation and sympathy with a solitary, homeless Redeemer. Dearest Lord! anything, everything Thou dost appoint, if it but link me closer with Thy life, and moulds me more perfectly to Thine image.

And, then, there are seasons of spiritual desertion and gloom through which many believers are called to pass. Apart from this peculiar stage of the divine life, we should lose a great portion of Christ's sympathy. Spiritual darkness is a portion of the discipline, more or less, of every child of the light. It is a distressing, dreary stage; nevertheless, there is light enough in it for faith to descry the footprint of the Shepherd and the flock, and this alone were sufficient to invest the gloomiest path with sunshine, and to awaken ten thousand echoes of love in the loneliest. But let no child of God, who may be in spiritual darkness and desertion of soul, cast away his confidence, or cease to hold fast firmly the profession of his faith. Our blessed Lord did not renounce His Sonship or loosen His hold of faith when in the hour of His deepest gloom He exclaimed, "*My God, my God, why hast thou forsaken me?*" Imitate your Lord and Master. Is your soul in a spiritual eclipse—the light of God's countenance hidden, the visible presence of your Saviour withdrawn, the strong consolations of the Spirit suspended, prayer distilling no dew, the promises speaking no comfort?—be it so. Yet, what is the message of your God to you?—"*Who is among you that feareth the Lord, that obeyeth the voice of his servant, that* WALKETH IN DARKNESS, *and* HATH NO LIGHT? *let him trust in the name of the Lord, and stay upon his God,*" (Isa. l. 10.) Here is the true, the sublime attitude of faith in spiritual darkness—the soul staying itself upon God the strong One, the unchangeable One, the reconciled One. The mental depression, the spiritual darkness, the soul desertion through which you are now passing, touches not your union with the Lord Jesus, affects not your adoption into God's family. You are still one who feareth the Lord—who obeyeth the voice of His servant—a child of light, though in darkness, beloved of God, and dear to Christ. "*Why art thou cast down, O my soul? and why art thou disquieted within me? Hope thou in God: for I shall yet praise Him who is the health of my countenance and my God.*"

Seasons of loneliness and solitude often prove among the most hallowed and precious in the experience of the believer. In the first place, the spiritual discipline is healthful and wholesome. The solitary are never really in solitude. They are never more with God, or God with them, than at that period. He not only "*setteth the solitary in families,*" as He often kindly does, but He makes it to be in reality no solitude to the soul by virtue of His own manifested presence, converse, and glory. Thus that which else might prove the most severe, indescribable source of anguish, becomes one of the highest, holiest, and sweetest enjoyments of which our renewed nature is susceptible. It is then that,

> "Contemplation prunes her ruffled wings,
> And the free soul looks down to pity kings."

This close intercourse with God, which sacred

solitude produces, must then stamp this otherwise painful discipline as a golden period of our Christian career. It is then, if ever, the soul is alone with God. And the believer, having once experienced this sacred luxury, ever after pants for it as the hart panteth for the water-brooks. In how many a spiritual mind, thus sighing for the Divine presence in secret, will these poetical thoughts awaken sacred echoes, tender and plaintive as Æolian breathings—

> Prostrate, O Lord, before Thy cross,
> I come to own my shame and loss,
> My nakedness and poverty,
> Because I'm ne'er alone with Thee.
>
> The fretting trifles of the day,
> Like droppings, wear my soul away:
> No lively frames—no spirit free—
> Because I'm ne'er alone with Thee.
>
> Thy daily mercies oft forgot,
> My conscience stain'd with many a spot;
> A broken reed behold in me,
> Because I'm ne'er alone with Thee.
>
> A day will come when I must be
> Alone, my Lord and God, with Thee;
> With shame I then shall bow my head,
> My only plea—Thy blood was shed.*

But it is not all lamentation with the child of God. His harp has chords which might arrest

* E. W.

an angel's ear. How often has solitude witnessed to the richest experience, the sweetest songs, the brightest revelations of the Church of God! David in his cave, Jeremiah in his dungeon, Paul in his jail, John in Patmos, form a part of a great cloud of witnesses to this page of Christian experience. In all these places of banishment and desertion, of loneliness and solitude, God, in Christ, was their sun and their shield. And it is to these periods, sequestered from earth, separated from man, and shut in with God, that the Christian Church is indebted for some of the richest truths, the most mellowed experiences, sweetest strains, and sublimest visions which the pen of inspiration has recorded. It is then, truly and emphatically, the soul is—ALONE WITH GOD

Alone with Thee! alone with Thee!
'Tis there, dear Lord, I oft would be:
Where can my throbbing heart find rest
But on my God and Saviour's breast?

Alone with Thee would I be found,
Where none can misconceive or wound,
Before Thine eye my soul to bare,
And roll on Thee each burthening care.

Alone with Thee when Thou dost bless,
Alone, in sorrow and distress
Alone with Thee, by day, by night,
I cannot live, save in Thy sight.

Yea, e'en amid the seraph choir,
While praising Thee with golden lyre,
My jealous heart shall crave to prove
Thy personal, unchanging love.*

Is this the way God is now leading you, my reader? Is your path shaded with grief, solitary with desertion? Have friends and kindred forsaken you? You are not all alone! Your mind needed the teaching of solitude, your heart the discipline of separation; and so Christ, who is preparing both for the place He has prepared for you, allured you into this wilderness that He might instruct, sanctify, and comfort you. It is in the calmer quietude of separation, alone with God, that Divine truth is often the best studied and understood. We read of Christ that, "*when they were* ALONE, *He expounded all things to His disciples.*" The Word of God, ever precious and instructive, is never so much so as when the circumstances that exile us from man shut us up exclusively and entirely to its study with God. How instructive, consolatory, and precious, then, grows this Divine Book! The mysteries of providence have helped to explain the mysteries of revelation; the bitterness

* E. W.

of sorrow has drawn forth the sweetness of the Divine promises; the crushed hopes of earth have brought the soul into a closer realisation of the assured hope of heaven; and the wintry chill and gloom of adversity has made us acquainted with the Brother born for it. Oh, who can describe the preciousness, the soothing, the sustaining power of God's Word in the direst, the extremest circumstances of calamity, exile, and woe? Among the countless ancient and costly treasures contained in the great national treasury of this land, the most ancient, rare, and precious is a copy of God's Word found among the relics of the Franklin Expedition. To whom it belonged is not known, nor, perhaps, ever will be; enough that, amid the awful solitude of the Arctic seas—surrounded by interminable fields of ice, robed with the dreariness and gloom of eternal winter—pining in loneliness and starvation—thoughts of home crowding the memory—an awful death fast congealing the life-current—the contents of this copy of God's Word, all thumbed and marked, cheered, comforted, and sustained its possessor as he laid him down to die amid the polar snows, with none to soothe the last hour of agony save Christ and His Word.

Enough! less will not suffice—more we cannot have, in that trying, that solemn hour. No! you will never be all alone with this blessed volume of your Father's love, and the Saviour's presence sharing and soothing your solitude.

How beautifully adapted, then, is the *sympathy* of Christ to seasons of desertion and solitude. Did Christ know what it was to be alone—to be unbefriended and deserted? Was He abandoned, forsaken in sorrow, all Divine and human consolation for the moment suspended? Then Christ is with me in my present position! I have Jesus side by side with me in the shaded path I tread. He is with me the companion of my solitude, the sharer of my grief, softening, sweetening, sanctifying it; deepening and maturing His work of grace in my soul, and, by putting far from me lover and friend, drawing me all the closer to Himself. "*When my father and my mother forsake me, tnen the Lord will take me up.*"

Fear not the hour when you will descend into the valley of death's shadow. Not all solitary and alone will you be then. Believer in Christ! Jesus will be personally, visibly with you at that moment. His arm will encircle you,

His bosom will pillow you, His voice will cheer you, His words will strengthen you, His rod and His staff will comfort you, and you shall fear no evil. In all the past stages of your pilgrimage never will you have been so conscious of the encircling, clinging presence of your Lord, never will you so fully have realised His sustaining grace and soothing love as at the moment that severs you from all that is human, and shuts you up to all that is Divine. A DIVINE REDEEMER, when heart and flesh are failing, will be the strength of your heart and your portion for ever.

"Rise, my soul, thy God directs thee;
Stranger hands no more impede;
Pass thou on; His hand protects thee—
Strength that has the captive freed.

"Is the wilderness before thee,
Desert lands where drought abides?
Heav'nly springs shall there restore thee,
Fresh from God's exhaustless tides.

"Light divine surrounds thy going,
God Himself shall mark thy way;
Secret blessings richly flowing,
Lead to everlasting day.

"God, thine everlasting portion,
Feeds thee with the mighty's meat—
Saved from Egypt's hard extortion,
Egypt's food no more to eat.

"Art thou wean'd from Egypt's pleasures?
God in secret thee shall keep,
There unfold His hidden treasures,
There His love's exhaustless deep.

"In the desert God will teach thee
What the God that thou hast found—
Patient, gracious, powerful, holy,
All His grace shall there abound.

"On to Canaan's rest still wending,
E'en thy wants and woes shall bring
Suited grace from high descending:
Thou shalt taste of mercy's spring.

"Though thy way be long and dreary,
Eagle-strength He'll still renew:
Garments fresh, and feet unweary,
Tell how God hath brought thee through.

"When to Canaan's long-loved dwelling
Love divine thy foot shall bring,
There with shouts of triumph swelling
Zion's songs in rest to sing.

"There, no stranger, God shall meet thee—
Stranger thou in courts above—
He who to His rest shall greet thee,
Greets thee with a well-known love."

CHAPTER XI.

CHRIST'S DEPENDENCE UPON HUMAN SYMPATHY.

"Then saith he unto them, My soul is exceeding sorrowful, even unto death: tarry ye here, and WATCH WITH ME."—MATT. xxvi. 38.

GOD has created us with a *social* nature, and its instincts prompt us to seek fellowship with our own. We can scarcely imagine an instance of the human repairing, in its depression and sadness, to the aid and sympathy of the angelic. There is nothing between the two natures affinitive and sympathetic. That these celestial beings are our ministering spirits, clustering around us, noiseless and invisible, each moment fulfilling some benevolent behest of God on our behalf, it is delightful to believe—but, to invoke an angel's sympathy, to cast ourselves upon an angel's compassion in a season of difficulty and sorrow, is a conception that not only never enters into the human mind, but is foreign to all the instincts and yearnings of our nature. What an illustrious and impressive instance have we of this before us! Our Lord was now in the garden which lay at the foot of the Mount of Olives, just outside, and north of the holy city. He was in solitude and sorrow. His mental anguish, His spirit-grief, had now in reality begun. The "hour of darkness" had flung its first cold shadow upon His soul, and the cup, that must not pass undrank, now pressed His lips. Listen to His touching words, "MY SOUL IS EXCEEDING SORROWFUL." And to whom, in this hour of unknown agony, of crushing grief, of overwhelming sorrow, does He turn? He is man—and to man He looks. He is human—and to the human He repairs. He is the Friend of man—and upon the friendship and sympathy of man He now casts Himself. "*And He took with Him Peter and the two sons of Zebedee.*" Favoured men! honoured disciples! And what did He ask of them?—their words?—their protestations of fealty and friendship? Oh, no!—but simply their quiet presence, their silent sympathy—"*tarry ye here and* WATCH WITH ME."

The discussion in the preceding pages renders it the less necessary that, in the present chapter, we enlarge at great length upon the *soul-sorrow* of Christ—the occasion of His present appeal to the sympathy of His disciples. It will suffice in brief terms to remark that it partook essentially of the sorrow which grew more intense and dark as He approached the goal of His passion. The cup was the same, but He had not reached its dregs. The physical element had not as yet been added—it was now all mental, all spiritual, all soul-sorrow. "*My* SOUL *is exceeding sorrowful, even unto death.*" The human soul undoubtedly was the seat of this agonising, exceeding grief. The Deity was unapproachable by suffering. Not a cloud shaded its glory, not a wavelet ruffled its repose. It was the human in Christ that now sorrowed, and in its sorrow turned piteously and beseechingly to the human for its sympathy. But in what light are we to view this "soul-sorrow even unto death" of our Lord? His soul was holy—He had never sinned—no atonement was needed for Himself. The answer is at hand—"It pleased the LORD to bruise him; he hath put him to grief: when thou shalt make *his soul an offering for sin*, he shall see his seed, he shall prolong his days, and the pleasure of the Lord shall prosper in his hand. He shall see of the travail of his soul, and shall be satisfied." (Isa. liii. 10, 11.) His *soul* was now *suffering for sin.* This is the solution, this the explanation of what on other grounds could never be solved or explained. Christ was suffering as the sin-bearing, sin-atoning Substitute of His Church. For this the waters were rushing into His soul, and He was sinking in deep mire where there was no standing—into deep waters where the floods overflowed Him. He was now by imputation bearing the exceeding sinfulness and malignity of sin—the bitter, burning nature of Divine wrath on its account—the assaults of the power of darkness—added to which was the withdrawment of all divine, sensible, and spiritual light and comfort from His soul. Beloved, behold your salvation! Your sins were on that sinless One—your sorrow was sinking that holy soul—all this darkness and desertion was for you—He loved you, and He gave Himself for you. The simple, full belief of this will lift your soul above all sorrow, distress, and alarm for sin. The Divine Redeemer's soul bore all, absolved all, and exhausted all penal grief in the place and stead of His people. The punishment was His, because, by suretyship and transfer, the sin was His. He took our sins, and made Himself answerable to Divine justice on their account. Our sins being thus found upon Him by imputation, when Justice paused at the cross, she exacted from Him the full equivalent, inflicted upon Him the full penalty. Surely, a Divine and sinless Redeemer could only have met this demand! The sorrow, then, was His, the joy ours. Sin-distressed soul! look at the distress of Christ's soul, and be joyful. Never shall your soul be as His was, "sorrowful unto *death*." Yours is a sorrow unto "*life*." The burden of sin you now feel shall be as wings to your soul bearing it to Jesus; the grief for sin you now experience shall be the occasion of your deepest, holiest joy. There is everything in a soul-sorrowing Christ to impress with joy, gladness, and hope the soul-sorrowing sinner. The deep, fathomless grief of His holy soul utterly forbids the existence of despair on account of sin in the heart of a truly-awakened, sensible sinner. After *such* sorrow as the Saviour experienced, the chief of sinners, stricken with godly penitence, may hope. Remembering His soul-travail, the sorrow unto death, think you that when, by one touch of His hand, one word of His mouth, one glance of His eye He can heal, assure, and save you, that He will repel your approach, reject your plea, and refuse to pardon and accept you? Oh no! Before you arrive at such a conclusion, you must ignore His sacrifice, and regard the story of His dying agonies, His soul-grief, His blood-shedding on the cross as mere fiction, a fable, and a myth. "*It is a faithful saying, and worthy of all acceptation, that Christ Jesus came into the world to save sinners; of whom I am chief.*"

But we must keep in view the subject of our more immediate study—our Lord's appeal to the sympathy of His disciples in this the hour of His soul-sorrow. Nothing could afford a stronger proof than this that the human soul of our Lord was the seat of His grief. His humanity was suffering, and with all the instincts of humanity it turned for succour to the human. "*Tarry ye here and* WATCH WITH ME." Was it, we ask, incongruous that, suffering as man, for man, and, in a measure, from man, our Lord should throw Himself upon the affection, and sympathy, and compassion of man for a portion of the soothing which should soften and mitigate His grief? By no means. It was true to nature, to our nature, the very nature which still yearns in us for sympathy from its own. Let us take each particular of this marvellous incident in our Lord's closing life. From whom did He ask this sympathy? Was it from the world? Oh no! He had never received aught from the world but a thorn-crown and a cross! It flung no flowers on His path, beamed upon Him no smile, rent not the air with His acclaim; but, hating and despising Him because He testified of it that its works were evil, it maligned and traduced His character, then insulted, tortured, and put Him to death. Oh believer, love not, imitate not, identify not yourself with a world which thus traduced and slew the Lord who bought you. But it was to His Church Christ turned for its holy watchings with Him in the hour of His soul-sorrow. It was to our renewed, sanctified, and redeemed nature—to His beloved disciples. None but the holy were admitted to share the loneliness, the solitude, the sorrow of that hour. He took with Him His chosen followers, His beloved apostles, a representative portion of His Church. In what a touching point of light does this present His love for, and clinging to, His people! That He should have admitted them to a confidence so sacred, to a sorrow so deep, to a scene so solemn, to a transaction so momentous—permitting them, in a sense, to share it, to sustain it, to sympathise with it,—oh the marvellous love of Christ for His people! And still He permits us to have "fellowship with Him in His *sufferings*," and to feel the "power of His *resurrection*." If this be so, see that you cultivate a tender, holy sympathy with Christ in His soul-sorrow for your sins. And manifest that sympathy by vowing eternal hate to all sin, and in seeking its crucifixion by that very cross on which your Lord and Saviour was crucified.

And what was the nature of the sympathy which our Lord now asked? "*Tarry ye here, and* WATCH WITH ME." "Watch with me!" He was alone! The clouds were darkening, the sorrow was swelling, the foe was advancing, the cup was brimming: in that hour he felt the need of human sympathy,—He flung Himself upon it,—He asked it. "WATCH WITH ME." How touching His exquisite conception of the true, the soothing, and the delicate in real sympathy! He asks no cheering words, no visible sign, no interposing action,—but simply and only their *silent presence.* This would relieve the dreariness of the scene, lighten the pressure of His load, and diffuse over His troubled spirit a measure of serenity and repose. To *feel* that they were near to Him,—to know that, with unslumbering eyes, they were keeping solemn vigils,—that their affections, their thoughts, and their sympathies, like holy sentinels, were hovering around Him on the spot where He lay prostrate in wrestling prayer,—oh, this, *this* would be solacing and soothing, and His weary, yearning spirit asked it! Who can describe the power and the tranquillising influence of a *mute* sympathy—the calm, quiet presence of a loving, gentle heart in the hour of grief and woe? And have *we* no need of fellow-watchers in our sorrow—the loving heart, the speaking eye, the unwearied patience, the silent sympathy? Surely, it is not weak to feel its want, nor sinful to ask its expression!

But how painful and sad was our Lord's disappointment! "*And he cometh unto the disciples, and findeth them asleep, and saith unto Peter, What, could ye not watch with me one hour?*" They were human, and *but* human; and our Lord was now learning the uncertainty and frailty of human reliance in the dark and bitter hour of the soul's grief. It was a reproof—but, oh, how gentle! It was a rebuke—but, oh, how considerate! "*The spirit indeed is willing, but the flesh is weak.*" The Lord Jesus is not only cognisant of our shortcomings, our frailties, failures in duty, in service, and in love, but He remembers that we are dust; He considers how limited are our powers, and how often our energies are overtasked and exhausted. The spirit with Him is everything, the flesh as nothing. And if He descries in us a loving heart, a willing mind, an honest intention of purpose, a ready spirit, He makes all allowance for the limit, the weariness, and the infirmities of the flesh, and graciously and condescendingly accepts, in our endeavours and strivings to serve Him, to watch with Him, and to glorify Him, the sincere desire of the will.

From this picture of our Lord's dependence upon human sympathy, we may gather much that is instructive and consolatory.

It is delightful to meet, among those already considered in this volume, yet another instance of the perfect identity of Christ's nature with ours. There is no wide chasm which separates Him from us. It is true, as we have again and again asserted, He was sinless; but as true, as we have again and again affirmed, that He was not the less human. His human nature, apart from our moral taint, was cast into the same mould as our own. It had all our social instincts, our sympathies, our sensitiveness, our cravings and yearnings for fellowship with its species. Let us, then, cultivate a closer intimacy with Christ in all our infirmities and sorrows, nor deem any weakness, or pressure, or craving of our nature too mean and insignificant to bear to Him.

We have already remarked that it cannot involve either a charge of weakness or sin, our felt reliance upon the sympathy, compassion, and help of our fellow-Christians. What God has provided, cannot be wrong in the indulgence. It is He who gives us friends, forms our friendships, governs our affections, and unveils to us those deep founts of feeling and sympathy which well up from the human heart, and gush forth in a thousand warm streams of succour, comfort, and soothing. The genius of Christianity, the nature of the gospel, the teachings and exhortations of Jesus, are all predicated upon the fact, that man is to help man, to strengthen man; that Christian is to succour Christian, to weep with Christian; that brother is to love brother, to share a brother's sorrow, supply a brother's want, and bear a brother's burden; that sister is to sympathise with sister, shield her weakness, veil her frailty, and comfort her grief. If such, then, be the wise, the kind, the benevolent provision of God for the wants of our nature, surely it is not, it cannot be wrong to avail ourselves of it.

And yet the Lord may, to discipline us to a higher, purer, and surer reliance, dry up this source of sympathy on which we had too firmly and too fondly relied. We may look for it, when we had a right to expect it, ask it, when we had every hope of receiving it, and yet meet with the bitter disappointment our Lord experienced when He found His watchers in sorrow slumbering at their post. Human sympathy is not a thing we can either create or command. It is not controlled by the laws of force. We can neither inspire nor invoke it. It must flow naturally and spontaneously, or not at all. There may, therefore, be occasions and circumstances in which all sympathy is withheld from us—sympathy with our position, sympathy with our enterprises, sympathy with our grief; we may ask but for the "one hour's" sympathy, and ask in vain! And what is the lesson the Lord would thus teach us? Ever to look to a higher source than the human—to look to Himself. There is a strong natural inclination in us to lean too reliantly upon the human arm, and too fondly upon the human heart. We repair first to man before we go to God. We counsel in our perplexities with a human wisdom, before we seek the wisdom which cometh from above. We repair with our burden of grief to man's sympathy, ere we take it to Christ's. Now the Lord would teach us that real strength, true consolation, pure, unmixed, sustaining sympathy is found only in Himself.

> "Man's wisdom is to seek
> His strength in God alone;
> And e'en an angel would be weak,
> Who trusted in his own."

It is possible, we repeat, that your Lord should see proper—for the holiest, wisest, and most loving end—to *withhold* from you the reciprocated affection, the responsive sympathy, the close, sacred intercourse for which your heart yearns. May it not be that another and a sweeter channel should be opened, another and a holier object should be supplied—even HIMSELF? Attempt not, then, to check those feelings, to suppress those yearnings, to veil those affections within the deep, lonely cloister of a morbid, self-consuming, wounded sensibility. Let them flow forth in unrestrained, unforbidden freedom, and rise to the source from whence they came. The heart's crushed affections, and earth's beclouded hopes, in the hallowed experience of the believer, but go to bloom in a kindlier soil and shine beneath a brighter sky in heaven.

The want of created strength, and of human sympathy, is only to be met by being brought into closer communion with the Invisible. The defect, the insufficiency, the failure of human friendship, human affection, human aid, and human sympathy only can be remedied and supplied by JESUS—the sufficiency, the fulness, the tenderness of whose grace, strength, and love can so fill the soul, so engage the heart that it shall not sigh for aught besides. Oh, with such a treasure so rich and so near,—with such a Friend and Father so mighty, yet so compassionate, whatever your sorrows or your loneliness may be,—forsaken and disappointed, wounded and deceived,—the void is more than filled, the want is more than supplied by the infinite sufficiency and eternal sympathy of your incarnate God. Blessed result of disappointment in the human, to find one's self absorbed in the Divine!

> "Who is alone, if God be nigh?
> Who shall repine at loss of friends,
> While he has One of boundless power,
> Whose constant kindness never ends;
> Whose presence felt enhances joy,
> Whose love can stop the flowing tear,
> And cause upon the darkest cloud
> The *pledge* of *mercy* to appear."

And yet we must not forget that He who has provided this sweet spring of comfort and succour—the affection and sympathy of a human heart—would not have us undervalue the precious gift. Our Lord Himself was not indifferent to it. He was not insensible to human sympathies. He loved man—He sought man's love, and He asked man's sympathy; and keen was the pang and bitter the disappointment when the friends and disciples He had chosen out of the world to be His companions and followers, forsook and failed Him in the hour of adversity. Affect not then, beloved, to be wholly independent of thy fellows, and regard not with cold indifference and ingratitude the tear that would flow with yours, or the hand kindly upraised to dry it. At the same time, be not too reliant upon this reserve of human sympathy and compassion. If the Lord supplies it, receive it with gratitude, use it with moderation, and employ it for His glory. If He withholds it, it is but to bring you into the experience of something infinitely better—the deeper experience of HIMSELF.

"Oh, ask not, hope thou not, too much
Of sympathy below;
Few are the hearts whence one sure touch
Bids the sweet fountains flow:
Few—and, by still conflicting powers,
Forbidden here to meet;
Such ties would make this life of ours
Too fair for aught so fleet.

"Yet scorn thou not, for this, the true
And steadfast love of years;
The kindly, that from childhood grew,
The faithful to thy tears!
If there be one that, o'er the dead,
Hath in thy grief borne part;
And watch'd through sickness by thy bed,
Call *his* a kindred heart."*

* Hemans.

But to what did Jesus resort when, sad and disappointed, He turned from this dried stream of human sympathy? He gave Himself again *to prayer*—He returned a third time to His Father. O blessed lesson He would thus teach us! We shall find *in prayer*, beloved, all, and infinitely more, that we sought, and failed to find, in the holy watchers around us. They, like the dear disciples in the garden, may grow weary,—we may, in the moment of our deepest woe, find them unconscious of the throes and anguish of our spirit. Whither shall we go? *In prayer to our Father!* Oh, the power, the solace, the charm of prayer! What magic influence it now had upon the Saviour's troubled spirit! After He returns from His third appeal to His Father, He no more asks their sympathy—He had found all He wanted in communion with God. The struggle was over,—the conflict was past,—His will and His Father's will were now perfectly one. He rose from the earth strengthened and solaced in His soul, a peace, like the calm of evening, stole over His spirit, and He went forth in dignity, energy, and repose to confront His betrayer and to meet His fate. "*Sleep on now, and take your rest.*" It is the way, my reader, God, by human disappointments, impels us to prayer, and by prayer allures us to Himself. You have the same Father that Jesus had to repair to in trouble. And when the creature-stream is dried, and human dependence fails, and the loving, tender sympathy upon which you had fondly relied becomes weary and exhausted by its watchings, the Fountain from whence that stream flowed—God's all-sufficiency—remains as full and changeless as ever. The hour of agony, ere this point is reached, may be long and dark. Not once, or twice, but thrice, you may repair with your soul-sorrow, your mental darkness, to the throne of grace before relief is felt; but the result, however agonising and protracted the wrestling, will be glorious—"THY WILL, not MINE BE DONE!"—and a halcyon peace, a sunlight joy, and a giant's strength will bear you on to meet the crisis,—to do, or to endure—to service, or to suffering,—that your holy, wise, and loving Father has ordained. Go, then, your way, clasping the robe of Christ's full sympathy closer and firmer around you, girded and strengthened with all might by His presence and grace promised and pledged to His disciples, always, and in all circumstances, to the world's end.

"When gathering clouds around I view,
And days are dark, and friends are few,
On Him I lean, who, not in vain,
Experienced every human pain.
He sees my wants, allays my fears,
And counts and treasures up my tears.

"If aught should tempt my soul to stray
From heavenly wisdom's narrow way,
To fly the good I would pursue,
Or do the thing I would not do;
Still, He who felt temptation's power
Shall guard me in that dangerous hour.

"If wounded love my bosom swell,
Deceived by those I prized too well,
He shall His pitying aid bestow,
Who felt on earth severer woe:
At once betray'd, denied, or fled,
By those who shared His daily bread.

"When vexing thoughts within me rise,
And, sore dismay'd, my spirit dies;
Yet He who once vouchsafed to bear
The sickening anguish of despair,
Shall sweetly soothe, shall gently dry,
The throbbing heart, the streaming eye.

"When sorrowing o'er some stone I bend,
Which covers all that was a friend;
And from his hand, his voice, his smile,
Divides me for a little while:
Thou, Saviour! seest the tears I shed,
For thou didst weep o'er Lazarus dead.

"And oh, when I have safely past
Through every conflict but the last,
Still, still unchanging, watch beside
My dying bed—for Thou hast died;
Then point to realms of cloudless day,
And wipe the latest tear away!"

CHAPTER XII.

CHRIST'S SYMPATHY WITH TEMPTATION.

"Then was Jesus led up of the Spirit into the wilderness to be tempted of the devil."—MATT. iv. 1.

THIS must be regarded as one of the most marvellous pages in the Saviour's history, and, to a large portion of the Church of God, not less precious and soothing. That the Son of God should be exposed to so personal, so searching, so trying, and so protracted an onslaught of the devil as this,—that He who was sinless and could not sin, who was almighty and could not fall, who with one word could have commanded back the foe to the regions from whence he came, or with a breath could have annihilated his being, should yet for forty days and forty nights have subjected Himself to this fiery, burning furnace—which, had He not been GOD would have utterly consumed Him—is the marvel of earth, and will be the wonder, the study, and the song of heaven through eternity. But it was a part of the suffering of our Lord by which He was to learn, even though He were a Son. That wilderness was to Christ both a school and a battle-field. He had not been perfected but for this suffering, He had not learned obedience but for this trial, He had not been complete, as the Head of His Church, but for this furnace. Had our Lord been exempt from temptation, had He known nothing of Satanic agency and power, what an essential defect would there have been in His mediatorial relation to the Church! How could He have met the case of a tempted member of His body, a worried sheep of His flock, a Satan-terrified lamb of His fold? Impossible! Whither, then, could these have turned for succour, aid, and deliverance in temptation? From whom, when the fiery darts fell thick and fast around and upon them, could they have obtained the skill to quench, the grace to support, the sympathy to soothe them in the conflict, and bring them through more than conquerors? Alas! not another being in the universe could have met the case! And it was necessary for the Church, His body, that Christ, its Head, should be in all points tempted like as we are, and yet be without sin. Reserving, for the present, the peculiar circumstances attending Christ's temptation, let us view the temptation itself, and then apply it as illustrating His sympathy with His tempted people.

In the first place, let us remark that Christ was *tempted of the devil.* He was confronted with the head, the apostle, the chief of the hierarchy of hell. It was proper that it should be so. To have met and defeated a foe of inferior rank, a subordinate agent of the Evil One, one of less authority or of less power, would have broken the Scriptures and compromised the Church. But "the Scripture cannot be broken," and the interests of the Church can never be imperilled. The sentence pronounced upon the serpent in Paradise involved a prediction which must be fulfilled,—"*I will put enmity between thee and the woman, ana between thy seed and her seed; it shall bruise thy head, and thou shalt bruise his heel.*" It was necessary, then, that, if our Lord be tempted, that temptation should come from the prince of the devils—the tall archangel of hell himself. Our temptations from Satan often flow from indirect sources, from sin within or incentives to sin without; our Lord's were direct from Satan. He had come to destroy the works of the Devil, but He must first confront, bind, and virtually destroy the Devil himself. It was by this malignant foe God had been accused to man, and it is by this same malignant foe man is accused to God; and it was proper that, by the God-man, he should be met and overthrown—himself accused and condemned. But how replete with instruction, and how full of consolation to the Church is this truth! Not the myrmidons, not the subordinate ministers and agents of the Devil have been defeated by Christ, but the Devil himself. The head has been bruised, the prince has been despoiled, the chief defeated by Christ's heel. Thus, from personal experience, our Lord learned who and what Satan is,—his subtlety, his malignity, and his power,—and is prepared to succour and sympathise, as no other being can, with those that are tempted. It was proper, then, that the Captain of our salvation should meet in conflict hell's chief; that the Head of the Church should meet face to face the head of hell, and so "*be led into the wilderness to be tempted of the devil.*"

And what were His temptations? They would seem to have been from every quarter and of every kind. The quiver of the artful foe lacked no darts. The moment one was winged and quenched, another, yet more potent, was upon the string. The devil is never at a loss for means and appliances. His resources are vast, his ingenuity versatile, his operations as rapid and as telling as the electric current. The wiles and devices of the devil are worthy a being of so vast yet so depraved an intellect. What, then, was his *first* assault upon our Lord?

It was the temptation *to distrust the providence of God.* After His long, exhausting fast our Lord *hungered.* He needed bread. He was man, and He felt as man. Oh, touching evidence of His real humanity! precious proof of His perfect oneness with us! Of this sinless infirmity of His nature Satan took advantage. Thus we read, "*And when the tempter came to Him, he said, If thou be the Son of God, command that these stones be made bread.*" The temptation was timely, plausible, and strong. It had been as easy for Christ to have established the fact—not *denied* by His adversary—of His Divine Sonship by turning the stones into bread, as subsequently

He did by turning the water into wine. But He would not! He had come to bring to our spiritually famished race Himself the Bread of life; to teach His disciples the lesson of a believing reliance upon the care and provision of their heavenly Father—His Father and their Father. To have yielded to this temptation, to have complied with this suggestion of the wily foe, would have been a practical compromise of the one, and a direct denial of the other. No! Christ would not break His fast upon such terms. He would endure the gnawings of hunger still rather than place the meat that perisheth above the meat that endureth unto eternal life, or throw the shadow of a shade of distrust upon a Father's care. How Godlike and sublime His reply, "*It is written, Man shall not live by bread alone, but by every word that proceedeth out of the mouth of God.*" And is there not a page in our experience corresponding to this? How often by the same Adversary we are assailed with the same temptation! It is one of the ingenious plans of our subtle foe to seize upon the present circumstances of believers, turning them to his own advantage, and to their discomfort, by constructing them into a weapon of point and power with which to assail them. Are we in affliction and sorrow?—he tempts us to question God's goodness and love. Are we prostrate on a sick and suffering couch?—he tempts us to doubt the wisdom and kindness of our Father. Is the mind in spiritual darkness, the soul painfully exercised, a cloud-veil thrown over the evidences of our union with Christ and our adoption into God's family?—he tempts us to ignore our past Christian experience as a delusion, and to yield ourselves to a present and dark despair. Are the providences of our God trying, painful, and mysterious?—he tempts us to carnal reasoning, and hard thoughts of the character and government of God, sometimes bringing us to the very verge of atheism and infidelity—impeaching His character, if not doubting His very being. Are our temporal resources straitened, our wants pressing, our position trying and critical?—he tempts us to unbelief, distrust, and despondency; to employ unwise, if not unlawful, means of extrication, and to purchase immediate and temporary relief by a compromise of integrity, reputation, and happiness. My reader, Satan knows your circumstances, is acquainted with the network of your trying and difficult position, and is prepared to forge from it a weapon of assault upon your principles, your well-being, and your peace. The Devil is marvellously strategic: his suggestions will have all the appearance of reason, fitness, and propriety; they will seem plausible, facile, and honest; nevertheless, they are *satanic*, are from beneath, and must not receive from you the consideration of a moment. "*Trust in the* LORD, *and do good; so shalt thou dwell in the land, and verily thou shalt be fed. Delight thyself also in the* LORD; *and He shall give thee the desires of thine heart. Commit thy way unto the Lord; trust also in Him; and He shall bring it to pass.*" The Lord can give you bread —and *no* good thing will He withhold from you —without the intervention of a miracle. The sustenance is all provided; no need, then, that He command the stones that they be made bread!

The second temptation of our Lord was—SELF-DESTRUCTION. This was its form,—"*Then the devil taketh Him up into the holy city, and setteth Him on a pinnacle of the temple, and saith unto Him, If thou be the Son of God,* CAST THYSELF DOWN: *for it is written, He shall give His angels charge concerning thee; and in their hands they shall bear thee up, lest at any time thou dash thy foot against a stone."* And still there is no *denial* of His Divine Sonship on the part of the devil. Alas that there should be on the part of man! He places the fact in a hypothetical point of light only,—"IF *thou be the Son of God,"*—for on a subsequent occasion the unclean demon could exclaim, *"I know thee who Thou art, the Holy One of God."* And yet, there was this fearful temptation of this Holy One. And what was its nature? *Suicide!* "CAST THYSELF DOWN — *destroy Thyself!* Presume upon the providence and power of God to preserve Thee. Commit the act, and leave Him to shield Thee from its consequences." Such, in substance, was the reasoning of this arch-fiend of darkness. With what holy horror must the Son of God have recoiled from the temptation to this rash, sinful, appalling crime! And yet with what dignity and power He repels and silences it! *"Jesus said unto him, It is written again, Thou shalt not tempt the Lord thy God."* There are few temptations by which our race is assailed more common, and none more dire, than this. And, as Satan loves a prominent and shining mark, the victim of his malignity is often placed upon a pinnacle of the temple, that the crime may be the darker, and his triumph the more conspicuous and complete. Therefore it is that God's saints, Christ's disciples, are not the exception, but generally the rule, of this appalling onslaught of the foe. How many of the saints of the Most High are, like their Lord and Master, thus assailed by the devil! My dear reader, it may be that this fiery dart has been hurled at *you.* Taking advantage of your position, your circumstances, your domestic anxieties, your pressing liabilities, the detractions of enemies, a nervous temperament, mental dejection, a frame tortured by suffering or enfeebled by disease, *this* may be the form of the temptation by which Satan approaches you. As "*there hath no temptation taken you but such as is common to man,*" and as both Christ and many of His disciples have been alike assailed as you may now be, it may not be considered out of place or unacceptable if we endeavour to meet and mitigate your present trial with such words and counsels as the Holy Spirit may suggest and apply.

The temptation that assails you is—*self-destruction.* "*Cast thyself down.*" With whom but with a spirit so inventive of crime, so depraved and malignant, could so unnatural a suggestion, so fearful a sin, originate? Every point of light in which we view it, every reason with which we assail it, every plea by which we dissuade from it,—its touching relation to the present, and its more solemn relation to the future,—conspire to render the act abhorrent and repelling. Reserving, for the present, its more religious aspects, regard the sin of suicide in the light of *nature.* There is not a stronger or more innate principle of the human mind than SELF-PRESERVATION. The love of life and the fear of death are feelings naturally and incontestably implanted in all beings. The irrational creation possess an instinctive principle of the kind engrafted in their nature by God. But it has been left for man to war against a principle of his nature which all other beings preserve inviolate; and, though endowed with reason, intelligence, conscience, and responsibility, yet, estranged from God, and the subject of a deranged organism, he is often swept on by the force of an irresistible current which lands him at the tribunal of eternity, the destroyer of a principle the most precious and solemn in the universe! It is a remarkable fact that in the abnormal state of society the idea of self-destruction is scarcely known; that it is only in nations of extreme civilisation and high intelligence that this crime the most greatly prevails. A distinguished French physician remarks that, when a captive in Russia, he once spoke to an intelligent peasant concerning this unnatural deed, and found him totally and blissfully ignorant of its existence.* In the rise of the Roman republic it was scarcely known, nor did it become frequent until after the battle of Pharsalia. Thus it would seem that, as society advanced in civilisation and refinement, not only modes of self-destruction became more refined, but the act itself more familiar. We need scarcely cite the cases of Regulus, Codrus, and Socrates as illustrating what have been termed virtuous and patriotic examples, but which, in no point of light, justify a crime as opposed to the instincts of man as it is condemned by the law of God. As we are not attempting a treatise on this melancholy subject, we forbear pressing our inquiry into the various motives or causes which may predispose the mind in the commission of so rash an act. Indeed, it would seem impossible to give anything like a proper analysis or classi-

* M. Chevrey.

fication of them. A few examples will shew this:—Adrian, Licinius, and Cœcinus destroyed themselves from excess of pain; Imilicar, Nasso, and Hannibal from excess of fear; Pontius Pilate from chagrin at the spread of Christianity; Maximian from despair at having oppressed its disciples; Judas from guilt and remorse at having betrayed its Author.* Others have been tempted thus to anticipate their future from the pressure of want, from the dread of exposure, from wounded pride, from crushed affections, from disappointed hopes, from hypochondriacism assuming a religious form, from sheer selfishness, and from a morbid disgust and weariness of life. These are some of the predisposing causes to which this prodigality of life may be traced. But it is with the temptation itself we have now to do.

* This feeling of remorse is thus finely described by our great national poet:—

"Some strange commotion
Is in his brain; he bites his lips, and starts;
Stops on a sudden, looks upon the ground,
Then lays his finger on his temples; straight
Springs out into a fast gait; then stops again,
Strikes his hard breast, and anon he casts
His eye against the moon."

We premise, however, that in most cases of this kind the melancholy subject of the temptation must be regarded in the light of an *irresponsible agent,* whose diseased and disordered mind has utterly destroyed the self-controlling power of the soul, and consequently annihilating the only basis upon which human responsibility rests—viz., a sound and healthful reason. The majority of suicidal cases must be thus resolved — the alienation of an unbalanced intellect obscuring the light of reason, and destroying the responsibility of the agent. Let nothing, therefore, which may be traced upon this page deepen the shade of sadness which still lingers upon the memory of the past; but let the profoundly mysterious act resolve itself in the righteous permission of the Divine will, quenching in its melancholy subject every vestige of human accountability. "*Shall not the Judge of all the earth do right?*" "*Even so, Father, for so it seemeth good in thy sight,*" must be the expression of our submission to so dark a mystery of providence. With regard to the temptation, if for a moment it be suggested to your mind, there is every argument drawn from the light of nature with which resistance may be strengthened, and the crime repelled. Let us briefly group them together. Your life is not your own. "*Behold, all souls are mine, saith the Lord.*" The possession of a power over your own life establishes no claim to ownership, any more than the same power over the lives of others invests you with a right to destroy them. God, therefore, "*in whom we live and move and have our being,*" as your sole Proprietor, alone has authority to dispose of you—demanding or retaining your life, as it pleases Him. "*There is no man that hath power over the spirit to retain the spirit; neither hath he power in the day of death.*" (Eccl. viii. 8.) "*None can keep alive his own soul.*" (Ps. xxii. 29.) What an impeachment, too, is this act of the wisdom, goodness, and righteousness of God! Deliberately and dispassionately to fling into His face a soul He had created in His own image; endowed with an intelligence second only to His own; and for whose culture, happiness, and preservation He had provided, in His infinite goodness, so amply, is to insult His majesty, to deny His faithfulness, and virtually to own a disbelief in His very being. It is an act, too, of extreme selfishness—selfishness utterly indifferent to the claims and feelings of those dependent upon our existence for their own, whose interests we compromise, and upon all the future of whose earthly happiness we cast the dark shadow of grief. What sad fruit, too, of pride, shame, and cowardice is this act, calmly, premeditatively done! Shrinking from meeting the eye of man, yet not afraid of rushing into the presence of God; seeking to escape from present embarrassments, afraid to face existing responsibilities, yet not shrinking from the responsibility of a sane suicide, braving the terror of God's tribunal before which the soul thrusts itself uncalled,—oh, it is a fearful temptation of the arch-foe of man, from listening to which for a moment every natural, reasonable, and moral argument and consideration powerfully and solemnly dissuades. Listen to the voice of God, echoed by reason and conscience—"**Do thyself no harm.**"

> "Against self-slaughter
> There is a prohibition so divine,
> That cravens my weak hand."

The language of a good man is, "*All the days of my appointed time will I wait until my change come.*" Let revelation and reason unite in winning back your thoughts to solemn reflection and self-restraint, that thus you may be doubly armed against this fearful temptation of Satan.

"Our time is fix'd, and all our days are number'd;
How long, how short, we know not; this we know—
Duty requires we calmly wait the summons,
Nor dare to stir till Heaven shall give permission.
Like sentinels that must keep their destined stand,
And wait th' appointed hour till they're relieved.
Those only are the brave who keep their ground,
And keep it to the last. To run away
Is but a coward's trick; to run away
From this world's ills, that at the very worst
Will soon blow o'er, thinking to mend ourselves
By boldly venturing on a world unknown,
And plunging headlong in the dark! 'tis mad;
No frenzy half so desperate as this." *

We have remarked that this is a temptation of Satan from which God's people are not totally exempt. A consideration of this will place before us the *religious* aspect of the subject. The Head of the Church thus tempted, the Church and the individual members of the Church must not expect to be absolved. "*Cast thyself down,*" was the temptation presented to Christ by Satan. "Destroy thyself," is the like dark thought often suggested by the Evil One to the

* Blair.

minds of Christ's disciples. Seizing upon your peculiar and pressing circumstances, or the physical and mental condition through which you are for the time passing,—your tried spirit, or embarrassed position, or bodily suffering, or spiritual gloom and despondency of mind,—Satan avails himself of it to present to your mind gloomy thoughts and distrustful feelings of God and His dealings, and to insinuate an easy and effectual mode of escaping from present difficulties and mental distress—the dark, the awful, the appalling one of anticipating the future by your own hand! The idea, the suggestion, the mode of its execution come from him the adversary, the accuser, the foe of God's saints. But not for the universe must an instigation so awful in its nature, so dishonouring to your Christian profession, so wounding to Christ, so denying of God, and investing life's close with a pall of woe so dark, find a moment's reflective response in your heart or mind. All the powers of your soul, every effort of self-resistance, every tender, holy consideration it is possible for you to command, must be summoned to the battle and aid you in the victory. Far beyond this, must you betake yourself to Christ the tempted One, tempted as you are now and by the same tempter, who is prepared to strengthen, aid, and fortify you against, and deliver you out of, this terrible onslaught of His foe and yours. No imagination can portray the tenderness, the compassion, the sympathy of Christ with you in this dark hour of your terrible temptation. All the boundless resources of His grace, power, love, and sympathy are enlisted on your side, and are at your command. How appropriate and precious are the Divine declarations of this truth written for *you*:—"*We have not an High Priest which cannot be touched with the feeling of our infirmities, but was in all points* TEMPTED LIKE AS WE ARE, *yet without sin. Let us therefore come boldly unto the throne of grace, that we may obtain mercy, and find grace to help in time of need.*" "*For in that He himself hath suffered,* BEING TEMPTED, *He is able to succour them that are* TEMPTED." Oh, yield yourself in this extremity to PRAYER. There is no weapon of resistance like this. With it, you can "*resist the devil, and he will flee from you.*" Meet the arch-foe with the name of JESUS, and he will quail before you. Uplift in faith the cross of Christ, and you will put to flight all the hosts of hell.

Christ has wounded, despoiled, and vanquished Satan on the cross and in the grave; and a yet more signal and a final triumph over him awaits the Son of God—and you have but to shelter your tried, tempted, trembling soul beneath His over-shadowing wing until this dark hour of temptation is past. Oh, what a soothing reflection is this—"The Son of God, my Saviour, was tempted to self-destruction, even as I am! Then, will He desert me in this hour of my weakness? will He leave me to combat the tempter alone? Will He not prevent me by His grace, aid me with His strength, comfort me with His love, soothe me with His sympathy, and deliver me by His great power? Most assuredly He will! He has trodden this very path Himself. He has been assailed by this very foe, and with this very temptation; and will He not succour me as no other being does, as no other being can? O sweet assault that opens to me the gentle heart of Jesus, into which I run, and am shielded by its power, soothed by its sympathy, and am lost in its love. Then, I will look to Jesus, cling to Jesus, trust in Jesus, who knoweth how to deliver the godly out of temptation, and who will deliver—*me!*"

Closely akin to this form of temptation of

Satan, is a modern manifestation popularly termed "Spiritualism," or the alleged power to unravel the mysteries of the spirit-world. To so great an extent has this delusion spread, and so disastrous has been its influence upon the mental and moral well-being of numbers of its victims, that, in touching upon the subject of satanic agency, we should be scarcely justified in passing it over in total silence. We do not assert that the senseless mummeries of spirit-rapping, table-turning, clairvoyance, and kindred delusions—professed *media* of communication with the invisible world—are the direct results of satanic power;—the manifestations are far too clumsy and transparent to conduct us to such a conclusion;—still, we avow our unhesitating belief that they are the conceptions of human depravity and the inventions of human fraud, working upon the imagination of the weak and the credulous, suggested, prompted, and abetted by the Evil One, who employs the sin that is in man to increase the amount of sin and misery that is in the world. Indirectly, then, we trace these ungodly arts, these awful delusions, to the "prince of the power of the air, who now worketh in the children of disobedience." From all such proceedings, then, it becomes the solemn duty of every believer in Jesus to turn with detestation and horror, as from the Evil One himself, and to have no fellowship with these works of darkness, but rather to reprove them. They are diabolical and satanic so far as they are a part of the machinery by which the Devil carries forward his government in this ungodly world, where for a season his seat is. That even some of the elect of God have been deceived by these delusions, it is mournful and humiliating to confess; and not a few cases have transpired in which domestic happiness has been blasted, spiritual peace has been destroyed, Christian hope has been beclouded, and the mind has succumbed either to moody despair, or to hopeless insanity, in some instances terminating in self-murder. Oh, be this our constant prayer, "*Keep back Thy servant also from* PRESUMPTUOUS SINS: *let them not have dominion over me.*" And to the Divine exhortation we do well that we take heed,—"*Put on therefore the whole armour of God, that ye may be able to stand against the* WILES *of the devil. For we wrestle not against flesh and blood, but against principalities and against powers, against the rulers of the darkness of this world, against spiritual wickedness in high places. Therefore take unto you the whole armour of God, that ye may be able to withstand in the evil day, and having done all, to stand.*"

The *third* temptation of our Lord was—IDOLATRY, with the promise of temporal territory, glory, and power. This was the form in which the Devil put it:—"*Again, the devil taketh him up into an exceeding high mountain, and sheweth him all the kingdoms of this world, and the glory of them; and saith unto him, All these things will I give thee, if thou wilt fall down and worship me.*" We pause not to notice the monstrous arrogance and mendacious insolence, together with the glaring falsehood, exhibited in the form of this assault. It is enough to notice the aspiring ambition of this proud Lucifer who now demanded the homage and worship of the Son of God, and thus aspired to be God: "*If thou wilt fall down and worship me!*" This would seem to have been the climax of horror, the sin of sins, to the holy Son of God. No sin has Jehovah so emphatically forbidden, or has marked with such signal and overwhelming indications of His hatred, displeasure, and wrath, as the sin of *idolatry.* And yet this was the climax to the series of temptations by which our Lord was assailed of the devil! Dwell upon the thought for a moment—devil-worship, offered, justified, and encouraged by the example of the Son of God! Can the imagination depict a temptation so fearful, or a crime so appalling? Again we remark, with what horror must the Saviour have met, with what indignation must He have repelled, and how instantaneously must He have quenched this fiery dart of the foe! Listen to His words: "*Thus saith Jesus unto him, Get thee hence, Satan: for it is written, Thou shalt worship the* LORD *thy God, and Him only shalt thou serve.*"

And are the saints of God entirely exempt from temptation akin to this? We believe not. Assailing us through our senses,—the eye fond of beauty, the heart ambitious of power, the mind dazzled with glory, the soul lusting for possession,—easy and accessible avenues are open to this arch-foe of Christ and of the Church. To what idolising of ourselves, and of the creature, and of worldly possessions, are the best of saints exposed! We may—so deceitful and wicked are our hearts—be beguiled, ere we are conscious of our sin, into a worshipping of our intellectual powers, of our acquired endowments, of our popularity, of our usefulness, of our very graces! Wherein else could have been the appropriateness and the force of the apostolic exhortation, —"*Wherefore, my dearly beloved, flee from* IDOLATRY." And again, "*Little children, keep yourselves from* IDOLS." And what is the homage paid by the ungodly to objects that are sinful, yea, to sin itself, but a worship unconsciously, but really, offered to Satan? It is against this the saints of God have need to be armed and fortified—to be vigilant and prayerful. He assails us through the affections—through the eye—the ear—the intellect, yea, through every bodily sense and mental faculty. The creature may become an idol of the heart, and learning an idol of the intellect; we may be so enamoured of the beauty of the arts, of the melody of music, of the fascination of science, as to be swept on by the resistless force of the passions to a point where we may worship and serve the creature more than the Creator, who is blessed for ever! Such is the natural tendency to idolatry of the human heart, such the power and influence of Satan, we have need to be acquainted, in some measure, with the deceitfulness and wickedness of the one, and not to be ignorant of the wiles and the devices of the other.

From this subject of our Lord's temptations, we may glean some lessons of holy instruction, and derive some streams of real comfort.

We learn that our great adversary and accuser is—*a defeated foe.* From this onslaught upon Christ he retired foiled, vanquished, and abashed. The Seed of the woman had bruised the serpent's head. It is true, "*Satan left Him for a season,*" to renew the battle on another and a more conspicuous field, and at a future and a more eventful time; but only to be more signally discomfited, more fatally wounded, and more completely overthrown. Tempted believer in Jesus! learn thus the paralysed power of your tempter, that you be not disheartened and dismayed. Remember that the Son of God has foiled him, that the Captain of your salvation has pierced him, signally and fatally; and that every fiery dart winged at your soul is plucked from a quiver all whose weapons, pointed at the believer, are tipped with the conquering blood of Christ, and are hurled by the stricken arm of an archer humbled and cowed by the consciousness of a signal and irrecoverable defeat!

Learn to meet Satan's suggestions, to answer his arguments, and to repel his temptations by the "*sword of the Spirit, which is the Word of God.*" He too can quote and apply Scripture, only to misquote and misapply it. You may, therefore, safely infer that if he seeks to give Scripture point and force to a vile insinuation,—quotes a promise or cites an example from the Word of God in support of some infernal suggestion, some dark design, some horrid temptation,—he has by fraud and subtlety stolen from the arsenal of truth weapons with which, by perversion and wicked ingenuity, to accomplish his dark, nefarious design. Lend not your ear for a moment to a temptation that comes clad in Scripture authority. Suspect the cloven foot of Satan. The Word of God is very pure. It is on the side of holiness, of uprightness, of goodness, of love. It inculcates the fear of God, confidence in God, and love to God. It teaches the protection, the sufficiency, and the sympathy of Jesus. It unfolds many exceeding great and precious promises; announces many gracious and free invitations; and it is designed to succour the tempted, to comfort the mourner, to soothe the sorrowful, to hold out the promise of pardon to the guilty, salvation to the lost, and to reveal the hope of glory to all them who humbly and simply believe in Christ. The moment, then, beloved, that a text of God's Word is suggested to your thoughts in favour of sin, of distrust of God, of disbelief of Christ, of self-injury, repel it with the holy indignation of a believer in Christ from the threshold of your mind, as from the Evil One, prompting you to evil, and seeking to slay you with the very arms God graciously provided for your defence! O yes! God's Word will fortify, strengthen, and succour you in temptation. It is the Book of the tempted. Like its Author, it is divine, invincible, and holy. It is the history of saints tempted like you, but from whose temptation God rescued them. "*The Lord knoweth how to deliver the godly out of temptation.*" The most gracious souls, the most eminent saints, have been *tempted* saints. Abraham was tempted, David was tempted, Job was tempted, Peter was tempted, Paul was tempted, Luther was tempted—and, above all, and greater than all, CHRIST was tempted; and all from the self-same foe—"Satan, the accuser of the brethren." All passed through this heated crucible, all were taught in this painful school, all bore to heaven the scars of the wounds in this battle with the devil—but out of all God delivered them. Think not, then, that some strange thing has happened unto you—that you tread a peculiar, solitary path, a path untrodden by the saints of God. O no! You are one of the "great cloud of witnesses" of whom it is recorded, "*they were tempted,*" and with them you shall testify to the power of faith in giving you the victory over all the assaults of the world, the flesh, and the devil. Fly, tempted one! to the precious Scriptures. They are your grand arsenal, richly stored with every species of weapon with which to foil and vanquish your powerful, sleepless, subtle foe. "*Thy word have I hid in my heart, that I should not sin against thee.*" Above all, fly to the Christ of the Scriptures, and nestle your tempted spirit beneath His sheltering wing.

And forget not what a girding of the soul in the temptations of Satan is—*prayer.* Take your temptation, drag the tempter to the throne of grace, and you are safe. The shadow of that spot is too divine, too pure and holy, for a temptation to live a single moment. There the Wicked One will cease to trouble you, there your weary soul will sweetly rest. Communion with God, the opening of your heart to Christ, flying into the very bosom of the Comforter, will put to flight all the hosts of hell. Oh, betake yourself, tempted child of God, *to prayer!* God invites you, the blood of Jesus gives you access, and the mercy-seat will cover you with its Divine and sacred shadow, beneath which God will keep you in perfect peace. "*Oh, how great is thy goodness, which thou hast laid up for them that fear thee; which thou hast wrought for them that trust in thee before the sons of men! Thou shalt hide them in the secret of thy presence from the pride of man: thou shalt keep them secretly in a pavilion from the strife of tongues.*" Resort, then, to prayer! "If he haunts thee with fears of thy spiritual estate, fly thee to the throne of grace, and beg a new copy of thy old evidence, which thou hast lost. The original is in the pardon-office in heaven, whereof Christ is Master; if thou art a saint, thy name is upon record in that count; make thy moan to God, hear what news from heaven, rather than listen to the tales which are brought by thine enemy from hell. Did such reason less with Satan, and pray over their fears more to God, they might sooner be resolved. Can you expect truth from a liar, and comfort from an enemy? Did he ever prophesy well of delievers? Was not Job the devil's hypocrite, whom God vouched for a nonsuch in holiness, and proved him so at last? If he knew that thou wert a saint, would he tell thee so? If a hypocrite, he would be as loth thou shouldest know it; turn thy back therefore on him, and go to thy God: fear not but sooner or later He will give His hand again to thy certificate. But look thou dost not pass rashly a censure on thyself, because a satisfactory answer is not presently sent at thy desire; the messenger may stay long, and bring good news at last."*

Designed as this volume is to set forth the sympathy of Christ with man, no illustration of this precious truth is more touching than *Christ's sympathy with the tempted.* The inspired allusions to it are few, but, oh, how pointed and precious! "*In that He* HIMSELF *hath suffered, being* TEMPTED, *He is able to* SUCCOUR *them that are* TEMPTED." "*We have not an High Priest which cannot be touched with the feeling of our infirmities, but was in all points* TEMPTED *like as we are, yet without sin.*" How schooled and trained to this work of sympathy with Satan-

* Gurnall.

tempted souls, then, is our great High Priest! What! is He not "touched?" will He not "succour?" And when Satan stands at your right hand to accuse, think you that He, your Advocate with the Father, will not put in a plea on your behalf that shall quash the indictment, silence the accusation, and condemn the accuser? Oh, enfold yourself, tempted believer, within the robe of your Saviour's sympathy! Hide you within its rich, its ample folds, until the temptation be past. Christ will not fail you. He may permit, for wise and holy ends, the messenger of Satan to buffet you, but He will restrain the enemy, permitting him to go so far and no farther, and will make good His promise, "*My grace is sufficient for thee, for my strength is made perfect in weakness.*" This very temptation of your soul may make you better acquainted with Christ than ever. For this end, doubtless, He permits it. You have learnt what Christ is in times of guilt, in times of sorrow, in times of want, in times of perplexity; now you are to learn what He is in times of *temptation.* New views of God will be opened to you, new treasures of truth unlocked, new promises applied, new discoveries and manifestations made to you of the love, the grace, the tenderness, the sympathy of Christ. You will have found some new niche in His heart of love and sympathy, unknown, undiscovered before, into which your weary, panting spirit will insinuate itself and nestle in assured safety and repose until the tempter flee. Every deluge has its dove, every dove its ark, every ark its Noah, every cloud its bow. And when the enemy shall come into your soul like a flood, the Spirit, the Comforter, will gently lead you to Jesus, and cloister you within the secret place of His loving, sheltering bosom. Hidden and resting there, the swelling waves may lift up their voice, but the Lord Jesus on high "*is mightier than the noise of many waters, yea, than the mighty waves of the sea,*" and you need not fear. Satan is more restless, earnest, malignant at the present moment than ever; yea, often assuming the form of an angel of light, seeing that his time is short. But the Lord is at hand! In a little while He will come and complete the victory begun in Paradise, continued in the wilderness, renewed on the cross, carried on through the long history of His Church, and consummated in the day of His personal, glorious, and triumphant appearing. Tempted child of

God! take heart—look up! You shall, through your conquering Head, bruise Satan under your feet shortly!

But slight allusion has been made in this chapter to the awful condition of the *unconverted*, still under the dominion and power of Satan, led captive by him at his will. We would not close it without a solemn word addressed especially to such. My dear reader, be your standard of morality, your religious creed, your education, your rank in society what it may, nothing modifies, softens, or alters, in the slightest degree, the appalling fact that an unrenewed, unregenerate soul is a soul yet the subject of Satan—the captive and slave of his power and service. What is the unerring testimony of God's Word? Addressing those who, through grace, were rescued from the power of Satan, the apostle thus speaks, "You hath he quickened, who were dead in trespasses and sins; wherein in time past ye walked according to the course of this world, *according to the prince of the power of the air, the spirit that now worketh in the children of disobedience.*" (Eph. ii. 1, 2.) What an appalling description of the unrenewed! Reader, it is a faithful portrait of you, if you are yet not born again of the Spirit. What need have we of further testimony? Surely this one passage, were there no other proof, is sufficient to fill with awe and alarm every unconverted reader of this page. The strong man armed, who is the Devil, has still possession of your soul in peace; and will remain in undisturbed, undisputed, and willing occupation, until a stronger than he enters, spoils him of his goods, and casts him out. (Luke xi. 21, 22.) "*The god of this world hath blinded the minds of them which believe not, lest the light of the glorious gospel of Christ, who is the image of God, should shine unto them.*" (2 Cor. iv. 4.) It is his aim and policy to keep your soul in carnal security, in false peace, in the stillness and insensibility of spiritual death. Mistake not your real condition! Mistake not cold ritualism for vital religion; dead formalism for spiritual life; carnal insensibility for Divine peace; rash confidence for humble faith; human excitement for holy love; groundless expectation for assured hope! Satan is a great counterfeiter! He not only can quote Scripture, but he can imitate grace. Every species of false religion, and every form of spurious Christianity, are his inventions. He will strive to retain possession of your soul, nor relinquish his hold without a long and a desperate struggle. Be you assured of this, that everything that is evil and false is of Satan. Every atheistical idea of God, every infidel thought of the Bible, every suggestion of sin, every prompting to evil, every new attraction of the world, every impediment in the way of your salvation, every argument and persuasive pleading for a postponement to a more convenient season, it may be to a sick and dying bed, of the great, the needful work of repentance and of faith, the solemn, the momentous preparation of the soul for eternity, all, *all* is of Satan. In all this you are "*led captive by him at his will.*" Oh, solemn, appalling thought—"My soul the palace of Satan! my intellect, my will, my heart all under his influence and at his command! My present and my future life not God's, not Christ's, not heaven's, but Satan's!" Oh, throw yourself at the feet of the Saviour, whose mission it is to destroy the works of the devil, and the devil himself, and beseech Him to rend the chain, to eject the usurper, and to claim and possess the throne and the kingdom of your soul as His own for ever! Hell shall not then be your everlasting abode, nor Satan your eternal tormentor. But He who came into this world "*to proclaim liberty to the captive, and the opening of the prison to them that are bound,*" (Isa. lxi. 1,) will claim you as His lawful prize, and when you die, heaven will be your home and God your Father. You shall live and reign with Christ for ever and ever. "*Be sober, be vigilant; because your adversary the devil, as a roaring lion, walketh about, seeking whom he may devour: whom resist stedfast in the faith.*" And then comes the final defeat and eternal doom of him who so long and so fearfully reigned and ruled, the god and despot of mankind—"AND THE DEVIL THAT DECEIVED THEM WAS CAST INTO THE LAKE OF FIRE AND BRIMSTONE, WHERE THE BEAST AND THE FALSE PROPHET ARE, AND SHALL BE TORMENTED DAY AND NIGHT FOR EVER AND EVER."

CHAPTER XIII.

CHRIST'S SYMPATHY WITH CHRISTIAN PERSEVERANCE.

"Then said Jesus unto the twelve, Will ye also go away?"—
John vi. 67.

When one views the perilous journey which conducts the believer to heaven, it seems a miracle that any should ever arrive there at last! Remembering that each one carries within his bosom the elements of his own destruction,—a moral magazine, a single spark lighting upon which, unextinguished instantaneously by the power of Christ, would annihilate every vestige of hope; when we remember, too, that the wilderness through which he passes is thronged with beasts of prey, headed by the prince of the power of the air, and how, at the very last gasp of life, he would, were it possible, pluck the trembling spirit from the hand of Jesus;

when to this is added the allurements of the world, the snares of one's daily calling, the offence of the cross, the seduction of false doctrines, the disguises of error, it does indeed appear a miracle—an especial and continuous intervention of Divine power, contrary to the law of nature and of sin—that a sinner should ever find himself in glory. It is an affecting thought that multitudes who appear to set out for heaven, moved by some powerful, undefinable impulse, eventually flag, halt, and finally turn back, and never touch the borders of the good land. They seem to make some spiritual progress, to bid fair to hold on their way to the end, but by and by, when the straitness, the difficulties, and the dangers of the way unfold themselves, they tire, and stumble, and gradually decline and walk no more professedly with Jesus. It were well, my reader, if we lay these things close to heart,—if they lead us to earnest self-examination as to our religion, our progress, our hope, lest at any time we should seem to come short. A solemn and striking instance of turning back from Christ is before us. Christ had been propounding truths unpalatable to some of his hearers—truths which uprooted their self-righteousness, laid their glory in the dust, removing the crown from the head of human merit and placing it upon the head of Divine grace. These doctrines gave offence; they were test truths,—truths which brought the principles, the grace, and the progression of these professing disciples to the proof, and when thus tested and proved they failed. His line of truth was this:—"*Many therefore of His disciples, when they had heard this, said, This is an hard saying; who can hear it? When Jesus knew in Himself that His disciples murmured at it, He said unto them, Doth this offend you? What and if ye shall see the Son of man ascend up where He was before?*"—(thus declaring His pre-existent deity.) "*It is the spirit that quickeneth*"—(thus teaching the doctrine of spiritual regeneration); "*the flesh profiteth nothing*"—(thus upholding the doctrine of man's moral impotence): "*the words that I speak unto you, they are spirit, and they are life*"—(thus asserting the Divine inspiration of His truth.) "*And He said, Therefore I say unto you, that no man can come unto me, except it were given unto him of my Father. From that time many of His disciples went back, and walked no more with Him.*" Thus early commenced the offence of gospel truth, the enmity and opposition of man's carnal mind to the doctrines and principles of grace. "From *that time*"—from the moment these Divine and distinctive doctrines were declared, which laid the axe at the root of human power, pride, and merit —"many went back, and walked no more with Him." It was at this trying and critical juncture that Christ manifested that touching sympathy with the Christian fidelity and perseverance of His true disciples, which prompted the affecting appeal, "*Will ye also go away?*" What a solemn, heart-searching question! What an exhibition of our Lord's sympathy with the Christian constancy and perseverance of His people! Our spiritual progress, our growth in grace, our Christian consistency and perseverance, cannot be a matter of indifference to Christ. That He should construct a beautiful vessel,—recreating, remodelling, and re-embellishing it from the ruins of the fall, for the purpose of restoring to it the Divine image, and of filling it through eternity with the Divine glory,—and should then feel and manifest no regard, sympathy, or care for its future safety and well-being, is a picture of Christ the Bible nowhere presents. Such a statement is belied by the words before us—"*Will ye also go away?*" What an impressive and exquisitely affecting view of the Saviour's holy, tender solicitude for His people's perseverance in grace! May its study quicken our sensibilities, stimulate our diligence, awaken our vigilance, and call forth the response, "Lord, to whom shall we go? thou hast the words of eternal life!" In considering this sympathy of Christ with the constancy of His disciples to His person and truth, and their perseverance in personal holiness and grace, it will be proper to place in the foreground the solemn fact, that there are professors of Christ who, assailed by certain hostile influences, go away and walk no more with Jesus. This will prepare us to consider true Christian perseverance, and Christ's tender, wakeful sympathy with it. "*Will ye also go away?*"

The sin implied in this affecting appeal of Christ is that of backsliding and apostasy from Him and His cause. With an unregenerate man, the whole life is one act of going from Christ. Our nature has been wandering from God, from Christ, and from heaven more and more, farther and farther, from the moment that it first broke from its grand centre—GOD. Supposing myself addressing personally such a one, in proof of this solemn statement as to your spiritual condition, let me remind you that you have never yet taken one actual step toward Christ; that you have never yielded to the attraction of His cross, have never felt the power of His love, have never tasted that the Lord is gracious. What is this but a turning the back upon the Saviour? The final condemnation of such a rejection of Christ will admit of no palliation or excuse. Your plea at Christ's bar will not even be that which we might suppose a heathen would present, whose shores the keel of the missionary ship never smote, whose valleys and whose rocks never echoed with the sounds of salvation—"I never heard of Thee, O Lord! The gospel of Thy salvation never saluted my ears. I never knew that I was a sinner, and never heard that Christ Jesus came to save sinners, and that I might be saved." You possess the Bible, have some intellectual knowledge of the truth, have heard the solemn warnings and the thrilling invitations of the gospel, and yet your whole life is one continuous act of wilful going away from Jesus. You reject His person, neglect His salvation, spurn His grace, and trample upon His bleeding heart. Listen to the solemn word of God:—"*How shall we escape, if we neglect so great salvation?*" "*There remaineth no more sacrifice for sin, but a fearful looking for of judgment and fiery indignation, which shall devour the adversaries.*" Oh, ponder these declarations before you take another step with your back upon Christ!

But there are those who, by a most solemn profession, have given in their adherence to Christ—have walked with Him in the observance of religious duties and ordinances—have appeared to exhibit some marks of grace, some signs of conversion—the bud, the blossom, the foliage—but, alas! whose "*goodness has been but as the morning cloud and the early dew, passing away.*" The bud was nipped, the blossom withered ere the fruit was set; and so they went back and walked no more, even professedly, with Jesus. To what cause shall we trace the spiritual inconstancy, defections, and backslidings of many who walk no more with the Lord?

Some forsake the way of the Lord *because of its growing straitness.* The extreme narrowness of the way does not fully appear to the believer on his first setting out in the Divine life. The Lord wisely and graciously reserves this for the more advanced and matured stages of grace. As the believer grows in grace, he grows in the knowledge of the difficulties of salvation, of the increasing straitness of the path, and of the necessity of working out his own salvation with fear and trembling. He comes to learn more fully what at first might have startled and discouraged him, that *"the righteous scarcely are saved."* This proves a test of real grace. True conversion will stand it. He that truly has Christ in his heart will never swerve from the Christian life because, as he advances, he finds the path become straiter, narrower, and more difficult. His growing knowledge of Christ meets the new intricacies of his Christian course. Indeed, Christ is his way; and while he grows in a closer intimacy with the way, he also grows in a closer intimacy with all his supplies for the way. I have remarked that the growing narrowness of the Christian way is a test of religious profession. This supplies one reason why so many religious professors after a while prove inconstant, and backslide from the way. Wearied with the practice of self-denial—tired of bearing the cross after Jesus—restive beneath His yoke—impatient of His burden—they slacken in the race, halt in the journey, and eventually altogether relinquish their profession. Such individuals never counted the cost of a Christian profession of Christ. They took not into consideration the self-denial demanded, the battle with sin involved, the crucifixion to the world required; and when these things came upon them, these half-hearted pilgrims swerved from their profession, and returned to the sins they professed to have renounced, and to the world they professed to have abandoned, and walked no more with Jesus.

The world is another fruitful cause of alienation from a religious profession. It is a deadly snare, a fatal rock to many a towering professor. Its seductions are so powerful, its disguise so successful, its pleas so plausible, its eddies so numerous, its vortex so powerful and absorbing, few who profess to have come out of and to have renounced it for ever, escape from its entire enthralment, and hold on their Christian course of daily dying to its fascination and power. Oh, *what* a snare to the Christian profession is the ungodly world! And is there not, at the present moment, cause for alarm at the growing encroachment of the world upon the professing Church of Christ? We verily think so. Are not worldly amusements—dancing, card-playing, private theatricals, concerts—rife among many who have openly and solemnly professed *His* holy name before men, "*who gave Himself for our sins, that He might deliver us from this present evil world?*" What means this eager pursuit of wealth, this love of display, this extravagance of living, this studied toilet, this conformity to the world in a hundred different ways, so conspicuous and so increasing among Christian professors? Wherein, save in an outward profession, do these avowed disciples of the Crucified differ from the unregenerate, ungodly, non-professing world around them? If these are true disciples of Christ, where are we to look for the worldlings?—if these are worldlings, where are we to look for the true followers of Christ? The Church in its worldly conformity looks so like the world, and the world in its religious forms looks so like the Church, we are at times embarrassed where to look for the one or for the other. But this amalgamation must not be. The true Church of Christ is a separate body, a holy nation, a peculiar people, a royal priesthood, the light and the salt of the world. And the precept that is to regulate its course as it regards this world is, "*Love not the world, neither the things that are in the world.*" "*If any man love the world, the love of the Father is not in him. For all that is in the world, the lust of the flesh, and the lust of the eyes, and the pride of life, is not of the Father, but is of the world.*" (1 John ii. 15, 16.) "*Be not conformed to this world: but be ye transformed by the renewing of your mind.*" (Rom. xii. 2.) "*Know ye not that the friendship of the world is enmity with God? whosoever therefore will be a friend of the world is the enemy of God.*" (James iv. 4.) "*If ye be risen with Christ, seek those things which are above, where Christ sitteth on the right hand of God. Set your affection* [mind] *on things above, not on things on the earth. For ye are dead, and your life is hid with Christ in God.*" (Col. iii. 1–3.) "*Wherefore, come out from among them, and be ye separate, saith the Lord, and touch not the unclean thing; and I will receive you, and will be a Father unto you, and ye shall be my sons and daughters, saith the Lord Almighty.*" (2 Cor. vi. 17, 18.) What can be more clear, more imperative, or more solemn than these injunctions to a nonconformity to the world?

To their entire disregard must be traced the apostasy from their solemn vows of Christian discipleship of multitudes of professed disciples of Christ. "*Demas hath forsaken me, having loved this present world.*" "*They went out from us, because they were not of us.*"

Offence because of the truth is another popular cause of inconstancy of religious profession and of apostasy from the faith. As the gospel becomes more unfolded to their view, and those truths and doctrines are propounded which teach eternal election, Divine sovereignty, free grace, effectual calling, spiritual regeneration, preceptive holiness, final perseverance, and cognate doctrines of grace, by and by they become offended, go back, and walk no more with Jesus. These were the truths our Divine Prophet taught the people. On one occasion so powerfully did they stir up the opposition of the natural heart and the enmity of the carnal mind, that they bore Him to the brow of a hill, and would from thence have hurled Him headlong to destruction. And what prevented the accomplishment of this murderous purpose? The inbeing of His Godhead! "*And all they in the synagogue, when they heard these things, were filled with wrath, and rose up, and thrust him out of the city, and led him unto the brow of the hill whereon their city was built, that they might cast him down headlong. But he, passing through the midst of them, went his way.*" (Luke iv. 28–30.)

The awful consequences of having professed Christ only to renounce Him, of swerving from Christian doctrines and profession, must be left for the pen of inspiration to portray. They will be found delineated with terrific and startling power in the sixth chapter of the Epistle to the Hebrews. That these solemn passages can be predicated of real Christians we do not aver, and have elsewhere taught.* The apostle supposes the hypothetical case of one who had so far professed Christianity as to bear a strong resemblance to its genuine truths and practice, but who yet eventually fell away and renounced both the doctrines and the precepts of Christ. Applied, as they originally are, to this class of religionists, they present a picture of so appalling a character as should make every religious professor in Christendom turn pale and tremble!

But there are those who go not from the

* *Vide* exposition of these passages in "Help Heavenward," pp. 249–262.

Saviour. To those He touchingly appealed,—"*Will ye also go away?*" What was the feeling our adorable Lord here betrayed? It was a deep, intense, earnest sympathy with the Christian progress and perseverance of His true disciples. "Will *you* leave and forsake me? Will *you* sever from my faith, no more walk with me, and henceforth cease to be my disciples?" Oh, what must have been the touching tenderness of that look, the melting tones of that voice, the winning power of that appeal when these words were spoken! We marvel not that the earnest and instantaneous response of His true disciples was, "Lord, to whom shall we go? If we forsake Thee, whither could we turn? Who could be to us such a Saviour, such a Friend, such a Portion as Thou art, if, Lord, we turn from Thee?" Now, what is the subject thus so dear to the heart of Christ?—with what is His sympathy so closely, so warmly entwined? It is the perseverance of His disciples in spiritual knowledge, grace, and steadfastness, resolving itself into a simple, single, and firm adherence to Himself. "Will ye also go away?" The subject is important—*Christian perseverance.* Let us present it to the reader in two or three particulars.

And first, perseverance in the growth of spiritual knowledge must necessarily occupy a prominent place in religious progress. "*Add to virtue* KNOWLEDGE." Real growth in experimental Christianity demands calm thought, mental abstraction, patient and prayerful study of Divine truth. Christian progression would be an anomaly not based upon, and accompanied by, Christian knowledge—an increasing knowledge of Christ, knowing more and more of the glory of His person, the excellency of His work, the sufficiency of His grace, and the depth of His love—knowing more and more of God in Christ as our Father, as God all-sufficient—knowing more and more of the fulness and preciousness of the Scriptures of truth—and knowing more and more of the depravity of our nature, and at the same time of the blood that cleanses from all sin—past, present, and to come. Religious progress, not guided and tempered by this, will be a progression in the wrong direction, in all probability landing the traveller upon the bleak and perilous shore of some essential error in doctrine, or wild extravagance in practice, which may prove fatal to his Christian profession, holiness, and hope! To our progress in Christian knowledge there is no limit in this life but life itself. The subjects of spiritual research and study are so infinite in their nature, rich in their wealth, and boundless in their range, the believer may be ever learning; and yet, when he comes to relinquish the limited for the illimitable sphere of knowledge, he will feel that, like the great philosopher, he has been all his lifetime but gathering pebbles on the shore, while the vast ocean of truth lay at his feet unsmitten by his barque, unsounded by his line. And yet, fathomless as are the depths, and boundless as is the range of spiritual truth, we are not to be discouraged in seeking, through the teaching of the Holy Spirit, to know more of God's revealed Word. The point from which we start, and the goal to which we aspire, are the same—a knowledge, spiritual and saving, of God and Christ. "*This is life eternal, that they might know thee, the only true God, and Jesus Christ whom thou hast sent.*" With this we commence our spiritual life, with this we close it on earth, and with this we prolong it through eternity, ever studying the glory the character, the love, the government of God and knowing more and more of the infinite Triune Jehovah. Lord, if this is to be Thy disciple, a humble learner in Thy school and at Thy feet would I ever be.

The ways by which God thus increases our spiritual knowledge are various. The great Instructor is the Holy Ghost, and the great school is sanctified affliction, and the great instrument is the Word. No child of God is perfected in the evidences of his adoption, and no disciple of Christ has made any very high attainments in experimental truth, until he has passed through trial. His Christianity must be tried—his grace must be tried—his faith must be tried, before he has any deep experience in godliness. Oh, how much is known of God in one mysterious providence! How much is learnt of Jesus in one painful affliction! How much is experienced of the Comforter in one deep sorrow! "*Blessed is the man whom Thou* CHASTENEST, *O Lord! and* TEACHEST *him out of Thy law.*" *Chastening* and *teaching* are always linked, as cause and effect, in the corrective dealings of God with His saints. He corrects and rebukes but to promote our spiritual education; that knowing His truth more *experimentally*, and becoming better acquainted with Himself, we may enter into more perfect peace and more real possession. "*Ac-*

quaint now thyself with Him, and be at peace, and so good shall come unto thee."

A faithful, consistent attachment to Christ also includes a firm, *unswerving adherence to His pure truth.* To compromise the gospel is to compromise the Christ of the gospel. To give heed to the teaching that causeth to err, to exchange truth for error, sound doctrine for false, to relinquish the evangelical system of truth, any part of it, for any one of the modern anti-evangelical systems or tenets, is to turn the back upon Christ. Adherence to truth and loyalty to Christ are inseparable. As error enters the mind, love to Christ leaves the heart. As antichristian doctrine obtains the ascendancy in the intellect, Christ sinks in the affections. Christ only maintains His supremacy in the spiritual affections of the soul as His pure, simple gospel dwells in the heart an element of life and holiness. The gospel is the heart of Christ speaking. The truth as it is in Jesus is the glory of Christ revealed; and as we swerve from the gospel and sell the truth, our love to the Saviour chills, our admiration for His person lessens, and our attachment to His cause and His disciples relapses into indifference, alienation, and neglect. Study the moral history of all who have turned from the way of vital truth into the way of deadly error, and mark how gradually their spirituality has deteriorated, their heavenliness declined, and their prayerfulness, humility, and Christ-like simplicity has given place to a dogmatical, self-sufficient, worldly spirit and carriage. It was to check this evil in the early Church that Paul thus expressed himself toward the Corinthian saints, "*I fear, lest by any means, as the serpent beguiled Eve through his subtlety, so your minds should be corrupted from the simplicity that is in Christ.*" (2 Cor. xi. 3.) My dear reader, before, then, you yield your ear to the ensnaring, seductive voice of error, listen to the gentle, persuasive voice of Jesus,—"*Will ye also go away?*" To go away from the truth is to go away from Him who is emphatically and essentially—"*the Truth.*"

Adherence to Christ includes also *adherence to the Church of Christ.* Christ and His Church are one, as the Church *per se* is one and indivisible. We cannot, therefore, in any way separate from the Church of Christ without compromising our union with Christ Himself. We do not say by this that the believer's union with Christ can ever be imperilled. This is impossible. Our union with the Head does not depend upon our union with the body, though it involves it; but our real and vital membership with the body, the Church, *does* depend upon our firm and vital union with Christ the Head. If we are truly united to Christ, that union involves another—union with all the members of Christ—with the one and the whole Church of God. We cannot deny the one without a virtual denial of the other. Nor does the true believer in Christ find this a hard saying or unwelcome truth. The sap ascends not from the root, through the trunk, to every branch, and twig, and fibre, and leaf of the whole tree more naturally and really than does the spiritual life that we derive from Jesus extend throughout the whole Church, permeating and vitalising all the members of the entire body, uniting each to the other, and all to Christ. How careful, then, should we be of unduly fostering and magnifying those ecclesiastical, sectarian differences of form, those varieties of judgment and interpretation in religious things, not vital and essential, which already to too great an extent exist to the deformity of the body, to the detriment of real religion, to the grieving of the Holy Spirit of God, and the dishonour of Christ. Let us, then, manifest the reality of our union with, and the sincerity of our love for, Christ, by sedulously cultivating brotherly love and Christian union with all who love our Lord Jesus in sincerity, though they belong not to *our* branch of Christ's Church. We go away from Jesus when we go away from His saints. They are dear, very dear, precious, priceless to His heart. They are as tender to Him as the apple of His eye; are engraved upon the palm of His hand, and are borne upon the breastplate on His heart. God is equally their Father, Christ equally their Elder Brother; and as you are, so are they, the temple of the Holy Ghost. Oh, then, evince your love to Jesus by the manifestation of your love to His disciples. Let not your affection, your confidence, and your intercourse be cold, suspicious, forced; let it be as spontaneous and as warm as light streaming from the sun; as free and as refreshing as the rain distilling from the clouds, as the stream flowing from the mountain spring. "*Beloved, let us love one another; for love is of God; and every one that loveth is born of God, and knoweth God. He that loveth not, knoweth not God, for God is love.*"

Let us, then, exhort you ever listen to this appeal of Jesus. In all times of temptation, in all times of trial, in all times of error, in all times of adversity, in all times of creature, worldly, sinful allurement may the tender, touching, melting words of Jesus penetrate our innermost soul—"*Will ye also go away?*" Oh, whatever betide, forsake not Christ! Walk so near to Him that you may feel He is at your side in every path and circumstance of life; lean upon Him so confidently that you may find yourself, with the disciple whom Jesus loved, reclining upon the very bosom of your Lord. Let your every-day life be a constant going to, rather than a going from, Jesus. Be humbled and mourn that you ever forsook, distrusted, wounded, and grieved Him. Times without number have we done this. Alas! our Christian profession of Christ has been chequered and uneven. Declension and revival, relapse and recovery, backsliding and restoring, have made up so much of our spiritual history; who would or could have borne with us as Jesus has? We have never forsaken Him and have returned, throwing ourselves at His feet deploring, confessing, bemoaning the sinfulness of our ingratitude, forsakings, distrustings, but He has graciously received us, gently raised us to His bosom, lovingly and freely forgiving all our sins.

> "Wretch that I am to wander thus
> In chase of false delight."

How touching, then, the sympathy of Christ with the difficulties, temptations, and progress of our Christian perseverance! "*Will ye also go away?*" He could not endure the thought that, among the many who went away and walked not with Him, any of His own true disciples should prove cold, false, and recreant. "*Will* YE *also go away?*" With what power and tenderness must this appeal to their attachment, fidelity, and love have pierced their hearts! He addresses it still to us! What multitudes in the present age of religious excitement and profession fall off and walk no more with Jesus! Weary of the cross, discouraged by reason of the way, possessing not real grace, true conversion, the indwelling of the Spirit, vital union with the Lord Jesus, they fall from the profession—not from the *possession*—of grace, (Gal. v. 4,) and return to the beggarly elements they had so openly and solemnly renounced. Oh, it is an appalling thing—apostasy from the faith! it is a fearful step—falling from a profession of Christ! Rather let us endure any self-denial, hardship, scorn, persecution or loss, yea, death itself, than deny the Lord Jesus, crucifying Him afresh, and putting Him to an open shame by turning from our solemn profession of faith and love. And yet, if ours be a profession of the Saviour *only*, unaccompanied with true change of heart, with real regeneration by the Spirit, let us not be content to meet the Bridegroom with this empty lamp! The sooner a mere profession of Christ is relinquished for what is real, vital, saving, the better. Oh let us not go down to the grave with a spurious religion, a false hope, a lie in our right hand! But, for the encouragement of the Lord's true people, let us remark that Christ has pledged the exercise of His power, the communication of His grace, the aid of His intercession on behalf of all His true disciples. Not one of these shall utterly backslide, not one shall finally fall, not one shall eternally be lost. His promise is, "THEY SHALL NEVER PERISH." Their vital union with Christ, the indwelling of the Holy Ghost, the power of Jehovah, the intercession of the High Priest in heaven, all the promises of God prove their security, and are pledges of their perseverance from grace to glory. In His strength, then, and aided by His grace, let our response be, "Lord, to whom shall I, to whom *would* I go, if I go from Thee? Who so lovely, who so attractive, who so worthy, who so precious as Thou? Who such a Friend, such a Brother, such a Redeemer, such a Portion? Heaven embraces, earth contains no being that can be what Thou art to my soul. To whom could I repair with my wants, upon whose arm could I suspend my burdens, upon whose breast could I breathe my sorrows, into whose ear could I pour my prayers, at whose feet could I confess my sins, and weep my love, but Thine, O Lamb of God? To go from *Thee* is—death! Rather let me yield my heart's fondest treasure, costliest, strongest attraction, life's sweetest charm, yea, life itself, than part, blessed Jesus, with Thee: "WILL YE ALSO GO AWAY? LORD, TO WHOM SHALL WE GO? THOU HAST THE WORDS OF ETERNAL LIFE." Saints of God—PERSEVERE! Every serious thought of time, every solemn view of eternity, bids you—PERSEVERE! All the promises of God, all the assurances of Christ, all the revelations of the gospel bid you—**PERSEVERE**! Angels winging their way from heaven, the spirits of just men made perfect bending from their seats in glory, the great cloud of witnesses around your path, bid you—PERSEVERE! Christ from His throne holds out the jewelled diadem, the palm, the robe, and bids you—PERSEVERE! "BE THOU FAITHFUL UNTO DEATH, AND I WILL GIVE THEE A CROWN OF LIFE." "*Will ye also go away?*" Blessed Lord, kept by Thy power, upheld by Thy grace, comforted by Thy love, soothed by Thy **sympathy**, I will never, no, *never* leave Thee!

"I'll not leave Jesus—never, never!
Ah, what can more precious be?
Rest, and joy, and light are ever
In His hand to give to me.
All things that can satisfy,
Having Jesus, those have I.

"Love has bound me fast unto Him,
I am His, and He is mine;
Daily I for pardon sue Him,
Answers He with peace divine.
On that Rock my trust is laid,
And I rest beneath its shade.

Without Jesus, earth would weary,
Seem almost like hell to be;
But if Jesus I see near me,
Earth is almost heaven

Am I hungry? He doth give
Bread on which my soul can live.

"Spent with Him, one little hour
Giveth a year's worth of gain;
Grace and peace put forth their power,
Joy doth wholly banish pain;
One faith-glance that findeth Him,
Maketh earthly crowns look dim.

"Oh, how light upon my shoulder
Lies my cross, now grown so small!
For the Lord is my upholder,
Fits it to me, softens all;
Neither shall it always stay,—
Patience,—it will pass away.

"Now He leads me wonderfully,
Right and left, through sun and rain,
Yet I know and trust Him truly,
It is always for my gain.
Yes, His wonder-road, indeed,
Always heavenward doth lead.

"Those who faithfully go forward,
In His changeless care shall go;
Nothing's doubtful or untoward
To the flock who Jesus know.
Jesus always is the same;
True and faithful is His name.

"Blinded world! if ye admire
Earthly trifles, ye are free!
Out of Jesus my desire
Never shall contented be:
I have sworn it in my heart,
I from Jesus will not part."

CHAPTER XIV.

THE DISINTERESTEDNESS OF CHRIST'S SYMPATHY.

"**Even Christ pleased not himself.**"—Rom. xv. 3.

No single principle of His own religion did our Lord more perfectly embody or more touchingly illustrate than its *disinterested benevolence.* The nature which, sinless He assumed, yet whose sinfulness He came to remove, was essentially and totally disorganised. To affirm, as the Scriptures of truth positively do, that it is originally and totally depraved, is but to portray it with every feature of its pristine nobleness, purity, and excellence utterly spoiled. When, therefore, our Lord made His advent to our world, He found man the living embodiment, the acting impersonation, the very incarnation of *fallen* self-love—self-love in the form of complete *selfishness.* The original Centre of the soul forsaken, He had become a centre to himself. The god he worshipped, was the deification of—*self.* The religion he professed, was the adoration of—*self.* The powers he cultivated were consecrated to—*self.* His whole existence was one act of service and devotion to—*self.* The Divine Centre, as we have said, abandoned, he knew no other god, acknowledged no other sufficiency, recognised no other end than—*himself.* Every faculty and thought, every affection and action, was made to contribute to the cloud of incense which rose as in one dense column before this little idol—SELF. Himself the first—himself the last—himself all in all! And is it not so now? Self, in some shape, is still the deity of the natural man. Selfishness is still the universal sin of our nature, exhibited in one or more of its thousand modifications, its endless forms. All are in pursuit either of wealth, or ambition, or pleasure, or honour, or gratification—each one urging his individual suit—under the rule of this "reigning law of the world ravaged and disorganised by sin"—the law of selfishness. A total *disregard* for the interests and enjoyment of others—an entire *oblivion* of what is due to another's feelings and well-being—the *possession* of a certain good, the *attainment* of a certain end at the expense of another's happiness and rights, is the only recognised principlend a rule of action which regulates the conduct of the great majority of our depraved species. The indictment is heavy, the picture is dark, the sin is awful, we admit; but it is borne out as much by daily observation and frequent experience, as by the faithful, unerring Word of God—"ALL MEN SEEK THEIR OWN." What means this self-exaltism—this egotism—this envy and jealousy—this attempt to supplant others in esteem, influence, and power—this prodigality and love of worldly show—this eager chase of wealth—this covetousness and penuriousness—this niggardly dole of charity—this cruel, heartless, grinding oppression—this growing sensuality and crime—this haughty inflexibility of will, impatience of contradiction, and acknowledging no superiority to its own—this love of ease and sloth—this sectarian exclusiveness which looks with coldness, jealousy, and distrust upon the spiritual prosperity of others?—what, we ask, is all this, and a thousand times more, but the one appalling, cancerous sin of *selfishness* existing in the very heart of depravity, and sending its fatal poison along all the fibres of human society? That there are noble modifications of this appalling description of our nature, we readily and thankfully concede; but they are the exceptions to the rule—the beautiful ivy intwining the decayed and crumbling trunk of our fallen humanity, reminding us of what man was in his first estate, and faintly foreshadowing what man in his restored state will be, when the Lord comes to make all things new.

Nor is this selfishness of our nature entirely uprooted, though greatly mortified, in the renewed man. The Divine precepts, admonitions, and exhortations of God's Word all imply its existence and working in the believer, and the need of incessant battle with the fallen principle. In nothing, perhaps, is its existence more marked than the perpetual collision of our will with the will of God. To please ourselves, and not God, in the path we tread, in the service we perform, in the cross we bear, in the suffering we endure, in the place we dwell,—to gratify our inclinations, to please our taste, to indulge our repose, to promote our self-interest, often at the expense of others,—is the baneful fruit borne by this corrupt tree. Oh, it is a humiliating truth, that though engrafted, through sovereign grace, as the believer is upon Christ, there should mingle with the "fruits of righteousness, which are by Jesus Christ," fruit so bitter and noxious. That, with the great, the lofty, the holy principle implanted within of living to please God, we should yet be brought into perpetual conflict with its opposite most low and degrading principle—living to please ourselves. And yet so it is. We marvel not, then, at the earnest and pointed exhortation of the apostle,—"*We then that are strong ought to bear the infirmities of the weak, and not to please ourselves. Let every one of us please his neighbour for his good to edification.* FOR EVEN CHRIST PLEASED NOT HIMSELF." This precept is in perfect harmony with the genius of the gospel of Jesus. The Divine religion He introduced into the world was in direct and close antagonism to the world's selfishness. It revealed to man a new and unearthly principle—the principle of unselfish love, disinterested sympathy, highminded, chivalrous benevolence and self-denial. He descended to earth, the reflection of heaven. He appeared to man, the incarnation of God—the embodied essence of the divinest, purest, loftiest affection in the universe. His gospel was unselfishness speaking—His life was unselfishness acting—His sympathy was unselfishness weeping—His death was unselfishness suffering, self-consumed amid its own sacrificial fires. "*The zeal of thine house hath eaten me up.*" And, then, when He had presented on the cross such a spectacle of disinterested love for man as angels could not have conceived, and such an outgush of unselfish sympathy as man had never seen—pure, sublime, unparalleled—He rose from the grave; and, ere He relinquished the scene of His humiliation for the home of His glory, He commissioned His apostles to traverse the world and tell its wondrous story as far as the empire of man and misery extended,—"*Go ye into all the world and preach the gospel to every creature.*" Such is the divine precept, and such its human embodiment we are about to study. "*Even Christ pleased not himself.*" May the Holy Spirit of truth, while we behold as in a glass this glory of the Lord, transform us into the same image, that henceforth we may be more like Christ in His unselfish love and disinterested sympathy. In what points did our Lord illustrate this Divine principle of His gospel? Trace first its higher forms.

In Christ there was perfect *submission to the supreme will of His Father.* Our Lord descended to this part of His Father's empire to erect no throne, to assert no will in opposition to God's. His language was, "*I came, not to do mine own will, but the will of Him that sent me.*" In *this* He pleased not Himself. He would have done so had there been the slightest dissonance of mind, or collision of will. But the union was essential—the harmony complete—between the will of Christ on earth and the will of God in heaven. It was the will of God that His elect should be redeemed—it was the will of Christ to redeem them. It was the will of God that His glory should be revealed—it was the will of Christ to reveal it. It was the will of God that His truth should be taught—it was the will of Christ to teach it. It was the will of God that Christ should be sacrificed—it was the will of Christ to die. "*Lo! I come to do thy will, O God,*" were the prophetic words which struck the first key-note to the harmony of God's will and Christ's will. "*Wist ye not that I must be about my Father's business?*" was a deeper intonation of the melody. "*Not my will, O my Father, but Thine be done!*" has its loftiest strain on earth. To do God's will from the heart, He was willing to forego the joys of heaven, to empty Himself of His glory, to sink to the deepest humiliation, to die the accursed death—and in all this, "*Christ pleased not Himself.*" Child of God, you reach the loftiest attainment in sanctification, you stand upon the highest round in the ascent of holiness, when *your will*, like Christ's, is thus blended with your Father's. No holier, no higher, no sublimer act of self-denial marks the believer than this. It was in this school of subjection to the Divine will that Christ's disinterested sympathy for us was trained. Had there been aught of self-seeking in Him, it would have been exhibited in the opposition of His will to the will of God. And the moment this hostility commenced, all disinterested benevolence for man would have ceased. The pure, deep spring of His self-consuming sympathy had its rise in the perfect union of His human will with the Divine. In addition to the sinlessness of the human nature of our Lord, it was also replenished with the Holy Spirit without measure, and He was the fulness of the Godhead bodily. Our Lord Jesus was thus the embodied revelation of infinite benevolence and love. In seeking, therefore, as man, to do the will of God, He clasped the object of His sympathy in a love that sought not its own but the happiness of the being it embraced. It is in this same school we, if moulded in Christ's image, are trained to love man, to sympathise with man, to aid man with an unselfish affection. In proportion as we are found doing the will of God, we rise superior to selfishness, and learn the difficult, yet God-like, lesson of looking not exclusively upon our own things, but in expansive, disinterested sympathy also upon the things of others. As we recede from the human and approximate to the Divine, we recede from selfishness and approximate to that disinterested love to man which manifested itself in the bestowment and sacrifice of its unspeakable gift: "*In this was manifested the love of God toward us, because that God sent His only-begotten Son into the world that we might live through Him.*"

In seeking the glory of God supremely, our Lord pleased not Himself. If ever there was the single eye, it beamed in Christ. He had no separate kingdom, swayed no rival sceptre, wore no divided crown separate from His Father. All that He embarked in, did, and taught converged to one common centre, pointed to one single aim, terminated in one great end—*the glory of God!* Had there been one thought or feeling of self-seeking in Christ, He might easily have erected a separate throne from His Father's, at whose feet kings, and princes, and potentates would have been proud to bring their treasures and lay their crowns. But no! His whole soul was swallowed up in God. "*I seek not mine own glory,*" was a declaration of unselfishness which found a living expression in every action of His life. To win back homage to the dishonoured law of God, to vindicate the outraged glory of His Father's government, to reveal His love, and accomplish His purpose in the salvation of His elect, and finally to bring to heaven all whom the Father had chosen to eternal life, to the endless honour and praise of His name, was the pole star which guided Him, the goal for which He pressed. To vindicate and uphold His Father's glory He was willing that His own should set in darkness, in ignominy, and in blood. Oh that this mind that was in Christ might be in us! What a powerful impetus, what a divine sanctity, what a lofty elevation it would give to every purpose, and act, and sacrifice, were it done with a more simple, pure, single aim to the glory of God! It would dignify the lowliest, and sanctify the loftiest service for Christ. Done solely and only for His glory, the cup of cold water which we offered to a disciple would be sweeter than nectar to him who drank it, and to Him in whose name it was given, precious and priceless above rubies. There is no greater, no more humiliating or visible form of selfishness than in placing our glory above God's. If we preach, or labour, or achieve, or suffer, or give with a view of making the world our pedestal, self the sole figure, mankind the admiring gazers, we are seeking but our own honour and glory, and God will consume the idol, and will make us drink the waters which the ashes of our self-deification and man-worship have embittered and defiled. Oh for the mortification of this sin! Oh for the crucifixion of this self-seeking that taints and deforms all that we do for God and for our fellows! In all this, "*even Christ pleased not himself.*"

Such, too, *was the tenor of His whole life*—it was a life of continuous and perfect self-denial. Every step He trod was another footprint in the path of disinterested benevolence. He went about doing good, scattering from the horn of blessing His favours and benedictions on friends and foes, on those who blessed, and on those who reviled, those who loved, and those who hated Him. Behold Him denying Himself of earth's comforts to promote the comfort of others; hungry Himself, yet feeding the famishing; weary, yet inviting and leading others to repose; Himself accused, yet vindicating the condemned. Was there ever such a spectacle of self-abnegation? Trace Christ, too, in service. There was no labour too toilsome or self-denying from which He shrank. He would walk forty miles in one day to take the living water to a poor sinner. He would stoop to unclasp the sandal and wash the feet of His erring disciple. He would stand still at the word of a blind beggar sitting by the wayside, and in response to his appeal, pour the light of day upon the sightless eye. He would go, when asked, to heal a sick servant. He would come, when bidden, to the house of mourning. He had an ear for every cry of sorrow, an eye for every spectacle of woe, a hand for every object of want, a heart for every appeal to human sympathy. Yea, there was no service so wearisome, or so distasteful, or so difficult, or so self-denying, in which He was not at home. The atmosphere most genial with His nature was laden with suffering, saturated with tears, vocal with sighs, and groans, and supplications. The homes most attractive to

Him were those where poverty, sickness, and grief had found an entrance. Such was the pure, self-denying benevolence of Jesus! Well may it be said, "*even Christ pleased not himself.*"

But the crowning act of His disinterested love and sympathy was, *His suffering unto death.* Marvellous and precious as were all the other expressions of His unselfish love, they pale and vanish before this the most marvellous, precious, and costly of all—the sacrifice of Himself upon the cross! What more could unselfish love do? What loftier form could it assume? What costlier sacrifice could it make? More than itself it could not give. Listen to the inspired confirmation of this: "*For when we were yet without strength, in due time Christ died for the ungodly. For scarcely for a righteous man will one die; yet peradventure for a good man some would even dare to die. But God commendeth His love toward us, in that while we were yet sinners, Christ died for us,*" (Rom. v. 6–8.) What more, we again ask, could love so unselfish, so disinterested do? Listen yet again: "*Christ also hath loved us, and hath given* HIMSELF *for us.*" "*Who gave* HIMSELF *for our sins.*" "*Christ also loved the Church, and gave*

HIMSELF *for it.*" "*Who gave* HIMSELF *for us, that he might deliver us from all iniquity.*" Oh what an infinitude of wealth and glory and blessing is included in these words—"GAVE HIMSELF!" Gave His Deity—gave His humanity—gave His obedience—gave His life—gave His heart's blood—gave His heaven of glory—all for poor, unworthy, self-destroyed, helpless sinners who had nothing to pay—pardoning them fully, justifying them freely, calling them graciously—keeping and eternally glorifying them. O Lord, my soul dissolves before this stupendous, this strange, this unparalleled spectacle of disinterested, self-sacrificing love! I blush to find myself so unlike it—I weep that my sins demanded it—I believe because it was Thou who didst die—my heart is won, my affections are captivated by a love which enchains to itself my whole being!

"Love celestial, ardent fire!
Oh extreme of sweet desire!
Spread thy bright, thy gentle flame,
Swift o'er all my mental frame.

"Sweet affections flow from thence,
Sweet above the joys of sense!
Let me thus for ever be
Full of gladness, full of Thee."

Before we speak of the consolation flowing to the saints of God from this view of Christ's disinterested sympathy, let us glean a few of the practical *lessons* it inculcates.

The first holy lesson it teaches is—*humility of mind.* Pride forms the root of all living to ourselves. And before our selfishness can be expelled, replaced by a new and divine principle, the power of Christ's cross must be brought into the soul, ruling, conquering the principle of pride. "*Though I be* NOTHING," will then be the echo of our hearts to the noble declaration of Paul. The moment this inflated bubble is pierced by the cross of Jesus, the collapse follows, and the disciplined, humbled believer is prostrate in the dust before God, in the spirit of self-abasement and self-surrender. Oh, let us cultivate a grace which assimilates us more than all others to Him who, "*being in the form of God, thought it not robbery to be equal with God: but made himself of no reputation, and took upon him the form of a servant.*" Never are we more truly conformed to Christ than when, emptied of self, we "*walk humbly with God.*" Oh, let us earnestly seek more fully to possess, with all our attainments, this, the highest and holiest of all—"THE MIND *that was in Christ Jesus.*" It will bring with it a happiness and a soothing real and indescribable. It will preserve us from those woundings, chafings, and mortifications to which the unslain pride of our hearts incessantly exposes us. Why do we feel so sensitively and so keenly the slight, the neglect, the depreciation of our fellows? Why, when thrust into the shade while others are more favoured and honoured and admired, do we, like Mordecai, "*retire to our house mourning, and having our head covered?*" Is it not because of the deification and worship of self within us? Oh to be emptied of self-complacency, self-seeking, self-exaltation!—this hydra-headed monster, which can only be effectually conquered and slain by a believing realisation of the self-denying love of Christ! Study this perfect annihilation of self in Jesus more closely, and you will imperceptably, yet really, transcribe the divine and beauteous lineament to your own soul. The power of Christ will be upon you visibly, the comeliness of Jesus will array you beauteously, you will feed in the greenest pasture, and gather the fairest flowers, and pluck the richest fruit, and drink the purest stream of spiritual blessing, because your daily walk will be in lowliness and love beneath the Saviour's cross—self-swallowed up in Christ, and Christ all and in all.

"Oh, hide this SELF from me, that I
No more, but Christ in me, may live;
My vile affections crucify,
Nor let one darling lust survive!
In all things nothing may I see,
Nothing desire or seek, but Thee!

"O love, thy sovereign aid impart,
To save me from low-thoughted care!
Chase this self-will through all my heart,
Through all its latent mazes there:
Make me thy duteous child, that I,
Ceaseless, may 'Abba, Father!' cry.

"Each moment draw from earth away
My heart, that lowly waits thy call;
Speak to my inmost soul, and say,
'I am thy Love, thy God, thy All!'
To feel Thy power, to hear Thy voice,
To taste Thy love, be all my choice."

But the deepest renunciation of self is in *the believing reception, as a sinner, of the Lord Jesus Christ.* All other acts of humiliation and self-denial apart from this are imperfect. Until the contrite and believing heart has received Christ, until the soul has subjected itself to the power of His gospel, until the law of the spirit of life in Christ Jesus has freed the mind from the enslaving law of self-justification, self may be mortified, but not humbled; wounded, but not slain. The very reception of God's free justification implies the surrender of that strong citadel of the soul of man—the principle of *self-righteousness*. And on no other ground will God capitulate with man in the great work of salvation. All human merit must be disclaimed, all creature worthiness must be abjured, and the one plea with which we may approach the Saviour is that of a sinner bankrupt and beggared of all personal righteousness, worthiness, and claim, looking only to Jesus, and resting simply and solely in His blood and righteousness for pardon and acceptance. Oh, what a real prostration and crucifixion of self is there in this one believing act of receiving Christ! The great mountain has been shaken to its centre before the power of the true Zerubbabel. Jesus has conquered. His grace has gotten the victory. His love is clothed with triumph, and another jewel is planted in His studded diadem. My reader, has there been such a revelation of the Lord Jesus to your soul as to stain the pride of your own glory? Has this Dagon self fallen before the divine Ark of your salvation? But let me remind the child of God that the principle of self in the renewed heart, though fatally wounded and destined eventually to die, yet retains much of its original vitality, and will, by occasional spasmodic acts, often seem to regain its original power and ascendancy. This must be met by a constant and close dealing with Christ. The principle of self-pleasing can only be kept in abeyance by strengthening its opposite principle—walking humbly with God, under the influence of the love of Christ, constraining us to live, not as seeking our own ease, advantage or honour, but with the single eye to God's glory both in service and in suffering, in all we do and endure. Oh hateful and hated act that terminates only in—*self!* If, to gratify the lust for human distinction and applause, if, to please self in any one of its many forms—self-esteem, self-complacency, self-exaltation—this thing has been done, better, far better, that it had been left undone, than that it should stand but as a monument to the pride and self-pleasing of our depraved hearts. And, oh, let us lay our mouth in the dust in the remembrance of our many failures touching this divine and holy precept. How much have we done for self, ostensibly done for Christ! How have we spoken and laboured and given in connexion with holy things, seeking our own glory and not the glory of God! But for the blood of atonement, whither could we look? The most righteous, most pure, most lowly act would witness against us at the tribunal of Christ, as having enough of the sin of self-pleasing to assign both it and us to God's eternal displeasure. What need have we to confess the sin, and wash in atoning blood, the moment we are conscious our self-complacency has been moved by the flattery and applause of our sinful fellows! O God! we blush to lift up our faces to Thee in the remembrance of our sin of self-pleasing! Lamb of God! wash out the deep, dark stain, and fill our soul with contrition, humiliation, and self-abhorrence, that we should ever have sought to carve our vile name upon Thy dear cross, while professedly uplifting only Thee!

The practical embodiment by us of this holy principle, thus so beautifully exhibited in our Lord, *will regulate our conduct towards others.* A disinterested sympathy, like His, will prompt us to seek the advancement of another's interest and well-being as well as our own. It is one of the characteristics of true charity, that she "*seeketh not her own.*" Like the Being from whence it flows, true love is disinterested and self-sacrificing. It looks with an eye of interest upon the estate of others. It will, so far as it righteously can, descend to their circumstances and infirmities, might it but promote their well-being. A striking example of this is presented in the conduct of Paul. The quotation is long, but one passage supplies a clue to the whole. "*Though I be free from all men, yet have I made myself servant unto all, that I might gain the more.*" (1 Cor. ix. 19–23.) Magnanimous man! thy love was like thy Master's, high-minded, chivalrous, and self-sacrificing. What abnegation of self in thy ministry! what a forgetfulness of self in thy labours! what a sacrifice of self in thy sufferings! Lord, may I follow Thine apostle as he followed Thee!

This Divine precept, so touchingly illustrated by Christ, also includes bearing the burdens, tenderness toward the infirmities, and sympathy with the sorrows and necessities of our brethren. In all this Christ has set us an example that we should follow His steps. To be Christ-like, in this particular, is to aspire to one of the loftiest and loveliest features of our religion. To supply, as far as in our power, the wants of Christ's poor—our brethren by a fraternal tie, closer and holier than nature's; to visit the sick and afflicted, the widow and the fatherless; to bear with the infirmities of those who, in religious things, are weak in judgment, in faith, and in practice; to identify ourselves with those who are suffering calumny, persecution, and loss for Jesus' sake,—oh, *this* it is to be like Him who went about doing good in the spirit of His own unworldly, unselfish religion! How touching is the apostle's exhortation,—"*We then that are strong ought to bear the infirmities of the weak, and not to please ourselves. Let every one of us please his neighbour for his good to edification. For even Christ pleased not himself; but, as it is written, The reproaches of them that reproached thee fell on me.*" May the Lord the Spirit write this holy, unearthly precept upon our heart! May we more deeply feel, more constantly realise, that, ransomed with so great a price as Christ's blood, we are not our own; and that, in the self-denying spirit of the gospel, living for the good of others, especially for the household of faith, we are, in reality, living for the Lord himself. The lowliest labour of love, the feeblest work of faith, the obscurest act of self-denying service, done in the Lord's name, is registered in His remembrancer, to be reproduced, acknowledged, and rewarded in the great day of account. Treading thus in the footsteps of Jesus, we shall experience a happiness and a blessing found only in a life of unselfish benevolence, of disinterested, expansive sympathy. And while others are living in the frigid region of self-pleasing, your spirit will rise to an atmosphere of the purest happiness and joy, unchilled and undimmed by the iciness and fogs of this sinful, heartless, selfish world. Assimilating with the spirit, you will also participate in the joy of Him who pleased not Himself, but lived and laboured, suffered and died for others. Oh, evidence and illustrate your union with the Lord by the studious and daily cultivation of this disinterested, self-denying sympathy! And, in addition to the evidence thus appended to your discipleship with Christ, it will return into your own soul with a sweet recompence of reward. Disinterested charity is sweetly and richly remunerative—blessing him who receives, with a powerful reflex influence, it blesses him who bestows. Would you experience the purest, the most exquisite and refined bliss the human heart is capable?—then, imitate Christ, and be merciful, sympathising, and kind; loving others as you love yourself, seeking and promoting their well-being and happiness, even though it curtail or sacrifice your own. "*Hereby perceive we the love of God, because He laid down His life for us; and we ought to lay down our lives for the brethren. But whoso hath this world's good, and seeth his brother have need, and shutteth up his bowels of compassion from him, how dwelleth the love of God in him? My little children, let us not love in word, neither in tongue, but in deed and in truth.*" Do this, and your own need will be met, your own sorrow soothed, your own wound healed, by the love and sympathy you have dispersed abroad, returning back in confluent streams upon yourself.

> "Art thou dejected? Is thy mind o'ercast?
> ———Go, fix some weighty truth;
> Chain down some passion; do some generous good;
> Teach ignorance to see, or grief to smile."

Then shall the benedictions of the widow, the fatherless, and the poor light upon you in gentle breathings; above all, and sweeter than all the hand of Him who submitted to a life of poverty and humiliation to enrich you with grace and glory, will pour the oil of gladness on your head.

"Blest is the man whose soft'ning heart
Feels all another's pain,
To whom the supplicating eye
Is never raised in vain.

"Whose breast expands with gen'rous warmth
A brother's woes to feel;
And bleeds in pity o'er the wounds
It wants the power to heal.

"He spreads his kind supporting arms
To every child of grief;
His secret bounty largely flows,
And brings unask'd relief.

"To gentle offices of love
His feet are never slow;
He views, through mercy's melting eye,
A brother in a foe.

"Peace from the bosom of his God,
My peace to him I give;
And when he kneels before the throne,
His trembling soul shall live.

"To him protection shall be shewn,
And mercy from above
Descend on those who thus fulfil
The perfect law of love."

We have equal reason to guard against *religious selfishness.* This is but another form of the fallen principle we have been endeavouring to combat,—it is selfishness in a Christian disguise. A child of God may be so exclusively enfolded within his own religious privileges and enjoyments as to overlook his obligation and pledge to promote the spiritual well-being of others. Satisfied of his own conversion—nourished in rich pastures—and experiencing high spiritual enjoyment, he may become selfishly and criminally indifferent to the multitudes within his reach living in sin and ignorance, destitution and neglect; hearing of no Saviour, possessing no Bible, attending no sanctuary; and each day passing into a hopeless eternity, uttering the fearful wail and the bitter reproof—"*No man cared for my soul!*" But this must not be. Forbid it, the religion and the love of Him who sacrificed Himself for us! What an example of self-denying, self-sacrificing, self-consuming, disinterested benevolence, sympathy, and labour was Christ's! He had griefs that needed assuaging, loneliness that needed cheering, depressions that needed soothing, wounds that needed healing, wants that needed supplying, weakness that needed strengthening, and yet, He buried all within the deep, silent cloisters of His own bosom, and went about doing good. Let us imitate Him! God converted us, that we might be instrumental in converting others.

Through grace we have found Jesus, that we may bring our fellow-sinners to Jesus. The light of life has been enkindled within our soul, that its bright shining might guide the steps of those who are stumbling on the dark mountains of death to the Saviour. The Lord, therefore, deposited this rich grace in our heart, that it might be dispersed abroad in self-denying efforts to win souls to Christ. Arise, then, and let us labour. This is a day of glad tidings, and we dare not hold our peace. We must not be satisfied with our own salvation, but seek also the salvation of others. We must love our neighbour as ourselves. And what is the nature of the love we are to cherish for him? A self-denying sympathy for his soul's eternal happiness. And who is our neighbour? Not simply him who dwells beneath the shadow of our own abode—but the sinner, the wanderer, the sufferer, the child of sorrow and of want, be he who and where he may. *He* is your neighbour! Be willing for a while to forego your own religious advantage, to relinquish some personal spiritual enjoyment, to find him out and tell him of Christ. How can you go to and fro to the rich banquet of the gospel, week after week, and feel no concern for, and make no effort in behalf of, those within your reach who are dying of spiritual starvation amid the plenty of which you have enough and to spare? This is religious selfishness of a fearfully responsible kind! The Lord deliver us from blood-guiltiness! You *must* deny yourself of some spiritual privileges for the spiritual benefit of others, if you are a true disciple and imitator of the Saviour. Restrict not your evangelical sympathy and labours within the limits of your own vicinity. At home or abroad, in your native or in a foreign land, be a herald of salvation, a missionary of the gospel, a witness for Christ, recognising him as your neighbour and your brother who needs a word of instruction, a look of kindness, an uplifting hand—the oil and the wine of Christian sympathy and love poured into a wounded and bleeding heart—in a word, some one to speak to him of—JESUS!

"Thy neighbour? It is he whom thou
 Hast power to aid and bless;
Whose aching heart or burning brow,
 Thy soothing hand may press.

"Thy neighbour? 'Tis the fainting poor
 Whose eye with want is dim,
Whom hunger sends from door to door—
 Go thou and succour him.

"Thy neighbour? 'Tis that weary man
Whose years are at their brim,
Bent low with sickness, cares, and pain,—
Go thou and comfort him.

"Thy neighbour? 'Tis the heart bereft
Of every earthly gem;
Widow and orphan helpless left,—
Go thou and shelter them.

"Thy neighbour? Meet'st thou a human form
'Less favour'd than thine own?
Remember, 'tis thy neighbour worm,
Thy brother, or thy son.

"Oh, pass not, pass not heedless by;
Perhaps thou canst redeem
The breaking heart from misery,—
Go, share thy lot with him.

Let us, also, be watchful against *denominational selfishness.* Other branches of the Christian Church than our own should share our sympathy, good-will, and prayers. We add nothing really to the ranks of Christ by proselyting from one denomination to another. Alas! there are those who deem it of much more importance to compass sea and land to draw over a convert to their own religious sect from another, than to make a single effort to win a convert to Christ from the world! What has Christ, or what has the gospel really gained by this? Nothing! To labour only to advance our own denomination, to seek exclusively the increase, the wealth, the prosperity of the body to which we belong, indifferent to the depression, or jealous of the increase and prosperity of other communions, is not the spirit of the gospel, is not the spirit of Christ. Oh for more largeness of heart! Oh for more of our Lord's disinterested sympathy! Let our love and intercessions embrace *all* Christian sections and congregations of the one Church of Christ, praying, "*Peace be within thy walls, and prosperity within thy palaces! For my brethren and companions' sake I will now say, Peace be within thee. Because of the house of the Lord our God I will seek thy good.*"

Nor would we fail to remind you that in proportion as self-pleasing in us decreases, pleasing God increases. In the same degree that the one is crucified, the other lives. "*I live, yet not I, but Christ liveth in me.*" And what is Christ living in the believer, but the believer living so as to please God? And, oh, to live as pleasing God is the holiest principle, the purest joy, the sublimest life. An angel, with soaring wing, could not ascend higher!

But for one moment let us refer to the *consolations* flowing from this subject If such is the disinterested sympathy of Christ, then, believe that you have not a want, nor a grief, nor a burden that He is not prepared to make all His own. Oh, how much have we yet to learn of the unselfishness of Christ's compassion — its self-denying, yearning, weeping tenderness! He would have you learn something of it in your present circumstances. For this end He has permitted them. Oblivious of all your past waywardness, ingratitude, and sin; forgetting your countless backslidings and base requitals of His love; and remembering only the kindness of your youth, the love of your espousals, how you once went after Him in the wilderness, and entered into a covenant to be His, which covenant you have broken times without number,—in the exercise of a love forgetful of Himself, and thinking only of you, He will cast around you the robe of a sympathy which soothes your sorrow, while it veils your sin, and which absorbs your infirmity, while it makes you comely through His comeliness put upon you. Let no sad memories, then, intercept your approach to the Saviour. So unselfish is His love, so disinterested His sympathy, not one look, or word, or motion of the hand will upbraid you for the past, or reprove you for the present. He will forget how you have wounded, grieved, and dishonoured Him; how your heart has again and again proved treacherous and inconstant as a broken bow; how, forsaking your first love, you have gone after other lovers and other confidences, and now retrace your steps and return to Him again, because the hand of affliction, of sorrow, and of chastisement is upon you—forgetting all this, He will receive you graciously, love you freely, and turn His anger away from you, clasping you to the bosom of a disinterested sympathy that writes your countless failures upon the sand, while it engraves your lowliest deeds of love eternal upon the rock.

CHAPTER XV.

CHRIST'S PARTING SYMPATHY.

"I say unto you, I will not drink henceforth of this fruit of the vine, until that day when I drink it new with you in my Father's kingdom."—MATT. xxvi. 29.

THERE is, to a feeling heart, something inexpressibly tender and touching in the *last* contact with what is dear and sacred. The *last* tearful look of home, the *last* fond glance of love, the *last* warm grasp of friendship, the *last* word of counsel and of prayer unlocks a spring of sensibility in the soul until that moment sealed—feelings of which the heart was before unconscious, scarcely suspecting their existence. In that moment of parting, what an oblivion transpires of every painful memory, every resentful feeling, of all that has injured, wounded, and grieved us. One thought, one feeling only occupies the whole soul—it is the thought, the feeling of—*parting;* and in the tenderness and agony of that thought, and of that feeling, all others are absorbed. Nothing now remains in the cell of memory, or engraved upon its tablet, but—how much we loved! "Men seldom appear so human, or in a position so advantageous to their humanity, as when they part. How few friends are there who endure a protracted separation without some abatement of warmth, or meet by appointment, without some precautionary anxieties, or continue together long without some accidental discontents; but none in any degree entitled to the character ever part without much regret! Even the cheerful and social are not always exempt from these momentary perturbations with which selfishness chills the pulse, or controversy overheats. The needle will oscillate a little from the just point of its affection; and though its polarity is never lost, it is seldom steady. Yet even the petulant, the irritable, and the more generous of the resentful, lose all unfriendliness as they pass away from each other—sighing at a conversation which, perhaps, they may have mutually desired. The last shake of the hand is sufficient to dissipate a hundred grievances. There are then no reproaches which we can recall, besides those against ourselves."

And these are pointed and poignant beyond expression! The thought that we should have inflicted a pang on the heart of one from whom we are now severing—and severing, it may be, for aye—the memory of harshness and neglect, of unkindness and wrong, received at our hands—oh the bitterness it infuses into that parting! Worlds would we give that it had never been! And yet who would lose the moral discipline of that moment? To have these sharp angularities of our nature smoothed — these rude, rough blemishes effaced—and the nobler, finer features which sin and infirmity had veiled, now exhibited and strengthened, and to realise how truly and deeply we had actually loved, were worth even the extreme grief and anguish of that parting moment!

> "Oh, who that from a friend must sever,
> For long, long years—perhaps for ever—
> Would wish to fly without possessing
> A parting look, a parting blessing!
> Though in that moment is combined
> All that can agonise the mind,
> Though lips cannot express their woe,
> Though tears may then refuse to flow;
> Though anguish, not to be express'd,
> Nearly o'erwhelms the throbbing breast!"

Studied in this light, how exquisite the beauty

and how instructive the lessons of Christ's farewell to His disciples at the Last Supper! It is true He met them again,—met them in Gethsemane, to which place He went from that table,—met them on Calvary,—yet again when He arose from the grave,—and for the last time on Mount Olivet, whence, in the act of breathing His final blessing, He was taken up into heaven;—yet *this* was the real farewell—the hour of His parting sympathy. In no subsequent interview was there such a tender, hallowed outflow of His sympathy as now. He was on the eve of His passion; it was the institution of His supper; the expressive memorials of His dying love, in beautiful simplicity, were upon the table; clustering around Him, in touching, clinging union, were His followers; one was reclining on His bosom; alas! another was meditating His betrayal—*that* was the hour of His parting sympathy! Then it was He uttered the memorable words—"*I will not drink henceforth of this fruit of the vine, until that day when I drink it new with you in my Father's kingdom.*" A brief meditation upon this sacred occasion and these expressive words will not prove, we trust, an inappropriate or unprofitable close to a volume the one theme of which is Christ's sympathy with man,—Christ's sympathy with His Church.

It was at the institution of this beautiful and solemn festival of the Lord's Supper that the Lord himself, for the first and the last time, presided. The occasion was well calculated to unfold, in its clearest and most winning form, the sympathy of Christ's love for His Church. It was His *last* feast of love on earth. That assemblage of disciples,—a type of the one Church of God,—gathered at the feet of their one Redeemer, Lord, and Head, to express, in these symbols of His death, of which *all* partook, their union with each other—the closer, dearer, union of all with Christ. No institution of Christ has been more mystified, misrepresented, or abused than the Lord's Supper. The infidel has scoffed at it, the world has prostituted it, the sacramentalist has exaggerated it, the unconverted have abused it, and the professing Christian has denied it; and yet it still continues, and will continue, until the twilight shadows of the Church on earth are lost in the noontide splendour of the Church in heaven, a memorial of love, a feast of communion, a symbol of unity, a pledge and first-frui of the great supper of the Lamb. Before we address ourselves more especially to the relation of the Lord's Supper to the Christian experience of the believer, tracing the tender, close communion into which it brings him with Christ, let us endeavour, briefly, to vindicate the institution from some of those unscriptural and erroneous views with which it is associated in the creed and practice of not a few.

In the first place, the Lord's Supper is not, as many suppose, *a sacrifice*, but rather *the commemoration of a sacrifice.* It is the glory of our divine and holy religion that the one and only sacrifice for sin is—the Lord Jesus Christ, who "*gave Himself an offering and a* SACRIFICE *to God.*" And so divine, so perfect, and acceptable was it, we read that, "*after He had offered* ONE SACRIFICE *for sins for ever, He sat down on the right hand of God.*" That one sacrifice of Christ, so completely met all the claims of God's moral government, rendered it so righteous, so glorious, on the part of God, to pardon sin and justify the sinner, that no more was required; and when Christ had offered this one, He ascended into heaven, and sat down at the right hand of God: "*for by one offering He hath perfected for ever them that are sanctified.*" It follows, then, that "*there remaineth no more sacrifice for sins;*" and that this one sacrifice wilfully and finally rejected, nothing remains to the rejector but a "*certain fearful looking for of judgment and fiery indignation, which shall devour the adversaries.*" Away, then, with the fearful notion that the Lord's Supper is a sacrifice! In no sense whatever is it so. A sacrifice is to propitiate, to atone, to render an equivalent for sin committed. Does the Lord's Supper do this? Preposterous idea! Oh no! We approach this ordinance as sinners pardoned, as enemies reconciled, as children adopted, as those whose sins and transgressions our Divine Surety bore, and with His atoning blood has for ever put away. We come to celebrate the offering of this one finished, glorious, accepted sacrifice of our incarnate God, in faith, gratitude, and love.

Nor is the Lord's Supper a *transubstantiated* institution, as taught by others. On this ground we seriously object to the expression, "holy mysteries," as applied to the elements. We cannot, perhaps, convey to the general reader, not conversant with the exact meaning of the term, a better idea of the error we seek to refute, than by quoting the authorised Roman statement of the doctrine as propounded by the Council of Trent; it is as follows:—"Inasmuch as our Redeemer Christ said, that that which He offered under the species of the bread was really His body, therefore the Church of God has ever been in the persuasion, and it is now again declared by this Holy Synod, that by the consecration of the bread and wine a conversion is made of the whole substance of the bread into the substance of the body of Christ our Lord, and of the whole substance of the wine into the substance of His blood, which conversion has by the Holy Catholic Church been conveniently and properly called *transubstantiation*." Without going at length into the refutation of this heresy, which the few remaining pages of this volume will not admit, we may remark, in brief but emphatic terms, that this notion is at once repugnant to taste, is opposed to reason, is contradicted by the evidence of sense, and is unauthorised and unsustained by the Word of God. We remark, then, at once, that in a *figurative*, and not in a literal sense, we are to interpret the words of our Lord, the Originator of this ordinance. When, therefore, Christ said, "*This is my body—this is my blood,*"

He spake the words in the same sense in which Isaiah did when he said, "*All flesh is grass.*" Did the prophet speak these words in a literal, or in a figurative sense? In a figurative sense undoubtedly. "*All flesh is grass,*"—that is, *as* grass—frail, fading, evanescent, cut down, and withered. Thus, then, "*This is my body—this is my blood,*" in other words, "This bread is the figure, the symbol of my body; this cup is the figure, the symbol of my blood." In a figurative, and not a literal sense, then, we are to interpret these words of our Lord. This is strictly in agreement with the general usage of Scripture language. Thus when Christ says, "*I am the vine;*" "*I am the door;*" "*Ye are the salt of the earth;*" "*Ye are the light of the world;*" and a thousand other figurative passages which might be quoted, who ever for a moment imagines that our Lord was *transubstantiated* into a vine, or into a door, or His people into salt and into light? If, then, we are to take, as undoubtedly we are, the general usage of Scripture language, and our Lord's language in particular, as possessing any value in interpretation, the doctrine of transubstantiation, as tested by it, falls to the ground. But not only is the doctrine of a real, corporeal presence of Christ in the elements opposed by the Word of God, but it is equally contradicted by the evidence of sense, as it is extremely revolting to our best feelings. The bread *is* bread, and the wine *is* wine. There is no change in the elements. They are simply bread and wine, and nothing more, our senses confirming the fact. But the doctrine we are confuting is not only contradicted by our senses, but is extremely revolting to our feelings. It is three times affirmed in the Bible of our Lord, that He was incapable of corruption. "*Thou shalt not suffer thine Holy One to see corruption.*" If the doctrine of the real, corporeal presence of Christ in the elements of the Lord's Supper be true, then this scripture is false! Which? But the Scripture cannot be broken. Let God be true, and every man who would impeach His veracity or contravene His word a liar. But a yet graver objection is alleged against the doctrine of transubstantiation. It identifies Christianity with one of the grossest forms of heathenism. Those who hold the idea of a literal and actual presence, cannot escape the sin, the terrible sin, of *idolatry*. They *worship* the bread and the wine, and are involved in one of the most God-dishonouring crimes to which the soul of man can be brought into subjection. It is impossible for the transubstantiationist to escape this logical conclusion,—he is emphatically an *idolater*. To ascribe Divine homage, adoration, and worship to the simple, material elements of the Lord's Supper, as we must do if we believe that they have been converted into the real body, and blood, and divinity of Christ, is to violate the second great law of the Divine decalogue, and to be involved, if unrepented of, in its inevitable and fearful punishment. How true and graphic of such is the description of the prophet: "*Yea, he kindleth it, and baketh bread; yea, he maketh a god, and worshippeth it.*" (Isa. xliv. 15.) And what is the final doom of all idolaters, be they those of heathendom or of Christendom? The Word of God alone reveals it: "IDOLATERS *shall have their part in the lake which burneth with fire and brimstone: which is the second death.*" But believers in Jesus, who approach the Lord's table in faith and love, enjoy the *real* presence, which is the spiritual, believing, realised presence of the Lord Himself. And a more blessed and honoured manifestation of the Lord in the ordinance is this, inasmuch as faith, in its present realisation of Jesus, is transcendently more glorious than sight. "*Blessed are they who have not seen, and yet have believed.*" Oh, approach that table, beloved, with an earnest desire, and with the full expectation of the realised presence of the Lord! Go, seeking and seeing Jesus only. It is with Him alone you have to do in this solemn feast. Jesus is its original, its substance, and its sweetness. Apart from a believing apprehension of Him, it is but an unmeaning symbol, a cold ceremonial, a lifeless picture—cold, shadowy, and unblest.

Equally unscriptural and erroneous is the idea that the Lord's Supper is a *converting* and *saving* institution. Neither of the two divinely-appointed rites of Baptism or the Lord's Supper were intended by Christ to accomplish this end; to interpret and employ them as such is to pervert their design, and to press them into the service of fostering a spurious and fatal hope. The Lord's Supper is a shadow, and not a substance; a sign, a symbol, a figure, an exponent of the most glorious Being and of the most august event in the universe. Beyond this, the elements possess no spiritual, quickening, gracious influences; and no act of the administrator, be he the most holy, spiritual being on earth, can possibly impart to them a miraculous change or a sacramental virtue. Real conversion is the work of the Holy Spirit alone; and he who is not born of the Spirit, and made a possessor of divine life, may partake of the Lord's Supper every day of the week, and at last perish in his unregeneracy and sins. Away, then, with the false and fatal idea that your observance of the Lord's Supper conveys to your soul one particle of grace, of holiness, or spiritual life. You may partake of it in health—in sickness—and in the hour of death, but it will serve you nothing, save as a seal of your greater condemnation, if you are not born again of the Spirit, apart from which neither meats nor drinks, circumcision nor uncircumcision, will avail you anything at the judgment-seat of Christ. But let your simple faith embrace the one glorious sacrifice of our divine and gracious Redeemer, of whom this ordinance is the expressive and sacred memorial, the lowly, life-like portrait, and you shall be saved.

It is a strictly logical and solemn inference from this, that *none but true believers in the Lord Jesus either are authorised or are quali-*

fied to partake of the Lord's Supper. It was originated by Christ for His Church, and not for the world. And who are His Church?—all, and none but those, who are born of the Holy Ghost, who possess a saving faith in Christ, and are living godly, righteously, and soberly, in this present evil world. These compose the one family of God, this banquet is the family feast, this the children's bread, of which none have a right to partake but true members of the family. The paschal lamb was commanded not to be eaten *until the posts of the house were sprinkled with the blood of it.* (Exod. xii. 7.) How significant! We must come in faith to the blood of sprinkling, ere we eat the flesh of the Lamb of God spiritually and in faith, as set forth in this ordinance. The individual who partakes of it without the application of atoning blood, the washing, the cleansing from sin and guilt through the atonement of Jesus, comes under the charge of "*eating and drinking unworthily,*" and occupies a position of fearful peril! The Lord's Supper is a seal. But a seal implies a covenant made, a promise given and accepted. Jehovah has made a covenant of salvation through the Lord Jesus on behalf of His Church. In that covenant He has promised pardon, adoption, acceptance, and heaven to all who truly and heartily believe in Christ. By faith we take hold of His covenant, and accept the promise. In the Lord's Supper, God seals this covenant of redemption to us, and we set our seal to the covenant. The promise of salvation, therefore, being only to those who truly repent and believe, the Lord's Supper becomes a seal of condemnation, and not of salvation, to all who partake of it in an unconverted, unbelieving, unsaved state. The language of the apostle is solemn and decided: "*Whosoever shall eat this bread, and drink this cup of the Lord unworthily, shall be guilty of the body and blood of the Lord. But let a man examine himself, and so let him eat of that bread, and drink of that cup. For he that eateth and drinketh unworthily, eateth and drinketh damnation to himself, not discerning the Lord's body.*" (1 Cor. xi. 27–29.) Let no timid, doubting believer in Jesus be discouraged by these words from approaching the Lord's table, and let none who in truth and sincerity love the Saviour, be deterred by them from making a profession of religion. We must, in their interpretation, bear in mind the distinction and the difference between the words *unworthy* and *unworthily.* The grammatical construction of the passage would seem to indicate this. The one word is an *adjective,* and refers to *personal qualification;* the other is an *adverb,* and refers to the *manner* in which the ordinance is observed. With regard to our personal worthiness to partake of the Lord's Supper, we possess none but what we have in and through the grace of Christ implanted in us by the Spirit, and the merits of Christ imputed to us through faith. This is our only personal qualification. We partake of this ordinance *unworthily* when we come to it without this renewing grace implanted in, and this justifying righteousness imputed to, us by the Lord Jesus. But let no individual suppose that because he may have partaken of the Lord's Supper unworthily, either through ignorance or wilfully, that, therefore, he has committed an *unpardonable* sin. Oh no! "*The blood of Jesus Christ cleanseth from* ALL *sin,*"—and this one among them. No contrite soul deploring in true penitence his unworthy partaking of Christ's Supper, and coming to the atonement of Christ, shall be excluded from the Divine forgiveness. The blood that the soldier shed pardoned the sin-of shedding it. The Lord's Supper, of which we may unworthily have partaken, is the symbol of His forgiving love, and His cleansing blood, whose ordinance we thus have dishonoured.

But while, for the honour of our Lord Jesus, we have thought it right to vindicate His institution, and to guard the reader against erroneous views respecting it, it will be a more pleasant duty to devote the few remaining pages of this work to two or three views of the Lord's Supper, tending to simplify and endear it to the hearts of those who truly love Jesus.

And let us first remind you that it is *a feast of hallowed and solemn memory.* With this view, among others, our blessed Lord instituted it. He would have His saints kept in memory of Himself. How simple and emphatic His words, "*Do this in* REMEMBRANCE *of me!*" And oh, how solemn and precious the memories clustering around this table! Our thoughts are wafted back to the hour of His agony and bloody sweat, His cross and passion, when, bearing our sins, He was led as a lamb to the slaughter, and was slain for us. There are some events in human life that are never effaced from its annals. Among the most solemn and precious are the death-memories of loved ones. Whatever other events transpire, this one stands alone in its own solemn, hallowed impressiveness; and we find it sanctifying and salutary often to remember the day and the circumstances that tore that fond one from our eyes. Transcendently more solemn and sanctifying than all is the memory of our Lord's death. To this end He left this memorial. And not of His death alone, but of the *love* that constrained Him to die, is it the sacred and lasting remembrance. It is a memorial of dying love,—love that could not, and that would not, do less than *die* for the object of its affections. Therefore may we regard it as the chief one of the Agapæ, or love-feasts, of the Christian Church,—a festival peculiar to the primitive Christians, and which conduced much to the early promotion of Christianity by the cultivation of mutual affection and sympathy, and which awoke the observation of heathen strangers,—"See how these Christians *love* one another!" How kind, and sacred, and considerate of Jesus to bequeath to us this Memento of love, knowing how often and how long we should allow other beings and objects to thrust Him from our thoughts! But the return of this season of communion recalls Him to our mind. Just as when we unclasp a casket, and gaze upon the image of an absent one, and there rushes back upon memory the loved features, the familiar tones, the cherished acts of kindness; so the Supper of our Lord—this fond and faithful remembrancer of one so dear—keeps us in tender, hallowed memory of Him whom our souls love until He come again. Lord, *we will remember Thy love; Thy love is better than wine.* Saints of God, beware, then, how you wilfully neglect this ordinance, seeing it is to keep you in vivid, grateful remembrance of Jesus. To neglect is to despise it, and to despise it is to turn the back upon HIM who should be entwined with our every affection, and blended with our every thought.

The Lord's Supper is also *a feast of present enjoyment.* Our Lord spread this table in love to a Church yet in the wilderness. In that wilderness, a dry and thirsty land, she would often be weary and faint. The toilsome march, the perils without, the fears within, the soul's hunger and thirst, would all conspire to render the table in this wilderness a banquet exceedingly welcome and refreshing to the saints. He who, when on earth, had compassion on the multitude who followed Him into the desert, and would not dismiss them fasting, lest they should faint by the way, was not likely to leave His Church in the world unfurnished with spiritual supplies. In addition to the rich provision of the gospel, He has instituted this feast of remembrance and of love, which, like perpetually descending manna, forms a continuous source of nourishment in the wilderness. The chief and the highest enjoyment flowing from the observance of the Lord's Supper is, *the Lord's presence at the table.* There is ever, on this hallowed occasion, an especial and peculiar manifestation of Christ to His saints, such as is vouchsafed and experienced nowhere else. The testimony of the Church is the same in all ages,—"*While the King sitteth at His table, my spikenard sendeth forth the smell thereof.*" It is emphatically *His* table, a banquet of His own originating and of His own furnishing. He provided the repast, and He Himself is there to sanction it, to welcome and bless the guests. And, oh, is not this the highest enjoyment on earth,—the manifested, realised, and precious presence of Christ? There is none other like it. What were heaven itself without it but a Christless and a joyless heaven? What is earth with it? It is the uplifting of this planet of sin and of woe, as it were, into the meridian and region of heaven. While the King, arrayed in beauty, overflowing with benignity and love, sitteth at His table, it is as though heaven in its glory had come down to earth, or that earth in its woe were upraised to heaven,—so divine, holy, and precious is the communion. No marvel that our spiritual graces put forth their power and their fragrance. It is the Sun of Righteousness warming into life and beauty, fertility and perfume, the holy and costly work of the Spirit in the soul. Our religion only becomes vitalised, vigorous, and fertile, as it closely deals with Christ. He is the source of our holiness, as He is the spring of our happiness and the anticipation of our glory. The beams of His grace and love flowing in upon the conservatory of the Spirit, the fruit and flower of the Holy Ghost appear, to the glory and praise of the heavenly Husbandman. "*Their soul shall be as a well-watered garden,*" is the Divine promise that crowns obedience to the Divine precept with its diadem of holy fruit. Approach, then, the Table of the Lord with the full expectation of meeting Jesus. Rise above the sign and the symbol to Him of whom it testifies, and quit not that Table until you have realised the presence, caught a glimpse of the beauty, and heard the voice of Him whom your soul loves.

Another present enjoyment at the Lord's Supper, of which we should avail ourselves, is the especial opportunity it affords for the presentation of particular requests in prayer. The soul is in close, confidential audience with Jesus. "*What is thy petition? and what is thy request?*" is the gracious, assuring language of the benignant glance He now bends upon each believer. Hasten, then, to pour every petition into His ear, every sorrow into His bosom. Jesus expects it. He waits to be gracious. He asks no preparation for your approach other than your felt need, and the longing of your heart for Him. And whether you come to confess your sins beneath His cross, or to rain upon His feet tears of love, or, while reclining upon His bosom, to bury in its deep sympathy your sorrows, cares, and wants, His gracious, loving heart bids you welcome. Oh, the solemn stillness, the sacred meditation, the precious communion, the confidential transaction of that moment when Jesus and the believer meet together at the Supper!

It is a feast, too, of *joyous anticipation.* Our

Lord has closely blended the past, the present, and the future of the Church in this Festival. These are the words which point to the coming glory—"*Ye do shew the Lord's death until* HE COME." The Second Advent, the glorious appearing of Christ, is interwoven with this memorial of humiliation, suffering, and death. The CROSS and the CROWN are strangely yet beautifully entwined together in this expressive institution. The dark shadow of the one, and the bright effulgence of the other, meet and mingle here. What play for the *trio* graces of the Spirit! *Faith* looks back to the sacrifice of Calvary—*Love* dissolves with holy affection to a present Christ —and *Hope*, with uplifted, unwearied wing, soars onward to the glorious future. Thus are we to eat the Lord's Passover, all sandalled and girdled for our heavenly march. This is not our rest, for here we have no continuing city, but we seek one to come, having Christ in us, the hope of glory. Thus, then, let us never merge the crown in the cross, nor the cross in the crown; but in all service and suffering, in duty and in trial, ever keep in view the truth, that if we now bear the cross, we shall then wear the crown,—if we suffer with Him here, we shall reign with Him hereafter. Oh, delightful, when we cluster around this sacred feast, to feel that it links us with the coming glory of Christ,—with the sorrowless, tearless, sinless, triumphant state of the spirits of just men made perfect, the general assembly and church of the first-born which are written in heaven, — and what will be ours when we shall relinquish the Supper of the Lamb on earth, for the marriage Supper of the Lamb in heaven. Then there will be no more ordinances! The symbol will merge into the reality, the shadow will melt into the substance, the river will be lost in the ocean, and the stars, which heralded His coming, and often led us to His feet, will vanish before the light and splendour of the meridian Sun. We shall be with Jesus then, and with Him drink the new wine of the kingdom; our holiness will be perfect, our happiness will be complete, and God in Christ will be our all in all.

"I love the windows of Thy grace,
Through which my Lord is seen,
And long to meet my Saviour's face,
Without a glass between.

"Oh, that the happy hour were come,
To change my faith to sight!
I shall behold my Lord at home,
In a diviner light.

"Haste, my Beloved, and remove
These interposing days;
Then shall my passions all be love,
And all my powers be praise."

There is one view of the Lord's Supper which should render it inexpressibly dear to our hearts—it is this, that it is not the table of a church, of a sect, of a party, but, emphatically, the Lord's Table, and, as such, belongs alike to the whole Church of Christ; and no priest or ecclesiastical body has an especial and exclusive right either to bless and administer its elements, or to appropriate and monopolise its communion. We approach this table, not to exhibit a badge, or to utter a shibboleth, or to assert a system, but to shew forth the Lord's death, in the goodly fellowship of apostles and prophets, of the noble army of martyrs, and the communion of all saints, until He come. And if there be one spot more appropriate and precious than all others from whence the prayer for Christian love and unity should ascend, surely it is *this*—and from this hallowed spot let it ever fervently and believingly be breathed!—

"O God, the Father of our Lord Jesus Christ, our only Saviour, the Prince of Peace, give us grace seriously to lay to heart the great dangers we are in by our unhappy divisions. Take away all hatred and prejudice, and whatsoever else may hinder us from godly union and concord; that, as there is but one body, and one Spirit, and one hope of our calling, one Lord, one faith, one baptism, one God and Father of us all, so we may henceforth be all of one heart and of one soul, united in one holy bond of truth and peace, of faith and charity, and may with one mind and one mouth glorify Thee, through Jesus Christ our Lord. Amen."*

"Hail, holy love! thou word that sums all bliss,
Gives and receives all bliss, emblem of God!
Overflowing most when greatest numbers drink;
Essence that binds the uncreated Three;
Chain that unites creation to its Lord;
Centre to which all being gravitates;
Eternal, ever-growing, happy love!"

How sacred, soothing, and precious, then, is the *parting* sympathy of Christ! It flows in silver streams around our path even to the last and latest of life. Having loved us in the world, He loves us to the end. His tender sympathy is with us when we part from places, from privileges, from friends, yea, from life itself. He

* Book of Common Prayer.

knows this peculiar sorrow; and, as if to meet and soothe it, He instituted this sacred and expressive ordinance, blending its past history with a present holy joy, and a future glorious hope. Oh, think you that when the last, the final, the *parting* hour comes that severs you from the home you have loved, from the being to whom so fondly, so inseparably you have clung, or from your life, now ebbing fast away—the deathless soul pluming her wing and poised for her awful, mysterious flight—think you that JESUS will not be there to clasp you in the arms of a SYMPATHY that shall solace that grief, sustain that hour, and enable you to say "farewell" without a sigh, and meet death without a quiver? Oh, yes! Jesus *will* be there; for He has promised, "LO! I AM WITH YOU ALWAY, EVEN UNTO THE END."

"Jesus, I need Thee all my life,
Through childhood's glee and manhood's strife,
In cloud or sunshine, joy or woe,
In wealth and power, or station low.
What other name such power to cheer;
What other voice so charms the ear;
What hand so gently leads as thine;
Whose heart so ready answers mine?
I need Thee *ever* by my side,
Supply *this* need, whate'er betide.

"Thus, when I read the holy page,
The guide of youth and staff of age,
I need a Teacher ever near,
To make the sacred message clear.
At Jesus' feet I fain would sit,
And ask *Him* to interpret it;
Then shall the Word a lamp become,
To light the pathway to my home.

"When fever'd pulse and throbbing brain
Seem to proclaim earth's healing vain,
I need the great Physician near,
To bid diseases disappear.
Once more my Saviour comes to me,
The wondrous Man of Galilee;
Then healthfully life's currents roll,
He speaks the word, and makes me whole.

"This changing world I cannot trust,
I need a friendship true and just;
One friend alone can hope impart—
The 'Friend of sinners' claims my heart:
Closer than any brother He
Accompanies and comforts me:
His love unchanging, strong, and pure—
The only friendship to endure!

"I am defenceless, weak, alone,
Cast down by foes, and overthrown;
I need a valiant arm—a shield,
While struggling on life's battle-field.
Then Jesus comes, a mighty King!
And now to arms I gladly spring;
His banner, o'er me in the fray,
Still leads me on a conquering way.

"I need my Saviour, when I mourn
O'er fleeting wealth or funeral urn:

When disappointments chill my soul,
And troublous billows angry roll,
With bleeding heart to Him I fly,
And once more find a helper nigh,—
With words of love, in accents sweet,
He cheers me at the mercy-seat.

"I need my Saviour when I die,—
Then *most of all* I wish Him nigh,
To bid me doubt and fear no more,
And bring me to the 'shining shore.'
There shall my needs be all supplied,
With harp and crown, at Jesus' side;
And ever more my rapture be,
That Jesus needed even me!" *.

* Anon.—Brooklyn.

CPSIA information can be obtained
at www.ICGtesting.com
Printed in the USA
LVHW100518120522
718524LV00004B/128

9 783375 00288